¡NO PASARÁN!

¡NO PASARÁN!

Writings from the Spanish Civil War

EDITED BY PETE AYRTON

SS

PEGASUS BOOKS

NEW YORK LONDON

¡No Pasarán!

Pegasus Books, Ltd.
148 West 37th Street, 13th Floor
New York, NY 10018

First Pegasus Books hardcover edition September 2016

ISBN: 978-1-68177-216-5

10 9 8 7 6 5 4 3 2 1

Printed in the United States of America
Distributed by W. W. Norton & Company, Inc.

This book is dedicated to Martin Chalmers, a
wonderful reader and fine translator

CONTENTS

Introduction   · Pete Ayrton   xi

Luis Buñuel · 'The Civil War (1936–1939)', from *My Last Breath*,
    translated by Abigail Israel   1

Muriel Rukeyser · 'We Came for Games', from *Savage Coast*   21

André Malraux · 'Hullo, Valladolid! Who's Speaking?', from *Days
    of Hope*, translated by Stuart Gilbert and Alastair Macdonald   34

José María Gironella · 'No More Delay!', from *The Cypresses
    Believe in God*, translated by Harriet de Onís   41

Ksawery Pruszyński · 'A Proletarian Bullfight', from *Inside Red
    Spain*, translated by Wisiek Powaga   50

Nivaria Tejera · 'More Important than a Law', from *The Ravine*,
    translated by Carol Maier   60

Arthur Koestler · 'Portrait of a Rebel General', from *Spanish
    Testament*   69

Langston Hughes · 'Laughter in Madrid', from *The Nation*   79

Mika Etchebéhère · 'Of Lice and Books', from *Ma Guerre
    d'Espagne à Moi*, translated by Nick Caistor   84

Drieu La Rochelle · 'A European Patriotism', from *Gilles*,
    translated by Pete Ayrton   91

CONTENTS

Manuel Chaves Nogales · 'The Moors Return to Spain', from
And in the Distance a Light…?, translated by L. de Baeza and
D. C. F. Harding   97

Laurie Lee · 'To Albacete and the Clearing House', from *A
Moment of War*   117

Pere Calders · 'The Terol Mines', from *L'Esquella de la Torratxa*,
translated by Peter Bush   127

Antoine Gimenez · 'Of Love and Marriage', from *Sons of the Night*,
translated by Pete Ayrton   139

John Dos Passos · 'The Villages Are the Heart of Spain', from
Journeys between Wars   144

Ana María Matute · 'The Master', from *El Arrepentido*, translated by
Nick Caistor   156

George Orwell · 'Two Memories', from 'Looking Back on the
Spanish War'   170

Joan Sales · 'Accursed Bourgeoisie, You Shall Atone for Your
Crimes!', from *Uncertain Glory*, translated by Peter Bush   174

Leonardo Sciascia · 'Today Spain, Tomorrow the World', from
Antimony, translated by N. S. Thompson   184

Jean-Paul Sartre · 'The Wall', translated by Lloyd Alexander   190

Manuel Rivas · 'Butterfly's Tongue', from *Vermeer's Milkmaid:
And Other Stories*, translated by Margaret Jull Costa   209

Francisco García Pavón · 'In Which Are Explained…', from *Los
Liberales*, translated by Nick Caistor   221

Curzio Malaparte · 'The Traitor', translated by Walter Murch   237

Mercè Rodoreda · 'Movie Matinée', from *Vint-i-dos-contes*,
translated by Peter Bush   248

Juan Goytisolo · 'The Empty Black Bag', from *Forbidden Territory*,
translated by Peter Bush   252

CONTENTS

Gamel Woolsey · 'Punctual Bombs', from *Death's Other Kingdom*   259

Medardo Fraile · 'An Episode from Natural History', from
Things Look Different in the Night, translated by
Margaret Jull Costa   272

Esmond Romilly · 'At the End of the Alphabet', from *Boadilla*   277

Dulce Chacón · 'The Missing Toe', from *The Sleeping Voice*,
translated by Nick Caistor   287

Victor Serge · 'Speak plainly, you know me', from *The Case of
Comrade Tulayev*, translated by Willard R. Trask   292

Pierre Herbart · 'My Gods Abandoned', from *La Ligne de Force*,
translated by Nick Caistor   302

Alberto Méndez · 'Second Defeat: 1940', from *Blind Sunflowers*,
translated by Nick Caistor   312

Arturo Barea · 'This War Is a Lesson', from *The Clash*, part 3 of
The Forging of a Rebel, translated by Ilsa Barea   328

Bernardo Atxaga · 'Marks', from *De Gernika a Guernica*, translated
by Margaret Jull Costa   338

Javier Cercas · 'There's nobody over here!', from *Soldiers of Salamis*,
translated by Anne McLean   350

Max Aub · 'January without Name', from *Cuentos ciertos*,
translated by Peter Bush   358

Jordi Soler · 'The Camp at Argelès-sur-Mer', from *The Feast of the
Bear*, translated by Nick Caistor   379

Jorge Semprún · 'Our War', from *Veinte años y un día* (*Twenty Years
and a Day*), translated by Margaret Jull Costa   384

Acknowledgements   389

Permissions   390

'It was in Spain that men learned that we can be right and yet be beaten, that force can vanquish spirit, that there are times when courage is not its own reward. It is this, doubtless, which explains why so many men, the world over, regarded the Spanish drama as a personal tragedy.'

Albert Camus

INTRODUCTION

THE SPANISH CIVIL WAR, a small war in comparison with the two world wars of the 20th century, continues to 'punch above its weight' in terms of cultural and political resonance. The richness and diversity of the texts collected in *!No Pasarán!* will help explain why this is the case.

The Civil War started on 17/18 July 1936 when units of the Army rebelled against the progressive policies of the Spanish Republic. The military coup began in Spanish Protectorate in Morocco and spread to mainland Spain. The coup was met with popular resistance especially in the urban centres and was defeated in Madrid and Barcelona. Rapidly the country was split in two. In late July, the Army of Africa, commanded by the Rebel General Francisco Franco, was airlifted to Seville in mainland Spain with planes provided by Hitler and Mussolini. France and Britain adhered to a policy of non-intervention, the only countries to support the Republic militarily were Mexico and the Soviet Union which agreed to ship arms in September.

At the time, many saw the Civil War as a crucial moment in the fight of democracies against fascism and many who supported the Republic did so on the grounds that its victory would send a clear signal to Hitler and Mussolini that fascism could be defeated. Artists, writers and workers from all over Europe and further afield took sides over the Civil War.

The majority of them supported the Republic but there were also some who took the Rebels' side – both are represented here. For many it was not only a matter of supporting the war through their art: some went to Spain to fight. As early as October 1936, volunteers from abroad began to arrive to enlist on the Republican side in the International Brigade: many were rushed into battle with few weapons and inadequate training.

So, the battle lines were drawn for a war that was to last for a thousand days until early 1939 when the Rebels made their decisive breakthrough: in January of that year, Barcelona fell to Franco and in March, it was followed by Madrid. Hundreds of thousands of Republicans fled to France in what is known as *La Retirada* –The Retreat.

Eighty years on, the Spanish Civil War continues to be the subject of much contemporary art and literature in Spain and elsewhere. There is a continued relevance of the themes it raises: the question of whether winning the war should take precedence over implementing fundamental social change, the use of carpet bombing of towns with the inevitable death of thousands of civilians, the relationship between the role of women and the war effort both on the Rebel and the Republican sides, the claims for independence of autonomous regions, for example, the Basque Country, Galicia or Catalonia.

Spain was already a deeply divided and unequal society when the Civil War broke out; but, by forcing the Republic to respond, the military uprising brought these divisions to a head. A process of social revolution was unleashed in the towns (the Hotel Ritz in Barcelona became a people's canteen) and in the countryside (the collectivization of land, the expropriation of estates), which the Republic was initially unable to control. It is because this cleavage – between reform and revolution – is here at its most visible that the Spanish Civil War has so powerful a claim to our literary and political imagination.

Why the Writers in *¡No Pasarán!*?

There have been several excellent anthologies in English on the Civil War – for example, *And I Remember Spain: A Spanish Civil War Anthology* edited by Murray A. Sperber and, more recently, *Spanish Front: Writers on the Civil War* edited by Valentine Cunningham, but neither of these anthologies (and others like them) feature any Spanish writers. This seems a strange omission.

Much well-known English-language coverage of the Civil War includes a succession of books and films about the love life of Ernest Hemingway and who slept with whom in the Hotel Florida in Madrid, the rivalry between Dos Passos and Hemingway, and so on. This kitsch packaging of the war was predicted with wry humour by a character in the Catalan writer Joan Sales' *Uncertain Glory*:

> 'But the worst side to the wars is the fact that they are turned into novels; at the end of this war – and I assure you it's a war as shitty as any – novels will be written that are especially stupid, as senti-mental and risqué as they come: they'll have wonderfully coura-geous young heroes and wonderfully buxom little angels. I don't mean you, Cruells; you'll not be stricken by one of these tomes. But foreigners … It's a pity you don't believe in my gifts as a prophet; I could tell you, for example, that foreigners will turn this huge mess into stirring stories of bullfighters and gypsies.'
>
> 'Bullfighters? I've never heard of mention of any, so far as I know …'
>
> 'Right, poor Cruells: a bullfighter has never been sighted in the army, let alone a gypsy, but foreigners have a good nose for business …'
>
> (From *Uncertain Glory*, Maclehose Press, 2014, p. 312)

For anglophone readers, most of our literary knowledge of the Civil War comes through writers such as Dos Passos, Stephen Spender, George Orwell, Ernest Hemingway and W.H. Auden. They are insightful writers and have much of value to say but this was a Spanish War and the over-whelming majority of combatants – active or passive – were Spanish. And so many of the contributors to *¡No Pasaran!* are Spanish: speakers of Castilian, Basque, Catalan and Galician. They include writers such as Arturo Barea, Max Aub and Mercè Rodoreda who lived through the war and those like Javier Cercas, Manuel Rivas and Bernardo Atxaga who are writing about it now. Many works in contemporary Spanish culture make reference to the Civil War; in fact, its importance is growing. This making up for lost time is no accident. From the end of the War in 1939 to the death of Franco in 1975, there was harsh censorship of the arts: exiled Spanish writers could publish in places such as Chile, Argentina or Mexico, but usually not in Spain, and the distribution of their work was very limited. Within Spain, the defeated Republicans kept silent for fear of weighing their children down with memories of a lost cause that could only bring them grief. After the death of Franco, the democratic parties overseeing the transition to democracy formulated the Pact of Forgetting (*el Pacto del Olvido*) which was an attempt to let bygones be bygones and concentrate on the future. It was given a legal basis in the 1977 Amnesty law. This attempt to sweep Franco's (and to a lesser extent Republican) crimes under the carpet lasted until 2000 when the Association for the Recovery of Historical Memory was founded by the sociologist Emilio Silva Barrera. Silva Barrera wanted to locate and identify the remains of his grandfather shot by Franco's forces in 1936 and he led a campaign for this to happen. In response to this pressure, the Socialist government of José Luis Rodríguez Zapatero passed in 2007 The Historical Memory Law which sought to remove symbols of Francoism from public buildings and provided a budget for public exhumations. The right-wing government (2011–2015) led by Mariano Rajoy did not repeal the law but cut off funds for its implementation. In November 2015, the city of Pamplona asked the courts to investigate crimes committed against its residents during the Civil War and the dictatorship of General Franco. This is the first time a public institution has decided to present a criminal complaint to the Spanish courts.

That the legacy of the war remains contested throughout Spain can be seen in the many defaced Francoist and Republican statues as well as in numerous books and films. The Historical Memory Law has led to new atrocities coming to light. As Bernardo Atxaga writes in a recent book *De Gernika a Guernica*:

In the newspaper *El País*, dated 4 November 2006, I read these words spoken by a man from Fuenteguinaldo, in the province of Salamanca:

INTRODUCTION

'Apparently, the Falangists asked the priest to draw up a list of all the reds and atheists in the village. On 7 October 1936, they went from house to house looking for them. At nine o'clock at night, they were taken to the prison in Ciudad Rodrigo, and at four o'clock in the morning, were told they were being released, but, at the door of the prison, a truck was waiting and, instead of taking them home, it brought them here to be killed.'

By now, the only surprising thing is how long it has taken for these facts to come to light: seventy years. A whole lifetime.

(p. 348)

The war at the front
The content of *¡No Pasarán!* reflects the different aspects of the Civil War. The war at the front is best known for accounts of armies engaging each other in combat. Within these accounts of battles, there are epic personal encounters like the one described by Chaves Nogales between a Republican fighter (the militiaman) and a Moor (the Caid) near Madrid:

The cunning Caid approached stealthily from behind and when, he was within striking distance, he charged and thrust his bayonet into the militiaman's back, at the same time as the latter raised the butt of his rifle to bring it down on another Berber's head. Neither the Moor nor the militiaman missed. Another fell to the mighty club, but the militiaman was pierced by the Moor's bayonet. As he toppled, his head fell against the chest of the victim and thus they fell together like skittles and lay on top of one another.

(p. 110)

The war in the countryside
In the countryside, years of feudal exploitation had led to poverty and class hatred; thousands starved for nine months of the year. In the war years in many parts of Spain peasant revolutionaries seized the land and organized collective farms. This process fundamentally changed relationships. Hierarchies crumbled and now it was the turn of the haves

to flee or, at the very least, to watch their step. The collectivization was part of a general revolutionary process that took place in the country-side often with a considerable degree of violence. When the war was over, the victors sought revenge. Jorge Semprún's *Twenty Years and a Day* (the sentence given to political prisoners under Franco) describes how the landowners, under Franco, forced rural workers to re-enact every year the violent murder of a landowner in 1936 – a ritual of submission designed to keep them in their place:

> They were not the murderers of 1936, but the ceremony, in a way, made them accomplices of that death, forcing them to take respon-sibility for it, to bring it back into the present, to bring it alive again.
>   A baptism of blood, you might say.
>   By perpetuating the memory the farm workers perpetuated their condition not only as vanquished but as murderers – or as children, relatives, descendants of murderers. They acted out the awful reason for their defeat by commemorating the injustice of the death that had treacherously justified their defeat and their reduc-tion to the ranks of the vanquished. In short that ceremony of atonement, which was attended by some of the provincial authori-ties, civil and ecclesiastical, helped to make sacred the very social order which the farm workers had thought rashly no doubt – fear-fully too, one imagines – they were destroying when they murdered the owner of the farm.
>
> (p. 387)

However, it is clear that the acts of violence of the rural landless were not on the same scale as the landowners' systematic use of terror during the Civil War to turn the clock back in the countryside.

The war against the Catholic Church
The Primate of Spain supported Franco, as did many local priests, monks and nuns. So the church, seen by many in the countryside as the source of their oppression, was another target of the revolutionaries. Many churches were destroyed. 'Priests and monks were killed because they

were seen as representing an oppressive Church historically associated with the rich and powerful whose ecclesiastical hierarchy had backed the military rebellion.' (Helen Graham, p.27*)

The popular vengeance exacted on the clergy was often brutal. This fury is captured by José María Gironella in *The Cypresses Believe in God*, his portrait of small town life written in 1953:

> The leaders of the mob broke into the house. Nobody there. Empty. In the waiting-room there was a table and, a huge chronological album of the popes. Santi was among the first in and he rang every bell his fingers could find. Down a gloomy corridor they came to the communicating door. They entered the church. Those who had remained outside were waiting for the immense door of the church to be thrown wide.
>
> When they heard the first blows, they rushed up the stairs unable to restrain themselves, and, as one man, flung themselves against the doors, trying to help those struggling with them inside. At the sixth try, the doors gave way. And at that moment all the lights went on. Santi had discovered the switches in the sacristy and had illuminated the festival. The temple was incapable of holding them all. Shots rang out.
>
> (p. 42)

The role of women

Initially the revolutionary militia woman was the role many young Republican women aspired to: she would wear blue overalls, have a rifle slung over her shoulder and go to the front to fight the Fascists. But the women fighters were aware of the ambiguity of their situation. Mika Etchebéhère, one of the few women to lead an army column, writes movingly:

---

* *The Spanish Civil War*, Helen Graham, OUP, 2005. Much of the important history on the Civil War has been written in English – by Paul Preston, Helen Graham, Herbert Southworth and Michael Richards, amongst others.

– Why should the militia men feel jealous?
– Firstly, I am mother to all of them, so they alone have the right
to be loved. On one side, and this is most subtle, I am wife to all of
them, untouchable, on a pedestal. But, if for one reason or another,
I go to visit other soldiers I leave my pedestal, I come back to earth
like other women, like them I am able to sin and be guilty of the
same illicit thoughts …

(Mika Etchebéhère, *Ma Guerre D'Espagne a Moi*, Actes Sud: Arles, 1998,
page 273).

This was the time of La Pasionaria's (the Communist leader, Dolores
Ibárruri) famous speech 'A salute to our militiawomen on the front
line', but the period of women fighters was short lived. It thrived as
long as making a revolution and waging a war were seen to go hand in
hand. By October 1936, this was no longer the case; it had become clear
to the Republican government that the priority was to win the war.
That required a conventional army and a return to a more traditional
division of labour captured in the slogan: 'men to the front, women to
the home front'. Women had to replace in the factories the men who
had gone to the front and also to find the food and supplies to feed
themselves and their children – a exacting task poignantly described in
Mercé Rodoreda's classic novel *In Diamond Square*.

The bombing of cities
Conditions on the home front were harsh and became harsher as food
supplies ran low and the towns in Republican areas were subjected to
the aerial bombardment of German and Italian planes. Juan Goytisolo's
mother was killed in one such air raid over Barcelona:

She had gone shopping in the center of the city and was caught
there by the arrival of the airplanes, near where the Gran Vía crosses
the Paseo de Gracia. She was a stranger, also, to those who, once the
alert was over, picked up from the ground that woman who was
already eternally young in the memory of all who knew her, the
lady who, in her coat, hat, and high-heeled shoes, clung tightly to

the bag where she kept the presents she had bought for her children, which the latter, days afterward, in suits dyed black as custom ruled, would receive, in silence, from the hands of Aunt Rosario: a romantic novel for Marta; tales of Doc Savage and the Shadow for José Agustín; a book of illustrated stories for me; some wooden dolls for Luis that would remain scattered round the attic without my brother ever touching them.

(p. 255)

For Laurie Lee, who witnessed the bombing of Valencia, it was clear that important lessons were being learnt by the Fascists:

Those few minutes bombing I'd witnessed were simply an early essay in a new kind of warfare, soon to be known – and accepted – throughout the world.

Few acknowledged at the time that it was General Franco, the Supreme Patriot and Defender of the Christian Faith, who allowed these first trial-runs to be inflicted on the bodies of his countrymen, and who delivered up vast areas of Spain to be the living testing-grounds for Hitler's new bomber-squadrons, culminating in the annihilation of the ancient city of Guernica.

(p. 123)

The bombing of Guernica on 26 April 1937, carried out by German and Italian air forces at the behest of Franco, was systematically planned to inflict maximum damage and loss of life to the region's inhabitants (for example, it took place on Monday, a market day). It became the most famous of the bombing raids through Picasso's mural commissioned by the Republican government for the World's Fair in Paris, and completed in June 1937 – a mural that then toured the world.

The Retreat/La Retirada
As the war advanced and Franco's forces occupied more and more of the country, many in the Republican areas saw no other way out than

to flee to France. After the fall of Bilbao in June 1937, 120,000 refugees fled the Basque Country and were taken by boat to ports on the Atlantic coast. Another several hundreds of thousands Republicans crossed the border into France from Catalonia after the fall of Barcelona in January 1939. The conditions of *La Retirada* were perilous and many died on the way. The French border guards were rough in their treatment of the refugees and made clear their contempt.

The French government of Daladier quickly recognized the legitimacy of Franco's triumph and was hostile to the refugees who were sent to internment camps from which they were offered the choice of joining the Foreign Legion or deployment into work brigades. Many of these brigades were sent to the North of France to work on strengthening the Maginot line fortifications against a German invasion. Conditions in the camps were brutal and totally inadequate to deal with the numbers of refugees – in March 1939, there were 260,000 Spaniards in the camps in the Roussillon, which was more than the local French population.

Today the camps are almost forgotten and over the years Republicans and their descendants have had to fight for an occasional plaque to remember their existence. Remembering is essential as Jordi Soler writes in *The Feast of the Bear.*

Besides, this is the twenty-first century, and Spain and France are no longer what they were in 1939; we don't have pesetas or francs anymore, and there isn't even a frontier between the two countries: to get to the place where the event was being held, I had climbed into my car, which was parked outside my house in Calle Muntaner in Barcelona, and driven for two hours without stopping once to Argelès-sur-Mer; in two hours I had completed the same journey it had taken my grandfather Arcadi and most of the Republican exodus several weeks to cover in 1939. The traces of that exile have been buried beneath a toll motorway you can drive along at a hundred and forty kilometres an hour, and a crowd of tourists who, smothered in cream, expose their bodies to the sun on the long beach of Argelès-sur-Mer. Very little can be done to ward off oblivion, but it is essential we do so, otherwise we will end up without foundations or perspective. That is what I thought, and that was the reason why in the end I gave up my domestic morning, took off my pyjamas and got into my car, still thinking obsessively of that verse from the Russian film I had memorized and which had robbed me of sleep; 'Live in the house, and the house will exist'.

(p. 382)

There are clear parallels in the treatment of Republican refugees in 1936 and the treatment of refugees and political exiles from Africa and Syria in Europe in 2015. Both are (were) treated harshly and made to feel unwelcome in the countries they escaped to.

The Civil War continues to attract the attention of artists and intellectuals: it divided regions, towns, villages and families and to an extent still does. It also reminds us that there can be times when not getting involved can have disastrous consequences. In 1936 this was recognized by a generation of idealists.. As Laurie Lee writes:

But in our case, I believe, we shared something else, unique to us at that time – the chance to make one grand, uncomplicated gesture of personal sacrifice and faith which might never occur again. Certainly, it was the last time this century that a generation had such an opportunity before the fog of nationalism and mass-slaughter closed in.

(p. 117)

The idealism of the International Brigades is very much a gold standard for altruistic behaviour. This idealism was disingenuously invoked by Hilary Benn, Shadow Foreign Secretary, in his speech in December 2015 in support of British government bombing in Syria: 'What we know about fascists is that they need to be defeated. It is why socialists, trade unionists and others joined the International Brigade in the 1930s to fight against Franco…'

The International Brigades, unlike the British air force, were fighting in support of a democratically elected government. Even so, those who went to Spain were threatened with the Foreign Enlistment Act of 1870. The British government warned that anyone volunteering to fight would be 'liable on conviction to imprisonment up to two years'.

Now, eighty years after the end of the Civil War, the issues that it raises are just as relevant. The strength of nationalist feelings in Catalonia, the Basque Country and Galicia, the desire of those who lost kith and kin in the war to know their fate, the need for a history that treats equally the vanquished and the victors, and an examination of the idealism that draws individuals into armed conflicts, are part of the legacy of the war. I hope the writings in *¡No Pasáran!* illuminate this legacy.

LUIS BUÑUEL

THE CIVIL WAR (1936–1939)

from *My Last Breath*

translated by Abigail Israel

IN JULY 1936, Franco arrived in Spain with his Moroccan troops and the firm intention of demolishing the Republic and re-establishing 'order.' My wife and son had gone back to Paris the month before, and I was alone in Madrid. Early one morning, I was jolted awake by a series of explosions and cannon fire; a Republican plane was bombing the Montaña army barracks.

At this time, all the barracks in Spain were filled with soldiers. A group of Falangists had ensconced themselves in the Montaña and had been firing from its windows for several days, wounding many civilians. On the morning of July 18, groups of workers, armed and supported by Azaña's Republican assault troops, attacked the barracks. It was all over by ten o'clock, the rebel officers and Falangists executed. The war had begun.

It was hard to believe. Listening to the distant machine-gun fire from my balcony, I watched a Schneider cannon roll by in the street below, pulled by a couple of workers and some gypsies. The revolution we'd felt gathering force for so many years, and which I personally had so ardently desired, was now going on before my eyes. All I felt was shock.

Two weeks later, Elie Faure, the famous art historian and an ardent supporter of the Republican cause, came to Madrid for a few days. I went to visit him one morning at his hotel and can still see him standing at his window in his long underwear, watching the demonstrations in the street below and weeping at the sight of the people in arms. One day, we watched a hundred peasants marching by, four abreast, some armed with hunting rifles and revolvers, some with sickles and pitchforks. In an obvious effort at discipline, they were trying very hard to march in step. Faure and I both wept.

It seemed as if nothing could defeat such a deep-seated popular force, but the joy and enthusiasm that colored those early days soon gave way to arguments, disorganization, and uncertainty – all of which lasted until November 1936, when an efficient and disciplined Republican organization began to emerge. I make no claims to writing a serious account of the deep gash that ripped through my country in 1936. I'm not a historian, and I'm certainly not impartial. I can only try to describe what I saw and what I remember. At the same time, I do see those first months in Madrid very clearly. Theoretically, the city was still in the hands of the Republicans, but Franco had already reached Toledo, after occupying other cities like Salamanca and Burgos. Inside Madrid, there was constant sniping by Fascist sympathizers. The priests and the rich landowners – in other words, those with conservative leanings, whom we assumed would support the Falange – were in constant danger of being executed by the Republicans. The moment the fighting began, the anarchists liberated all political prisoners and immediately incorporated them into the ranks of the Confederación Nacional de Trabajo, which was under the direct control of the anarchist federation. Certain members of this federation were such extremists that the mere presence of a religious icon in someone's room led automatically to Casa Campo, the public park on the outskirts of the city where the executions took place. People arrested at night were always told that they were going to 'take a little walk.'

It was advisable to use the intimate 'tu' form of address for everyone, and to add an energetic *compañero* whenever you spoke to an anarchist, or a *camarada* to a Communist. Most cars carried a couple of mattresses tied to the roof as protection against snipers. It was dangerous even to hold out your hand to signal a turn, as the gesture might be interpreted as a Fascist salute and get you a fast round of gunfire. The *senoritos*, the sons of 'good' families, wore old caps and dirty clothes in order to look as much like workers as they could, while on the other side the Communist party recommended that the workers wear white shirts and ties.

Ontañon, who was a friend of mine and a well-known illustrator, told me about the arrest of Sáenz de Heredia, a director who'd worked for me on *La hija de Juan Simón* and *Quién me quiere a mí?* Sáenz, Primo de Rivera's first cousin, had been sleeping on a park bench because he was afraid to go home, but despite his precautions he had been picked up by a group of Socialists and was now awaiting execution because of his fatal family connections. When I heard about this, I immediately went to the Rotpence Studios, where I found that the employees, as in many other enterprises, had formed a council and were holding a meeting. When I asked how Sáenz was, they all replied that he was 'just fine,' that they had 'nothing against him.' I begged them to appoint a delegation to go with me to the Calle de Marqués de Riscál, where he was being held, and to tell the Socialists what they'd just told me. A few men with rifles agreed, but when we arrived, all we found was one guard sitting at the gate with his rifle lying casually in his lap. In as threatening a voice as I could muster, I demanded to see his superior, who turned out to be a lieutenant I'd had dinner with the evening before.

'Well, Buñuel,' he said calmly, 'what're you doing here?'

I explained that we really couldn't execute everyone, that of course we were all very aware of Sáenz's relationship to Primo de Rivera, but that the director had always acted perfectly correctly. The delegates from the studio also spoke in his favor, and eventually he was released, only to slip away to France and later join the Falange. After the war, he went back to directing movies, and even made a film glorifying Franco! The last I saw of him was at a long, nostalgic lunch we had together in the 1950s at the Cannes Festival.

During this time, I was very friendly with Santiago Carrillo, the secretary of the United Socialist Youth. Finding myself unarmed in a city where people were firing on each other from all sides, I went to see Carrillo and asked for a gun.

'There are no more,' he replied, opening his empty drawer.

After a prodigious search, I finally got someone to give me a rifle. I remember one day when I was with some friends on the Plaza de la Independencia and the shooting began. People were firing from rooftops, from windows, from behind parked cars. It was bedlam, and there I was, behind a tree with my rifle, not knowing where to fire. Why bother having a gun, I wondered, and rushed off to give it back.

The first three months were the worst, mostly because of the total absence of control. I, who had been such an ardent subversive, who had so desired the overthrow of the established order, now found myself in the middle of a volcano, and I was afraid. If certain exploits seemed to me both absurd and glorious – like the workers who climbed into a truck one day and drove out to the monument to the Sacred Heart of Jesus about twenty kilometers south of the city, formed a firing squad, and executed the statue of Christ – I nonetheless couldn't stomach the summary executions, the looting, the criminal acts. No sooner had the people risen and seized power than they split into factions and began tearing one another to pieces. This insane and indiscriminate settling of accounts made everyone forget the essential reasons for the war.

I went to nightly meetings of the Association of Writers and Artists for the Revolution, where I saw most of my friends – Alberti, Bergamín, the journalist Corpus Varga, and the poet Altolaguirre, who believed in God and who later produced my *Mexican Bus Ride*. The group was constantly erupting in passionate and interminable arguments, many of which concerned whether we should just act spontaneously or try to organize ourselves. As usual, I was torn between my intellectual (and emotional) attraction to anarchy and my fundamental need for order and peace. And there we sat, in a life-and-death situation, but spending all our time constructing theories.

Franco continued to advance. Certain towns and cities remained loyal to the Republic, but others surrendered to him without a struggle. Fascist repression was pitiless; anyone suspected of liberal tendencies was summarily executed. But instead of trying to form an organization, we debated – while the anarchists persecuted priests. I can still hear the old cry: 'Come down and see. There's a dead priest in the street.' As anti-clerical as I was, I couldn't condone this kind of massacre, even though the priests were not exactly innocent bystanders. They took up arms like everybody else, and did a fair bit of sniping from their bell towers. We even saw Dominicans with machine guns. A few of the clergy joined the Republican side, but most went over to the Fascists. The war spared no one, and it was impossible to remain neutral, to declare allegiance to the utopian illusion of a *tercera España*.

Some days, I was very frightened. I lived in an extremely bourgeois apartment house and often wondered what would happen if a wild bunch of anarchists suddenly broke into my place in the middle of the night to 'take me for a walk.' Would I resist? How could I? What could I say to them?

The city was rife with stories; everyone had one. I remember hearing about some nuns in a convent in Madrid who were on their way to chapel and stopped in front of the statue of the Virgin holding the baby Jesus in her arms. With a hammer and chisel, the mother superior removed the child and carried it away.

'We'll bring him back,' she told the Virgin, 'when we've won the war.'

The Republican camp was riddled with dissension. The main goal of both Communists and Socialists was to win the war, while the anarchists, on the other hand, considered the war already won and had begun to organize their ideal society.

'We've started a commune at Torrelodones,' Gil Bel, the editor of the labor journal *El Sindicalista*, told me one day at the Café Castilla. 'We already have twenty houses, all occupied. You ought to take one.'

I was beside myself with rage and surprise. Those houses belonged to people who'd fled or been executed. And as if that weren't enough, Torrelodones stood at the foot of the Sierra de Guadarrama, only a few kilometers from the Fascist front lines. Within shooting distance of Franco's army, the anarchists were calmly laying out their utopia.

On another occasion, I was having lunch in a restaurant with the musician Remacha, one of the directors of the Filmófono Studios where I'd once worked. The son of the restaurant owner had been seriously wounded fighting the Falangists in the Sierra de Guadarrama. Suddenly, several armed anarchists burst into the restaurant yelling,

'*Salud compañeros!*' and shouting for wine. Furious, I told them they should be in the mountains fighting instead of emptying the wine cellar of a good man whose son was fighting for his life in a hospital. They sobered up quickly and left, taking the bottles with them, of course.

Every evening, whole brigades of anarchists came down out of the hills to loot the hotel wine cellars. Their behavior pushed many of us into the arms of the Communists. Few in number at the beginning of the war, they were nonetheless growing stronger with each passing day. Organized and disciplined, focused on the war itself, they seemed to me then, as they do now, irreproachable. It was sad but true that the anarchists hated them more than they hated the Fascists. This animosity had begun several years before the war when, in 1935, the Federación Anarquista Ibérica (FAI) announced a general strike among construction workers. The anarchist Ramón Acin, who financed *Las Hurdes*, told me about the time a Communist delegation went to see the head of the strike committee.

'There are three police stooles in your ranks,' they told him, naming names.

'So what?' the anarchist retorted. 'We know all about it, but we like stooles better than Communists.'

Despite my ideological sympathies with the anarchists, I couldn't stand their unpredictable and fanatical behavior. Sometimes, it was sufficient merely to be an engineer or to have a university degree to be taken away to Casa Campo. When the Republican government moved its headquarters from Madrid to Barcelona because of the Fascist advance, the anarchists threw up a barricade near Cuenca on the only road that hadn't been cut. In Barcelona itself, they liquidated the director and the engineers in a metallurgy factory in order to prove that the factory could function perfectly well when run by the workers. Then they built a tank and proudly showed it to a Soviet delegate. (When he asked for a parabellum and fired at it, it fell apart.)

Despite all the other theories, a great many people thought that the anarchists were responsible for the death of Durutti, who was shot while getting out of his car on the Calle de la Princesa, on his way to try to ease the situation at the university, which was under siege. They were the kind of fanatics who named their daughters Acracia (Absence of Power) or Fourteenth September, and couldn't forgive Durutti the discipline he'd imposed on his troops.

We also feared the arbitrary actions of the POUM (Partido Obrero de Unificación Marxista), which was theoretically a Trotskyite group. Members of this movement, along with anarchists from the FAI, built barricades in May 1937 in the streets of Barcelona against the Republican army, which then had to fight its own allies in order to get through.

My friend Claudio de la Torre lived in an isolated house outside of Madrid. His grandfather had been a freemason, the quintessential abomination in the eyes of the Fascists. In fact, they despised freemasons as heartily as they did the Communists. Claudio had an excellent cook whose fiancé was fighting with the anarchists. One day I went to his house for lunch, and suddenly, out there in the open country, a POUM car drove up. I was very nervous, because the only papers I had on me were Socialist and Communist, which meant less than nothing to the POUM. When the car pulled up to the door, the driver leaned out and... asked for directions. Claudio gave them readily enough, and we both heaved a great sigh of relief as he drove away.

All in all, the dominant feeling was one of insecurity and confusion, aggravated, despite the threat of fascism on our very doorstep, by endless internal conflicts and diverging tendencies. As I watched the realization of an old dream, all I felt was sadness.

And then one day I learned of Lorca's death, from a Republican who'd somehow managed to slip through the lines. Shortly before *Un Chien andalou*, Lorca and I had had a falling-out; later, thin-skinned Andalusian that he was, he thought (or pretended to think) that the film was actually a personal attack on him.

'Bunuel's made a little film, just like that!' he used to say, snapping his fingers. 'It's called *An Andalusian Dog*, and I'm the dog!'

By 1934, however, we were the best of friends once again; and despite the fact that I sometimes thought he was a bit too fond of public adulation, we spent a great deal of time together. With Ugarte, we often drove out into the mountains to relax for a few hours in the Gothic solitude of El Paular. The monastery itself was in ruins, but there were a few spartan rooms reserved for people from the Fine Arts Institute. If you brought your own sleeping bag, you could even spend the night.

It was difficult, of course, to have serious discussions about painting and poetry while the war raged around us. Four days before Franco's arrival, Lorca, who never got excited about politics, suddenly decided to leave for Granada, his native city.

'Federico,' I pleaded, trying to talk him out of it. 'Horrendous things are happening. You can't go down there now; it's safer to stay right here.'

He paid no attention to any of us, and left, tense and frightened, the following day. The news of his death was a terrific shock. Of all the human beings I've ever known, Federico was the finest. I don't mean his plays or his poetry; I mean him personally. He was his own masterpiece. Whether sitting at the piano imitating Chopin, improvising a pantomime, or acting out a scene from a play, he was irresistible. He read beautifully, and he had passion, youth, and joy. When I first met him, at the Residencia, I was an unpolished rustic, interested primarily in sports. He transformed me, introduced me to a wholly different world. He was like a flame.

His body was never found. Rumors about his death circulated freely, and Dali even made the ignoble suggestion that there'd been some homosexual foul play involved. The truth is that Lorca died because he was a poet. 'Death to the intelligentsia' was a favorite wartime slogan. When he got to Granada, he apparently stayed with the poet Rosales, a Falangist whose family was friendly with Lorca's. I guess he thought he was safe with Rosales, but a group of men (no one knows who they were, and it doesn't really matter, anyway) led by someone called Alonso appeared one night, arrested him, and drove him away in a truck with some workers. Federico was terrified of suffering and death. I can imagine what he must have felt, in the middle of the night in a truck that was taking him to an olive grove to be shot. I think about it often.

At the end of September, the Republican minister of foreign affairs, Alvarez del Vayo, asked to see me. Curious, I went to his office and was told only that I'd find out everything I wanted to know when I got to Geneva. I left Madrid in an overcrowded train and found myself sitting next to a POUM commander, who kept shouting that the Republican government was garbage and had to be wiped out at any cost. (Ironically, I was to use this commander later, as a spy, when I worked in Paris.) When I changed trains in Barcelona, I ran into José Bergamín and Muñoz Suaï, who were going to Geneva with several students to attend a political convention. They asked me what kind of papers I was carrying.

'But you'll never get across the border,' Suaï cried, when I told him. 'You need a visa from the anarchists to do that!'

The first thing I saw when we arrived at Port Bou was a group of soldiers ringing the station, and a table where three somber-faced anarchists, led by a bearded Italian, were holding court like a panel of judges.

'You can't cross here,' they told me when I showed them my papers.

Now the Spanish language is capable of more scathing blasphemies than any other language I know. Curses elsewhere are typically brief and punctuated by other comments, but the Spanish curse tends to take the form of a long speech in which extraordinary vulgarities – referring chiefly to the Virgin Mary, the Apostles, God, Christ, and the Holy Spirit, not to mention the Pope – are strung end to end in a series of impressive scatological exclamations. In fact, blasphemy in Spain is truly an art; in Mexico, for instance, I never heard a proper curse, whereas in my native land, a good one lasts for at least three good-sized sentences. (When circumstances require, it can become a veritable hymn.)

It was with a curse of this kind, uttered in all its seemly intensity, that I regaled the three anarchists from Port Bou. When I'd finished, they stamped my papers and I crossed the border. (What I've said about the importance of the Spanish curse is no exaggeration; in certain old Spanish cities, you can still see signs like 'No Begging or Blaspheming – Subject to Fine or Imprisonment' on the main gates. Sadly, when I returned to Spain in 1960, the curse seemed much rarer; or perhaps it was only my hearing.)

In Geneva, I had a fast twenty-minute meeting with the minister, who asked me to go to Paris and start work for the new ambassador, who turned out to be my friend Araquistán, a former journalist, writer, and left-wing Socialist. Apparently, he needed men he could trust. I stayed in Paris until the end of the war; I had an office on the rue de la

Pépinière and was officially responsible for cataloguing the Republican propaganda films made in Spain. In fact, however, my job was somewhat more complicated. On the one hand, I was a kind of protocol officer, responsible for organizing dinners at the embassy, which meant making sure that André Gide was not seated next to Louis Aragon. On the other hand, I was supposed to oversee 'news and propaganda.' This job required that I travel – to Switzerland, Antwerp (where the Belgian Communists gave us their total support), Stockholm, London – drumming up support for various Republican causes. I also went to Spain from time to time, carrying suitcases stuffed with tracts that had been printed in Paris. Thanks to the complicity of certain sailors, our tracts once traveled to Spain on a German ship.

While the French government steadfastly refused to compromise or to intervene on behalf of the Republic, a move that would certainly have changed the direction of things, the French people, particularly the workers who belonged to the Confédération Générale de Travail, helped us enormously. It wasn't unusual, for instance, for a railroad employee or a taxi driver to come see me and tell me that two Fascists had arrived the previous night on the eight-fifteen train and had gone to such-and-such a hotel. I passed all information of this kind directly to Araquistán, who was proving to be by far our most efficient ambassador.

The nonintervention of France and the other democratic powers was fatal to the Republican cause. Although Roosevelt did declare his support, he ceded to the pressure from his Catholic constituency and did not intervene. Neither did Léon Blum in France. We'd never hoped for direct participation, but we had thought that France, like Germany and Italy, would at least authorize the transport of arms and 'volunteers.' In fact, the fate of Spanish refugees in France was nothing short of disastrous. Usually, they were simply picked up at the border and thrown directly into camps. Later, many of them fell into the hands of the Nazis and perished in Germany, mainly in Mauthausen.

The International Brigades, organized and trained by the Communists, were the only ones who gave us real aid, but there were others who simply appeared on their own, ready to fight. Homage should also be paid to Malraux, albeit some of the pilots he sent were little more than mercenaries. In my Paris office, I issued safe-conduct passes to Hemingway, Dos Passos, and Joris Ivens, so they could make a documentary on the Republican army.

There was a good deal of frustrating intrigue going on while we were making a propaganda film in Spain with the help of two Russian cameramen. This particular film was to have worldwide distribution, but after I returned to Paris, I heard nothing for several months on the progress of the shoot. Finally, I made an appointment with the head of the Soviet trade delegation, who kept me waiting for an hour until I began shouting at his secretary. The man finally received me icily.

'And what are *you* doing in Paris?' he asked testily.

I retorted that he had absolutely no right to evaluate my activities, that I only followed orders, and that I only wanted to know what had happened to the film. He refused to answer my question and showed me rather unceremoniously to the door. As soon as I got back to my office, I wrote four letters – one to *L'Humanité,* one to *Pravda,* one to the Russian ambassador, and the last to the Spanish minister – denouncing what seemed to be sabotage inside the Soviet trade delegation itself (a charge that was eventually confirmed by friends in the French Communist Party, who told me that it was 'the same all over'). It seemed that the Soviet Union had enemies, even within its own official circles, and indeed, some time later, the head of the delegation became one of the victims of the Stalinist purges.

Another strange story, which sheds a curious light on the French police (not to mention police all over the world), concerns three mysterious bombs. One day, a young and very elegant Colombian walked into my office. He'd asked to see the military attaché, but since we no longer had one, I suppose someone thought I was the next best thing. He put a small suitcase on my desk, and when he opened it, there lay three little bombs.

'They may be small,' he said to me, 'but they're powerful. They're the ones we used in the attacks on the Spanish consulate in Perpignan and on the Bordeaux–Marseille train.'

Dumbfounded, I asked him what he wanted and why he'd come to me. He replied that he had no intention of hiding his Fascist sympathies (he was a member of the Condor Legion) but that he was doing this because he despised his superior!

'I want him arrested,' he said simply. 'Why is none of your business. But if you want to meet him, come to La Coupole tomorrow at five o'clock. He'll be the man on my right. I'll just leave these with you, then.'

As soon as he'd gone, I told Araquistán, who phoned the prefect of police. When their bomb experts got through with their analysis, it turned out that our terrorist had been right; they were more potent than any others of that size.

The next day, I invited the ambassador's son and an actress friend of mine to have a drink with me at La Coupole. The Colombian was exactly where he said he'd be, sitting on the terrace with a group of people. And as incredible as it may sound, I knew the man on his right, and so did my friend. He was a Latin American actor, and we all shook hands quite amicably as we walked by. (His treacherous colleague never moved a muscle.)

Since I now knew the name of the leader of this terrorist group, as well as the hotel in Paris where he lived, I contacted the prefect, who was a Socialist, as soon as I got back to the embassy. He assured me that they'd pick him right up; but time went by, and nothing happened. Later, when I ran into the boss sitting happily with his friends at the Select on the Champs-Elysées, I wept with rage. What kind of world is this? I asked myself. Here's a known criminal, and the police don't want any part of him!

Shortly afterward, I heard from my Colombian informant again, who told me that his leader would be at our embassy the next day applying for a visa to Spain. Once again, he was correct. The actor had a diplomatic passport and got his visa with no trouble whatsoever. On his way to Madrid, however, he was arrested at the border by the Republican police, who'd been warned ahead of time; but he was released almost immediately on the protest of his government. He went on to Madrid, carried out his mission, and then calmly returned to Paris. Was he invulnerable? What kind of protection did he have? I was desperate to know.

Around that time, I left on a mission to Stockholm, where I read in a newspaper that a bomb had leveled a small apartment building near the Etoile that had been the headquarters of a labor union. I remember the article saying quite precisely that the bomb was so powerful the building had simply crumbled to dust, and that two agents had died in the blast. It was obvious which terrorist had done the job.

Again, nothing happened. The man continued to pursue his activities, protected by the careful indifference of the French police, who seemed to support whomever had the upper hand. At the end of the war, the actor, a member of the Fifth Column, was decorated for his services by Franco.

While my terrorist was cheerfully going about his dirty work in Paris, I was being violently attacked by the French right wing, who – believe it or not – had not forgotten *L'Age d'or.* They wrote about my taste for profanity and my 'anal complex,' and the newspaper *Gringoire* (or was it *Candide?*) reminded its readers that I'd come to Paris several years before in an effort to 'corrupt French youth.'

One day, Breton came to see me at the embassy.

'*Mon cher ami,*' he began, 'there seem to be some disagreeable rumors about the Republicans executing Péret because he belonged to POUM.'

POUM had inspired some adherence among the surrealists. In fact, Benjamin Péret had left for Barcelona, where he could be seen every day on the Plaza Cataluña surrounded by people from POUM. On Breton's request, I asked some questions and learned that Péret had gone to the Aragón front in Huesca; apparently, he'd also criticized the behavior of certain POUM members so openly and vociferously that many had announced their firm intention of shooting him. I guaranteed Breton that Péret hadn't been executed by the Republicans, however, and he returned to France soon afterward, safe and sound.

From time to time, I met Dali for lunch at the Rôtisserie Périgourdine on the place St.-Michel. One day, he made me a bizarre offer.

'I can introduce you to an enormously rich Englishman,' he said. 'He's on your side, and he wants to give you a bomber!'

The Englishman, Edward James, had just bought all of Dali's 1938 output, and did indeed want to give the Republicans an ultramodern bomber which was then hidden in a Czechoslovakian airport. Knowing that the Republic was dramatically short of air strength, he was making us this handsome present – in exchange for a few masterpieces from the Prado. He wanted to set up an exhibition in Paris, as well as in other cities in France; the paintings would be placed under the warranty of the International Tribunal at The Hague, and after the war there would be two options: If the Republicans won, the paintings would be returned to the Prado, but if Franco was victorious, they'd remain the property of the Republican government in exile.

I conveyed this unusual proposition to Alvarez del Vayo, who admitted that a bomber would be very welcome, but that wild horses couldn't make him take paintings out of the Prado. 'What would they say about us?' he demanded. 'What would the press make of this? That we traded our patrimony for arms? No, no, it's impossible. Let's have no further talk about it.'

(Edward James is still alive and is the owner of several châteaux, not to mention a large ranch in Mexico.)

My secretary was the daughter of the treasurer of the French Communist party. He'd belonged to the infamous Bande à Bonnot, and his daughter remembers taking walks as a child on the arm of the notorious Raymond-la-Science. I myself knew two old-timers from the band – Rirette Maîtrejean and the gentleman who did cabaret numbers and called himself the 'innocent convict.' One day, a communiqué arrived asking for information about a shipment of potassium from Italy to a Spanish port then in the hands of the Fascists. My secretary called her father.

'Let's go for a little drive,' he said to me two days later, when he arrived in my office. 'I want you to meet someone.'

We stopped in a café outside of Paris, and there he introduced me to a somber but elegantly dressed American, who seemed to be in his late thirties and who spoke French with a strong accent.

'I hear you want to know about some potassium,' he inquired mildly.
'Yes,' I replied.
'Well, I think I just might have some information for you about the boat.'

He did indeed give me very precise information about both cargo and itinerary, which I immediately telephoned to Negrín. Several years later, I met the man again at a cocktail party at the Museum of Modern Art in New York. We looked at each other across the room, but never exchanged a word. Later still, after the Second World War, I saw him at La Coupole with his wife. This time, we had a chat, during which he told me that he used to run a factory in the outskirts of Paris and had supported the Republican cause in various ways, which is how my secretary's father knew him.

During this time I was living in the suburb of Meudon. When I got home at night, I'd always stop, one hand on my gun, and check to make sure I hadn't been followed. We lived in a climate of fear and secrets and unknown forces, and as we continued to receive hourly bulletins on the progress of the war, we watched our hopes slowly dwindle and die.

It's not surprising that Republicans like myself didn't oppose the Nazi–Soviet pact. We'd been so disappointed by the Western democracies, who still treated the Soviet Union with contempt and refused all meaningful contact with its leaders, that we saw Stalin's gesture as a way of gaining time, of strengthening our forces, which, no matter what happened in Spain, were sure to be thrown into World War II. Most of the French Communist party also approved of the pact; Aragon made that clear more than once. One of the rare voices raised in protest within the party was that of the brilliant Marxist intellectual Paul Nizan. Yet we all knew that the pact wouldn't last, that, like everything else, it too would fall apart.

I remained sympathetic to the Communist party until the end of the 1950s, when I finally had to confront my revulsion. Fanaticism of any kind has always repelled me, and Marxism was no exception; it was like any other religion that claims to have found *the* truth. In the 1930s, for instance, Marxist doctrine permitted no mention of the unconscious mind or of the numerous and profound psychological forces in the individual. Everything could be explained, they said, by socioeconomic mechanisms, a notion that seemed perfectly derisory to me. A doctrine like that leaves out at least half of the human being.

I know I'm digressing; but, as with all Spanish picaresques, digression seems to be my natural way of telling a story. Now that I'm old and my memory is weaker, I have to be very careful, but I can't seem to resist beginning a story, then abandoning it suddenly for a seductive paren- thesis, and by the time I finish, I've forgotten where I began. I'm always asking my friends: 'Why am I telling you this?' And now I'm afraid I'll have to give in to one last digression.

There were all kinds of missions I had to carry out, one being that of Negrín's bodyguard from time to time. Armed to the teeth and backed up by the Socialist painter Quintanilla, I used to watch over Negrín at the Gare d'Orsay without his being aware of it. I also often slipped across the border into Spain, carrying 'special' documents. It was on one of those occasions that I took a plane for the first time in my life, along with Juanito Negrín, the prime minister's son. We'd just flown over the Pyrenees when we saw a Fascist fighter plane heading toward us from the direction of Majorca. We were terrified, until it veered off suddenly and turned around, dissuaded perhaps by the DC-8 from Barcelona.

During a trip to Valencia, I went to see the head of agitprop to show him some papers that had come to us in Paris and which we thought might be useful to him. The following morning, he picked me up and drove me to a villa a few kilometers outside the city, where he intro- duced me to a Russian, who examined my documents and claimed to recognize them. Like the Falangists and the Germans, the Repub- licans and the Russians had dozens of contacts like this – the secret services were doing their apprenticeships everywhere. When a Repub- lican brigade found itself besieged from the other side of the Gavarnie, French sympathizers smuggled arms to them across the mountains. In fact, throughout the war, smugglers in the Pyrenees transported both men and propaganda. In the area of St.-Jean-de-Luz, a brigadier in the French gendarmerie gave the smugglers no trouble if they were crossing the border with Republican tracts. I wish there'd been a more offi- cial way to show my gratitude, but I did give him a superb sword I'd bought near the place de la République, on which I'd had engraved: 'For Services Rendered to the Spanish Republic.'

Our relationship with the Fascists was exceedingly complex, as the García incident illustrates so well. García was an out-and-out crook who claimed to be a Socialist. During the early months of the war, he set up his racket in Madrid under the sinister name of the Brigada del Amanecer – the Sunrise Brigade. Early in the morning, he'd break into the houses of the well-to-do, 'take the men for a walk,' rape the women, and steal whatever he and his band could get their hands on. I was in Paris when a French union man who was working in a hotel came to tell me that a Spaniard was getting ready to take a ship for South America and that he was carrying a suitcase full of stolen jewels. It seemed that García had made his fortune, left Spain, and was skipping the continent altogether under an assumed name.

García was a terrible embarrassment to the Republic, but the Fascists were also desperate to catch him. The boat was scheduled for a stop-over at Santa Cruz de Tenerife, which at that time was occupied by Franco. I passed my information along to the ambassador, and without a moment's hesitation he relayed it to the Fascists via a neutral embassy. When García arrived in Santa Cruz, he was picked up and hanged.

One of the strangest stories to emerge from the war was the Calanda pact. When the agitation began, the civil guard was ordered to leave Calanda and concentrate at Saragossa. Before leaving, however, the officers gave the job of maintaining order in the town to a sort of council made up of leading citizens, whose first venture was to arrest several notorious activists, including a well-known anarchist, a few Socialist peasants, and the only Communist. When the anarchist forces from Barcelona reached the outskirts of town at the beginning of the war, these notable citizens decided to pay a visit to the prison.

'We've got a proposition for you,' they told the prisoners. 'We're at war, and heaven only knows who's going to win. We're all Calandians, so we'll let you out on the condition that, whatever happens, all of us promise not to engage in any acts of violence whatsoever.'

The prisoners agreed, of course, and were immediately released; a few days later, when the anarchists entered Calanda, their first act was to execute eighty-two people. Among the victims were nine Dominicans, most of the leading citizens on the council, some doctors and land-owners, and even a few poor people whose only crime was a reputation for piety.

The deal had been made in the hope of keeping Calanda free from the violence that was tearing the rest of the country apart, to make the town a kind of no man's land; but neutrality was a mirage: it was fatal to believe that anyone could escape time or history.

Another extraordinary event that occurred in Calanda, and probably in many other villages as well, began with the anarchist order to go to the main square, where the town crier blew his trumpet and announced: 'From today on, it is decreed that there will be free love in Calanda.' As you can imagine, the declaration was received with utter stupefaction, and the only consequence was that a few women were harassed in the streets. No one seemed to know what free love meant, and when the women refused to comply with the decree, the hecklers let them go on their way with no complaints. To jump from the perfect rigidity of Catholicism to something called free love was no easy feat; the entire town was in a state of total confusion. In order to restore order, in people's minds more than anywhere else, Mantecon, the governor of Aragón, made an extemporaneous speech one day from the balcony of our house in which he declared that free love was an absurdity and that we had other, more serious things to think about, like a civil war.

By the time Franco's troops neared Calanda, the Republican sympathizers in the town had long since fled. Those who stayed to greet the Falangists had nothing to worry about. Yet if I can believe a Lazarist father who came to see me in New York, about a hundred people in Calanda were executed, so fierce was the Fascists' desire to remove any possible Republican contamination.

My sister Conchita was arrested in Saragossa after Republican planes had bombed the city (in fact, a bomb fell on the roof of the basilica without exploding, which gave the church an unparalleled opportunity to talk about miracles), and my brother-in-law, an army officer, was accused of having been involved in the incident. Ironically, he was in a Republican jail at that very moment. Conchita was finally released, but not before a very close brush with execution.

(The Lazarist father who came to New York brought me the portrait Dali had painted of me during our years at the Residencia. After he told me what had happened in Calanda, he said to me earnestly, 'Whatever you do, don't go back there!' I had no desire whatsoever to go back, and many years were to pass before I did in fact return.)

In 1936, the voices of the Spanish people were heard for the first time in their history; and, instinctively, the first thing they attacked was the Church, followed by the great landowners – their two ancient enemies. As they burned churches and convents and massacred priests, any doubts anyone may have had about hereditary enemies vanished completely.

I've always been impressed by the famous photograph of those ecclesiastical dignitaries standing in front of the Cathedral of Santiago de Compostela in full sacerdotal garb, their arms raised in the Fascist salute toward some officers standing nearby. God and Country are an unbeatable team; they break all records for oppression, and bloodshed.

I've never been one of Franco's fanatical adversaries. As far as I'm concerned, he wasn't the Devil personified. I'm even ready to believe that he kept our exhausted country from being invaded by the Nazis. Yes, even in Franco's case there's room for some ambiguity. And in the cocoon of my timid nihilism, I tell myself that all the wealth and culture on the Falangist side ought to have limited the horror. Yet the worst excesses came from them; which is why, alone with my dry martini, I have my doubts about the benefits of money and culture.

∽

The great Spanish film-maker **Luis Buñuel** was born in 1900 in Calanda, a small town in the province of Teruel. In 1917, he went to the University of Madrid, where he ended up studying philosophy and befriending Federico Lorca and Salvador Dali. Buñuel moved to Paris in 1925, where he made *Un Chien Andalou* (with Dali) and *L'Age d'Or* (without Dali, who objected to its anti-Catholicism). In 1934, Buñuel returned to Spain and started to make commercial films for Filomofono. By then, he was a communist fellow-traveller. At the outbreak of the Civil War, Buñuel was sent by the Republican government first to Geneva and then to Paris where, he produced *España 1936*, a moving documentary that won much support for the Republican cause. He then went to Hollywood to give advice on films being made about the Civil

War and was still there when the war ended. Buñuel returned to Spain in 1961 to make *Viridiana* – a film that bizarrely was passed by the government censors, who requested only a minor change to the ending. The film won the Palme d'Or at Cannes, provoked great controversy and was banned in Spain for the next 17 years – until the death of Franco.

> When De Sica saw it in Mexico City, he walked out horrified and depressed. Afterwards, he and my wife Jeanne went to have a drink, and he asked her if I was really that monstrous, and if I beat her when we made love.
> 'When there's a spider that needs getting rid of,' she replied, laughing, 'he comes looking for me.'
>
> (*My Last Breath*, page 238)

Buñuel died in Mexico City in 1983.

MURIEL RUKEYSER

WE CAME FOR GAMES

A Memoir of the People's Olympics, Barcelona, 1936

from *Savage Coast*

W E COULD SEE VERY LITTLE from the train. But what we could see was full of sunlight and mystery at the same time: the Water-polo team out there on the station platform doing exercises, and all the yellow flowering mimosa trees full of little boys trying to see into the windows of the compartments.

There was the station, and the row of houses beyond. We showed no sign of starting. The engineer, somebody said, was sitting on the steps up front, eating bread and sausage.

I could hear a radio playing Bing Crosby songs, and then a wild yodeling broke in; it was the Swiss team in the car ahead.

An old Catalan woman said, 'This train isn't going to move, not anymore.'

I say 'we,' but I had been sent down from London by myself. It was the hot, beautiful summer of 1936, my first time out of America, with all the smiting days and nights of the month in England.

I was working for the people who had brought me over with them, and I had driven across to London from the landing in Liverpool on the first morning. Then the first tastes: many people who came to my friends' flat, people who afterward would be the Labour government, and the people I saw, poets and refugees and the League of Nations correspondent for the *Manchester Guardian*. A brilliant performance of *The Seagull*, and the Russian Ballet, and a tithe-marchers' day, all silent, with the signs reading WE WILL NOT BE DRUV. The feeling of Hitler in the sky, very highly regarded by many, the feeling of Mussolini. Adventures in meaning, too; curiosity about the cooperatives, for my friends were working on a book about co-ops in England and Scandinavia as well as in the U.S.; curiosity about Russia; all-absorbing delight and storm about people, for me, and my own wish not to be 'druv,' for I was driven.

When the editor of an English magazine said, 'Will you go to Barcelona for me?' I put away a chance to go to Finland and Russia with my friends. The Olympic Games were to be held in Hitler's Berlin early in August, and there were going to be Games in Barcelona as a peaceful assertion and a protest. France had asked for more money for these Games than the sum allotted to the big Olympics, and the United States and many other countries were going to send teams. The wedding of the other editor of the magazine, a woman I had never met, came at that moment too – and my editor would have to go to the wedding. I told my editor I would go. He came to the station with me, and gave me a handy black and orange book, a *Guide to 25 Languages of Europe*.

Now that book was being passed among us on the train.

On the way south, there was a tantalizing hour in Paris, glimpses of avenues and buildings seen in movies and paintings and dreams, and kiosks with posters advertising gas masks for children. A change of trains, and the night, and the Spanish frontier at Port Bou, and then this train, going slowly, with a flash of the Mediterranean, and shoulders of olive hills, and a Catalan family in the wooden compartment with me. Slowly, and the olive, yellow-strapped uniform of the Civil Guard; the grins over English cigarettes and the Olympic teams, whom everybody had noticed at the frontier because one or two had some difficulty about the collective passports under which they traveled.

The train had gone more and more slowly, and then stopped here, Moncada. A small station after Gerona, a clearly unimportant town. The Spaniards begin to talk to the Hungarian athletes, partly in French, partly in a mixture of sign language and *25 Languages*. But the phrase-book language, 'One o'clock exactly. Thank you very much,' would not carry the questions about the Olympics, or politics. The Spaniards said, 'The

Army. Some on one side, some on the other. Not good to talk.' These are not Spaniards; they are Catalans. Their own nation, their own language (not in the orange and black book), and they have been preparing for these Games, these *Jocs*, for a long time. People are hurrying to Barcelona from Paris, from Switzerland, from America, from all over France, from England, whose unions have sent a tennis team and some track people.

The train does not go. On the station platform, there are armed civilians patrolling, and now the small boys are climbing the little blossoming trees. Rumors begin to go through the train, and the Catalan family sitting with me begins to make a plan. The heavyset fine father talks to his mother, who agrees; he pats his young olive-colored son on the head. The boy is eleven; he looks at me with iodine-color eyes as his father invites me to come into the town with them. His father says, 'It is General Strike.'

At that moment two Americans come through the train. They have heard that an American woman is here. The lady from Peapack, New Jersey, had shared my compartment on the French train; she is up front, and is concerned about me. I decided for the train, and told the Catalan family I would find them later.

We went through the train, talking; really we were collectors of rumor. The engineer was in charge of us now, and the stationmaster spoke for the town. No, he could not say how long the strike would last. But the shooting had begun at the barracks in Barcelona that morning. It had something to do with the Games, they said; or something to do with the moment of the Games, at which several thousand foreigners were expected in the city. Some of the soldiers, at the appeal of the crowd before them, had refused to fire and had turned against their officers, to immense cheers. There was something about generals, a general flying in from the Islands.

The tourists, frightened and inconvenienced, murmur, make a kind of flutter and try to plan.

Who is on this train? Conspicuously, Catalan families on their way from town to town or back to Barcelona, and the two teams, the Hungarian water-polo team from Paris and the Swiss team. The Catalans leave the train, almost without exception, and find quarters in the town.

There is a German who has come to run in the Games, on his own, from France where he has been working as a cabinetmaker. Bavarian, with a broad strong face like a man in a Brueghel picture – or a Käthe Kollwitz – his cheekbones stand out. He smiles, a very dark brown flashing. He had been a *Rotfrontkämpfer* who left Germany soon after Hitler came to power.

In first class, there are Italian businessmen, and a German family with two children who are hitting each other; a very beautiful woman from South America; the French deputy, M. de Paiche, who has come officially to the Games, and his male secretary; two rather attractive English couples on their way to Mallorca on holiday, from a bank and from *The New Statesman*, and others in the two cars who are not at once identifiable. In the one Pullman, there are Hollywood people, a director and two cameramen.

A Spanish doctor emerges from the Pullman and tells us about the Hollywood men; he has offered to hire a car, and to go with them to the city. But they do not want that. They want to go back to the frontier.

The mayor of the town appears on the platform; very grave, wearing in his lapel a black ribbon of mourning. There have been deaths of men from this town today.

A tall man, distinguished face, thin, with fine movements, climbs down the steps of the train. We see him speaking for a while to the mayor, as the long evening closes down. The birds begin; the boys whistle from the trees. Word comes back: the tall man is a professor of philosophy from the University of Madrid. He will act as go-between for the train.

First of all, household arrangements. The two English couples bring basins of water and the little cakes of soap they carry with them, for the use of the train.

'But we can wash on the train!' says the lady from Peapack. She has five white rawhide valises, I admired them in the compartment, one is a hatbox.

No, we can't wash on the train; that water was used up hours ago.

We sleep on the train. As we choose places – we have all moved to first class – the two teams are playing soccer outside. There is a rattle of guns from the olive grove on the hill. A dark figure moves to the steps where the professor of philosophy has stood. After about an hour, he comes out again; his face cannot be seen, but his shoulders are in grief.

The station is dark, except for three or four lights and the slight movement of mimosa flowers, shadow and yellow in a slight breeze coming down cool from the Pyrenees.

Night. Two families, the father wounded, walk in from Barcelona with news of a tremendous battle. The radio goes on at half-hour intervals: Beethoven's *Fifth*, government bulletins, tangos, *You're Driving Me Crazy*, sardanas, Catalan songs. As long as the radio goes, the government is in control. And now, over that booming, scratching sound, a tired voice. The general who had tried to take Catalonia. There are four of them: Goded, Mola, Sanjurjo, Franco. Sanjurjo has been killed; this is Goded. He sounds to me like the businessmen during the Crash, an endless tiredness in his defeated voice. He is telling his followers to lay down their arms. There has been enough bloodshed, he says.

We write a letter on the train – to the town – and take up a collection for the wounded. We each give a little, the athletes do, too. No, not the German family, not the Italian businessmen, not the Cockney shoe salesman; not the six platinum blondes, the Rodney Hudson Young Ladies, who were supposed to open tonight in Barcelona. The passenger whose help counts most turns out to be a League of Nations observer from Switzerland. He revises our letter to the town, putting it in perfectly acceptable diplomatic language.

We take it into Moncada, to the next street over from the station, past the finer houses belonging to people who live in the capital and come there for weekends sometimes. In the next street, the Committee is in session at the mayor's office. The mayor accepts the money with a speech of thanks, and turns the letter over to the Committee – formed of members of the two unions, and the Anarchists. Catalonia is Anarchist country, the first I have ever seen. They say there has been fighting for a hundred years, but never like this.

One of us begins to speak in sympathy for the town, but the mayor puts his hand up, stopping him flat. 'No,' he says. 'No foreign nationals can intrude in revolutionary situations.'

The passengers' committee and the Committee shake hands, and we go back to the train.

The roosters crowed all night, after the radio shut down. At four-forty-five the train shook, and the branches of the trees. A spire of black smoke could be seen off to the side; the church had been bombed.

Now we begin to hear the story. The dark figure who had come to the train last night had been the priest, come to ask the professor to hide him. For an hour, the professor had considered, and had finally given his answer: this was an international place, the church had been storing ammunition for the officers' revolt, and he could not. Years later, in America, I heard Spaniards debating this incident. The professor had become an ambassador by then; but this incident had become one of the most well-known and a node of argument of the war, with the death of Lorca. The train had become famous for the story of the priest and the professor of philosophy.

Five officers had been shot that morning in Moncada, we heard, and before their deaths, one had said, 'Do what you want with me. I've killed two or three hundred of your men already.'

Gun cars begin to appear, with U.G.T. and C.N.T. painted on their sides – the initials of the united trade-union groups. The guns bristle, pointing at us as we walk in the town. The Committee has suspended the strike for an hour, to allow buying of food. Ernie and Rose, the American couple, face guns. He is a labor lawyer from New York, and he is comforting her. She is terrified of the guns this morning. I see her again at four in the afternoon, as the gun cars come through again. She is standing with her back to them, eating chocolate. The fear is absorbed very quickly.

The teams are doing exercises on the station platform. A member of the Committee comes to ask us not to come out of the train anymore. I am in third class when the word of the change of control in Moncada comes through. A Catalan woman has made a fire here, and is cooking soup. The Member of the Committee will speak for the town from now on, and Otto, the German, is speaking for the train.

The town has given the engineer permission to drive the train a hundred feet down the track, toward Barcelona. Damn fool passengers have been using the toilets; they must stop, and something must be done. The English couples have done all they can to get people to use the lavatories in the station but some few people are not listening, and PASSENGERS WILL PLEASE REFRAIN is not widely known. The town has two wells, and is giving us one of them. It also is giving us the use of the schoolhouse, the most modern building in Moncada. We can sleep on the tables. The two teams move to the schoolhouse at once; they have a playing field, too, even though they are warned not to go out for more than two hours, now. Officers and rebel men are escaping northward from Barcelona, and running battles are expected.

There is a sound of cannon from Barcelona.

One of the Englishmen comes back as the stores close, with a supply of gunnysacks to sleep on. 'So cheap – really such a bargain,' he commends them to us. 'They're really clean.'

The people on the train are becoming very jumpy. Now we all go to the schoolhouse, for trucks have been promised to take the two teams into Barcelona; but they do not come.

Otto and I begin to talk in the late afternoon, in a complex immediate closeness. He does not speak English, and my freshman German is very bad, clumsy, full of mistakes. I have never wanted language so much. We try, and laugh, and hand the orange and black book back and forth. We try the pale yellow section, English, Spanish, French, the Romance tongues; we can both speak French of a sort. Then the pale blue: German, Dutch, the Scandinavians, and English. Then the buff: Russian, Polish, Czech, Serbo-Croatian, Bulgarian, always English. And the green, that the Hungarians have been using (but Ernie speaks Hungarian, with the languages that most of us speak), with Finnish, Estonian, that group. And the orange, Greek, Turkish, Albanian, Arabic, Esperanto. English always. Never Catalan.

With our language of many colors, we make a beginning.

The French newspapers lie on the floor of the train aisle. A tiny paragraph can be read if you pick up the paper. It says that shooting broke out yesterday in Spanish Morocco. But you don't have to pick the paper up to see the big picture of the feature story. It is Nijinsky in his

Swiss sanatorium, against the background of black cloth unrolled in the shape of a cross, dancing his black dance of the world.

Rattle of machine guns, in the town, all night.

The soldiers reappeared, as loyal troops. Civil Guard, for the government, patrolling the train, their yellow straps shining dark in the light from the platform.

In the morning a car came – not for the Hollywood men, who are shouting by now, but for the little Spanish doctor, who is needed in Barcelona. It goes off in that direction, the purple-faced director staring.

Now a curious panic begins on the train. Rumor has followed rumor, and now we hear that the looting has begun. 'Rape,' says one of the Rodney Hudson blondes, and the shoe salesman comforts her.

Down the street of houses belonging to absentee landlords, and facing the train, a methodical process, perfectly visible to the passengers. A group of young men – rather like the young men who went off in an open truck the first night to fight in Barcelona, no two firearms alike – go from door to door. Systematically, one opens the big heavy door with its black knocker in the shape of an iron hand dropped to sound on the door. If his key does not work, he forces the lock. Two young men go in, and after a moment, they can be seen with two or three religious prints and a hunting rifle and a pistol, perhaps. This goes on; the scene repeats. Suddenly, a boy of five or so ducks under the arm of the leader and disappears for a minute. Still running, he comes out with a heap of towels and cuts down the street. We all watch. 'Spanish looting,' says Ernie.

Halfway down the block, his mother catches him, walks in the sight of all to the young leader, returns the towels and makes her short speech.

Far off, among the olive trees on the hill, a man can be seen. He is running too. Shouts hurrah on the slopes. A plane flies far to one side, but one pulls one's head in. Everything is visible to the naked eyes, one feels.

At this moment the trucks arrive. There are two of them, open, with railings and stakes. They are for the teams and for anyone else who wants to try the ride. A car precedes them, a Communist Party car. The Americans wonder about being saved by the Communist Party, each with his own feelings before that prospect. Two American school teachers, who have been reading pamphlets on *The Problems of the Spanish Revolution*. The two teams; Otto and I; Ernie and Rose; some of the others in the second truck. There is actually a united front now in Catalonia, Socialists, Communists, Anarchists, all backing the government.

The valises are set up around the sides of the truck for fortification. The Swiss team amazes the town with a burst of yodeling, part of our thanks. A machine-gun truck goes down the road; we are to follow in two minutes.

Sudden spasm of nerves and laughing. Ernie, in the voice of Groucho Marx − 'Of course they know this means war!' A tiny boy in his shirt, holding his penis. Ernie − 'Vive le sport!' And the truck starts off to Barcelona.

The road has fortifications, thrown-up bales of hay, later there are barricades of paving stones flying the red flag for unity. There are machine-gun nests, dead horses, dead mules, terrible spots that I cannot identify at several crossroads. A Ford sign on the way into the city.

As we reach Barcelona, the white flags are at all windows − towels, sheets, tablecloths hung over the windowsills for peace. Shooting is heard again and again − not cannons or machine guns (except once), but guns. My teeth feel the shots, and everything else, too; a nerve in my leg jumps. Ahead of us, a man falls, and our truck swerves and turns, taking a detour as some street-corner battle opens.

We are taking another road to the Hotel Olympic − immense building requisitioned for the athletes.

In the streets, there are no cars that are not armed and painted with initials or titles. VISCA (that's Viva) CATALUNYA.

Overturned cars, dead animals, coils and spires of smoke rising from burning churches. The coils of color climbing the architectural heart of the city, Gaudí's marvelous church, untouched by harm. The Chinese Quarter, money-set.

From the roof of the hotel, the city is laid out before you, the wide avenues to the port, the Rambla, and there Columbus on a gilded ball and the water beyond. The heights over the city, Tibidabo, are very beautiful, the squares are illuminated, and the bullring, Monumental y Arena across the way, still a perfect place for snipers.

Look down, you can see the teams arriving still. Cars are overturned, here in the Plaza España, one of the two centers of the fighting. Guards stream into the building, and girls with rifles take their places in the cars.

In the dark, we set out for dinner at the stadium, with M. de Paiche (whose stomach has been badly upset by the diet of beans and soda) and his secretary. The windshield of the car we drive in is spangled by bullets, and there is blood on the cushion behind me. I sit upright; but the car goes up a winding road, and I can't help learning back.

Two thousand foreigners, thrown on the city as civil war began, are to be lodged and fed here.

The stadium is filled with athletes and stranded nationals. We eat beans; they are delicious. News goes around. We meet the English team, and at last the American team. Block parties have been held for months, and tryouts at Randall's Island – and here they are: Dr. Smith and George Gordon Battle in charge, and Al Chakin, boxing and wrestling; Irving Jenkins, boxing; Frank Payton, Eddie Kraus, Dorothy Tucker, Harry Engle, Myron Dickes, all track; Bernie Danchik, gymnast; Julian Raul, cycling; Charles Burley, William Chamberlain and Frank Adams Hanson.

In the meetings that night, the decisions are made to leave – the French, whose M. de Paiche says, 'We have much to learn from Spain' – and many others, to take the burden of thousands (some say twenty thousand) of foreigners off the government at this crucial and bloody moment. The French leave the next day on the *Chellé* and *Djeube*; we all see them off, waving from the dock. Even the gypsies, in red and pink, salute with clenched fists up. At the last moment, as on the deck the arms all rise together, the ship we watch appears to lift up on the sea.

The American and British athletes decide to stay, and ask us to come with them, to clear the Olympic building of as many people as possibly can go. The British are wonderful, brave, droll – they are feeling particularly humiliated, for they have had to lie down on the tennis courts while they were shot at – *lie down on the courts!* We go with them into the narrow streets, with barricades thrown breast high, paving torn up, the crowds in lyric late nighttime Catalan – to the Hotel Madrid in the Calle de Boqueria. Here, on the street, in the hotel and the two restaurants, the Condal and our own, we have the next days. We send our cables; the Telefónica, run by American business, is proud of a continued service.

At the American consulate, Drew Franklin tells us that Companys has asked him to supervise our leaving. There is no safe conduct, the consul tells us, don't try to go to the border by car. An art professor and a correspondent are there; the men should leave off their jackets, the women should not wear jewelry – 'They will think you are proletarians.' The hysterical reports have begun to register. Our three Hollywood men have reached the frontier, and have told reporters that they saw wild scenes of looting from the train, that they suffered deprivations and saw horrors.

Some of the athletes are talking of joining the fighting forces, which now include many members of the Assault Troops in their blue uniforms, the Civil Guard, and men and women who a week ago had been civilians.

We walk, going back always to the Madrid, talking with Otto, with the English athletes, smoking *Bisontes* (the Spanish relative of Camels) and drinking wine. There was a moment outside a house in Moncada, when they taught me the double-spouted drinking; I learned laughing how to bite off the free-pouring drink. My practice drink was water, not wine, and they were shooting at the house – real practice conditions. We went in the house, and I learned. Now we drank from glasses, and from the pouring too; we came to our decisions in these days. It cleared and deepened between us; it was certain for Otto. He had found his chance to fight fascism, and a profound quiet, amounting to joy, was there; it was the German chance, in or out of Germany.

We talked with the athletes about what might happen. It was a matter of doing what we did *entire*, with our whole selves committed. What about King Edward, said the English. There was a rumor that something was happening so that his life was at last coherent, politically and erotically; it had something to do with the American woman, Mrs. Simpson, but there was a lot more besides.

Who would help the government and the people of Spain against the generals and the officers, the Fascist revolt backed by Germany and Italy? The checks and guns had been found in the Fascist strongholds. News of all this was published in the papers, which were coming out whole after the first days in which front-page stories were torn out, and sometimes hardly anything but the lists of the dead and wounded appeared. The death of the dancer La Argentina, whom I had loved to watch, was noted in a tiny paragraph.

But who would help? Not England, we thought. The English interests in cork, wine, many valuables, were visible. Her leaders liked Mussolini – 'gentle,' Churchill called him – and thought Hitler would improve. But the French were naturally and politically friendly. And America would surely be the friend of the Republic. 'We can count on you,' the poet Aribau had said.

The army begins to go. 'A Zaragoza,' is the word.

The city is under martial law. We are called to a meeting of the Olympic people remaining, in a smaller square. The Norwegian speaks, briefly, and the Italian representative of his team. The Catalan speaks, in the language that is beginning to break open to us, glints like French, flashes like Spanish:

'This is what the Games stand for,' not only to work against what is about to happen in Berlin, what is happening in Germany and through Hitler, but the true feelings of the Games, their finality: '*Amor i fraternitat entre els homes de tot el món i de totes les races.*'

And Martín, the organizer of the Games, has the last word. He speaks to us as foreigners, as ourselves. He is speaking to me directly, at least that is how I hear his open words:

'The athletes came to attend the People's Olympiad, but have been privileged to stay to see the beautiful and great victory of the people in Catalonia and Spain.

'You have come for the Games, but you have remained for the greater Front, in battle and in triumph.

'Now you will leave, you will go to your own countries, but you will carry to them…' the tense sunlit square, Martín about to start for Saragossa, the people in the streets, the train, the teams, the curious new loving friendship, the song of the *Jocs*:

No és per odi, no és per guerra
Que venim a lliutar de cada terra

'…you will carry to your own countries, some of them still oppressed and under fascism and military terror, to the working people of the world, the story of what you see now in Spain.'

⌇

Muriel Rukeyser was born in 1913 in New York, where she died in 1980. Poet, activist and journalist, Rukeyser was sent to cover the People's Olympiad, a protest event against the 1936 Olympic Games being held in Berlin during the Nazi regime. In addition to the usual sporting events, the Barcelona games were to feature chess, folk dancing, music and theatre. Six thousand athletes from all over the world registered for the games, which were due to start on 19 July 1936, the day after the Civil War began. The games were cancelled and most of the athletes sent home. Some, including the German contingent, stayed on to fight for the Republic. Rukeyser said that these days in Spain were when 'I began to say what I believed'. Her whole life she wrote about the Spanish revolution in essays, poems and a powerful novel, *Savage Coast*. In 1937, the novel was rejected for publication for, among other reasons, having a protagonist who is 'too abnormal for us to respect'. This meant a politically committed feminist who enjoys sex! To make matters worse the novel was experimental in form. Rukeyser continued to work on *Savage Coast* until her death in 1980 but it was not published until 2013, when the manuscript was found in her archives. On its publication, *Savage Coast* was hailed by critics and recognized as a book which enriches and widens our understanding of the Civil War.

ANDRÉ MALRAUX

'HULLO, VALLADOLID! WHO'S SPEAKING?'

from *Days of Hope*
translated by Stuart Gilbert and Alastair Macdonald

ALL MADRID WAS ASTIR in the warm summer night, loud with the rumble of lorries stacked with rifles. For some days the Workers' Organizations had been announcing that a Fascist rising might take place at any moment, that the soldiers in the barracks had been 'got at', and that munitions were pouring in. At 1 a.m. the Government had decided to arm the people, and from 3 a.m. the production of a union-card entitled every member to be issued with a rifle. It was high time, for the reports telephoned in from the provinces, which had sounded hopeful between midnight and 2 a.m., were beginning to strike a different note.

The Central Exchange at the Northern Railway Terminus rang up the various stations along the line. Ramos, the Secretary of the Railway Workers' Union, and Manuel were in charge. With the exception of Navarre – the line from which had been cut – the replies had been uniform. Either the Government had the situation well in hand, or a Workers' Committee had taken charge of the city, pending instructions from the central authority. But now a change was coming over the dialogues.

'Is that Huesca?'

'Who's speaking?'

'The Workers' Committee, Madrid.'

'Not for long, you swine! *Arriba España!*'

Fixed to the wall by drawing-pins, the special late edition of the *Claridad* flaunted a caption six columns wide: *Comrades To Arms!*

'Hullo, Avila? How's things at your end? Madrid North speaking.'

'The hell it is, you bastards! *Viva El Cristo Rey!*'

'See you soon. *Salud!*'

An urgent message was put through to Ramos.

The Northern lines linked up with Saragossa, Burgos, and Valladolid.

'Is that Saragossa? Put me through to the Workers' Committee at the station.'

'We've shot them. Your turn next. *Arriba España!*'

'Hullo, Tablada! Madrid North here, Union Delegate.'

'Call the jail, you son of a gun. That's where your friends are. And we'll be coming for you in a day or two; we want to have a word with you.'

'*Bueno!* Let's meet on the Alcalá, second dive on the left. Got it?'

All the telephone operators were staring at Manuel, whose devil-may-care manner, curly hair, and grin gave him the air of a jovial gangster.

'Hullo, is that Burgos?'

'Commandante, Burgos, speaking.'

Ramos hung up.

A telephone-bell rang.

'Hullo, Madrid! Who's there?'

'Railway Workers' Union.'

'Miranda speaking. We hold the station and the town. *Arriba España!*'

'But *we* hold Madrid. *Salud!*'

So there was no counting on help from the North, except by way of Valladolid. There remained the Asturias.

'Is that Oviedo? Yes? Who's speaking?' Ramos was getting wary.

'Workers' Delegate. Railway Station.'

'Ramos here, the Union Secretary. How are things your end?'

'Aranda's loyal to the Government. It's touch and go at Valladolid. We're entraining three thousand armed miners to reinforce our lot.'

'When?' A clash of rifle-butts drowned the answer. Ramos repeated the question.

'At once.'

'*Salud!*'

Ramos turned to Manuel. 'Keep in touch with that train, by tele-phone.' Then called Valladolid.

'Is that Valladolid?'

'Who's speaking?'

'Station Delegate.'

'How's it going?'

'Our fellows hold the barracks. We're expecting a reinforcement from Oviedo. Do your best to get them here as soon as possible. But don't you worry; here it'll all go well. What about you?'

They were singing outside the station; Ramos could not hear himself speak.

'What?' Valladolid repeated.

'Going well! Going well!'

'Have the troops revolted?'

'Not yet.'

Valladolid hung up.

All reinforcements from the North could be diverted there.

The air was thick with engine-smoke and the reek of hot metal – the door stood open on the summer night – and a faint odour of card-board files came from the office shelves. Manuel noted down, amongst official messages concerning points and sidings – of which he could make little – the calls coming in from the various Spanish towns. From outside came bursts of song, a clatter of rifle-butts. Time and again he had to have the messages repeated. The fascists merely rang off. He noted down the various positions, on the railway-map. Navarre was cut off; all the east of the Bay of Biscay – Bilbao, Santander, and San Sebas-tian – was loyal; communications were cut at Miranda. The Asturias and Valladolid, however, were with the Government. The telephone rang ceaselessly.

'Hullo! Segovia! speaking. Who are you?'

'Representative of the Union.' Manuel looked at Ramos doubtfully; after all, what was his real position here?

'We're coming along to bite 'em off.'

'We shan't notice it. *Salud!*'

Now it was the turn of the fascist stations to start ringing up: Sarracin,

Lerma, Aranda del Duero, Sepulveda, Burgos again. From Burgos to the Sierra, threats came pouring in faster than the reinforcement trains.

'Ministry of the Interior speaking. Is that the North Station Exchange? Inform all stations that the Civil Guard and the Assault Guard are with the Government.'

'Madrid South speaking. Is that Ramos? How's it going in the North?'

'They seem to be holding Miranda and a good many places further south. Three thousand miners are going to Valladolid. That district looks pretty good for us. How's things your way?'

'They've occupied the stations at Seville and Granada. The rest's holding out.'

'Cordova?'

'We don't know. There's fighting going on in the suburbs of the towns where they hold the stations. We're in the hell of a jam at Triana. At Pennaroya, too. Look here, what you say about Valladolid's a bit staggering; sure they haven't taken it?'

Ramos changed over to another telephone.

'Hullo, Valladolid! Who's speaking?'

'The Station Delegate.'

'Oh!... We'd heard the fascists were in.'

'You heard wrong. All's well. What about you? Have the troops revolted?'

'No.'

'Hullo, Madrid North. Who's speaking?'

'In charge of transportation.'

'Tablada here. Didn't you ring us up?'

'We heard you were all shot, or in jug, or something of the sort.'

'We made a getaway. It's the fascists who're in jug. *Salud!*'

'Casa del Puelbo speaking. Inform all loyal stations that the Government, supported by the popular militia, is master of Barcelona, Murcia, Valencia, and Malaga, all Estremadura and the Mediterranean coast.'

'Hullo! Tordesillas here. Who's speaking?'

'Workers' Council, Madrid.'

'Ah! Bastards of your sort are shot! *Arriba España!*'

Medina del Campo; same dialogue. The Valladolid line was the only main line of communication with the South still open.

'Hullo, Leon! Who's speaking?'

'Union delegate. *Salud!*'

'Madrid North here. Has the miners' train from Oviedo passed?'

'Yes.'

'Do you know where it is?'

'Somewhere near Mayorga, I guess.'

Outside in the Madrid streets all was songs and the clash of rifle-butts.

'Is that Mayorga? Madrid this end. Who's speaking?'

'Who are you?'

'Workers' Council, Madrid.'

The receiver clicked dead. What had become of the train?

'Is that Valladolid ? Are you sure of holding till the miners arrive?'

'Dead sure.'

'Mayorga doesn't answer.'

'That don't matter.'

'Hullo, Madrid? Oviedo speaking. Aranda's just revolted. Fighting going on.'

'Where's the miners' train?'

'Between Leon and Mayorga.'

'Hold on a moment!' Manuel rang up, Ramos beside him. 'That Mayorga? Madrid here.'

'Who's that?'

'Workers' Council. Who are you?'

'Company Commander, Spanish Falangists. Your train's gone by, you fools. We hold all the stations up to Valladolid. We're waiting for your miners with machine-guns. Aranda's been cleaned up. See you soon!'

'The sooner the better!'

Manuel rang up all the stations between Mayorga and Valladolid, one after the other.

'That Sepulveda? Madrid North this end; Workers' Committee.'

'Yes, your train's gone through, you god-damned fools. And we're coming this week to cut your... off, you silly bitches.'

'Sounds like you'd got your genders mixed, my lad. Still... *Salud!*'

The calls continued.

'Hullo, Madrid! Is that Madrid? Navalperal de Pinares here. Railway Station. We've rushed the town again. Yes, we disarmed the fascists; they're in clink. Pass the good news along. Their people telephone us every few minutes to know if the town is still theirs. Hullo! Hullo!'

'We must send false news out everywhere,' Ramos said.

'They'll check up on it.'

'Still, it'll always give them something to scratch their heads over.'

'Hullo, Madrid North? U.G.T. here. Who's speaking?'

'Ramos.'

'We're told a train-load of fascists is on its way, with up-to-date armament. Coming from Burgos, they say. Have you any news of it?'

'We should know about it here; all the stations up to the Sierra are in our hands. Still we'd better take precautions. Hold the line a moment.'

'Manuel, call the Sierra.'

Manuel called one station after another, sawing the air with a ruler as if he were beating time. The whole Sierra was loyal. He called up the General Post Office Exchange. Had the same answer. Obviously, on the near side of the Sierra, either the fascists were lying low, or they'd been crushed.

Still, they were holding half the North. In Navarre, Mola, the former Chief of Police at Madrid, was in command; three-quarters of the regular army, as usual, were against the Government. On the Government side were the populace, the Assault Guard, and possibly the Civil Guard as well.

'The U.G.T. here. Is that Ramos?'

'Yes.'

'What about that train?'

Ramos passed on the news. 'And how's things generally?' he asked.

'*Bueno!* Excellent. Except at the War Ministry. At six they said that all was over bar the shouting. We told them they were barking up the wrong tree. But they claim that the militia's sure to scuttle. Anyhow, we don't give a damn for their opinion... The men here are making such a shindy singing, I can hardly hear you.'

In the receiver Ramos could hear the songs across the noises of the railway station.

Though the attack had obviously been launched almost every-where at the same moment, it seemed as if an army on the march were sweeping down; the railway stations held by the fascists were getting nearer and nearer Madrid. And yet there had been such tension in the air for several weeks, the dread of an attack which they might have to face, unarmed, had weighed so heavily on all the populace that tonight's warfare came as an immense relief.

⁓

André Malraux was born in Paris in 1901. A surrealist in his twenties, Malraux's commitment to left-wing politics began in Indochina, where he saw close up the effects of French colonial rule. When the Civil War broke out, Malraux went to Spain to help train the small, poorly equipped Republican Air Force. *L'Espoir (Days of Hope)*, written in 1937 and filmed (by Malraux and Boris Peskine) in 1945, is the account of the early days of the war and the heroic fight of the Republicans to defend Madrid, take Teruel and win the battle of Guadalajara. In this autobiographical novel, Malraux is Mangin, a French intellectual torn between the demands of his moral code and the need for efficient military discipline. The novel, a gripping evocation of the battle front, ends with this dilemma unresolved. In the Second World War, Malraux, after being captured in the Battle of France, escaped and joined the Resistance – for his work with British liaison officers in the Dordogne, he was awarded the Distinguished Service Order. A long-time admirer of General de Gaulle, Malraux was Minister of Cultural Affairs in the De Gaulle government from 1958 to 1969. From this period come his influential writings on art including *The Metamorphosis of the Gods*. He died in Créteil in 1976. In 1996, his ashes were moved to the Panthéon, a rare honour.

JOSÉ MARÍA GIRONELLA

NO MORE DELAY!

from *The Cypresses Believe in God*

translated by Harriet de Onís

THE NERVOUSNESS OF THE CROWD, which could not hear the dialogue, was mounting by the minute as the distance between it and the prisoners increased. The officers and the guards had already turned the corner of the Municipal Plaza. 'Now what do we do, now what do we do?' The reserves of available energy were inexhaustible.

Just then honkings were heard. The truck that had gone to deposit the arms at Communist Party headquarters was coming back jammed with members, those wearing handkerchiefs around their heads like pirates. Every one of them had a submachine gun. Gorki rode in the middle. Cosme Vila recognized among them the man who worked in the dry-cleaning establishment who had said: 'If it was my wife, I'd want to know what for.'

In spite of his potbelly, Gorki gave a flying leap from the truck and rushed over to Cosme Vila. 'Our people are dying by the hundreds in Madrid. The army and the priests have barricaded themselves in the Montaña Barracks.'

The priests, the priests – it was the magic word. This was Gorki's psychological triumph.

'Comrades, the people are giving their blood. In Gerona the people have been victorious. Let's clean out the lairs of the opposition!'

Cosme Vila, in shirtsleeves, with his wide belt and sandals, set off in the direction opposite to that taken by the officers. He had reached a decision. The thing to do was to level every church in the city. No more weighing pros and cons. No more delay!

He was making for the Church of the Sacred Heart, the church of the Jesuits. It was the nearest. The crowd caught on at once and with amazing ease forgot about Major Martínez de Soria. Julio caught on, too, and inconspicuously detached himself, making his way to police headquarters. Amid shouts, cheers, *vivas*, and *mueras*, Cosme Vila drew the thousand fanatics after him. The church loomed up before them. The sight of its serene gray towers and, above all, its huge locked door threw them into a frenzy. 'They've locked up; they knew what to expect!' Beside the church was the deserted rectory. Someone knew that there was a passageway between it and the temple.

The leaders of the mob broke into the house. Nobody there. Empty. In the waiting-room there was a table and a huge chronological album of the popes. Santi was among the first in, and he rang every bell his fingers could find. Down a gloomy corridor they came to the communicating door. They entered the church. Those who had remained outside were waiting for the immense door of the church to be thrown wide.

When they heard the first blows, they rushed up the stairs, unable to restrain themselves, and, as one man, flung themselves against the doors, trying to help those struggling with them on the inside. At the sixth try, the doors gave way. And at that moment all the lights went on. Santi had discovered the switches in the sacristy and had illuminated the festival. The temple was incapable of holding them all. Shots rang out. El Responsable was firing his revolver at the Sacred Heart on the main altar. He did not miss a shot, and yet the image did not fall. Most of the times he hit it in the mouth, so that with each shot the expression of the image changed, which aroused the crowd more and more. The side altars and benches were broken up by others of the raiders. La Valenciana had drenched her face in holy water. Gorki had climbed up on one of the pulpits, and with a long stick someone handed him was trying to reach the great central chandelier with its tinkling prisms.

The obsession of most of the mob was the confessionals. On each of them was a card with the name of the confessor. 'If only a few of them were inside!' The wood was hard and unyielding. The rifle butts hardly made a dent on it. Some of the crowd sat inside the stalls, others knelt beside them. 'The things that have gone on here!'

Future was the athlete. He was the first to approach the immense crucifix at the entrance. Taking hold of its base, he called for aid. 'Into the river with it, into the river!' he shouted. Dozens of willing hands were raised. 'Gangway, gangway!' The caravan set out. Christ lay flat, his feet higher than his head, for those bringing up the rear were taller than Future. When they came to the river embankment, the Oñar spread out muddy before them. To throw the cross over, they had to rest it on the railing, and raise it by a superhuman effort. 'Heave-ho!' Christ fell, describing a complete half-turn. He fell, and stood cleaving the mud like an arrow. The wooden arms of the cross pointed pathetically in all directions. The image rested head-down, like St. Peter.

Inside the church the struggle of man against matter was at its height. Everything was of such good quality that there was no choice but to employ fire. Cosme Vila put the first match to the high altar. He decided on this because he calculated that, in view of the thickness of the stones, the building would not burn, so there would be no danger to the neighborhood. Only the altars would go. All the hangings took fire. A confessional burned, then several benches. El Responsable was firing at the chandelier, and he had many imitators. Seeing Gorki in the pulpit, Cosme Vila suddenly thought: 'No question about it. He's the one for mayor.'

Professor Morales had not realized that it was so easy to destroy things that were centuries old. And what most impressed him was that everything was being done almost without the intervention of the human voice. Everyone was using hands and feet, pushing obstacles out of the way with his stomach, shooting. Some were laughing. Others were remembering that they had been married here. A tray gave an echo like a gong, arousing superstitious fears lest something fall and crush them. There was the legend *Ave Maria Gratia Plena Dominus Tecum* following the concavity of the crypt; colors; tactile surprises; but almost no intervention of the human voice. Professor Morales smiled as he watched the activity of Raimundo, the barber. Why were hypocrites taking part in this work?

Suddenly the flames shot up. The smoke was growing thick. All, including Cosme Vila, realized that it had been a mistake to set off the blaze so fast. Now they would have to get out. With all the games they could have made up in there! Nobody was satisfied with his achievements. Except Future. Future was smashing the organ pipes.

'Everybody out! Out!'

They obeyed reluctantly. The fire was so aromatic. The whole temple gave off exciting smells – wood, incense. A good smell. At that moment the main chandelier crashed to the floor, and by a miracle the child of one of the Murcians was not brained.

When Cosme Vila came out of the door, he had a great surprise. He had imagined that those of the crowd who had not been able to get into the church would be waiting outside, but they were not. 'Where are they?' he asked. Aside from those who had been inside, there was almost no one.

'They've gone,' someone informed him, 'to the other churches.'

That was what had happened. They had been unable to endure the torment of doing nothing, and another column had quickly formed, headed by Blasco, with the Church of the Carmen as its objective.

Cosme Vila was enraged. He had wanted to organize everything methodically, but that had not been possible. It was then that El Responsable realized that Cosme Vila was directing the orchestra. With all there was to do in the city! He made a sign to his followers and without saying a word set off in a different direction, as though he had just had an inspiration. Before leaving the street, he looked back and saw the first gigantic flame shooting out of the main entrance. Odd that one should not even care to see the crowning of one's labors, that one should tire so quickly of operating in the same spot! An embarrassment of riches. All the lairs of the opposition that were just waiting for his purifying touch!

While the Jesuit church was being gutted by the flames, the same scenes, but perfected by experience, were being repeated in the Church of the Carmen, which Blasco and his gang had taken over. El Cojo, who hated to imitate – and especially to imitate Cosme Vila or Gorki – instead of mounting the pulpit and performing other cheap tricks, had made straight for the ciborium, smashing it with the butt of his rifle. His idea was to get at the chalice. He took it in his hands and turned around. '*Fratres, fratres!*' he shouted, raising it as high as he could. He called to all to gather around him. The militiamen drew near, though for the moment they did not know what El Cojo was up to. Suddenly it flashed into their minds. Communion! El Cojo was calling them for that. Some of them knelt, others remained standing. El Cojo assumed a solemn air and came limping over to the communion rail. He began handing out a communion wafer to each of them, murmuring as he did so: '*Miserere nobis.*' When he reached the twelfth, he could not restrain himself any longer. He let out a roar of laughter and, ripping open the shirt of Blasco, who was acting as his acolyte, emptied the remaining wafers between his shirt and skin. Blasco writhed like a dancer. The bootblack took one of the wafers and tried to stick it on his forehead. It seemed to him that the most fun would be when he started to run and the white disks began falling through his pants' legs.

El Cojo then climbed the steps of the high altar. With a push he threw down the image of the Virgin of the Carmen. Then he climbed into the niche it had occupied and stretched out his arms like a preacher. Someone had turned on the lights, which threw into relief the livid scabs on El Cojo's lips. Veritable volleys of shots rang out, their targets the images. El Cojo began to fear he might be mistaken for a saint. 'Hey, be careful!' and he gave a leap. The wood of the altar gave way under his feet, and he found himself buried up to his waist, bleeding from deep scratches. Several comrades had to help him get loose. He was furious. On the floor gleamed a frame and glass. He stamped them to pieces with his heel. It was the Gospel according to St. John.

This group of vandals seemed to have more imagination. It was gold that had dazzled Cosme Vila's contingent. The gold of the candelabra, of the crowns, of the monstrance. To move about among gold objects they could destroy! El Cojo and his hordes were more given to horseplay. Thus, instead of dragging the main crucifix into the streets, they dragged out two confessionals. And a Communist came out of one of them with a collection of dirty postcards in his hand, saying he had found them in the confessional. Another claimed to have found a wine flask. 'Sure,

sure, to wash away the sins.' And he raised it to his lips. They all wanted to share in the fun. Some of the passers-by laughed.

The wife of Casal, whose flat was close by, came to the window and called out: 'Do any of you know where Casal is? Do you know where Casal is?' Nobody paid any attention to her. Flames were beginning to lick out of the temple. Huge flames, monsters' tongues of different colors. The building materials here seemed more inflammable than those of the Sacred Heart, the odors less pungent.

A kind of contest had developed all over the city. What had begun as a multitude had now broken up into groups of from fifty to one hundred. The sense of being free had aroused in many the idea of making themselves leaders. They were not content to help Future throw Christ into the river. They wanted to operate on their own.

As a result, in less than two hours eight churches in the city had been set afire and three convents had been destroyed. The desk at which Pilar had studied had been smashed to splinters, and the nuns' beds and pianos urinated upon, the pianos of those convents whose Mothers Superior had not followed Mosén Alberto's advice. Where had the nuns got to? The militiamen did not find a single one, but they did find out their secrets. At the Congregation of Mary, food supplies for five years; in the Convent of the Heart of Mary, an underground passage.

'The catacombs, the catacombs they were talking about!'

'Catacombs my ass. I'll bet this communicates with the sacristy of San Félix, with the priests. Did you think they slept by themselves?' The leader of that group was Ideal. With a flashlight he groped along the dark passage. The others followed him, convinced that at last they were going to come upon the secret center where the ecclesiastical orgies and tortures took place. But they began to notice that it was growing damp and that water was seeping in. 'How is this possible when it's much higher than the river here?'

'They've probably flooded it, they've flooded it so we can't see anything!' They turned back angrily. But they soon discovered a side passage. Following this a few steps, they came to a kind of rectangular court with flagstones set into the wall, and mounds of loose earth. Ideal stopped. He was accompanied by Sergeant Molina of the People's

Militia. 'What's here?' Someone brought a pick and hammer, and they easily pried loose one of the flagstones. 'Skeletons!' There they were. 'The beasts! That's where they hid the bodies!'

'The corpses of babies they got caught with,' someone said. No question about it. They were rickety skeletons, as though shriveled up. One after another the stones were loosened. Ideal buried his hands in the bones of one of the skeletons, and it crumbled away. Others, however, were whole in their wooden coffins. 'Get this outside, get it outside.' They pulled out the coffins and carried them up to the convent. 'Where shall we put them?'

'Out there on the sidewalk so everybody can see them!'

'The dirty sows!'

'Bring that little one, the one of the baby!'

The exhibit of skeletons on the sidewalk fired the imagination of all. Murillo, who had led his Trotskyite cell into the convent across the way, the rich Convent of the Congregation of Mary, was informed of the discovery made in the Heart of Mary. It seemed to him that his cohorts would look very silly if all they did was to break everything they could get their hands on and eat up a five years' food supply. The dissenter must always go his adversaries one better in everything. His second in command was Salvio, the sweetheart of Don Emilio Santos's maid. Murillo had seen too much broken plaster of Paris in his decorator days for smashing or even shooting images to make any impression on him. Besides, from that part of the city four other burning churches could be seen, the nearest that of San Félix. He had to do better than that. The convent square opened on the stairway to the Cathedral. The setting was therefore grandiose. Murillo and several others went into the sacristy, where they all put on religious vestments. Murillo pulled on an alb that came halfway up his leg, then a chasuble with gold embroidery and an old biretta he found on a hatrack. Salvio put on a surplice, which he tied around his waist with a red sash. And then a chasuble. Not one of them but found himself a chasuble. They took the aspergillum, two censers, and the missals. And then the pallium. Someone came upon a small pallium the nuns used when the Bishop visited their chapel. And then the monstrance, which Murillo took in his two hands. Thus attired, they went outside.

On the sidewalk on the other side of the street, the skeletons. On this side, the improvised procession, chanting '*Misereri nobis.*' All of them were singing '*Miserere nobis.*' In the center the sweeping stairway to the Cathedral, then the soaring, majestic façade, and then the bell-tower, which went on telling the hours the same as always, the same as when Matías Alvear listened sleepless at night.

The news of what was taking place reached Ideal's ears. He came out to watch the show with the others. Under the canopy Murillo was ascending the Cathedral stairway. The censers bobbed in the air. Those carrying them were unskilled in their use and banged themselves on the knees, giving rise to great hilarity. Suddenly Murillo turned around. His walrus mustache gave him a ferocious air. At that moment he became bored with the whole business. To tell the truth, he felt that none of all that was a patch on the skeletons Ideal had stumbled upon. He tossed the monstrance into the air and started quickly down the stairs as though a wonderful idea had just come to him. But the chasuble interfered with his movements, making everybody laugh. Those holding the pallium were left deserted. Fortunately, someone was passing around a chalice filled with wine. This cheered everyone, though in a few minutes both groups were looking around, as though admiring what they had done and seeking new things to do.

It didn't seem possible that one could get so little fun out of a monstrance. Ideal had thought it would afford jokes for a lifetime; but once it was broken, it was nothing but a piece of junk like any old thing Blasco had in his room.

The four fires, however, were growing and kept spirits high. 'Let's go see what's happened in San Félix!' All together, Murillo and his group, the anarchists, and the others rushed down the street. Only two or three women stayed with the skeletons, standing guard over the bones, and repeating: 'Did you ever see such a thing! The sows!'

The Church of San Félix smelled of blood. The flames were bursting from crevices everywhere, and there was a crowd in the square looking on. The bell-tower was as beautiful as when in other days, on St. John's Eve, it had been illuminated by lights from below.

〜

José María Gironella was born in Darnius near Girona in 1917. A fervent Catholic, he fought on Franco's side in the Civil War. Arrested for smuggling in the post-war period, he illegally walked over the Pyrenees in 1948 and stayed in France until 1952, during which time he wrote *The Cypresses Believe in God*, a powerful attempt to capture objectively the passion and loyalties of the Civil War. The book, which sold over three million copies when it was published in the 1950s, made Gironella a household name. His publisher Planeta said that the sales of Gironella's books saved his business. Although not as impartial as the author claimed, the book is an ambitious attempt to capture the war on both sides. Gerald Brenan wrote in his review in the *New York Times*: 'The sane and the moderate, caught helplessly in a dilemma they did not ask for, must throw in their lot with one violent party or another till mercifully the passions of the war submerge them and confirm their decision. It is this tragic unfolding of events which concerns this novel.' Wealthy and famous, Gironella died in Arenys de Mar in 2003.

KSAWERY PRUSZYŃSKI

A PROLETARIAN BULLFIGHT

from *Inside Red Spain*

translated by Wisiek Powaga

Arriba, parias de la tierra

The train pushes its way through yet another tunnel – and out into another flash of sunshine, mountains and the sea. Harvest on the French vineyards has just begun. It's only September. We stop at the large station of a small border town. The police – customs, security, political – stretch in a long line along the platform. Out of the train exit two passengers. All that magnificence of officialdom, the entire manpower of document and passport examiners that populate all border crossings, throws itself at the meager prey dropped off today at the Spanish station of Portbou.

A young Spanish woman, returning from Exeter in England via Paris, goes first. Opening of suitcases, checking of the passport and the visa. Done. Now they are opening my suitcase, examine everything carefully and professionally, leaving the packed things in perfect order. Exemplary job. They take the passport, look through the visas, extensions of validity, as if measuring their weight in hand.

'*Un instant, s'il vous plait.*'

My passport is taken away somewhere through a side door while the assigned to it body lingers on dolefully in the customs chamber. The office is large, completely empty. On the walls hang huge black-and-red manifestos and two brilliant, graphically perfect posters. One of them shows a laughing soldier in a battle dress without epaulettes, pulling at the strings attached to an officer-marionette donning a glittering uniform with a massive sabre on fancy slings. The officer is sporting hussar mustachios like yet another mark of power but it's the soldier who makes him dance a frisky jig. The other poster is not made for laughs, more like a horror, or a monster tale. A big-bellied, nightmarish beast with goggling eyes of a frog puts its apish hand to a huge ear. The beast has brown skin the colour of a monk's habit, a cross hanging on a rosary around his neck, and on its head – a royal crown, a small one, like the one on the Erdell monkey from the shoe wax ad. It's revolutionary art warning that the enemy has his feelers, his eavesdropping ears and spying eyes everywhere.

'*Suivez moi, s'il vous plait.*'

My passport is back from a mysterious walkabout but its separation from my body and soul – of which it is a policing extension – continues. An official brought it back, but instead of returning it he escorts me out on to the platform. The platform is long, we are walking in silence. I feel I ought to break it. From under the station's roof emerge mountains covered in olive groves bathed in sunshine. I turn to the official – 'I look forward to exploring the new country.' He replies coldly – 'Do you now' – and looks at me as if I were one of those feelers and ears, an embodiment of that brown beast from the poster. Not good.

We are in a small office room. Behind a desk sits a man who says he is not letting anyone into Spain, journalists especially. The one who has my passport stands behind me, by the door. Next to the desk sits another man, easily a creature from one of the posters, and further back on a small sofa – another one; he in turn wouldn't be out of place on an engraving from a French Revolution. It may be just a bureaucratic routine but they all could pass for a tourist attraction; after all it's Spain.

So, the one sitting next to the desk is an army man, tall, black-haired and swarthy, but his army must be an odd sort. He is wearing breeches, a semi-military jacket, his rifle resting peacefully against the civilian office desk. (O, those birthing days of new nations and ideological systems before everything limps, cools and sets in a formula!) On his head he has something that should be photographed or no one would ever believe me. It's a kind of forage cap, black over one ear, red over the other. On each side three big letters, red on the black, black on the red – FAI. Carnival, you'd say? Nope. You would not take this man for a harlequin, trust me.

The soldier of revolution, a militiaman, member of the Catalonian *Federación Anarquista Iberica* (FAI), takes up my case. I don't understand a word he is saying but I'm under the impression he is on my side. He addresses not so much the man behind the desk but the fellow sprawled on the sofa. The sofa friend also cuts an interesting figure, though of a different kind. He wears an odd garment between a frock coat and a stroller, something from the previous century, sometimes seen on a pensioner in a small provincial town. But out of this dried plank of a body grows a bull's neck, wrapped in a black-and-red cravat (again: the colours of the all-powerful in Catalonia FAI) and on it – a big head, large fleshy face with a muscular nose and relatively small eyes, peering out from under the folds of old wrinkled skin. Above it all unfurls, rather unexpectedly, a great whirl of hair, a thick black mane like Beethoven's. But no, he's a Marat, the legend of the French National Convention, the dangerous Marat. I instinctively feel it is this man I need to convince.

The small room has suddenly erupted into a big battle for Portbou, in the name of Polish journalism. In this battle the main adversary is the gentleman behind the desk in civilian clothes; no forage cap or black-and-red scarf, just a trace of red in the lapel. This man demands a proof that I am a journalist. I show him my professional credentials, Polish and international. The man doesn't know what it is. Enter Marat, who begins to say something that sounds conciliatory. The desk man looks irritated, again takes my passport and soon discovers a German visa. What was I doing in Germany? I take my passport back from him and show him it was a transit visa. We all calculate the time trapped between foreign stamps and the calculation supports my claim. It's my turn to attack: I pull out heavy artillery in the form of my recommendation letter, discarded a minute ago without perusal, from the newly appointed ambassador of Spain to Paris, Luis Araquistain. The forage-capped militiaman wants to make sure it is the new, just appointed, ambassador but the Marat dismisses all the doubts in the matter. A spirit

A PROLETARIAN BULLFIGHT

of reconciliation rises over the battlefield. At any rate, both anarchists are on my side. The plain-clothes official tries to negotiate a honorable defeat and save his face by demanding that I surrender the ambassador's letter. Inconvenient but what can I do? I exchange the letter for three round seals in my passport. The man who had escorted me here and who was giving me such little hope for my stay in Spain, now leads me back to the doorway. The three inquisitors send me on my way with three raised fists.

There is still plenty of time before the departure of the Barcelona train. In a huge waiting hall there are nine waiters to serve one young Spanish woman and myself. The mood is family-friendly, and revolutionary. The posters on the walls overflow with colours, red flags in the windows, the barlady's kid is sitting on the counter playing with a lobster shell. The little town lies below the railway station, descending like an amphitheatre into a small fishing port. The church is shut, on the door a note informing it has been 'appropriated', that is sequestered by the militia and Popular Front. At last the Barcelona train arrives at the platform, all carriages covered in revolutionary posters and slogans. I load my baggage into a big car, its walls displaying a revolutionary fusion of literature and religion: a popular novel of Blasco Ibanez and the great work by Saint John – the Four Horsemen of the Apocalypse. Inside the carriage, though, no sign of the revolution or the Apocalypse: just four workmen whiling the stop away with a game of bezique.

The train moves. Its colourful carriages begin to bore their way through tunnels, veer suddenly away from sea shores and fly over olive groves and fields. Villages flash past like white splashes, punctuating the flow of stone-walled fields on hillsides, sleepy stations, Shell and Dunlop ads. The field-workers greet us raising their hands clenched into fists. But after a while it gets tedious. The chessboard of vineyards and fields, manifestly well-tended but small, looks more like Germany, or at least Polish Wielkopolska,* which instead of rolling out flat swells into hills and puckers into earth terraces. The only exotic feature are two tall carts

---

*Wielkopolska – western part of partitioned Poland (1772–1918) under German occupation (transl.).

on huge wheels pulled by mules and asses. One can grow skeptical about that revolution, which at Portbou greeted me so colourfully, loudly, dangerously, but here merely administers the land of industrious ants, bees or termites. I doze off, wake up to a passport control, very civil this time, doze off again, and then at last – Barcelona.

It's only 8 o'clock in the evening but the night has fallen, black as ink, the way southern nights can. At the railway station a milling crowd of militiamen and workers. Red arrows direct to places where foreigners who come to fight for the revolution report. I take a cab across the huge town, badly lit and full of people. The hotel, to whose owner I have recommending letters, has not – luckily – been 'appropriated' like that church in Portbou, or like many other Barcelona hotels. I am given a tiny quiet room on one of the top floors, with a view onto a grey wall of another tall building. I'm worn out by the journey and take to bed early. Suddenly, mid-sleep, a huge, inhuman – industrial – voice begins to roar straight into my ear. It fires the words and complete sentences with the speed of a machine gun. The voice penetrates the wall, completely blocking out the whir of the city, filling my little room and all its nooks and crannies until it overflows like water in a bathtub. The radio megaphone stops for a moment but then, in a somewhat changed tone of voice, begins to spew words again. Outside, on the black street of Barcelona, people gather around the loudspeaker to hear the latest news from the front. But this doesn't sound like a news bulletin. More like speeches, homilies, incantations. The soft, supple like steel Spanish language comes out of the speaker heavy as lead. The words are falling through the air like iron tiles knocked off the roofs down onto the stone pavement of the street. I don't understand practically any of them, and that's what increases the sense of strangeness further still. Through the black night, out of darkness emerge contours of familiar words – revolution, proletariat, *España, el pueblo, fascismo, muerte*. Sometimes, though rarely, I manage to link one contour with another floating immediately behind out of the invisible loudspeaker, and tie them up with an invisible string of sense. But it doesn't happen often. I'm too tired, I simply lie there, on a bed in a hotel room, in a strange city, in the middle of the unbelievably black night that pours in through the window and with it a wave of bizarre, grating sound. At last, the weariness grows heavier than the wave. I fall asleep rocked by the echoes of its thunderous verbosity, weighed down by sheer physical exhaustion wrapped in darkness, swept by a tsunami of foreign words which now, dying down, pulls me slowly into some unfathomable deep. One thing I've learned for sure now is that in the revolutionary Spain I'll never be alone, not even for a moment. That wherever I go I'll be feeling the presence of light or darkness, followed by cries and pleas; that always and everywhere I'll be tossed like an odd piece of debris on this huge, swelled sea which has flooded everything.

The whole next day I spent in the biggest city of revolutionary Spain, the city where the revolution has been the bloodiest, the cruelest but also the most heroic. It is a big and beautiful city, rich too, and all that has now become the backdrop for the new brave world. The posters from Portbou have multiplied into thousands of colourful blots on the walls, glistening in the sun. The motorcars with huge unfurled flags whiz past, covered in slogans, emblems and anagrams of the two main trade unions, political parties and other revolutionary institutions which had 'appropriated' them, daubed on with white paint. Inside the cars sit the militiamen dressed in blue *monos* or battle dresses, or some garb in the process of becoming uniforms. But above all – the *mono*. In the gates of townhouses, especially the gates of big banks, post offices and government buildings, one can always spot a group of people's militiamen bearing rifles and donning the *mono*. The *mono* has been raised to the status of uniform, in fact the *mono* has dethroned the uniform. The *mono* is simply a one-piece overall, worn by workers and also by aircraft pilots. Now the *mono* has come out of factories and hangars. It's become an accessory of power as once epaulets were.

It's a Sunday and the crowds are bigger than normal. Imagine that one day the whole of Warsaw's Powiśle, the whole of working Praga and the red Wola poured into Aleje Ujazdowskie.* Just like now, out

---

* Powiśle, Praga, Wola – traditionally working-class districts of Warsaw; Aleje Ujazdowskie – Warsaw's central boulevards along the Royal Park of Łazienki, lined with palaces, government buildings and embassies (transl.).

of the remote suburbs, the port districts and the narrow streets of old
Barcelona the crowds spilled out onto the boulevards of Rambala, wide
pavements of Paralelo, into Plaça de Catalunya, flowing in front of the
palatial stores and their elegant vitrines. And they are armed crowds.
It's hard to picture a bigger number of people armed with rifles out
on a stroll in a big city. It's hard to imagine a complete mobilization
of motorcars by the working classes! Spain is the motherland of the
baronial Hispano-Suiza and now I'm seeing dozens of those luxu-
rious limousines decorated with Soviet emblems, hammers and sickles,
scratched by an untried hand in wonky lines on the glossy black paint.
At the feet of the Columbus monument sandbags stacked into a barricade, four heavy machine guns eyeing four streets. The crowds flow on
under the black-and-red flags of the Iberian Anarchist Federation and
the red hammer and sickle of the Trotskyist POUM – *Partido Obrero de
Unificación Marxista*. From the windows of the hotel Colon, where the
army soldiers fought and died, hang banners of the unified socialist and
communist parties. The walls of the great hotel are scarred with bullets
but the pockmarks are relatively few. These people, who every day are
sent in groups by the People's Tribunals to be shot, these people imprisoned inside 'Uruguay', the white ship seen in the port, didn't really put
up much of a fight here.

The crowds overflow the streets, conscious of their victory, and of
their power. The posters ridicule army officers and newspapers announce
daily new sentences passed by workers' tribunals. The churches saved
from burning display placards: *patrimonio de público* – public property.
The palaces of the ship magnates of this great merchant port are 'appropriated' and tenanted by workers' organizations. The illustrated 'Ahora'
carries a picture of a worker-militiaman sleeping in the royal bed of the
Pedrales palace. In front of the palace of a Catalan press baron, who bore
a title of *conde*, stands a row of five Packards. Not because it's a magnate's
palace but because it's the headquarters of the metalworkers' union.
In another grand 'appropriated' building lives the army chief, colonel
Sandino. Can't help feeling it looks like Sankt Petersburg in the spring
of 1917, the Petersburg of Kronstandt sailors, gallivanting about town in
the imperial limousines, the Petersburg of Madame Krzesińska's palace

'appropriated' by the communists.* Out of the loudspeakers flows the
Internationale. The crowd greets it with raised fists; as the song descends
on them from above they pick it up and up it goes in a fractured chorus.
This September evening has the scent of that Russian spring.

Among the posters I spot something very Spanish – a poster advertising a bullfight. Tonight's bullfight. The revolution has not disturbed the
ways of traditional entertainment. Well, except in two ways: it says the
bulls of today's corrida will be supplied from the stables of *ex-marqueses*
and *ex-condes*. The revolution, this last true revolution, added the 'ex-'.
It's also this revolution that has added the sentence that the corrida is
organized in partnership with People's Militia. The tanks that crushed
the churches have now stopped at the gates of an arena. Not to be
missed.

I'm a few minutes late, running under the huge arches of the outside
cloister and into the staircase, I'm out on the galleries, pushing my way
up step by step through the crowd filling the amphitheatre. Suddenly
the crowds stand up and raise their fists. I look back. Before me the
arena: a yellow, sandy ring, a semicircle full of people, portraits of tore-
adors hanging from above. The military band strikes out the hymn of
proletarian revolution.

> *Arriba, parias de la tierra,*
> *En pie, famélica legión,*
> *Atruena la razón en marcha*
> *Es el fin de la opresión.*

The *Internationale*, just like before in the street, now sweeps around
the bullring. The crowd picks it up with enthusiasm. The fists are stuck
into the air. From underneath the hanging portraits of the famous
toreros rises the song:

---

* The palace belonging once to Matylda Krzesińska, the famous *prima ballerina
assoluta* at the Mariyski Theatre, born into a Polish aristocratic family, a mistress of
the future Tsar Nicolas II; it was from the balcony of her palace that Lenin addressed
the revolutionary crowds on his return from Finland (transl.).

Agrupémonos todos
en la lucha final;
el género humano
es la International!

[...]

And then something odd happens, something that accidentally mixes and fuses the Hispanic spectacle with the proletarian revolution. Apparently, it was assumed that the orchestra would stop playing – into the ring runs a big bull. The public shouts. Some sit down, others keep their fists in the air. Two red *banderilleros* approach the bull, which is standing still, as if stunned and blinded. But people around me keep on singing, picking up the echoes of the orchestra and lifting up the song again:

Ni en dioses, reyes ni tribunes
está el supremo salvador
nostros mismos realicemos
el esfuerzo redentor.

[...]

For centuries Catholic holy days were celebrated with corridas, canonizations of saints were preceded with 'running of the bulls' which went on for days. Until recently, children going to their first communion, on that same day in the afternoon were taken to see their first bullfight. In this country of magnificent temples, of Saint Theresa and Ignatious Loyola, Catholicism slipped over the corrida like water off a duck's back while all its holidays got mired in bullfight. One would expect something different from a faith which itself went through human corridas and revealed itself to the world on the fighting arena, the ancestor of this one today. One would expect something more from a faith whose saints addressed wolves as 'brothers'. The corrida, honoured by Catholicism, the corrida rooted deeply in the Iberian paganism, kept alive in Roman provinces, universally popular under the Moors – survived them all.

The tank of history that crushed church portals has now stopped at the gates of the arena. We shall have a corrida on the First of May and each anniversary of the October Revolution, on Lenin's Day, Rosa Luxembourg's and Liebknecht's, just as we had on Corpus Christi. Except now it's 'Arise, ye damned of the Earth...' that will open a bullfight.

∽

Ksawery Pruszyński was a Polish journalist, publicist, writer and diplomat. He was born in 1907 in the Volhynia (now Ukraine) into a landowning family who after the Russian Revolution settled in Kraków. Pruszyński studied law at the Jagellonian University and, while continuing his academic career, started working for a newspaper, *Czas* (*Time*), as a proofreader. In 1930 he made his debut as a reporter with a series of articles from Hungary, and in 1932 with a book, *Sarayewo 1914, Shanghay 1932, Gdańsk 193?*, which presented his argument that Gdańsk would be the cause of a world war. Throughout the 1930s he travelled in Poland and Europe and published, among others, *Bunt Młodych* (The Youth Revolt). In 1933 he travelled to Palestine; the resulting book, *Palestine for the 3rd time*, made him a popular and respected journalist. In 1936/37 he was a war correspondent from Spain; *Inside Red Spain* records his experiences of the Civil War. During the Second World War he fought as a soldier, taking part in the Battle of Narvik (Norway, 1940) and the Battle of Falaise (France, 1944) but also worked as a diplomat in London and in Moscow (1941/42). After the war he decided to stay in the new communist Poland and joined its diplomatic corps, first at the UN, later as ambassador to the Netherlands. Pruszyński died in 1950 in a car crash in Germany.

NIVARIA TEJERA

MORE IMPORTANT
THAN A LAW

from *The Ravine*
translated by Carol Maier

EVERYTHING'S CONFUSED FOR ME, everything inside there was confused for me. But I'm sure we waited an hour in that room full of people, waited for something to happen that I didn't understand. Finally a door opened and Papa appeared, accompanied by six other prisoners and, through another door, men in long black kimonos, who looked like the witches you see in storybooks. 'They're the magistrates' robes,' Auntie said, frightened. The lights blazed overhead and above them, the fan made the shadow of the flag and the shadows from people's heads move across the ceiling. This was the assembly room, because that's what a sign over the entry said, and when the men sat down around a large table it seemed that everything would get dark. It was a very important place, so there were several priests. I recognized don Eutimio and don Tarife. They visit us and Grandpa's said we must always respect them. 'They're a different kind of priest. They tell jokes and they'll pass up the bishop's thin wine for an excursion or to visit a sick person. Besides,' he adds, 'they talk like anyone else and understand God's weaknesses.' One morning don Tarife didn't enter with 'God grant us a good day' but 'God sure prescribes strong purgatives,' because there were thunderclaps, which he laughingly called purgatives. Grandpa enjoyed those stories, even felt important because they showed that he and don Tarife thought the same way. But other priests appeared too, asking in low voices why they were bringing the prisoners loose like that when they should bring them tied, which made Grandpa tense his cheeks and praise 'such a Christian statement' between his teeth. I don't think they were brought loose. I could see that the prisoners were walking two by two, holding their hands together and going to sit on a long bench. 'They have them handcuffed, like criminals,' Mama said. Papa looked all around until he found us. I could feel by his eyes that he was hugging us, but I felt chilled too. He seemed more alone than before, more a prisoner. Outside, in the street, there were some children skating. I could hear them clearly and would have gone out if that hadn't been 'Papa's trial.' I'd have gone out for sure if I'd known that Papa would be set free. But at that moment Papa was suffering, he was in danger, and right then that was all I could think of.

I saw some strangers enter. They had to be witnesses for the other prisoners. There was a hunchback walking with them, and he looked like a dwarf. I was afraid of him but then I felt sorry for him because he didn't know what to do and because everyone was watching him. He sat down to our right under a big clock. He seemed uneasy and was probably protecting himself from the cold. When the clock struck the hour three times, its pendulum was the hunchback swinging above our heads from one side of the room to the other. Or maybe some child came in to skate up in the air.

It started. An usher read the paper where Papa and the others were harshly accused for attacking the Bishop's holy residence and also the Seminary. Then everyone began to shout, extending long fingers toward the accused on their bench, wanting to knock it over. The prisoners tried to defend themselves, but there was so much screaming they sat down again. Things went on like that for hours. I'm sure Papa wanted to explain how that day he was there by chance, because he'd come from the other island to see us. There was a huge burst of shouting and now the fingers looked like knives.

I listened to them talking at home about a denunciation and I knew a different truth. They'd detained him for his political campaigns in the newspapers and meetings. I also knew that don Pancho wanted Papa to be accused for this assault on the bishopric instead, in order to keep him from falling into the hands of the 'military authority.' But my ears had a hard time getting used to the words 'criminal delinquent assailant red' and to other words that must be bad because people said them with such disdain. Suddenly I felt a great calm inside because Papa was looking right at us and he was sparkling. The usher's voice stayed far away then, and the only thing hurting my eyes were the gold buttons on his uniform.

Then the little bell rang and the robes flapped like frightened crows and the faces got more hook-shaped, as if they were lying in wait as they asked each other questions. There was the sound of chairs and nervous moving around. People talked about 'the great lawyers and great cases, the grandeur of the multitudes, and authority in the world.' The word 'guilt' made the spectators' knees, the pendulum on the clock, the blades in the fan, and Papa's handcuffs all flap; and it seemed to be sucking up the little eyes of those men in the tribunal. 'Guilty, not guilty?' they asked, shaking the word just like when Chicho was born and everyone said 'boy or girl?' all at the same time. ('What can they be guilty of? Why do the men at the table know and not the men on the bench?' Papa must know as much about guilt as they do.) A list of names was read by the usher in a loud voice. The presiding magistrate had a kind face. It never occurred to me to think about why each person needs to have a name. They all answered immediately and went forward with curiosity, as if they'd been waiting until that moment to know each other close up. I looked around. When the magistrates argued, you had the impression that their faces were about to fall off. The fan moved slowly, scaring the flies. I watched the audience, which was very attentive and seemed bewildered. One person was smoking a cigar, a little old man whistled through his nose every time he breathed, some people were asleep and others scratched themselves nervously between their legs or tugged at their ears. I couldn't figure out why they liked sitting there so much. But all of them seemed to be guards and to have some task. Maybe they like knowing 'the law' because they're afraid and this way they'll be able to watch out for themselves by watching over it. I looked at all those people again and again. Read the signs above the big table one more time. Each one indicates an important position. Magistrate, Public Prosecutor, Defending Counsel, Presiding Magistrate. At that moment the prosecutor was requesting five years' imprisonment for some and three years for others 'because the freedom of these men is considered pernicious.' For Papa's name there was respect.

Finally they called the witnesses and everyone startled. First Papa's old friends walked by the bar, swearing they'd seen him lead the attack. I felt a pit open in my stomach when don Eustaquio maintained that Papa was 'a subversive element and a declared enemy of the "Glorious National Movement."' He's Juanela's father; I've sat on the roof terrace of his house and flown kites from his knees. Besides, he made the newspaper with Papa and even wanted to be my godfather. Traitor! Traitor! I would have liked to spit at him from my seat. (I won't be Juanela's friend anymore.)

They called one after the other until it was Mama's turn; she cried a lot, wanting to convince everyone that he'd come that day only to visit us and his sole reason for going by the bishopric was to prevent accidents, that Santiago was a good man, that he was a great man, repeating tirelessly how he'd come that day solely to visit us and how he was a great man. But they made her sit down.

Auntie cried too because 'my beloved brother had always been the vitality and intelligence in the family, that he had studied many things and that he even traveled to America, which is why you had to understand his restlessness and the adventurous spirit that prompts natural struggle, because the natural struggle of men,' and here she got stuck and spent a long time searching for a word that would not come to her, until she continued with 'the natural struggle of men is like a force spurring the growth of cities that with the influence of these men are, since they're since they're,' and she got stuck again then went on to say that 'they're odd but, which is why my beloved brother should be respected, esteemed, decorated, instead of executed (that would definitely be an execution of *in*justice) like a war criminal, since, as one of those exemplary men, he had been instrumental in establishing the cultural basis of a city like La Laguna, and for all those things he deserved unlimited freedom.' To which they answered that her city of such importance does not appear on any map of this earth, even if you study all the maps.

I thought that Auntie was saying too much and that she would never convince the tribunal. Along the table they were fidgeting impatiently, although this too seemed unjust. When she sat down, Auntie didn't look so fat.

The smoke in the room was even reaching the members of the tribunal, erasing them. Above the table everything dazzled, like a large mirror held to the sun. The glasses of the presiding magistrate, the prosecutor's bald spot, a ring waving accusatorially beside the glasses, the brass gleaming on the signs, the eyes of all the fidgeting men on the bench. For a minute Papa's astonished face appeared and the rest was opaque. Then the room returned again. And again, countless times.

I realized immediately how important it was to choose your words carefully. Wished I were big and could say things naturally, the way those shy peasants who are Grandpa's clients talk, because they don't know many words. 'Papa's innocent, he's always been an innocent person,' to say that many times until those people believed it.

The little bell rang to announce that something would start soon. Your ears nearly burst, and you didn't know how to block out that unbearably clear tone. It made people pay attention in a strange way, everyone stopped talking as if they hoped to be called. Then, you could hear a heavy murmur behind us. I realized that all those people must have wanted to testify. There was a truth in each one of them and now they spoke it in low voices, but it had nothing to do with the law and this made them happy.

The pendulum on the clock made a row of hunchbacks roll across the wall. They passed along the ceiling that divides the room in half, cast a watchful eye, and collapsed slowly, as if they felt cold. Papa felt nothing. Kept his back turned, motionless. From time to time he looked at us intensely; then his figure just gave you the impression of slow, humble waiting. I looked below the clock. It was still walking toward the next hour, and there the first hunchback was a strange hulk leaning against the wall.

Then they called Grandpa. Grandpa was weak and I was afraid of what he might tell them. He walked to the place they told him and looked at Papa as if he wanted to stop near him. Pinching his felt hat, he turned it around and folded it so many times you could hardly see it. The interrogation was always the same but each time it was faster. Grandpa shook his head yes or no, and I thought that he'd get confused because of his age, since he takes his time making packsaddles and spends an hour eating his bowl of oatmeal. But I felt sure he'd confess what I would have said if I could have testified. A bold fly began to torment him and he whacked his nose hard with his hat, which made the magistrates laugh. I laughed too, but it's because I realized he acts comical when he's nervous. Alido intervened, demanding proper respect and the presiding magistrate banged his gavel on the table a few times, which made the noise die down.

I remembered that Grandpa's reserved and he needs to weigh his sentences quietly before he pulls them out. Substitutes his voice for the needle he uses to sew packsaddles. But when Papa tried to keep him from talking, Grandpa got a set look in his eyes and his words were crystal clear. He protested, pretending to be angry, although he was really frowning from tenderness. 'Jijo, everyone here wants to pull out the lining in his heart.' Some people laughed again and others began to clap. But Grandpa doesn't hear when he's busy looking for 'his words,' and then I smiled and he caught 'the knot by its hole' as he says. Now he was very serious.

I was tired. I wanted to hear Papa, wanted that to end. Grandpa told the story starting from the day of the 'Movement,' which began with the entrance of those insurgents: 'Gentlemen, those guys were indeed insurgents, since they came in stamping on everything, same as my clients the mules.' There was some laughter again. This time it made me angry or feverish and I wanted to run out of there really bad. The doors started to fall down like that day, there was shouting and planes, a mixed sound of doors being bolted and windowpanes breaking. And Grandpa was shouting 'the war, the war,' with his mouth open very wide, until he swallowed me up little by little.

'No, Grandpa, no,' I shouted, creating a vacuum around me between

Mama and Auntie; the two of them suggested taking me out to the street for some fresh air. 'There is no street today, there is no street today,' I kept hearing in my head. Remembered everything while Grandpa swallowed me. It was the war moving in my memory and everything happening there was because of the war, Chicho was still repeating 'Ma-ma-ma-ma,' same as then, Grandpa went on being old, and everyone talked with isolated words. 'Why, why,' in the name of all the laws in the world, they tirelessly asked guilt, the fan, Grandpa's hat. I felt the wrinkles on Grandpa's neck jumping all over my face again, like ants. It was that day again, all over again. A pile of bright straw rose on the table at the back of a black cloth shed. But instead of rotten packsaddles, there were uniformed rifles in red, blue, and black, elongated by the fan, shadows flying across the ceiling.

When we went back to the hall again after getting some fresh air, the men in dark robes were whispering among themselves. Grandpa was still waiting for more questions. One of the men stood up and shouted for him to get to the point, since there wasn't much time left and they didn't want to waste it on such vague names. Grandpa wiped away the sweat. It hurt me that those witches didn't know that Grandpa talks with animals more than with people, that they didn't know what a mule means for him. He looked at the row of faces out of the corner of his eye and then he stopped at the platform where a lot of feet tapped restlessly, raising dust. Trembling, he fixed his bony hand in Papa's direction and began his story again. Said that the handcuffed man they saw there was his favorite jijo. Of course he grew up, but he was not like Grandpa. 'I know him better than you do, as naturally you know *your* sons,' he explained; 'I know what he's made of and know he's incapable of making a racket for the fun of it, because he always had a powerful reason for his actions, and if he didn't, he didn't act. Besides,' he said, 'considering the attack that smashed the windowpanes in my home and how peaceful things were in town the day of the "Coup," it's unfair to demand order from others because there's the same right, since each person has his own personal ideas.' And he repeated that his jijo had a good reason for his actions. They asked him to be briefer and Grandpa recalled Papa as a child and how he used to punish him, "cause I've always been a brute and he'd hide so I wouldn't make 'im work on my packsaddles, since I didn't realize he could benefit from time away from there; 'cause you men know that a father believes an jijo's time belongs to his father, and he wanted to study, get himself an education and get his thoughts together his own way.' Grandpa was tired and he breathed with his chest, walking the whole length of the bar and finally leaning on the magistrates' table. He stopped near don Eutimio and don Tarife. They talked about when Papa was an altar boy and he borrowed books from the library. 'Gentlemen, gentlemen,' Grandpa repeated, 'this is my jijo and he must be allowed his ideas, he must be believed when he says that something is true, because this is a total disgrace, it's a disgrace that now you're going to imprison him for years and years...' He even walked close to Papa, who was all hunched over, and asked in a loud voice if they would take off Papa's handcuffs, stroking his hands like Samarina and I do. But Alido was listening to Grandpa very attentively, and he brought him over to where we were sitting, because Grandpa was crying and order had been disturbed, which made the magistrates' little gavel bang on the table. 'Grandpa.' (I wished I could hug him hard, curl up in his oldness under his dirty lapel.)

But things continued. Movement of chairs. Papa and Alido chatted while the witnesses for the other prisoners waited. They patted us on the shoulder a few times, which meant we should meet with them. We went into a large room where there were pictures of hunched-over figures and the smell of old books. There were fat sofas covering the areas along the walls. A man in a suit was scratching his beard furiously. It all seemed like the buzzing of flies.

I felt dizzy. Through the door that led into the tribunal, you could hear the little bell, the scraping of chairs, and small blows on and under the big table. Even the sound of a sob carried that far. I looked at Papa and felt that he'd soon be free. But the thick sound coming through the door was like a battle raging in my head. I thought how from that moment on I would have him forever. Remembered how the presiding magistrate turned his monocle impatiently and tugged at it on a little chain. Pressed myself carefully against Papa's hand, afraid of finding a hollow. Something incomprehensible had his hands tied within.

At the end of an hour a guard came in to get us. Then everything was easy. They took off Papa's handcuffs and his free arms hugged us awkwardly. Alido was giving Grandpa little pats on the back and couldn't stop laughing. (His broad stomach shook contentedly and he was friendly.) He congratulated Grandpa for having moved the tribunal. 'That's more important than a law,' he said.

∿

Nivaria Tejera was born in Cienfeugo, Cuba, in 1929. Her father was from the Canary Islands and the family moved back to Tenerife when Nivaria was two. The father was taken prisoner at the outbreak of the Civil War and not released until 1944, when the family returned to Cuba. *The Ravine*, first published in France in 1958, is a magical attempt to convey from a child's point of view the confusions and fractures of the Civil War. Tejera said about the book:

> At the beginning of the 1950s, I decided to narrate my experiences as a child during the Spanish Civil War in the small city of La Laguna… I wrote as a witness both real and imaginary, the young narrator who tells of the catastrophe foregrounded in the novel's opening paragraph: 'the war started today opposite Grandpa's house.'… I believe that the goal running through the pages of *The Ravine* is timelessness, a secret hope that both the life fragmented by the war in Spain and the fragmented language I used to portray it will symbolize an eternal present found in subsequent but only slightly different situations.

Indeed, for the author, the narrator's point of view is 'a dialogue between past and present': the voice of the little girl fusing with the adult voice of the author herself. In the early 1960s, Nivaria Tejera served as cultural attaché for the Cuban government in Rome. In 1965, she broke with the Castro government and returned to Paris. She died in January 2016.

ARTHUR KOESTLER

PORTRAIT OF A
REBEL GENERAL

from *Spanish Testament*

A T THIS TIME GENERAL QUEIPO DE LLANO was one of the most famous broadcasters in the world; every evening millions of adherents and opponents listened in to his talk from Seville, with mixed feelings, but with rapt attention. Never, probably, in the whole history of wars and civil wars has a general made speeches to the world – and such picturesque speeches too; and even if his accounts of the strategic situation are frequently contradicted by the facts on the very next day, they have never been lacking in a certain artistic charm. Here are some samples, taken at random:

July 23rd, 1936. 'Our brave Legionaries and *Regulares* have shown the red cowards what it means to be a man. And incidentally the wives of the reds too. These Communist and Anarchist women, after all, have made themselves fair game by their doctrine of free love. And now they have at least made the acquaintance of real men, and not milksops of militiamen. Kicking their legs about and struggling won't save them.'

August 12th. 'The Marxists are ravening beasts, but we are gentlemen. Señor Companys deserves to be stuck like a pig.'

August 18th. 'I have to inform you that I have in my power as hostages a large number of the relatives of the Madrid criminals, who are answerable with their lives for our friends in the capital. I likewise repeat what I have already said, namely, that we have a number of the miners from the Rio Tinto mines in our prisons... I don't know why we are called rebels; after all, we have nine-tenths of Spain behind us. And since we have nine-tenths of Spain behind us, I fancy that those on the other side are rebels and that we should be treated as the legal government by the rest of the world.'

August 19th. 'Eighty per cent of the families of Andalusia are already in mourning. And we shall not hesitate, either, to adopt even more rigorous measures to assure our ultimate victory. We shall go on to the bitter end and continue our good work until not a single Marxist is left in Spain.'

September 3rd. 'If the bombardment of La Linea or one of the other coastal towns is repeated, we shall have three members of the families of each of the red sailors executed. We don't like doing this, but war is war.'

September 8th. 'I have given orders for three members of the families of each of the sailors of the loyalist cruiser that bombarded La Linea to be shot... To conclude my talk I should like to tell my daughter in Paris that we are all in excellent health and that we should like to hear from her.'

I had heard a few of these gems before my departure from Paris, and had pictured the speaker as a kind of Spanish Falstaff or Gargantua – coarse, jovial, red-nosed, fat and apoplectic. And now he was actually standing five paces away from me, in front of the microphone; on a lanky, gaunt, almost ascetic frame was poised a head with expressionless, sullen features; a thin-lipped mouth, covered by a short, scanty moustache, and grey cold eyes in which a smile was seldom, a peculiar and disconcerting flicker frequently, visible. The contrast between the extremely grave and restrained, if crabbed personality of the General and his spicy, burlesque way of expressing himself at the microphone was not merely staggering, it was positively uncanny.

His talk had now come to an end; while it was being translated into Portuguese, the General led me across the courtyard to his room. His first question was whether reception of Seville was good in Paris and London, and whether his talks came over well.

On my answering in the affirmative he continued ruminatively:

'I am told that I can scarcely be heard anywhere in Central Europe. Atmospherics are supposed to be responsible. But I am rather inclined to think there is deliberate interference from other stations...'

A somewhat painful pause ensued. Then, before I had time to put my first question, Queipo de Llano asked me rather brusquely:

'How is it that you've come to Seville?'

I reminded the General that I had received a 'Salvo Conducto' signed by Gil Robles in Lisbon.

'Don't talk to me about Gil Robles,' interrupted His Excellency ill-humouredly. 'When we are victorious, Spain will be governed by a military cabinet; we shall sweep away all the parties and their representatives. None of these gentlemen will be members of the Government.'

'Not even Señor Gil Robles?'

'I can assure you that Señor Gil Robles will not be a member of the new Government.'

I turned the conversation round to foreign affairs. What would happen in the event of a victory of the military party? The answer was short and succinct:

'Spain will maintain the closest friendly relations with Germany, Italy and Portugal, all of which states support us in our struggle and whose corporate constitution we intend to imitate.'

To my next question, what would be the relations of the new Spain to those countries which adhered strictly to the Non-Intervention Agreement, His Excellency's answer was no less precise. It consisted of two words:

'Less friendly.'

Finally I questioned him as to the origin of the German and Italian planes, 'the activities of which on the Nationalist side had aroused such lively comments abroad'.

'We bought those machines in Tetuan,' replied Queipo de Llano with a smile. 'It's nobody's business.'

'Whom did you buy them from in Tetuan?'

'From a private trader, who buys and sells aeroplanes off his own bat.'

I failed to discover from His Excellency the name of this curious private individual in Tetuan who apparently was in a position to deal in dozens of the most up-to-date foreign war-planes. I also failed to get in any further questions, for the General broke off abruptly and proceeded immediately to a description of the atrocities committed by the Government troops.

For some ten minutes he described in a steady flood of words, which now and then became extremely racy, how the Marxists slit open the stomachs of pregnant women and speared the foetuses; how they had tied two eight-year-old girls on to their father's knees, violated them, poured petrol on them and set them on fire. This went on and on, unceasingly, one story following another – a perfect clinical demonstration in sexual psychopathology.

Spittle oozed from the corners of the General's mouth, and there was the same flickering glow in his eyes which I had remarked in them during some passages of his broadcast. I interrupted again and again to ask him where these things had happened, and was given the names of two places: '*Puente Genil*' and '*Lora del Río*'. When I asked whether His Excellency had in his possession documentary evidence with regard to these excesses, he replied in the negative; he had special couriers, he said, who brought him verbal information with regard to incidents of this kind from all sectors of the front.

Unexpectedly the flood ceased, and I was given my *congé*.

Some days later the Spanish Consul in Gibraltar told me that on the occasion of an officers' banquet in Tetuan in the year 1926 he had seen Queipo de Llano in an epileptic fit.

Although Seville swarms with soldiers, it is not the army that chiefly impresses its character on the town. The dominant element is the Phalanx.

The headquarters of the Phalanx in Seville is in the Calle Trajano; on the afternoon of August 28th I myself saw a lorryload of prisoners from the Río Tinto mines being taken there. The scene was terrible; about half the prisoners were wearing bandages soaked through with fresh blood; and they were bundled out of the lorry like sacks. The street was cordoned off by a double file of Civil Guards; behind them the crowd stood looking on in silence. Speechless, grim, it lingered outside the building for another half hour, staring at the walls and the pale sentries; then it dispersed. It had been waiting for the sound of shots from within. But it had waited in vain; executions are carried out at night.

In the cafés in Seville two notices hang side by side; the first forbids anyone to talk politics, the other makes an appeal for volunteers for the National Militia, the pay offered being three pesetas a day. (In Portugal volunteers for Spain are promised twelve to fifteen pesetas.) I had an opportunity of watching a recruiting commission at work for about an hour. About thirty candidates had queued up, no more. The first question that was put to each of them was whether he could read and write. The illiterates, of whom there were about ten, were lined up in a special file, and about half of them were accepted. (They were nearly all labourers and agricultural workers.) Of the literates only one, a peasant lad, was accepted, all the rest being rejected. The recruiting commission had orders to turn down any suspicious character; by 'suspicious characters' are understood industrial workers, unemployed, anyone wearing spectacles, and agricultural labourers with that indefinable something in their appearance that betrays contact with revolutionary ideas. The recruiting officers, and still more so the sergeant-majors, knew how to detect 'this something'. I saw how this procedure worked out in practice during the hour I spent there; out of what was in itself, for a whole morning, a ridiculously small number of thirty candidates, only five were accepted. Andalusia is a poverty-stricken province with social contrasts of medieval intensity, and every second person has that 'something' in his gaze. And here we touch upon the chief problem of the rebels: their chronic lack of man power.

Franco and his generals were unable to introduce conscription on any considerable scale. They knew that they had the masses against them; they knew that every bayonet that they forced into the hands of the peasants of Andalusia and Estremadura might be turned against them at a suitable moment. The Spanish Army never has been a people's army; as we shall see in a later chapter there has always been a disproportionately large number of officers in it, a characteristic which has been still further intensified during the course of the Civil War. At the end of a year's fighting the Moors (estimated at about eighty thousand), the Italians (estimated at about a hundred thousand) and the picked troops of the Foreign Legion constitute the backbone of the infantry in Franco's army. Then come, in the order of their numerical strength, the political formations: the *Falange Española* and the *Requetes*. The actual Spanish regular infantry counts last in Franco's army.

This chronic lack of man power has been more than compensated for from a strategic point of view by supplies of the most up-to-date war material from abroad. On July 15th, 1937, almost exactly a year after the outbreak of the Civil War, the 'Daily Telegraph' wrote:

General Franco continues to rely principally on relatively small forces supported by very heavy armaments. In some quarters it has been estimated that there was one machine-gun to every four men. This is probably an exaggeration. Nevertheless, the Insurgents used very large numbers of machine-guns in proportion to their effectives.

The situation on the Government side was exactly the opposite. Madrid had at its command an infinite supply of men and for a time was numerically twice to three times as strong as the rebels. But these forces were without training, without discipline, without officers and without arms.

On the rebel side there were companies with one machine-gun to every four men. On the Republican side there were companies where four men shared a single rifle.

My stay in Seville was very instructive and very brief.

My private hobby was tracking down the German airmen; that is to say, the secret imports of planes and pilots, which at that time was in full swing, but was not so generally known as it is to-day. It was the time when European diplomacy was just celebrating its honeymoon with the Non-Intervention Pact. Hitler was denying having despatched aircraft to Spain, and Franco was denying having received them, while there before my very eyes fat, blond German pilots, living proof to the contrary, were consuming vast quantities of Spanish fish, and, monocles clamped into their eyes, reading the 'Völkischer Beobachter'.

There were four of these gentlemen in the Hotel Cristina in Seville at about lunch time on August 28th, 1936. The Cristina is the hotel of which the porter had told me that it was full of German officers and that it was not advisable to go there, because every foreigner was liable to be taken for a spy.

I went there, nevertheless. It was, as I have said, about two o'clock in the afternoon. As I entered the lounge, the four pilots were sitting at a table, drinking sherry. The fish came later.

Their uniforms consisted of the white overall worn by Spanish airmen; on their breasts were two embroidered wings with a small swastika in a circle (a swastika in a circle with wings is the so-called 'Emblem of Distinction' of the German National-Socialist Party).

In addition to the four men in uniform one other gentleman was sitting at the table. He was sitting with his back to me; I could not see his face.

I took my place some tables further on. A new face in the lounge of a hotel occupied by officers always creates a stir in times of civil war. I could tell that the five men were discussing me. After some time the fifth man, the one with his back to me, got up and strolled past my table with an air of affected indifference. He had obviously been sent out to reconnoitre.

As he passed my table, I looked up quickly from my paper and hid my face even more quickly behind it again. But it was of no use; the man had recognized me, just as I had recognized him. It was Herr Strindberg, the undistinguished son of the great August Strindberg; he was a Nazi journalist, and war correspondent in Spain for the Ullstein group.

This was the most disagreeable surprise imaginable. I had known the man years previously in Germany at a time when Hitler had been still knocking at the door, and he himself had been a passionate democrat. At that time I had been on the editorial staff of the Ullstein group, and his room had been only three doors from mine. Then Hitler came to power and Strindberg became a Nazi.

We had no further truck with one another but he was perfectly aware of my views and political convictions. He knew me to be an incorrigible Left-wing liberal, and this was quite enough to incriminate me. My appearance in this haunt of Nazi airmen must have appeared all the more suspect inasmuch as he could not have known that I was in Seville for an English newspaper.

He behaved as though he had not recognized me, and I did the same. He returned to his table,

He began to report to his friends in an excited whisper. The five gentlemen put their heads together.

There followed a strategic manoeuvre: two of the airmen strolled towards the door – obviously to cut off my retreat; the third went to the porter's lodge and telephoned – obviously to the police; the fourth pilot and Strindberg paced up and down the room.

I felt more and more uncomfortable and every moment expected the *Guardia Civil* to turn up and arrest me. I thought the most sensible thing would be to put an innocent face on the whole thing, and getting up, I shouted across the two intervening tables with (badly) simulated astonishment:

'Hallo, aren't you Strindberg?'

He turned pale and became very embarrassed, for he had not expected such a piece of impudence.

'I beg your pardon, I am talking to this gentleman,' he said.

Had I still had any doubts, this behaviour on his part would in itself have made it patent to me that the fellow had denounced me. Well, I thought, the only thing that's going to get me out of this is a little more impudence. I asked him in a very loud voice, and as arrogantly as possible, what reason he had for not shaking hands with me.

He was completely bowled over at this, and literally gasped. At this point his friend, airman number four, joined in the fray. With a stiff little bow he told me his name, von Bernhardt, and demanded to see my papers.

The little scene was carried on entirely in German.

I asked by what right Herr von Bernhardt, as a foreigner, demanded to see my papers.

Herr von Bernhardt said that as an officer in the Spanish Army he had a right to ask 'every suspicious character' for his papers.

Had I not been so agitated, I should have pounced upon this statement as a toothsome morsel. That a man with a swastika on his breast should acknowledge himself in German to be an officer in Franco's army, would have been a positive tit-bit for the Non-Intervention Committee.

I merely said, however, that I was not a 'suspicious character', but an accredited correspondent of the London 'News Chronicle', that Captain Bolín would confirm this, and that I refused to show my papers.

When Strindberg heard me mention the 'News Chronicle' he did something that was quite out of place: he began to scratch his head. Herr von Bernhardt too grew uncomfortable at the turn of events and sounded a retreat. We went on arguing for a while, until Captain Bolín entered the hotel. I hastened up to him and demanded that the others should apologize to me, thinking to myself that attack was the best defence and that I must manage at all costs to prevent Strindberg from having his say. Bolín was astonished at the scene and indignantly declared that he refused to have anything to do with the whole stupid business, and that in time of civil war he didn't give a damn whether two people shook hands or not.

In the meantime the Civil Guards had actually arrived on the scene, with fixed bayonets and pugnacious expressions, to arrest the 'suspicious character'. Bolín angrily told them to go to the devil. And to the devil they went.

I decamped there and then from the confounded Cristina. Arrived at the hotel, I began hurriedly to pack. I had hardly finished when a French colleague of mine came up to my room and privately advised me to leave for Gibraltar as quickly as possible. He was obviously acting as the mouthpiece of some higher authority; but he refused to say whom. He merely said that he had heard of the shindy and that the whole affair might turn out very seriously for me.

Eight hours later I was in Gibraltar.

Twenty-four hours later I learned from private sources that a warrant for my arrest had been issued in Seville.

So Strindberg junior had had his say after all.

I don't care two hoots, I thought. Seville has seen the last of me.

There I was wrong.

Arthur Koestler was born in Budapest in 1905. In 1927, after a year in Palestine, Koestler returned to Berlin and began to work for the Ullstein group of newspapers. In 1931, he was appointed foreign editor of the Berliner *Zeitung am Mittag* and that year joined the Communist Party of Germany. Koestler spent the next years in Paris engaged in anti-fascist activity for the Comintern, and in 1936 was sent undercover to visit Franco's headquarters in Seville – his cover was credentials from the *News Chronicle*. In Seville, Koestler found decisive evidence of the involvement of Fascist Italy and Nazi Germany on Franco's side – at the time something the Rebels denied. In 1937, Koestler returned to Spain and was in Málaga when it fell to Franco. He was captured and imprisoned in Seville under sentence of death – his *Dialogue with Death* is an account of this imprisonment. An international campaign for his release led to him being exchanged for a Nationalist prisoner held by the Republicans. Koestler's experiences in Spain led to disillusion with communism and the Party, from which he resigned in 1938. Later that year he started writing, in Paris, *Darkness at Noon*, his most famous novel, which was published in 1940; it is a searing critique of communism and Stalin's purges. The prison scenes are inspired by Koestler's imprisonment in Spain. By now a committed anticommunist, Koestler settled in the UK in 1953. In 1983, he committed suicide in London with his wife. This extract is from 'Portrait of a Rebel General', originally published as part of *Spanish Testament*.

LANGSTON HUGHES

LAUGHTER IN MADRID

from *The Nation*, 29 January 1938

THE THING ABOUT LIVING IN MADRID these days is that you never know when a shell is going to fall. Or where. Any time is firing time for Franco. Imagine yourself sitting calmly in the front room of your third-floor apartment carefully polishing your eyeglasses when all of a sudden, without the least warning, a shell decides to come through the wall – paying no attention to the open window – and explodes like a thunderclap beneath the sofa. If you are sitting on the sofa, you are out of luck. If you are at the other side of the room and good at dodging shrapnel you may not be killed. Maybe nobody will even be injured in your apartment. Perhaps the shell will simply go on through the floor and kill somebody else in apartment 27, downstairs. (People across the hall have been killed.)

Who next? Where? When? Today all the shells may fall in the Puerta del Sol. Tomorrow Franco's big guns in the hills outside Madrid may decide to change their range-finders and bombard the city fan-wise, sending *quince-y-medios* from one side of the town to the other. No matter in what section of the city you live, a shell may land in the kitchen of the sixth-floor apartment (whose inhabitants you've often passed on the stairs), penetrate several floors, and make its way to the street via your front room on the third floor.

That explains why practically nobody in Madrid bothers to move when the big guns are heard. If you move, you may as likely as not move into the wrong place. A few days ago four shells went through the walls of the Hotel Florida, making twenty that have fallen there. The entrance to the hotel is well protected with sandbags, but they couldn't sandbag nine stories. All this the desk clerk carefully explains to guests who wish to register. But most of the other hotels have been severely bombed, too. And one has to stay somewhere.

The Hotel Alfonso a few blocks away has several large holes through each of its four walls but is still receiving guests. One of the halls on an upper floor leads straight out into space – door and balcony have been shot away. In one of the unused bedrooms you can look slantingly down three floors into the street through the holes made by a shell that struck the roof and plowed its way down, then out by a side wall into the road. Walking up to your room, you pass a point where the marble stairs are splintered and the wall pitted by scraps of iron; here two people were killed. Yet the Hotel Alfonso maintains its staff, and those of its rooms that still have walls and windows are occupied by paying guests.

The now world-famous Telefonica, Madrid's riddled skyscraper in the center of the city, is still standing, proud but ragged, its telephone girls at work inside. The Madrid Post Office has no window-panes left whatsoever, but the mail still goes out. Around the Cibeles Fountain in front of the Post Office the street cars still pass, although the fountain itself with its lovely goddess is now concealed by a specially built housing of bricks and sandbags, so that the good-natured Madrileños have nicknamed it 'Beauty Under Covers,' laughing at their own wit.

Yes, people still laugh in Madrid. In this astonishing city of bravery and death, where the houses run right up to the trenches and some of the street-car lines stop only at the barricades, people still laugh, children play in the streets, and men buy comic papers as well as war news. The shell holes of the night before are often filled in by dawn, so efficient is the wrecking service and so valiantly do the Madrileños struggle to patch up their city.

A million people living on the front lines of a nation at war! The citizens of Madrid – what are they like? Not long ago a small shell fell in the study of a bearded professor of ancient languages. Frantically his wife and daughter came running to see if anything had happened to him. They found him standing in the center of the floor, holding the shell and shaking his head quizzically. 'This little thing,' he said, 'this inanimate object, can't do us much damage. It's the philosophy that lies behind it, wife, the philosophy that lies behind it.'

In the Arguelles quarter to the north, nearest to the rebel lines – the neighborhood that has suffered most from bombardments and air raids – many of the taller apartment houses, conspicuous targets that they are, have been abandoned. But in the smaller houses of one and two stories people still live and go about their tasks. The Cuban poet, Alejo Carpentier, told me that one morning after a heavy shelling he passed a house of which part of the front wall was lying in the yard. A shell had passed through the roof, torn away part of the wall, carried with it the top of the family piano, and buried itself in the garden. Nevertheless, there at the piano sat the young daughter of the house, very clean and starched, her hair brushed and braided, her face shining. Diligently she was beating out a little waltz from a music book in front of her. The fact that the top of the piano had been shot away in the night did not seem to affect the chords. When passers-by asked about it, calling through the shell hole, the child said, 'Yes, an *obús* came right through here last night. I'm going to help clean up the yard after a while, but I have to practice my lessons now. My music teacher'll be here at eleven.'

The will to live and laugh in Madrid is the thing that constantly amazes a stranger. At the house where I am staying, sometimes a meal consists largely of bread and of soup made with bread. Everybody tightens his belt and grins, and somebody is sure to repeat good-naturedly an old Spanish saying, 'Bread with bread – food for fools.' Then we all laugh.

One of Franco's ways of getting back at Madrid is to broadcast daily from his radio stations at Burgos and Seville the luncheon and dinner menus of the big hotels, the fine food that the Fascists are eating and the excellent wines they drink. (Rioja and the best of wine areas are in Fascist hands.) But Madrid has ways of getting even with the Fascists, too. Mola, a lover of cafes, said at the very beginning of the war that he would soon be drinking coffee in Madrid. He was mistaken. Then he said he would enter Madrid by the first of November. He didn't.

Then he swore he would enter the city on the eighth of December. He didn't. But on the evening of the eighth some wag remembered, and the crowds passing that night in Madrid's darkened Puerta del Sol saw by moonlight in the very center of the square a coffee table, carefully set, the coffee poured, and neatly pinned to the white cloth a large sign reading 'For Mola.'

Bread and coffee are scarce in Madrid, and so are cigarettes. The only cigarettes offered for sale more or less regularly are small, hard, and very bad. They are so bad that though they cost thirty centimos before the war they bring only twenty now despite their comparative scarcity. The soldiers call them 'recruit-killers,' jocularly asserting that they are as dangerous to the new men in the army as are bombs and bullets.

Bad cigarettes, poor wine, little bread, no soap, no sugar! Madrid, dressed in bravery and laughter; knowing death and the sound of guns by day and night, but resolved to live, not die!

The moving-picture theaters are crowded. Opening late in the afternoon and compelled to close at nine, they give only one or two showings a day. One evening an audience was following with great interest an American film. Suddenly an *obús* fell in the street outside. There was a tremendous detonation, but nobody moved from his seat. The film went on. Soon another fell, nearer and louder than before, shaking the whole building. The manager went out into the lobby and looked up and down the Gran Via. Overhead he heard the whine of shells. He went inside and mounted the stage to say that, in view of the shelling, he thought it best to stop the picture. Before he had got the words out of his mouth he was greeted with such a hissing and booing and stamping of feet and calls for the show to go on that he shrugged his shoulders in resignation and signaled the operator to continue. The house was darkened. The magic of Hollywood resumed its spell. While Franco's shells whistled dangerously over the theater, the film went its make-believe way to a thrilling denouement. The picture was called 'Terror in Chicago.'

～

Langston Hughes was born in Missouri in 1902. A leading member of the Harlem Renaissance, Hughes went to Spain in 1937 as a correspondent for Afro-American newspapers.

On his way to Spain, he spoke at the Second International Writers Congress in Paris on the links between fascism and racism: '...I come from a land whose democracy from the very beginning has been tainted with race prejudice born of slavery, and whose richness has been poured through the narrow channels of greed into the hands of the few.'

As a black man, Hughes understood the very special oppression of the Moors, African soldiers enlisted to fight in Franco's army. In his 'Letter from Spain', he explains the feelings of the black soldiers of the International Brigade about fighting the Moors:

And as he lay there dying
In a village we had taken.
I looked across to Africa
And seed foundations shakin'.

Cause if a free Spain wins this war,
The colonies, too, are free –
Then something wonderful'll happen
To them Moors as dark as me.

Hughes' stature in the Hispanic world grew from this moment on and his writings were translated and celebrated throughout the Spanish-speaking world. He died in New York in 1967.

MIKA ETCHEBÉHÈRE

OF LICE AND BOOKS

from *Ma Guerre d'Espagne à Moi*
translated by Nick Caistor

A NIGHT SPENT COUGHING and scratching is even longer than one when you can't sleep, because it's impossible to fill it with thoughts, memories or ideas. If only I could have the luxury of really coughing, of getting rid of this choking sensation I feel in my chest all the time. I cover my head, cough under the blanket, I feel I'm suffocating, my temples are about to explode, I want to throw up. At the same time, I scratch until I feel my fingernails are wet with blood.

In the morning, I tell myself, I'll go and see the doctor. I won't eat any more tinned stuff, and I'll ask him for a cream. But where and when could I spread it on? I haven't undressed for three weeks… I could ask the male nurse to leave me on my own in the clinic for a moment, but that would only emphasize my difference to the others, the fact of being a woman.

My skin is burning, my eyes sting, my back hurts. Very slowly, I wrap myself in the blanket and start to crawl towards the door. Suddenly, I hear Rogelio's voice:

'Where are you going? I'm as wide-awake as you. Would you like me to heat up some coffee?'

'No, I'm just going outside for a while so I can cough properly. Sleep, I don't want any coffee. In the morning if I'm not better I'll go and see the doctor. Let me go out.'

'It's so cold out there you'll catch pneumonia. Stay here and cough all you like, you're not disturbing anyone: just listen to the commander snore. I can't sleep because of my stomachache. Have a spoonful of cough medicine, come on, do as you're told.'

I swallow the cough mixture, sit with my back against the wall, and end up dozing off in a kind of torpor, interrupted from time to time by coughing fits. A stabbing pain in my right shoulder jerks me fully awake. Is it muscular, or does it come from somewhere deeper? It doesn't get any worse when I breathe in, so I decide it's because of the position I'm sitting in. It's time to get up anyway, Rogelio and the commander are already having breakfast.

'I heard you coughing a lot in the night,' says the commander. 'It's time you went to see a doctor in Madrid. You're not getting any sleep, or hardly any at all; you can't go on like this.'

'I'm sure it's nothing more than a heavy cold, or at worst a touch of bronchitis, it's not serious because during the day I hardly cough at all. It's not so much the cough as the urticaria that worries me, I'm sure it's the tinned food.'

'Or the lice,' says Rogelio. 'I don't see why you wouldn't have them like everybody else. Those little creatures are no respecters of rank.'

'But my head doesn't itch ...'

'That's because you've got them on your body, like all the rest of us,' Rogelio insists. 'If I were you I'd go and undress in the first-aid post to check.'

'It could indeed be lice,' the commander says. 'That's one more reason to go to Madrid. You could also take advantage of the journey to fetch some new books. It was a good idea to give the militia something to read, and an even better one to set up a school. When I told Colonel Tomás about it, he said he would give the order for it to be adopted by the whole brigade. He wants you to go and tell him the best way to put it into practice.'

'I'll go with you,' Rogelio says. 'If we arrive in time for breakfast the colonel's wife will give us some fried bread with chocolate, like the last time. If you want to change socks, here's a dry pair.'

We are out of luck, and arrive too late. Colonel Tomás and his wife have already had breakfast. Everything in the room is very tidy. It's obvious there is a woman in charge of the household. Lots of the men are unhappy about family life like this at the front, but not me. Besides, I like the wife a lot. She has a soft voice, looks you straight in the eye, and has the manners of a well-behaved child. The only thing I find shocking is that she is so young. She can't be more than twenty, whereas the colonel must be around forty.

Colonel Tomás asks me how to obtain books and school equipment. I explain that the Madrid bookshop owners give everything for free when they're told it's for the front, and suggest what I think are the most suitable kinds of book: romances, adventure novels or thrillers, and illustrated magazines, even foreign ones, provided they have good reproductions. As for the school at the front, it isn't just for those who can't read or write. We have had to organize a course at a higher level for the militiamen who want to improve their handwriting or their knowledge of arithmetic. We ought to extend the libraries and the school to wherever a lack of action allows it, not simply as an antidote to monotony, nostalgia and the harshness of life in the trenches, but to promote an education that doesn't require many resources.

'I'm so convinced you're right,' says Colonel Tomás, 'that straightaway today I'm going to send a message to the other battalions in the brigade, recommending they create a school and a library.'

'Wouldn't you care for some coffee?' the colonel's wife suggests in her gentle, melodious voice.

'Thank you very much, it'll have to be some other day,' I say, 'it's already late.'

I don't know if my voice betrays it, but all of a sudden this peaceful conjugal scene irritates me as an injustice, a lack of respect for all the men who have neither home nor wife, the ones scratching day and night at their lice in the trenches.

My anger is directed not at the young girl with humble gestures, but to the man, the colonel, the leader who gives himself permission to disregard the harsh law imposed by the solitude and misery the mass of combatants have to suffer. On our return journey, I won't allow Rogelio to talk of 'the good life that fellow enjoys.'

'It could be that he's ill,' I say, 'and he needs to have someone with him who can take care of him and look after him. His skin is so yellow he could well have liver problems. Let's leave it at that. There are women as well at Puerta de Hierro, and nobody thinks that's odd.'

'That's because there the militia women cook and clean for everyone, they're not the wives of any particular officer; they're not there to sleep with them.'

We have more visitors at the command post. They are officers from a battalion in our brigade who want to learn more about the libraries. Two of them are primary school teachers and are especially interested in our school. As is only fair, before we begin discussing important matters, we drink a glass of the horrible brandy which has popularly become known as 'rat poison', apparently made from pure alcohol.

I start scratching furiously, excusing myself by saying I must have eczema caused by the tinned food, some sort of vitamin deficiency. I slip my hand into my sleeve to scratch my arm, and up by my elbow I feel something crawling on my skin. I grasp it between thumb and first finger, thinking it must be a small scab, but of course it's an enormous, monstrous louse with a dark, striped back. It is waving its legs desperately in the air, and looking me in the eye, yes, looking at me, even if nobody believes that a louse can look.

Humiliated, not knowing what to do with this ghastly creature I'm clutching in my fingers – I can hear the others laughing and saying 'That's some deficiency!' – I rush out to the first-aid post, where fortunately I find no-one. I squash the louse under my nail on the edge of a table, and start to strip off. My brassiere is crawling with lice. I stamp on it furiously, then put my jersey and oilskin back on. I return to the command post, where the commander asks if I want to go to Madrid.

'At once, if possible. I'll have time to see the doctor, have a bath, change my underwear. And bring back some books. Now I've got over my fear, I prefer lice to a lack of vitamins; they're easier to deal with.'

At the hospital, the delousing process consists of several stages: an antiseptic bath, anti-parasite cream on the head after a fine-tooth comb has been run several times through the closely-cropped hair, then a cicatrizing lotion on the wounds, followed by lots of talc all over the body.

To avoid the wool rubbing, I am given a fine cotton shift that covers me from neck to ankle. It feels as though I'm in a shroud: perhaps I am, who knows?

'Now,' I say, 'can I be given something for my cough, a medicine so that I can sleep at night and let others sleep as well?'

'The doctor is expecting you,' the nurse replies gently. 'Come with me as you are. That shift suits you, it's like a wedding dress...'

'Or a dress for a funeral: it looks like a shroud. I feel as if I've already been buried.'

'Don't talk nonsense, and above all, don't take it off. If you put your woollen clothes directly on to your skin, the sores on your chest will get infected.'

The doctor listens to my breathing carefully, then peers at my X-ray. He explains that I have bad bronchitis but that it hasn't affected my lungs. He says I need to spend a week in bed.

'The week in bed will have to be when our men are relieved, which must be soon,' I say. 'For now all I want is for you to give me medication, especially something to help me sleep. If I'm still coughing when I return to Madrid, I promise to take good care of myself.'

'It would be better to do it now, or are you so indispensable at the front that you can't be away for a week?' the doctor replies irritatedly.

'I'm not indispensable, or even necessary, but in our trenches there are dozens of militiamen who are coughing like me, and are covered in lice just as I was an hour ago. If they can't leave their posts, there's no reason for me to abandon mine. It's a simple matter of equality, or discipline if you prefer.'

The doctor does not deign to reply, but writes out a prescription, hands it to the nurse, gives a brief nod of the head and hurries out of the consulting-room.

'I think we've got everything the doctor wants here,' says the nurse.

In a short while, she comes back with bottles, tubes of pills, boxes of cream and a big packet of iodised cotton similar to what I put on Hippo's chest when he was coughing.

'I put in two or three times as much of everything,' says the gentle girl, 'in case other people need them. They're very good medicines; and besides, I'll pray for you all. The medicines will be more effective that way.'

'You're religious, aren't you? It's obvious from your manners and your voice.'

'I used to be a nun, and there's no reason I should hide it. When I took the veil it was against the wishes of my family, who are all left-wing. Whatever happens, I won't go back to that, but I haven't lost my faith. I pray to God every day for Him to protect my two brothers who are fighting on the Andalusian front. I've heard that Málaga is about to fall. I've lit ten candles to the Virgin in my heart so that she doesn't allow the Fascists to enter Málaga, because if they do they'll carry out the same slaughter as at Badajoz. God will not permit it, I'm telling you that God will not permit it. I'm sorry for all this pointless chatter, Málaga may already have fallen, so it's possible that I lose my faith even in the Holy Virgin.'

Somebody pushes open the door. It's an old man, probably the porter, who cries out in anguish: 'Málaga has fallen; it's just been announced on the radio. The Italian air-force is bombing the roads packed with civilians. What a crime, Lord, what a terrible crime!'

I embrace the nurse and run out to get to the bookshop on Calle Preciados, where the car is waiting for me. The driver already knows that Málaga has fallen. So does the bookseller. They both say the government is to blame because it didn't send the troops and weapons needed for the defence of the city in time.

We pick up the packages of books already made up for us, then call in at two other bookshops. We give up on the idea of paying for the black market meal we had promised ourselves, and rush back to our positions as quickly as possible as if we are fleeing the Italians bombing the roads around Málaga that are full of women and children.

'There's talk of betrayal in the high command,' the driver complains, 'and of struggles between different workers' organizations. Just think: allowing Málaga the Red to fall! It's all well and good to defend Madrid: but while we're sitting waiting on our own in our trenches, the Fascists are taking all the other cities one by one!'

~

Mika Etchebéhère was born Michele Feldman in 1902 in Argentina into a middle-class Jewish family. Studying at Buenos Aires she met Hippolyte Etchebéhère, whom she later married. Both anarchists, the couple went to Europe in 1931, were active in left-wing circles in Berlin and went to Madrid in July 1936, where they enlisted in the POUM. After Hippolyte was killed in the siege of Sigüenza in August 1936, Mika was elected head of the company in his stead, the only woman to command a column in the war. Her book *Ma guerre d'Espagne à Moi* (My Spanish War) was published in France in 1975. Her column consisted of men from Extremadura, fearless macho fighters who loved Mika dearly but insisted that she act as if she were their mother; they did not want to be teased for being led by a woman! Her account of her war experiences is rich in the many sides of the social revolution – teaching the soldiers to read and write, helping the peasants cultivate their lands, and delousing. After the fall of Madrid, Etchebéhère fled first to France and then to Argentina. She returned to France in the 1950s and, as an anarchist activist, took part in the 1968 general strike and revolt. She died in Paris in 1992, venerated by the French extreme left.

DRIEU LA ROCHELLE

A EUROPEAN PATRIOTISM

from *Gilles*

translated by Pete Ayrton

TWO DAYS LATER, Walter was on the Irishman's boat sailing to France. O'Connor was to drop him off in Marseille, then he and the Pole would put the boat at the service of Franco. It was dark; the three men were in the salon, drinking and smoking after their meal. Perhaps because of recent violent emotions, Walter was less susceptible to sea-sickness.

He had left Ibiza with a clear conscience. The pilot and the radio had been found and Escairolle had escaped in a fishing-boat with the leaders and rank and file of resourceful or determined reds ready to go off to fight elsewhere. Cohen was out of sight and mind. Walter no longer thought about him.

He looked with contentment at his companions. His last pleasure in life would be like his first: the companionship of men, both highly strung and self-conscious, entirely focussed on themselves. In the past, on the front, two or three men had given him this satisfaction. Not always intellectuals. One enjoys the collective sacrifice to something that, as the danger grows, becomes closer to one's heart whilst also crucial to all. It is wondrous to be able to see oneself reflected in others and to appreciate others in oneself. A miracle so fragile and fascinating that soon only death could seal it with certainty.

He shouted out: 'Strange that we met given that we are up against the same problem.'

'We have each made the voyage necessary for this meeting,' replied the Pole.

O'Connor poured whiskey in the three glasses and joked: 'Each of us is fighting for a lost cause.' Walter looked at this face devoid of melancholy but lit up with jocular animation.

'What? You think it impossible that the Church recognises the lasting, universal reach of Fascism?'

'For a while now, the Church does not understand what is happening in the world. The Church took a century to understand Democracy and came round to it when the latter was becoming history.'

'Every time I meet a Catholic intellectual, they are anti-clerical. Do you think that the Church is committed to opposing Fascism?'

'And vice versa,' hummed the Pole.

'But really, look at Spain,' Walter replied. 'The Catholics are fighting for Franco.'

'Not the Basques,' complained the Irishman.

'You Irish must understand the Basques. They are like the Irish in the Great War: I side with the enemy of my enemy whoever he may be.'

'You are right there,' O'Connor agreed, but continued: 'There is no doubt that Hitler and Mussolini have a score to settle with the Pope.'

'The feeling is mutual,' added the Pole.

Walter reflected on what had just been said.

'I am not convinced. In any case, you want to remain a Fascist and a Catholic.'

The two men agreed with silent mirth. Walter, more pensive and gloomy than his companions, continued: 'What if the Church ordered you to fight Fascism?'

'We would not fight it.'

'Even if Fascism ordered you to destroy the Church?'

'The Church cannot be destroyed,' shouted the Pole. Walter shrugged his shoulders.

'This is not an answer. Put priests in prison?'

'Yes, if they are more committed to communism than to the priesthood,' exclaimed O'Connor. 'In any event, priests must atone for their sins: they recognise this themselves. That's why they are so keen on the communists.'

Walter looked at him with concern. Was he a frivolous dilettante? Or was he aware of the subtlety of his contradictions? A strong faith is aware of the contradictions it embraces.

The Pole continued: 'The Church is indestructible: it will overcome its present errors and be strengthened through persecution. It will remain alive in the hearts of Fascist Catholics.'

'But if you were ordered to renounce your faith?'

'We would renounce it for political gains.'

'Exactly so,' Walter sneered.

'Yes,' sighed O'Connor, 'there always comes a moment when one must sacrifice one part of one's faith to another.'

'What is your faith?'

'I believe that Fascism is an immense, salutary revolution and that the Church should take advantage of this moment it is offered to be completely renewed. Walter, from the first moment we met, you expressed perfectly my opinions: we are in favour of the virile Catholicism of the Middle Ages.'

'Bravo,' said the Pole.

Walter stirred on the bench he was sitting on.

'Fascism is a proper revolution, which could mean a complete overhaul of Europe through a mixture of the very old and the very new which includes the Church: but if it rejects…'

'And if the Church rejects it,' whispered the Pole, 'then…'

'…Then the world will await better days. It will wait for the Church and Fascism to see that they were made for each other,' joked O'Connor, downing a shot of whiskey. 'But I'm not worried. When Fascism is the master of Europe, it will need Catholicism and it will recast it.'

'Until then you Fascists would renounce the Church before you renounced Fascism?'

'Yes,' said the Pole. 'Fascism needs our help more than the Church. If the Church errs politically as it often has in the past, we would for the time being abandon it. You can take or leave the Church: it is eternal. If the Church were to ask us to fight with the Communists against the Fascists – that never. We would be excommunicated as many good Christians have been.'

'But if the government of your country asks you to fight with the Communists against the Fascists?'

The two men bowed their heads in anguish. They turned to Walter in the hope that he would be able to find a solution.

'I think,' Walter said, 'that you can make for Fascism the same distinction you make for the Church. In the same way as for the Church you do not conflate its political and its spiritual leadership, so for Fascism you would not place its universal principle on the same level with the powers that embody and, at times, misuse it. If you cannot bring about the triumph of Fascism in your respective countries, you will bear the terrible consequences of your failure and if needs be, you will defend these countries against Fascist powers with the danger of bringing about the victory of anti-Fascist forces. Like the Church, Fascism can wait but you cannot sacrifice to the powers that use Fascism in your homelands.'

'If Poland allies herself with Russia against Germany, if she allows herself to be invaded by the reds, I could no longer fight for Poland. It would be to sacrifice not only Fascism but also the Church. Look at what is happening here: to save the Church, the foundation of Europe, the good Spaniards have to call for help from Italy, Germany.'

'But the triumph of Fascism is not the same as the triumph of one nation over other nations,' said Walter.

'The hegemony of an idea is always conflated with the hegemony of a nation,' responded the Pole. 'The hegemony of democracy was for a century or two conflated with the hegemony of England. In the end, a choice has to be made between Nationalism and Fascism.'

'Nationalism is outdated,' was O'Connor's comment after a moment of thought. 'What the democratic powers could not bring about at Geneva, the Fascist powers will. They will achieve the unity of Europe.'

'But would not the defeat of the Fascist powers establish the hegemony of Russia? Or of one of the vile democracies of France, England, America,' shouted O'Connor. 'For me the triumph, after a world war, of the United States would be as bad as the triumph of Russia.'

'It would be the same thing,' acknowledged Walter.

'So?'

'So…'

Walter looked at both of them.

'For my part, I have withdrawn from what occurs between nations. I belong to a new military and religious order established somewhere in the world which strives against all odds for the reconciliation of the Church and Fascism and their joint triumph over Europe.'

The two men looked at him with fear and trembling.

'But,' the Pole took up again, 'how would you avoid the hegemony of Germany?'

'During the last century, peoples learnt Nationalism and Democracy from the French and turned it against them. We will turn Fascism against Germany and Italy. In any case, it is not possible that Germany does not foresee what will happen at a certain point in the next world war. A European patriotism will have to be born against the invasion of Europe by the Russian army. This spirit will only be born if Germany has in advance morally guaranteed the integrity of homelands, of all European homelands. Only then will it be able to effectively carry out the role it is allotted due to its might and by the tradition of the Holy Roman–Germanic Empire to set out a way forward for Europe.'

'Amen,' said the Pole.

'I'm off to bed,' said the Irishman.

⌒

Born in Paris in 1893, **Drieu La Rochelle** is a controversial figure in French literature. After the First World War in which he was wounded three times, Drieu went to Paris, where he was close to Dada and the Surrealists. As he grew older, his politics moved to the right. In the 1920s, he denounced the 'decadent materialism' of democracy and in 1934 he declared himself a 'Fascist Socialist'. After a visit to Germany in 1935, he embraced National Socialism as an antidote to the mediocrity of liberal democracy.

A collaborator during the war, Drieu hoped that the Nazis would lead a 'Fascist International'. After the liberation of Paris, Drieu had to go into hiding and he committed suicide in 1945. Never translated into English, *Gilles* is Drieu's masterpiece. A corrosive portrait of France in the first half of the 20th century, *Gilles* is an autobiographical novel of the coming of age of a Fascist aesthete. The anti-Semitic narrator, disgusted by the decadence of his social and intellectual peers, leaves for Algeria, where he finds for the first time love and contentment. However, political events in Europe force him to return home and declare his commitment to fascism. When the Civil War breaks out in Spain, he must go and redeem himself fighting for Franco.

MANUEL CHAVES NOGALES

THE MOORS RETURN TO SPAIN

from *And in the Distance a Light…?*

translated by L. de Baeza and D. C. F. Harding

'PAISA* IN THE NAME of the Big God, do not shoot… Me red, red.'

Mohamed showed by his gestures that he was giving himself up. His arms were raised high above his head, fingers wide-spread, and one of his legs was red with blood from a wound, a scarlet flower blooming amidst the baggy rags which were his trousers. He looked like a terrifying scarecrow, only his eyes were alive, shining like two green points of fire. He had thrown down his rifle to indicate that there was no more fight left in him and stood behind the big boulder he had used as cover to defend himself. The reds, fearing some ruse, hesitated to come out into the open and kept firing at him from their shelter behind the surrounding boulders. From time to time the bullets tore chips from the rock close by. The Moor's amazement at not having already been hit a dozen times grew with each badly aimed shot.

'Stop firing!' he kept on shouting. 'Me be red, me be Republica.'

And still the reds kept firing at him, as if at target practice, but no bullet touched him. Mohamed, astonished to see the shots whizzing past

---

* 'Paisa' is the word that a Moor gives to anyone who is fighting other than a Moor and 'hebreo' to any non-combatant.

his head, began to feel profound contempt for such clumsy marksmen. He could have scored a bulls-eye with every shot. Such a poor opinion did he form of them that it flashed through his mind that he might as well pick up his gun again and go on fighting; so sure was he of being able to defy such poor warriors. At last one of them dared to come into the open very cautiously and shout:

'Give yourself up!'

Three others, peeping out from behind their cover, echoed the cry – 'Give yourself up!'

Mohamed who, as a matter of fact, had given himself up a long time ago, could not understand why four armed men should take so many precautions against an unarmed one, and wounded at that. When he saw the four men round him still afraid, and when he noticed their poor physique and small stature, Mohamed, the stubborn, magnificent Berber warrior, utterly despised them and, in spite of his wounded leg, prepared to fight them.

He let them approach closer, little by little. Hidden in the folds of his burnous he still had his scimitar, and his loaded rifle was in easy reach of his hand. He waited for the right moment then, rapidly pulling out his dangerous weapon, he plunged it, like lightning, full into the chest of his nearest assailant. He then stooped to grasp the rifle and, crouching, shot down a second man and turned to aim at a third who threw down his sporting-gun and started to run. But he had no time to shoot. The fourth militiaman, a goat-herd from the Sierras, stocky and strong, charged him head foremost like an infuriated ram and they fell to the ground in an embrace of hatred, both brimming with the lust to kill. They fought rolling and twisting; serpent and mongoose. The green eyes of the Berber were fixed on the dark eyes, injected with blood and bile, of the Castilian peasant. The Moor's eyes flinched before the monstrous ferocity of the Spaniard's look as the spirit of his ancestors had fallen in that other mortal embrace that lasted for eight centuries and ended with the conquest of Granada. The goat-herd stretched his short neck and, opening his jaws like a beast of prey, sunk his sharp, strong, wolfish teeth into the throat of the Moor who, in agony, made a supreme effort to rise, with his enemy still grasped in his arms and to throw him off; the strong jaws and teeth were tearing at his flesh. He tore himself away and with knife in hand he advanced to kill, but the goat-herd had seized a large sharp-edged stone and flung it at him, catching him on the forehead with a blow which felled him. Then, in blind fury, the Spaniard squeezed the Moor's throat until his eyes bulged in their sockets.

The goat-herd only let go when he heard one of his wounded comrades call to him for help. He was bleeding from the knife-wound which was, however, less serious than it looked. The other militiaman had also had a narrow escape with a superficial flesh wound in the arm. The third militiaman had come back by then and, between the three of them, they lifted the Moor up and took him to a hut a short distance away where they threw him across a mule in order to take him in triumph to the nearest village.

They thought he was dead. Mohamed, however, had undoubtedly more than one life. In spite of a bullet through his leg, a ghastly wound in the forehead, a lacerated neck and the deep marks of the goat-herd's hands on his throat, he was still alive; so much so, that when they halted for a moment to light a cigarette, he jumped to his feet with a supreme effort, but this proved too much for him and he fell down.

'Shall we finish him off?' asked the militiaman who had run away in a panic. He caught hold of his sporting gun by the barrel and was ready to use it on the Moor's head as a club.

'No. Let us take him alive to the village,' said the goat-herd.

'When I killed a wolf in the Sierras and brought him to the village, they paid me twenty-five pesetas. For a live Moor they ought to give us one hundred at least.'

While still discussing how much they would get for their quarry, they replaced the Moor across the back of the mule, and tied his hands together with a stout cord, and started off in the direction of Montreal, the village whose church spire could be seen in the distance.

Secured with a rope to the mule's pack saddle, the Moor's head dangled near the ground, and their progress was marked by a bloody track.

The village was situated at the bottom of a valley under the shadow of the Gredos mountains, and the Almanzor and Galayos peaks stood like gigantic sentinels, barring the passage of the rebel armies. Franco's troops had their headquarters in Avila, in the Sierras some miles from Madrid, and from there they were trying to cross the passes in order to be able to descend into the valleys occupied by the loyalists. In this way the advance on Madrid would, they imagined, be a simple matter. The militiamen guarding the passes with advanced posts were considered strong enough to prevent the advance of the enemy and so, in the villages of the valley twenty to twenty-five miles away, the people felt secure and continued to live their ordinary uneventful and peaceful lives.

The four men had found Mohamed in one of the wildest spots in the Sierras. To the villagers, the presence of a Moor in those parts was staggering and unbelievable. It was thought that the rebel troops were still on the other side of the mountains. The passes, for all they knew, had not been forced. The peasants did not know, however, that the previous night the rebels had thrust a wedge of Moors and Legionaries through an almost inaccessible pass of the Sierras, and that these were advancing on enemy territory so as to take the militiamen by surprise in the rear. Mohamed, straying apart from the troops, possibly to indulge in some private marauding of his own, had been discovered by the patrol of one of the recruiting stations dotted about to round up anyone suspected of fascist sympathies.

The entrance of the Moor and his captors in Montreal was indeed spectacular. The villagers had on other occasions seen their hunters return from the Sierras carrying across the back of a mule a wild goat of the Capra Hispanica species. At times they had been shown big brown foxes which had been caught in the pine woods or even some lonely wolf; but they could not realise that the quarry could be a Moor – a strange creature more dangerous than a wild animal. They surrounded the hunters in admiration, the children with wide-open eyes shouted:

'Look! Look! they have caught a black man, a Moor,' while the women, in fear and rancour, approached the wounded prisoner to hurl insults at him.

The patrol halted in front of the Revolutionary Committee Room. Mohamed was released from the mule and taken before the leaders for questioning. But the Moor knew only a few words of Spanish and kept repeating them in a confused and monotonous sing-song.

'No matar Moro (No kill the Moor)… In the name of Dios Grande no matar Moro,' he kept saying, imploring them to spare his life. 'Moro be red… be Republica.'

A long argument started between the members of the Committee as to what to do with the unusual case. The republicans argued that the best thing to do was to take the prisoner to Madrid and deliver him into the hands of the proper authorities; the anarchists said that the logical thing to do was to let him go free so that he could in this way be redeemed from his past slavery and eventually become a free citizen and a decent member of the anarchist community; the communists were of opinion that the man must be attended to, his wounds taken care of, and when he was healed and restored to his normal strength, he should be enlisted in the fighting militia and sent to the front in defence of the people. There was one more opinion: outside the Committee Room the excited voices of the villagers and militiamen shouted that they wanted the prisoner and that he belonged to them, to deal with as they pleased, which was to kill him without any further delay.

There was such a pandemonium of angry voices, hoarse and violent, and cries of hysterical women round Mohamed that he became confused and weak and it was clear that at any moment he might die, thus frustrating the plans of all. He looked so ghastly that even those who clamoured for his immediate death thought better of it; it wouldn't be much fun as there was so little of Mohamed left to finish. It was therefore decided that the wounded Moor should be rushed to the local hospital, which was already filled to overflowing. Two militiamen took hold of him by the arms and half-dragged, half-carried him to the hospital, followed by a mass of villagers and militiamen who continued to discuss the situation. On the way, a militiaman asked them to stop for a second. He explained that he was taking pictures for the papers and that a photo of the Moor would be a good subject. Mohamed was placed against a wall to be photographed but every time the cameraman tried to get his camera ready the Moor started to scream and to jump at him, believing that he was going to be shot with some kind of mysterious weapon. The cameraman who wanted a posed photograph had to be contented with a snapshot of a wild man.

In the hospital they placed him on the operating-table and for two hours doctors and nurses in white overalls tended him with great care. They did all in their power to alleviate his suffering and to hurt him as little as possible while tending his wounds. The face of the savage African relaxed as he realised dimly that the figures in white, like so many ghosts, were being kind and gentle to Mohamed. He began to smile at them tentatively, the large-mouthed childish grin of his kind. Surely those nurses with such gentle hands were Houris of Mahomet's Paradise.

The members of the Committee, however, were not satisfied with the result of their arguments. It was considered necessary to go back to the Committee Room for more arguing, and the villagers and militiamen assembled again outside to continue their agitated discussions.

The leader of the overflow meeting was the goat-herd whose guttural voice dominated the turmoil. 'He was right,' contended some other goat-herds, muleteers and lumbermen friends of his – 'Enough with the arguing of the Committee. The Moor belonged to the people. The militiamen who had captured him were villagers. He was not going to be sent to Madrid nor was he going to be let go free or enlisted in the fighting militia.'

The goat-herd was appointed to go to the Committee Room to demand that Mohamed should be delivered to the villagers. The members resisted and tried to convince the goat-herd, who, after cursing and swearing against 'that b— lot of politicians,' ran from the Committee Room and shouted to the crowd 'come on!... let us get the Moor!'

They ran like a pack of wolves, forced an entry into the hospital, overpowered the resistance offered by the doctors and nurses, found Mohamed in one of the beds still smiling as though he were in Paradise, and dragged him out amidst vociferations and curses.

They placed him against a wall. Mohamed, with his slow wits enfeebled by weakness, could not realise what was happening and on what could be seen of his face amongst the white bandages, there still lingered a smile of satisfaction. He imagined perhaps, that as he was against the wall, they were going to perform some kind of gentle rite. To take his picture with a box, like the other man who, he now realised, had not meant to hurt him. He had not much time to wonder, for the militiamen pointed their rifles at him and he fell, pierced by a score of bullets, the smile just waning from his half-hidden face.

Soon Mohamed would be wandering in his Paradise in search of Mahomet, to ask for the solution of the riddle: 'Will you tell me, oh great and wise Prophet, why they were so kind as to take the trouble to try to heal me if they had meant all the time to kill me in the end?'

That night the 'Caids' (chieftains) of the 'mehalla' (company of Arab troops) waited in vain in their tent for Mohamed to serve them mint-tea as usual. A patrol watched and waited all through the night. At the break of dawn, when all hope of finding him was lost, one of the Caids, resting in a corner of the tent and smoking a pipe of hashish, was dreamily evoking the splendid figure of the lost Mohamed, who was a valiant young warrior, for many years his loyal henchman, and more like his brother-at-arms than a servant. Both had been born in the hamlet of Ait el Jens on the Southern side of the Atlas mountains where the courageous blue-eyed Berber warriors made war from birth to death with the Desert nomads. Mohamed and the Caid, who had drunk milk from the same breast, had never been separated from one another. They had fought together ever since they were youngsters; first to counter the raids made by the hungry inhabitants of the Sahara who wished to take possession of the fertile meadows of the Sus and the Nun, afterwards, under the Blue Sultan who led them from victory to victory before Marrakeech and, still later, in the chivalrous encounters between the warlike tribes of the Bu Amaran; and finally in the disastrous campaign against the French, that for four years had kept them on the run until they were forced to retreat across the Draa river to the boundary of the Desert.

When the Spanish soldiers had taken possession of the Ifny territory, soon after the advent of the Republic had spared the Berber warriors the hard necessity of having to take refuge in the Sahara in their flight from the victorious French army, those indomitable fighters had, with great pleasure, taken up service with the Spanish soldiers who offered them not only a possibility of revenge on the French, but good money in payment as regular colonial troops and, above all, new rifles and plentiful ammunition.

The Spanish soldiers who had occupied Ifny were controlled by fascist officers who were plotting against the republican régime, so that when the 1936 rebellion broke out, they told the Berber warriors that they must go to Spain to fight against the reds who were being helped by France and Russia. These born fighters, loyal as are all good Moslems to pacts of friendship, accepted gladly the chance to fight for the rebel cause on Spanish soil.

Equipped with splendid new weapons of German origin, they were shipped to Spain where they saw, for the first time, great cities with large houses and shop windows displaying untold riches. The watchmakers' shops containing thousands of watches and the jewellers' shops full of golden objects and precious stones of every kind glittered and sparkled before their dazzled eyes, conjuring up to their simple minds visions of abundant booty which they hoped would materialise. The Berbers kept their promise of loyalty and, under an iron discipline, fought with great courage against the enormous masses of red soldiers hurled against them. But the reds had not learned the art of war and either let themselves be killed like heroes, or ran away like herds of frightened deer.

Proud of their brilliant rôle of 'conquistadores' they allowed themselves to be made a fuss of by the women and by those whom they called the 'Hebrews'... timid people unfitted to take up arms. Wherever they passed they were the object of special acclamations. The women presented them with religious pictures and scapularies which they accepted with the supreme indifference of true believers. Allah was God and Mahomet was his prophet! Had any of the ladies who so kindly fêted and fussed over the Berber warriors guessed at their innermost thoughts and true feelings, their Christian and civilised souls would have been truly horrified.

The Caid, saddened by the disappearance of his beloved Mohamed, left the tent where the other Moorish officers were asleep and strolled up to the mountain; the light of the moon pierced the outspread branches of the pine-trees dappling the earth with deep shadows. The thin air of the Sierra Gredos caressed and stimulated the dark-skinned Caid's hot brow. The camp fires had been extinguished one after the other. Only one ray of light was left in the whole camp. It shone in the tent of the European officers, and the Caid, attracted by the light and noise, walked slowly in that direction. The officers were celebrating the victory of the day and were toasting their next triumph. Their bursts of laughter and their songs added to the Caid's sadness. The African warrior stood near the tent for a long time thinking deeply, and the joyful sounds and the strange speech sank into his dormant consciousness, arousing a strong emotion of disdain and hatred towards these alien people. Dumbly he resented their drinking and singing to celebrate victories bought so dearly with the blood of his brother warriors while he wandered alone and disconsolate, his heart grieving over the loss of his loyal friend Mohamed, whose death only he would mourn.

Someone lifted the flap covering the entrance to the tent and came outside. The Caid tried to hide himself, but had no time to do so.

'What on earth are you doing here, Caid?' asked the officer.

'I was sad and deep in thought,' he answered.

'Well, come in and drink with us. That will sweep away the cobwebs.'

Another officer came out and they insisted on taking him with them. They offered him wine which he refused.

'The Caid is sad,' explained an officer, 'because this afternoon the reds hunted down one of his most valiant "mejaznies," Mohamed the courageous.'

At this the Caid nodded his head in assent and smiled ceremoniously, as though trying to excuse himself for his weakness.

'Never mind, Caid... forget it. Drink a little, that will help you.'

'Leave him alone,' said an officer of the Foreign Legion who was already well-soused. 'The Moors are a lot of fools, they won't chase away troubles by drinking... They don't know how good it is to drown sorrow in booze. One of the Caid's men has been killed and until he is avenged he will not be happy again. Am I not right, Caid? You want revenge, don't you? Well, you won't have to wait long… to-morrow at the latest. How many ears of red militiamen do you want my men to cut off to-morrow in memory of your loyal Mohamed? How many did you say? A thousand? Ten thousand? Do you want us to bring you the ears of the President of the Republic? Don't be so sad, Caid! You shall have them. I swear it. On my honour, Caid. On the honour of the Legion… I swear it!'

And the Foreign Legion officer went on repeating this. He made a great fuss of the Berber warrior, toasted him, glass in hand, his bloated face close to the noble and serene visage of the Caid, his lips puffed and his speech thick. The Caid sat unmoved, even when he felt the drunken officer's loathsome spittle spraying against his face.

When it became evident that the vanguards of Moors and Legionaries had forced the mountain passes in a surprise attack and were invading the valleys, it was too late to organise any serious resistance. The only loyal forces were the local militias who were armed with all kinds of obsolete weapons. The news that the Moors and Legionaries had advanced, leaving behind them a trail of desolation and death without quarter, was brought by the villagers and peasants of the terrorised villages. The men were ready to resist to the end.

'Give us arms! Arms!' they shouted in despair.

But all was in vain, for there were no arms to give them. Masses of peasants armed with sticks, slings, scythes and old sporting-guns were nevertheless ready to fight. At the last moment the Madrid Government sent a column of militiamen and the most courageous amongst the peasants and villagers joined their ranks eagerly.

'Comrade Commander,' they asked, 'let us join the troops.'

'But you know I have no rifles for you. How are you going to fight?' answered the Commander.

'It doesn't matter; we will march behind the militiamen and pick up the rifles of those that fall.'

Thus was organised a column intended to stop the advance of the Moors and Legionaries along the valley. Behind each man bearing a rifle there marched another man unarmed, who, with clenched fists, waited for the tragic opportunity of picking up a gun. History has seldom shown the spectacle of a people more determined than these to resist an invader. Moved by a ferocious hatred for their foes, these peasants of the heart of Castile, these shepherds and lumbermen of the Sierras of Gredos, marched side by side, breast forward, so as to form a living wall against the advance of the colonial troops.

The heroic resistance collapsed with terrific slaughter, as it was fore-doomed to do. Courage is not enough in modern warfare; efficient arms and iron discipline are main factors. The peasants were routed, but their stubborn resistance exasperated the enemy officers, who gave their men licence to ravage the valley, spreading a devastating torrent of death and desolation. Groups of peasants and villagers sought sanc-tuary in the tortuous paths and caves afforded by the mountains, but even there they were found by the invaders and killed without mercy. No prisoners were taken, and until well into the night the pine woods in the mountains near Montreal resounded with the pitiless volleys of execution squads.

The officers of the victorious column began to concentrate on the principal square of the village. The last to arrive was the Caid. He was leading a small group of Moors with wide shining eyes and hanging jaws; their shoulders, bent under the weight of heavy burdens, indicated that they had been looting to their hearts' content. Some had their naked arms covered as far as the elbow with wrist-watches taken from the dead militiamen, for the puerile and barbarous covetousness of the Moors was particularly attracted to timepieces of all kinds – a reaction, perhaps, to the undivided eternal flow of unreckoned hours in their desert camps and mountain solitudes.

When the Caid approached the group of officers and stood to attention, giving the military salute with his right hand touching his fez, he saw the Foreign Legion officer who, the previous night, had offered to avenge the death of Mohamed. He advanced towards him with outstretched arms. The officer patted him gaily on the back and said:

'Well done, Caid – you and your men have fought like true Berbers. Don't think for a moment that I have forgotten to keep my promise.

My men could not cut off the ears of the President of the Republic, at least not yet… but we got a good collection for you as a first instalment.'

He called a batman who brought a bulging haversack which he took from him and threw at the feet of the Caid.

'There you are!' he laughed, 'there is a good vengeance for the death of your "mejazni"… A hundred ears of marxists!'

On touching the ground the haversack fell half-open and out of it rolled some bloody unrecognisable lumps of human flesh.

The soldiers soon established law and order in the valley. Their methods were simple and drastic. The peasants who had survived returned cowed to their usual work. There were no more strikes nor quarrels over wages. Work from dawn to sunset, the traditional custom in the country-side, was re-enforced. Instead of the clenched fists they gave the open fascist salute. The Civil Guard were once more masters of the country-side whilst the fascists reorganised all the villages that came within the iron girdle of their new discipline. The prisons that had been opened to incarcerate the reactionaries were now used by fascists to imprison the reds.

After a few days the troops left that part of the country. The Caid and his men were sent to the Madrid front where they fought in the first line with the great courage, tenacity and resistance to the hardships of the campaign that made them the greatest asset of the rebel army. The Moors knew this and inwardly were very proud of it. Their vanity was satisfied. Spain, with her masses of 'hebreos' incapable of putting up a fight, was falling before them. The valiant Berbers! An old instinct like an ancestral voice, a vehement desire for revenge unsatisfied for genera-tions, was now urging them on. The Arabs and Berbers, moved by these obscure impulses, charged in the open against the trenches of the reds and were happy. The mere fact that they could kill infidels and be praised for it by those hated Europeans who had subdued Islam, made risking their lives worthwhile and, in the bargain, they had the proud delight of seeing them run in panic before their overwhelming onslaughts.

So the Caid and his men advanced almost without resistance to the suburbs of Madrid. There they entrenched, ready for a last sally on the coveted capital. From the hill where they awaited the zero hour they could see the compact mass of buildings basking in the clear light so often painted by Velazquez. Madrid offered itself to their astonished eyes like a fantastic city of the Thousand and One Nights. When they looked at it through the veils of dusk and saw how that immense expanse resembled a starry sky with its myriads of lights, they revelled in the thought that the world of treasures within the city was at their mercy, as a well-deserved reward for their courage. A satanic pride filled the hearts of these warriors from the Rif Yebala and the Atlas, who had always been ready to kill or be killed for the mere conquest of a miserable 'aduar,' a meadow where their meagre cattle could graze, or for the trickle of water that sprang from an oasis of the Sahara. The conviction that they, the wretched Kabils who had been systematically humiliated and vanquished by the superior fire-arms of the Europeans, were now the deciding factor in the fate of that great city that was waiting to be stormed and plundered, increased their ardour and enthusiasm twofold.

The first day of the storming of Madrid the Moors attacked with an overwhelming fury. Displayed in open formation, leaning forward and howling to kill, they advanced under an inferno of fire from the enemy. Twice they had to retreat under the hail of bullets from the red trenches, and each time they returned to the attack with more determination and rage. At last they reached the first-line trenches of the republican militiamen and there, for the first time, the barbaric African warriors found their foe standing ready to fight them in an epic hand-to-hand duel. There, also for the first time, the Berbers received what to them was an appalling surprise: the fighters of the proletariat of the great European city did not run away. That day the Moors learned, to their cost, that not all Spaniards were miserable 'hebreos' and that, in that Spain which in their haughty superiority as warriors they disdained, there existed a soul as hard as steel with a vital impetus that could be compared to the devastating hurricane of the Desert.

During the storming of the trenches the Caid surprised a militiaman who, crouching behind some sand-bags near a breach in the trenches made by the explosion of a shell, was lying in ambush ready for the

Moors who might try to invade the trenches by that breach. He was a tall strong fellow, dressed in the blue overalls of a mechanic, his shirt-sleeves rolled up baring brawny arms which had been made strong and muscular by the constant use of the forging hammer. Holding his rifle tightly by the barrel he wielded it with great force above his head. A radiant expression of mad joy was on his face and every time he brought down his rifle, like a mighty club, on the head of an unsuspecting Moor who tried to force his way into the trenches, he felt proud of his unerring adroitness. With every mortal blow he jumped for joy like a child and, with the fluent lingo of a true son of the lower quarters of Madrid, he let flow a torrent of words with which he urged himself on to his death-dealing job.

'Ole! Viva! there goes another darkie,' he shouted. 'Another Moor for Allah's Paradise. God-speed, my friend! That was a good one, eh?… Come on, damn you… I want more heads to smash… Come on, come on… Ole! Viva!… There it is… Smack… another one!!'

The cunning Caid approached stealthily from behind and, when he was within striking distance, he charged and thrust his bayonet into the militiaman's back, at the same time as the latter raised the butt of his rifle to bring it down on another Berber's head. Neither the Moor nor the militiaman missed. Another victim fell to the mighty club, but the militiaman was pierced by the Moor's bayonet. As he toppled, his head fell against the chest of his victim and thus they fell together like skittles and lay on top of one another. The militiaman made a desperate effort to raise himself, but he fell back and this time his face was pressed against the face of the Moor. Their veiled eyes met and the look of terror and agony on the twisted features of the dying Moor inspired him to find strength to jeer his last defiant sarcasm:

'Good gracious, if you are not an ugly son of a bitch!' then resigning himself to die cheek to cheek with his enemy, he murmured without bitterness:

'Well, we both got it this time, friend!… Bad luck old blackamoor, eh?'

Over their dead bodies the Moors entered the trench, while the Caid kept the opening clear. The trench was speedily evacuated by the reds who were once more on the run. The Berbers had won another victory.

But the stout resistance of the militiamen had only failed on that spot where the Moors had attacked in force. The rest of the republican lines withstood the advance and the Foreign Legionaries, the Phalangists and the Requetes forming the rest of Franco's army failed to break the spirit of Madrid's defenders. The advance made by the Moors formed a dangerous salient and there was the possibility of their being cut off at any moment. The commanding officer of that sector, trusting to the courage and resourcefulness of the Moors, neglected to rectify the line in that direction and they were left for the night in possession of the trench they had captured.

But the reds gave them no peace and kept firing at them all night. At dawn the Government artillery found the range and opened a terrific and relentless fire on the Moors who, seeing that they were being killed like flies, tried to advance and were mown down from the enemy trenches which they tried vainly to reach. No reinforcements came to their aid, and the Caid gave the order to retreat.

It was too late, however. The Moors had been caught in the pincers of two simultaneous and well-directed flank attacks, and the survivors were forced to surrender. The group now consisted of some thirty men and they swarmed round the Caid while the reds continued killing them off, one after another. They had no more resistance left in them and the Caid, realising this, tried once more to force a way. He urged his men forward but he was the only one with enough courage to advance towards what was certain death. Suddenly from the red trenches came the order 'Cease fire!' Only a stray shot here and there was heard and a militiaman jumped out of the trench and, covering the Caid with his pistol, shouted:

'Give yourself up or I shoot!'

The Caid, with the fatalism of his race, believed this moment was ordained and, throwing down his rifle, put up his arms and went forward towards the enemy trench, still covered from behind by the militiaman's pistol.

To capture the rest of the group of Moors was easy enough. They were surrounded by militiamen and driven like dejected cattle into the trench. Their morale had failed them all of a sudden. Their eyes, so fierce and proud before, looked at their captors with the same sad and beaten look of wild animals caught in a trap.

One of the Moors, in order to spare himself any more nasty jabs with a rifle-butt, lifted his left fist and gave the red salute, shouting at the same time:

'Long live Republica... Me red, me your side!'

'Moros estar reds, we all be reds!' shouted the other Moors, hoping thus to save their skins. The militiamen found it a great source of entertainment to see these African warriors declaring themselves reds and lifting their clenched fists above their heads and shouting, in the only Pidgin-Spanish they knew, that they were the most devoted of all republicans.

One militiaman, with a face as hard as a hatchet and wings of grey hair on his temples, approached the Caid, who had not spoken a word nor clenched his fist, and asked him:

'And you?... You "estar rojo" also... One of us, eh?'

The Caid fixed his clear eyes on him and answered:

'No, me estar a Moor.'

'Kill him! Let us shoot the swine!' shouted the militiamen around him. One of them pressed the muzzle of his rifle against the Caid's breast, but the grey-headed veteran pushed the weapon away:

'Why are you going to kill him?... Are you going to murder him because he at least is honest?'

'I will kill him just because I want to,' answered a militiaman in a fury – 'And I will kill you too, if you are not careful.'

At this moment the old man went for the other, pistol in hand, and a nasty quarrel ensued between those who sided with him and those who backed his opponent. The trouble was only ended by the swift intervention of the more level-headed and it was decided to take the prisoners to the nearest commanding officer, but it was hard work to prevent them being killed on the way. At the commanding officer's post they were submitted to a severe questioning and later on it was decided that they should be taken to Madrid in a lorry.

Amongst the militiamen sent to guard the Moors was the veteran who had saved the Caid from certain death. He was a man of about fifty years of age, tall, lean and well-built. During the weeks he had been in the trenches he had grown a beard which, together with his bronzed skin, gave him a certain physical similarity to the Caid. Seated next to each other in the lorry one would have said that both belonged to the same race. It was as though the intervening eight hundred years had been wiped away – here was a man obviously descended from the time when the Moor was all-powerful and ruled over the Iberian Peninsula.

When the lorry entered the main Madrid streets the astonished Moors got up to stare at the big city. The Caid, who had dreamt of entering Madrid in triumph, did not move and hardly looked about him. But he took the opportunity, while he was sure that his men would not notice the gesture, to catch hold of the militiaman's hand and say to him:

'Moor be thankful.'

The militiaman, deeply touched, tried to appear indifferent and avoided the Caid's eyes.

'They will kill you, Moor. Do not hope for mercy.'

The militiaman tried to make his meaning clear by drawing one of his fingers across his throat. The Caid remained impassible and answered:

'Never mind, Moor be thankful to you.'

The lorry with its load of prisoners had arrived at its destination in the centre of Madrid. It was five o'clock in the afternoon and at that time the central streets were filled with the usual animated and noisy crowds in spite of the enemy at the very gates. The Moors, who stood in a compact group in the lorry, made an unexpected side-show for the crowd. Soon the lorry was surrounded by people of all kinds. The Madrid street urchins and hooligans passed amusing and caustic remarks about their personal appearance. When the lorry stopped at last in the Gran Via, a sea of humanity surged round the prisoners eager to see them, to touch them, to say something to them.

They had arrived in the nick of time to uplift the morale of the people. Someone ordered the driver of the lorry to drive round the streets and stop at certain places, and everywhere the Moors went they were surrounded by crowds who rejoiced to see the prisoners lifting their clenched fists to give the red salute.

'These are only a sample of what we took,' said a typical braggart. 'We have captured more than ten thousand of them!'

'They have revolted against Franco,' said another Madrileño. 'They have cut Franco's throat, you know, and joined us.'

'Of course, the Moors are a lot of bolsheviks... Is that not so, Mustafa?' said a 'chula' – a woman of the people – smiling in a friendly way at the prisoners who, by this time, were rather confused in their minds at the unexpected reception they were getting. They thought that all they had to do was to shout still louder:

'Viva Republica!' 'Vivan rojos!'

There were some in the crowd, however, who were less friendly. Some grumbling old woman with a good growth of hair on her upper lip, or some sullen-faced militiaman, said, on seeing the Moors:

'The thing to do with that crowd of murderers is to shoot them in the back.'

To this there was always someone who replied:

'Those who brought them to Spain are the ones who ought to be shot like dogs. The fascists, those are the real murderers.'

The fact was that the Moors did not provoke a great deal of exasperation in the people of Madrid. All the good-natured Madrileños saw were unwilling instruments used by the fascists. They did not realise how the Moors would have killed and looted without mercy; they looked so quiet and docile. They looked down on them as though they were poor beasts enticed from their own country on a fool's errand. They felt a kind of commiseration for them and when they saw the prisoners lifting their clenched arms in a tragic-comic gesture, they offered them peanuts as if they were monkeys in the cages in the Madrid zoo.

Knowing very little of the truth, as is always the case with the masses, they would willingly have let the Moors go free. But war has its inflexible laws and the Spanish Civil War had reached a terrible pinnacle of cruelty. The death of the Moors had been decreed in the name of the people, whose opinion was not asked. When night began to fall and the streets were deserted by the swarming day-time crowds, the Moors were taken to a lonely spot in the Madrid country-side. The exhibition for propaganda purposes had come to an end and the moment had arrived to get rid of that useless load of unwanted humanity.

The Caid, who had remained all the time seated near the red veteran who was guarding him, caught his hand again and asked him:

'Now they kill Moors, eh?'

The militiaman assented, nodding his head gravely.

'Allah is good and Mahomet is his prophet,' was the only comment made by the Moor.

After a while the militiaman said:

'I would like you to live. You are a real man. But I can do nothing for you.'

'Me sabe, me understand,' replied the Caid, again pressing gently the hand of the militiaman. Each knew without words the sympathy that existed between them, that mutual recognition which comes unknown and unwanted but cannot be ignored.

'Moor sabe that you be friend and no want to kill Moor, but must. Moor has to kill also. They be things of war... and things of men, inshallah! Allah alone is great. May his name be praised for ever.'

They were placed, unresisting, in a row against a wall and mown down like blades of grass at the time of harvest.

꙰

Manuel Chaves Nogales was born in Seville in 1897. He was an excellent journalist who, when the war broke out, stayed in Madrid editing the Republican newspaper *Ahora*. Of his time as editor during the war, Chaves writes:

I then placed my services at the disposal of the workers just as I had in the case of my Capitalist Boss, that is to say, on a basis of loyalty towards them as towards myself. I made it quite clear that I lacked the revolutionary spirit and I protested against all kinds of Dictatorships, including the Proletariat

Dictatorship, and I undertook only to defend the cause of the people against Fascism and Military Rebels.

(Preface to *And in the Distance a Light...?*, page 4)

His stories are among the great war stories of the 20th century. Chaves wrote about the atrocities and acts of generosity committed by both sides. What triumphs in his stories is the unexpected, the ability of individuals to empathize with the enemy, the infinite shadings of black and white. When the Republican government moved to Valencia in November 1937, Chaves Nogales went into exile in Paris. Because of his many articles denouncing the advance of German fascism, he was on the Gestapo list when the German army approached the French capital and he had to flee to the UK. He lived in London during the war writing for the *Evening Standard*, the BBC and his own company, the Atlantic Pacific Press Agency. He died there in 1944. His stories, first published in Chile in 1937, are now being rediscovered and celebrated in Spain.

LAURIE LEE

TO ALBACETE AND THE
CLEARING HOUSE

from *A Moment of War*

TEN DAYS AFTER MY ARRIVAL at Figueras Castle enough volunteers had gathered to make up a convoy. By that time we were sleeping all over the place – in tents in the courtyard, under the mess-hall tables, or the lucky ones in the straw-filled dungeons. Day after day, more groups of newcomers appeared – ill-clad, crop-haired and sunken-cheeked, they were (as I was) part of the skimmed-milk of the middle-Thirties. You could pick out the British by their nervous jerking heads, native air of suspicion, and constant stream of self-effacing jokes. These, again, could be divided up into the ex-convicts, the alcoholics, the wizened miners, dockers, noisy politicos and dreamy undergraduates busy scribbling manifestos and notes to their boyfriends.

We were collected now to be taken to where the war was, or, at least, another step nearer. But what had brought us here, anyway? My reasons seemed simple enough, in spite of certain confusions. But so then were those of most of the others – failure, poverty, debt, the law, betrayal by wives or lovers – most of the usual things that sent one to foreign wars. But in our case, I believe, we shared something else, unique to us at that time – the chance to make one grand, uncomplicated gesture of personal sacrifice and faith which might never occur again. Certainly, it was the last time this century that a generation had such an opportunity before the fog of nationalism and mass-slaughter closed in.

Few of us yet knew that we had come to a war of antique muskets and jamming machine-guns, to be led by brave but bewildered amateurs. But for the moment there were no half-truths or hesitations, we had found a new freedom, almost a new morality, and discovered a new Satan – Fascism.

Not that much of this was openly discussed among us, in spite of our long hours of idle chatter. Apart from the occasional pronunciamentos of the middle-Europeans, and the undergraduates' stumbling dialectics, I remember only one outright declaration of direct concern – scribbled in charcoal on a latrine wall:

The Fashish Bastids murdered my buddy at Huesca.
Don't worry, pal. I've come to get them.
(Signed) HARRY.

The morning came for us to leave. But it wouldn't be by cami-ones after all. The snow was too heavy. We would go by train. After a brief, ragged parade, and when we had formed into lines of three, the Commandant suddenly appeared with my baggage. 'It's all there,' he said, strapping it on to my shoulders, 'all except the camera, that is.' He gave me a sour, tired look. 'We don't expect much from you, comrade. But don't ever forget – we'll be keeping our eye on you.'

The Castle gates were thrown open, sagging loose on their hinges, and in two broken columns we shuffled down to the station. A keen, gritty snow blew over the town, through the streets, and into our faces. We passed Josepe's whose windows were now boarded up and outside which an armed militiaman huddled. On the station platform a group of old women, young girls, and a few small boys had gathered to see us off. A sombre, Doré-like scene with which I was to become familiar – the old women in black, watching with watery eyes, speechless, like guardians of the dead; the girls holding out small shrunken oranges as their most precious offerings; the boys stiff and serious, with their clenched fists raised. The station was a heavy monochrome of black clothes and old iron, lightened here and there by clouds of wintry steam. An early Victorian train stood waiting, each carriage about the size of a stage-coach, with tiny windows and wooden seats. Every man had a hunk of grey bread and a screwed-paper of olives, and with these rations we scrambled aboard.

As we readied to leave, with clanking of buffers and couplings, and sudden jerks backward and forward, the girls ran up and handed us their little oranges, with large lustrous looks in their eyes. The small boys formed a line, shouting, 'Salud, companeros!' The old women waved and wept.

I shared a compartment with a half-dozen muffled-up soldiers who had only arrived the day before, including an ill-favoured young Catalan whose pox-pitted cheeks sprouted stubble like a grave in May. Garrulous – as we all were – he declared himself to be an anarchist, but one with a pivotal sense of nationalism, which made him boast, quite properly, that having been born in Barcelona, he was no more Spanish than the rest of us.

For this reason he'd joined the Brigade. He kept slapping his chest. 'Pau Guasch,' he said. 'International Catalan, me! International damn Chinese-Russian-Catalan-Polish. No damn father, damn mother, damn God.' He'd helped burn down three churches in Gerona, he said. He'd scattered petrol, thrown a match, and said, 'Woosh!'

In the end we told him to shut up, his spluttering English was too much for us. He seemed in no way put down. He took a potato from his pocket, crossed himself before eating it, and muttered, 'Damn Trotsky, King of the Jews.'

The train jerked and clattered at an unsteady eight miles an hour, often stopping, like a tired animal, for gasping periods of rest. We moved through a grey and desolate country crossed by deserted roads and scattered with empty villages that seemed to have had their eyes put out.

It was then that I began to sense for the first time something of the gaseous squalor of a country at war, an infection so deep it seemed to rot the earth, drain it of colour, life and sound. This was not the battlefield; but acts of war had been committed here, little murders, small excesses of vengeance. The landscape was plagued, stained and mottled, and all humanity seemed to have been banished from it. The normal drive of life had come to a halt, nobody stirred, even the trees looked blighted; one saw no dogs or children, horses or girls, no smoking fires or washing on lines, no one talking in doorways or walking by the river, leaning out of windows or watching the train go by – only a lifeless smear over roof and field, like something cancelled or in a coma; and here and there, at the windswept crossroads, a few soldiers huddled in dripping capes. Worse than a country at war, this one was at war with itself – an ultimate, more permanent wastage.

Night came, and darkness, outside and inside the train. Only the winter stars moved. We were still smoking the last of our Gauloises Bleues, stripping them down and re-rolling them into finer and even finer spills. Our faces, lit by the dim glow of our fags, hung like hazy rose masks in the shadows. Then one by one, heads nodded, fags dropped from sagging mouths, and faces faded from sight.

It was a long broken night, the windows tight shut, our bodies drawing warmth from each other. But there were too many of us packed into this tiny old carriage, and those who chose to lie on the floor soon regretted it. Long murmuring confidences, snores, sudden whimpers of nightmare, a girl's name muttered again and again, Pau Guasch howling blasphemies when a boot trod on his face, oaths in three languages when someone opened a window.

It may have been twenty hours later – waking and sleeping, arguing, telling stories, nibbling bread and olives, or just sitting in silence and gazing dully at each other – that the train slowed down to less than a walking pace and finally halted in a gasp of exhausted steam under the cheese-green lights of Valencia station.

We were to change trains here, and were promised hot food. The time was about midnight, and the great city around us showed no light as though trying to deny its existence, its miles of dark buildings giving off an air of prostration, pressed tight to the ground like turtles.

We had pulled up in a siding. A late moon was rising. Some women arrived with buckets of stew. They moved in a quick, jerky silence, not even talking to each other, ladling out the thin broth in little frightened jabs. Suddenly one of them stopped, lifted her head, gave a panicky yelp like a puppy, dropped her food bucket and scampered away. She had heard something we had not, her ears better tuned already to the signals of what was to come.

Following her cry and departure, the others fled too. Then the station lights were switched off. An inert kind of stillness smothered the city, a stretched and expectant waiting. Then from the blank eastern sky, far out over the sea, came a fine point of sound, growing to a deep throbbing roar, advancing steadily overhead towards us. Such a sound that the women on the platform had learned to beware of, but which to us was only an aircraft at night. And which, as we listened, changed from the familiar, casual passage of peace to one of malignant purpose. The fatal sound which Spain was the first country in Europe to know, but with which most of the world would soon be visited.

Franco's airfields in Majorca, armed by Italian and German warplanes, were only a few minutes' flight from the mainland. Barcelona and Valencia lay as open cities, their defences but a few noisy and ineffectual guns.

As the bombers closed in, spreading their steady roar above us, I felt a quick surge of unnatural excitement. I left the train, and the roofed platform, and wandered off alone to the marshalling yards some distance away. This was my first air-raid, and I wanted to meet it by myself, to taste the full brunt of it without fuss or panic. We'd already seen posters and photographs of what bombs could do to a city, slicing down through apartment blocks, leaving all their intimacies exposed – the wedding portrait on the wall, the cheap little crucifix, the broken bed hanging bare to the street – the feeling of whole families huddled together in their private caves being suddenly blasted to death in one breath. New images of outrage which Spain was the first to show us, and which in some idiot way I was impatient to share.

The bombers seemed now overhead, moving slowly, heavily, ploughing deep furrows of sound. A single searchlight switched on, then off again quickly, as though trying to cancel itself out. Then the whole silent city woke to an almost hysterical clamour, guns crackling and chattering in all directions, while long arcs of tracer-bullets looped across the sky in a brilliant skein of stars. This frantic outburst of fire lasted only a minute or two, then petered out, its panic exhausted.

The airplanes swung casually over the city, left now to their own intentions. Just a couple of dozen young men, in their rocking dim-lit cabins, and the million below them waiting their chance in the dark. A plane accelerated and went into a dive, followed by the others in a roaring procession. They swooped low and fast, guided perhaps by the late moon on the water, on the rooftops and railway tracks. Then the bombs were released – not from any great height, for the tearing shriek of their fall was short. There followed a series of thumping explosions and blasts of light as parcels of flame straddled the edge of the station. I felt the ground jump at my feet and smelt the reek of burnt dust. A bomb hit the track near the loading sheds, and two trucks sailed sideways against a halo of fire, while torn lines circled around them like ribbons. Further off an old house lit from inside like a turnip lamp, then crumpled and disappeared. A warehouse slowly expanded in the gory bloom of a direct hit, and several other fires were rooted in the distance. But it was over quickly – a little more of the city destroyed, more people burnt or buried, then the bombers turned back out to sea.

I found I'd stood out in the open and watched this air-raid on Valencia with curiosity but otherwise no emotion. I was surprised at my detachment and lack of fear. I may even have felt some queer satisfaction. It was something I learned about myself that night which I have never quite understood.

Once the planes had gone, there was little to be heard but the crackling of flames and the distant bells of a fire-engine. I was joined by two of my companions from the train, both silent, both fresh to this, as I was. A railwayman crossed the lines, grouping about, bent double. We asked him if he was all right, and he said yes, but he needed help. He shone a torch on his left hand, which was smashed and bleeding, then jerked his head in the direction of the nearby street. We ran round the edge of the burning warehouse and found two little houses, also well alight. They were small working-class shops, blazing tents of tiles and beams from beneath which came an old man's cry.

'My uncle,' said the railwayman, tearing away at the smoking rubble with his one undamaged hand. 'I told him to sleep in the cinema.' The roofs collapsed suddenly, sending a skirt of sparks riffling across the road.

The old man's cries ceased, and we staggered back while great curling flames took over. 'The fault is his,' said the railwayman. 'He would have been safe in the cine. He used to go there every afternoon.' He stood doubled up, staring furiously at the blazing ruin, his clothes smoking, his hands hanging black and helpless.

Walking back towards the station, we stumbled over a figure on the pavement, lying powdered white, like a dying crusader. His face and body were covered in plaster dust, and he shook violently from head to toe. We rolled him on to a couple of boards and carried him to the main platform, where several other bodies were already spread out in rows. A moaning woman held a broken child in her arms; two others lay clasped together in silence, while a bearded doctor, in a dingy white coat, just wandered up and down the platform blaspheming.

It was a small, brief horror imposed on the sleeping citizens of Valencia, and one so slight and routine, compared with what was happening elsewhere in Spain, as to be scarcely worth recording. Those few minutes' bombing I'd witnessed were simply an early essay in a new kind of warfare, soon to be known – and accepted – throughout the world.

Few acknowledged at the time that it was General Franco, the Supreme Patriot and Defender of the Christian Faith, who allowed these first trial-runs to be inflicted on the bodies of his countrymen, and who delivered up vast areas of Spain to be the living testing-grounds for Hitler's new bomber-squadrons, culminating in the annihilation of the ancient city of Guernica.

About four in the morning, with fires still burning in the distance, we were rounded up by our 'transport officer', who was rather drunk and wearing a Mongolian jacket. Round his neck, somewhat oddly, he'd slung binoculars and a tape-measure, and he scurried about, shooing us back to the train, as though our departure was part of some major logistic.

Some of the men had loud, over-excited voices, shining eyes, and brave tales of survival. Some were quiet and staring, others appeared to have slept unaware through everything.

Our new train was drawn up in another part of the station, where we found Pau Guasch carrying a basket of bread. Once crammed into our compartment he handed chunks of it round, saying we were not fit to eat such victuals. He was half-right there; the bread must have been several weeks old, and was coated with soot and plaster. He looked smug and benign as we tried to gnaw away at his bounty; in the end we swallowed it down.

The night was long and cramped as the train lumbered inland, slowly circling and climbing the escarpment of Chiclana to reach the freezing tableland of Mancha. I had known part of this plateau in the heat of high summer when it seemed to blaze and buckle like a copper sheet. Now it was as dead as the Russian steppes, an immensity of ashen snow reflecting the hard light of the winter moon. No gold path of glory, this, for youth to go to war, but a grey path of intense disquiet.

Apart from Pau Guasch, all the men in my compartment were volunteers from outside – British, Canadian, Dutch. And poor Guasch, the only true native son of the Peninsula, found himself squashed between his own natural assumption of leadership and our teasing contempt for him – the 'foreigner'. So we used him as the butt of our mindless exhaustion, pushed him around, tripped him up, trod him under our feet, and stuffed his shirt with crumbs and crusts of bread.

Fear, exasperation and cruelty gripped us, and we continued to taunt the furious little Catalan till we tired, at last, of our mirthless game and slumped one by one to sleep. We slept stiffly, uneasily, propping each other bolt upright, or toppling sideways like bottles in a basket. We were not warriors any more, but lumps of merchandise being carried to a dumping-ground.

In a bitter dawn we approached Albacete on the plain, clanking through tiny stations where groups of snow-swept women watched us dumbly as we passed them by. A lad at a level crossing, with a thin head-down horse, lifted a clenched fist for a moment, then dejectedly dropped it again. Silent old men and barefooted children, like Irish peasants of the Great Hunger, lined the sides of the tracks without gesture or greeting. We were received, as we trundled towards our military camp, not as heroic deliverers, or reinforcements for victory, but rather as another train-load of faceless prisoners seen through a squint-eyed blankness of spirit.

But as we steamed at last into Albacete station, we found that someone, at least, had dredged up some sense of occasion. We fell stiffly from the train and lined up raggedly on the platform, and were faced by a small brass band like a firing-squad. In the dead morning light they pointed their instruments at our heads and blew out a succession of tubercular blasts. Then a squat mackintoshed Commander climbed on to a box and addressed us in rasping tones. Until that moment, perhaps, cold and hungry though we were, we may still have retained some small remnants of courage. The Commander took them away from us, one by one, and left us with nothing but numb dismay.

He welcomed us briefly, mentioned our next of kin (which we were doing our best to forget), said we were the flower of Europe, thanked us for presenting our lives, reminded us of the blood and sacrifice we were about to bestow on the Cause, and drew our attention to the sinister might and awesome power of International Fascism now arrayed against us. Many valiant young comrades had preceded us, he said, had willingly laid down their lives in the Struggle, and now rested in the honoured graves of heroes in the battlefields of Guadalajara, Jarama and Brunete. He knew we would be proud to follow them, he said – then shook himself like a dog, scowled up at the sky, saluted, and turned and left us. We shuffled our feet in the slush and looked at each other; we were an unwashed and tattered lot. We were young and had expected a welcome of girls and kisses, even the prospect of bloodless glory; not till the Commander had pointed it out to us, I believe, had we seriously considered that we might die.

Our group leader came striding along the platform leading a squealing Pau Guasch by the ear. He wanted to go home, he cried; he'd got arthritis and the gripe. The group leader kicked him back into line. We formed up in threes and, led by the coughing and consump- tive band, marched with sad ceremony through the streets of the town. We saw dark walls, a few posters, wet flags, sodden snow. Sleet blew from a heavy sky. I had known Spain in the bright, healing light of the sun, when even its poverty seemed coloured with pride. Albacete, this morning, was like a whipped northern slum. The women, as we passed, covered their faces with shawls.

∽

Laurie Lee was born in Stroud, Gloucestershire, in 1914. His first trip to Spain in 1935 is the subject of *As I Walked Out One Midsummer Morning*, the second part of his autobiographical trilogy which also includes *Cider with Rosie* and *A Moment of War*. He returned to Spain in 1937 as a volunteer in the International Brigades. Lee suffered from epilepsy and was in Spain only for nine weeks. The events of this grim winter provide the material for *A Moment of War*, first published in 1991, from which this extract is taken. In this book, Lee captures the idealism of the ill-prepared volunteers who came 'to make one grand, uncomplicated gesture of personal sacrifice and faith which might never occur again'. Lee's writing on Spain is all the more powerful for its absence of ideology. It poignantly captures the fear experienced by individuals in situations over which they have no control. Laurie Lee died in 1997 in Slad, Gloucestershire, a village to which he had first moved with his parents at the age of three.

PERE CALDERS

THE TEROL MINES

translated by Peter Bush

I'S BEEN GETTING COLDER over the last few days. In La Galiana, in the Villastar area, it's reached eight below zero.

The full moon lights up marches and troop formations; at night, some streets in the city of Terol look unscathed. We like to stroll, eyes half closed, imagining we are in a city at peace. We walk by the ruins of the Seminary and stare at the remains hit by our front-line guns. It's really exciting: a car headlight will switch on, or a moonbeam slant down, and our machineguns immediately sweep that fragment of landscape and the lights go out. It doesn't seem like war. Perhaps it's the night-time or the silence over the city; it's hard to know what to put it down to, but this concert of lights and weaponry seems like one big game.

'Hey, they'll arrest us if we're caught walking the streets.'

'The order was for nobody to wander around the city.'

It's all very well but we don't like that one bit. They ordered a brigade of frontier police to enter Terol. Our brigade obeys, enters, and of the original four battalions only two remain and they've been decimated. And now a mobile brigade arrives, sets up in Terol and stops us police from going for a walk.

These mobile shock brigades have got a better deal. They move around, and have much more to do. When a front is under attack, they're dispatched there; they finish the job and off they go for a rest!

If I ever have another chance to be soldier, the mixed brigades won't catch me.

Some people complain all the time, but the fact is we can't contravene military instructions. They sent us into the city centre, at top speed and seemingly to something related to our work.

The cold has penetrated our clothes and our flesh and we're really suffering. Our feet hurt so much we start crying and begin to feel the cold destroying our will and producing a kind of listlessness that kills off any wish to do anything. Then we realize we can't light a fire in the command post, and that we only have one blanket and are in for a horrible night. Wars shouldn't be fought in winter. We all agree on that, and when we all manage to agree on something, it's always something highly sensible.

When we cross the Plaza del Torico, we see a big bonfire in the Café Salduba. Through the empty window frame we see a group of men warming themselves. How we envy them!

'So why don't we go in and warm ourselves up a bit?'

'We can't. It's a guard post.'

'Let's try. If they won't let us in, it's their loss…'

That makes sense. We're carrying tins of jam from the Santa Teresa convent. If they let us in, we'll share our jam with them.

Against all the odds the Café Salduba has preserved echoes of its past glory. The door has a good quality brass handrail, and what remains of the glass in the frame is thick and superior, the sort that costs a lot of money.

The men on guard duty let us in. They're half asleep as if poisoned by the smoke fumes; our arrival gees them up slightly.

'So, you're the frontier police?'

'You got it.'

They're in a joking mood.

A corporal is in charge: 'Josep, bring chairs for the gentlemen.'

They're dynamiters from the shock troops. Very young lads, some under sixteen, who walk the world with a belt full of hand grenades. They clear a space for us around the bonfire and we warm up our hands and feet. As the cold goes, we feel like expressing our gratitude.

'Thanks, *camaradas*.'

'No, not *camaradas*. Acquaintances in war will do. You have to earn the right to be a *camarada*.'

This seems the right cue to offer them some jam. We open our cloaks and place the tins on a chair.

'If you like, you can try some of this.'

'You bet, comrades. We'd really like to.'

The marble tables in the Café Salduba are strewn with wine and water glasses, plates, small spoons, special tools for eating aperitifs, broken soda siphons, sets of dominoes and chess-pieces, dice and cards. The walls and ceiling are blackened by smoke; we don't know if that's the result of a fire caused by the war or the bonfires lit by the dynamiters. In any case, as all there is left of the building is this room in the café, no point being too fussy.

We each take a plate and a spoon, clean off the dust with a handkerchief or sleeve, and share the jam out. It's good, healthy food made by the hands of a nun.

One of the dynamiters is licking his lips and gives us a cheeky grin.

'So you frontier police find rich pickings, I guess?'

'Well, less than people think. A lot of flesh was given up for these tins.'

'Which brigade are you?'

'The eighty-seventh.'

'Dynamiters?'

'No.'

'Just as well. That's much better for you.'

He speaks with a hidden agenda. But we know what he's referring to: from the perspective of their military know-how, these dynamiters have a bone to pick with the dynamiters of the eighty-seventh. When our people placed the first mines under the Civil Government building, it was so cold the dynamite wouldn't light and had to be warmed up; that's something that's easily done, but on that occasion the fire caused a mine to explode and the charges went off before time. Several of our people died and many were injured.

We can't allow anyone to criticize our *compañeros*.

'Our people have done extremely well and deserve to be forgiven for any mistakes they might have made.'

A lad who's speaking for the first time adopts a conciliatory tone.

'Your people and ours are all one and we shouldn't lose our tempers.'

Enemy artillery has been shelling our lines for some time. Their automatic cannon shoot eight times on the trot, like a giant machinegun. Some of the mortars fall on the city and smash up things that were already smashed up even more.

When we've seen off the jam, the dynamiters offer us a great Italian vermouth and it's a nice touch.

'Did you find that here?'

'Of course, it wasn't all soda siphons.'

We start talking about things to eat. One dynamiter describes in great detail a rice and rabbit he made in Guadalajara. He didn't have many of the ingredients, but from what he says, it was a great paella. Our mouths water; week after week we've been eating bread and tinned meat, and mostly cold at that. Rice and rabbit!

'We could get rice, but rabbit…'

There's a fifteen-year-old from Madrid who really guzzled the jam; he looks at us and speaks up: 'Don't you believe it. The other day a lad in my squad comes in and says: "Hey, bring grenades and a gun and follow me. I've found two fantastic rabbits. One's grey and the other's black and white." I asked him where they were and he said in an abandoned house. I grabbed the stuff and went off with him. We walked down a narrow alley and when we reached the top he grabbed my arm: "See that doorway? It's there. Open the door and you'll see the cage with the rabbits. I'll stay here and keep an eye out." I left him, pushed open the door and saw there really was a cage with two rabbits. But there was also a lady sat knitting next to it. She looked me up and down and froze me cold. "Sorry," I said, "I took the wrong turning."'

'You mean civilians are still living here?'

'You bet. And more by the day. People who escaped to the mountains and villages, and, now they can, they're coming back.'

'And what about the rabbits?'

'I let them be. But there's got to be food around somewhere. If we searched the galleries we'd find lots of things.'

He's referring to the passageways that run all under the whole of Terol. You can go from one house to the next underground; they link up streets that are separate above ground and bring together distant neighbourhoods. These galleries have played an important role in the battle of Terol and are becoming mythical.

'I wouldn't go down those passages for anything in the world. Last week five police and a lieutenant went down to inspect them. Four days later they found the corpses of three of the police in the vicinity of the station. There's been no news of the lieutenant and the other two lads.'

'Do you believe that witches exist?'

'No, but we have proof that fascists do. A number didn't manage to escape but didn't fall into our hands. Where are they? You must agree that the underground tunnels are a good hiding place. Besides, whatever happened to the three assault guards who escaped?'

It was true. Three assault guards went down to explore the mines and were never seen again. We're frightened by these underground paths; we'd prefer they didn't exist.

The young dynamiter from Madrid reacts there and then: 'You know, if it's all the fault of the fascists, I'm not scared. If we're not scared of them in broad daylight, I don't see why they should scare us when they're hiding a few metres underground. And if a fascist and I come eyeball to eyeball, he'll have more reason to be worried than me.'

He's wearing a belt with eight hand grenades and looks athletic and determined. What he says is quite right.

'But you don't know the layout of these galleries, and we don't know what surprises they might have in store. An enemy who knows the terrain has a lot going in his favour.'

'Never mind,' we interrupted, 'if what we're imagining is true, we have a duty to clean out these mine shafts and catch the people hiding there. They could give us some nasty surprises. We've heard that some unexplored areas hide fascists who've got hold of dynamite charges.'

We were warming up. We soon agreed that if we didn't go down the mines, we'd not be able to show our faces we'd be so ashamed. As the conversation ran on, everybody kept raising the stakes, suggesting slightly bolder deeds; we were only limited by what was possible. We finally came to an agreement: tomorrow night we'll enter the mine shafts, through a point of entry in a house near the Plaza del Torico. We won't tell anyone; we must go in alone, so the glory from the expedition won't be spread too thinly.

The Madrid lad has brought along two long thick candles from the cathedral. With what they'll last, we'll have time to visit the circuit of passageways six or seven times and make a detailed examination.

Lit by a round, generous moon, the nights are still bright. We're armed; the least armed of us carries a pistol and has a pocket full of ammunition. The dynamiters have enough to re-structure the whole subterranean network.

Apart from the noise from the front, the only sound is the hum of the dynamos lighting the military offices. We pass under the arches on the square, glued to the wall and one by one, because groups out at night are suspected of looting and the police keeps an eye out for them. We don't know what we want to do, or why we're doing it; we don't know if we're going after danger or fascists, or committing a serious act of indiscipline or a heroic feat. In fact, the only thing we are clear about is that we are doing what we do to protect our own reputation, which we prize way above our own selves.

We are seven in total. There's no need to be alarmed; no enemy in hiding is waiting for us, and we feel powerful. When we come to the designated house, we go in warily so as not to be seen; we've entered a fishmonger's, that's been blown to pieces, destroyed in battle. One companion stumbles over the arms of scales that had been thrown to the ground and we have to catch him to stop him from falling down: the scales make a loud clatter that reaches the square and echoes beneath the arches.

The floor is covered in paper and small willow baskets. A mattress between the counter and the wall in the entrance to the back of the shop hobbles our feet and slows down our progress. Once we're across that and are sure the light can't be seen from the street, we light the candles; before we do that, however, I touched something dry and withered when I leant on a box to keep my balance. I now see they are mummified fish rushing from the box, their eyes popping out of their heads, as if they wanted to escape; they crack when squeezed by my fingers. They stink terribly.

The lad who's acting as guide goes in front and we follow, on tenter-hooks and holding our breath. We'd go back if our reputation wasn't on the line. We pass through what's left of a dining-room with a vase of faded flowers miraculously still in place on the table. Before we get that far, on the left, is a grey door that's shut; our guide gestures to us to go in but the rubble jams the door and it won't budge. We push at it with our shoulders, making as little noise as we can.

'If they catch us and don't like our excuses, they'll execute us for looting.'

'Shut up, you idiot.'

Our voices whine, which isn't what we'd prefer in a situation like this. But we are stubborn. We push that door as if a reward was waiting for us on the other side, and finally the hinges squeak, give and we go in.

We presumed it was safe to enter like that; it was a small wash-room, full of dirty clothes and damp that went straight to our lungs. However, we found what we were looking for: our guide crouched down and lifted up a wooden cover to reveal stairs. He scampered down to the bottom.

'Right, you lot, in you come.'

And we go in, one after another, saying nothing. We prick up our ears and focus our eyes, on the alert for whatever, even ready to take a jump if our instincts tell us to; we go down, placing the soles of our feet firmly on each step, feeling the walls with our hands. Our senses are hyped up and if danger blows our way, we'll smell it coming.

The flames of the candles flicker when there's a gust of wind, but they don't ever burn our skin. The smell of wax permeates the area and blots out any other smell. When the stairs end and we touch the ground, we feel a long way from the world above, and quite unpro-tected. Nobody would hear if we shouted and, if they did, and so what.

From here on in, we don't know the way. Our guide only knew how to get into the cave. In any case, as we don't know where we're going, any route seems like a good one.

We walk along the shaft that had been opened up by pick-axes. A warm draught circulates, coming from a way off and linking up with other mines. Sometimes, on a bend, the draught seizes our hair and shakes it gently, like jelly fingers stroking our head. Whenever this happens, a chill hits the napes of our necks and runs down our backs.

Our footsteps keep echoing round the vaults, in an eardrum shattering din. Apparently beset by the fear we ought to be provoking in the enemy we unconsciously quicken our pace and are forced to protect the flames of the candles in the palms of our hands.

The gallery lengthens out, forks, criss-crosses other networks. In some stretches rudimentary wood and brick structures reinforce the ceiling and our hearts sink at each new change. We find a large empty food tin, the remains of a recent meal and fine-tune our cautious movements even further. The Madrid lad takes a hand grenade from his belt and grips it tight in his hand.

'If you throw that in here, we'll be crushed to death like little chicks.'

'But the others will keep us company.'

Occasionally the idea that *the others* might have their own problems isn't sufficiently re-assuring. Our voices now reverberate in a strained, if hollow way; the surrounding earth compresses and lifts the sound around us. If we'd been ordered to go on this mission, we'd be thinking somebody wanted us out of the way, that we were victims of a great injustice. But right now, despite everything, we don't want to backtrack and a tremendous curiosity drives us on.

At a bend in the mine, to our right, we come across a half-closed door. A ham-bone on a string is hanging on a nail knocked into the wood, and, underneath, a notice says: 'If you'd like some more, come on in'. It's a macabre joke; a large pool of blood has seeped under the door and dried on the earth and a strong smell of dead bodies hits our senses.

'Shall we go in?'

'No need to bother. We can appreciate the sparkling wit of the author of this notice from here.'

'We might be able to identify a corpse.'

'And what good would that do? We can't bring it back to life.'

We don't feel like going in and continue walking. We've been making steady progress and are already a long way from where we started. We've twice had to retrace our steps because rubble blocked our path. They're places where powerful explosive charges were laid to blow up particular buildings. There are stretches that are the result of high blocks of flats collapsing under the ground and blocking entrances to the mine. Once we've even seen the sky through a narrow open slit above our heads. A bright moonbeam entered the gallery and the light on the candle-wicks turned pale. A metal helmet from our side lay on the ground; it's peppered with machinegun holes.

'What will we do if we meet a group of fascists?'

Everyone has thought of that likelihood and imagined the way he'd survive it.

'For the moment, we're a bit scared, but they must be too. We must be on the alert and react and shoot before they do. Besides, if...'

We hear voices and footsteps and break off our conversation. There are people very close. We are breathless. Our spirits are choking in our throats; we're afraid the candle light will give us away, but even more afraid of being in the pitch-black.

Something drives our wills on, beyond any reaction or feeling, forcing us to press on. We hold our weapons at the ready, put our feet on the floor ever so warily, entrusting our lust to live to our eyes and ears.

The mine now begins a steep descent, in one long, almost straight stretch. We don't know if we're sinking deeper into the earth or if the gallery runs parallel to surface terrain. Some stairs giving access to the mine are leaking dirty water and detritus that give off a horrible stench. We hear a persistent drip that echoes off the walls and reaches an absurd high pitch. That sound becomes an obsession, gives us headaches.

A huge explosion shakes the gallery ceiling; we've been half-covered in earth and our faces show that we are terrified of being buried alive.

'That's a mortar shell that's exploded outside. We must be very close to the surface.'

We quicken our pace, our hearts beating so loudly we're scared the noise will give us away. The voices sound nearer and nearer.

In front, the path ahead swings blindly round to the right. A sudden, total silence. What can be happening? Maybe they've seen the light from our candles and are about to give us a nasty surprise. We decide to snuff out the flames and grope along in the dark. Right now we can't believe we'll ever see the light of day again, let alone breathe fresh air.

As our eyes get used to the dark, we see a vague light entering from around the corner, like a moonlit clearing. We advance a few steps, then accelerate to the bend hoping our primed guns will frighten the men we think are waiting for us.

A blast of cold air penetrates our clothes and makes us shiver; we don't have time to recover our composure before a powerful reflector is dazzling us and preventing us from seeing anything outside the disk of the spotlight and its luminous glow.

'Don't move. There's a machinegun aimed at you. One move and we'll shoot.'

That firm, confident voice froze any spirit we had left. For a moment we stay stiff and still against the ground, our eyes bulging. We hear a loud, shrill laugh from behind the spotlight, and that hurts us much more than any sense of our complete impotence.

Half-hidden by a companion in front, the Madrid lad inches his hands up his back. He's holding a grenade and his fingers reach out to the detonator catch; he moves imperceptibly. The fingers of each hand reach out, reducing the distance separating them millimetre by millimetre.

The man behind the spotlight shouts out again: 'Hey, you fascists, drop your weapons on the ground!'

Fascists? Life rushes back to our lips in cries of relief that resound through the whole mine.

'Don't shoot, comrades! We are frontier police, dynamiters from the shock brigade.'

The people who'd so paralyzed us now exchange a few words: 'They're wearing armbands, they're ours'; 'They've got stars on their helmets'.

'Walk forward, *compañeros*. Don't be afraid.'

We take a few steps and, past the spotlight, find ourselves in the middle of the street, a broad sky overhead with the stars lighting up the world. We immediately recognize where we are: in the immediate area around Terol station.

'What were you doing down there?'

'We decided to hunt down fascists off our own bat.'

'Your timing was superb. We were within a whisker of hunting you down.'

We laugh. But we haven't recovered enough to enjoy our laughter.

Along the track there's a row of Falangists tied up that our *compañeros* dragged out of the mine to put at the disposition of the commander. On the ground, near to us, we see a pile of shapes, covered by a piece of tarpaulin.

'So what's that?'

'They're the bodies of the guards who disappeared.'

Our voices clam up and we find it hard to swallow.

'Can we be of any help?'

'No, the best you can do is clear off. If the officer sees you when he comes back and he doesn't like your bright idea, he'll give you a hard time.'

'All right. Keep well. And thanks a lot, *camarada*.'

Crestfallen, they start the trek up the slope to the city. Small fires blazing at the top of some houses near the station give the impression that they're still inhabited.

Before we enter Terol, the Madrid lad looks back towards the station.

'If we'd taken a second longer to realize we'd got it all wrong, I'd have chucked that grenade, and not even heavenly angels would have got to them in time.'

⌇

Pere Calders, born in Barcelona in 1912, was trained as a graphic artist and set designer. During the 1930s, he contributed articles and cartoons to the Catalan press and began writing fiction, publishing a novel and short story collections. He belonged to the Catalan Socialist Party and enlisted in the Republican army in 1937. He was sent as a cartographer to the Teruel region. From this experience comes the 1938 story published here, as does the very fine collection of writing on the Civil War, *Unitats de xoc (Pieces of*

Conflict). In 1939, Calders went into exile in Mexico, where he stayed until 1962, before returning to Catalonia. Dagoll Dagom's *Antaviana*, a theatrical version of some of Calders' stories, brought his work to a wide audience and made possible his recognition as a major 20th-century Spanish writer. He died in Barcelona in 1994. This story is included in the excellent anthology of Civil War writing *Partes de Guerra*, edited by Ignacio Martínez de Pisón.

ANTOINE GIMENEZ

OF LOVE AND MARRIAGE

from *Sons of the Night*

translated by Pete Ayrton

THE SPEAKER BEGAN.

'Comrades, I ask forgiveness in advance from those who will be shocked by what I plan to tell you. Marriage, an institution, I was going to say, a million years old but in any case, more accurately, many centuries since the coming of Christianity. Marriage, in its current form, is the tomb of love. A wife must obey a husband, submit herself to his will since he is the master. In exchange, it is his duty to feed her and, since she belongs to him, to defend her as he must defend his herd. I am talking about all women; those who are born in the lap of luxury as well as those who since the very beginning lie on these rough beds. In this society that we want to destroy, the proletarian marries to have a maid by day, a woman by night and to perpetuate the race of slaves and paupers who drag their feet the world over. And this for the great good of the ruling classes that crush us.

'Working class women, worn out by work, weakened by a lack of food, deformed by too many pregnancies, are old at thirty. If you don't believe me – look around you. Yes, I know what you tell yourselves; a girl without a husband is a plant without leaves, a tree without fruit... and to escape your father or your brothers, hoping to gain some little freedom, you are ready to give yourself in exchange for a name. NO. I am against all prostitutions, even those made legal by the mayor and blessed by the priest. The cause is these prejudices that come from long ago that the female of the species, heavy with child and unable to sustain herself, needed someone to hunt, fish, climb trees in search of food, defend her and her child against wild animals if necessary. She was obliged to accept the severe law of nature that everything must be done for the species to survive. And the species did survive.

'Through the generations, mankind has multiplied, invaded the world, invented machines, tamed lightning and domesticated fire. Males have imposed the law of the strongest and made of women a plaything, a servant or a beast of burden. She was conditioned by centuries of submission so that still today there are countries where a man buys a wife or parents exchange their daughter for goods, beasts or food. In our so-called civilized society, it is often the case, if not always, that marriages are made in which what matters are property, capital, the wealth of parents and in no way the emotional choices of the engaged couple. If a man has many mistresses, it is said of him: "what a stallion." If a woman has a lover, it is said of her: "what a whore." I demand for womankind, for all women, the same rights that us men have. I demand for half of humanity the right to free love, to free maternity.'

This did not go down well with some in the audience, especially with the older males. In Spain, young women were far from having the freedom of their sisters in France and other countries of Europe. To not offend their parents, they kept quiet.

Young and old men were in heated discussion, the former in favour, the latter against. Some women joined in. Questions were asked of the speaker. He was asked what his reaction would be if he were married and found out that his wife had a lover.

'Listen, *amigo*, if my wife is also a libertarian and has the same respect as I do for her liberty and for mine and informed me of her wish to sleep with another man for sentimental or physical reasons, we would decide together how things should proceed. If my wife does not share my views, she would not confide in me and were I to learn about it, I would have to ask myself the following questions.

'1. Do I satisfy her erotic needs? If not, it is fair that she seeks else-where what I cannot provide. An example: I invite you for dinner. You leave still hungry. Should I be angry if after leaving me you buy yourself a sandwich. Surely not. Sexual needs are like nutritional ones. They vary from person to person. Some have a large appetite, others are sated with very little. All I can do is keep my peace; perhaps, reproach her for not telling me.

'2. Does she look for a lover to satisfy her material needs, necessary or invented, and I am to blame since I am not able to earn enough so that she can get what she wants?

'In both cases, what should my behaviour be? In the first case, there is nothing I can do; nature has not given me the necessary strength to satisfy her and I would be a right bastard if, taking advantage of the power given to me by written law and morality, I prevented her from enjoying the pleasures of the flesh just because of my pride. In the second case, what can I do? Keep quiet and acquiesce? No… because I would be taking advantage of her beauty, her elegance, her wealth, unwillingly for certain, but I would feel myself to be the moral equivalent of pimps, of ponces who live off the work of whores like capitalists live off the work of workers, since prostitution is the oldest profession in the world. So I would leave her, however great the affection, love and friendship I had for her.'

'You do not experience jealousy?'

'Indeed, I am jealous of my mistresses. No contract binds me to them. We are only together in the search for erotic pleasure. It is normal that when this pleasure ebbs or disappears, we part company to find with other partners this pleasure that nature dictates is necessary for the psychological stability of each one of us. I am jealous of my mistress since I hate lies and hypocrisy. I hate the gratuitous, unnecessary lie that we commit only for the pleasure of hiding what we have done from those close to us, as if we did not think we had the right to do it. As if we were not free and responsible for our actions.'

From the beginning of his answer, there was silence. A young woman had come closer and listened, all the while looking at him. Dolores, a young woman of around 25, seamstress by trade asked:

'Pedrito, what would you think of a woman who here on this very spot was to say "I love you"?'

'I would think she was an intelligent and free woman. I would think she was well ahead of her time and for this, I would admire and respect her even if instead of talking to me, she had talked to someone else. Is this what you wanted to know?'

'Yes, but also, what would be the motivations that had led her to this statement?'

'They are many. You know them as well as I do. In general, they are the same for men as for women: desire, curiosity to know how an individual reacts in a given situation, the wish to know the virile prowess of the chosen one. All this can, in the last resort, be mistaken for love which makes us all think that we seek the happiness of the loved one, when in fact all we are looking for is the flowering of our subconscious. And, as the way we see things is always different, they collide, come into conflict, clash… and it's marital hell with its tears, complaints, gnashing of teeth. So, the need to part, to seek elsewhere the fulfilment of our hopes, the achievement of the fancies that haunt us.'

'You don't believe in a love that lasts a lifetime?'

'Yes, if it is based on frankness, on understanding, on the tolerance of all things that can divide a couple: differences of material or aesthetic tastes, moral or intellectual aspirations. It is very rare that two people with the same tastes, the same aspirations come together to make what is called a "family".'

The conversation ended very late. All those with work to attend to the next day had long ago gone to bed.

Antoine Gimenez was born Bruno Salvadori in the province of Pisa, Italy, in 1910. In 1922, the year the Fascists came to power, Antoine saved a school-friend in a street-fight and was taken to his friend's home where he met Errico Malatesta, a prominent figure of Italian anarchism. So began the extraordinary political life of this anarchist rebel who in July 1936 joined the International Division of the Durruti Column and fought until the retreat at the end of the war. After crossing the border, Gimenez was interned in the camp set up by the French government at Argèles-sur-Mer. Like many other Civil War fighters, he was active during the Second World War in the French Resistance around Royan. After the war, Gimenez moved with his family to Marseilles, where he worked on building sites. It was at that time that he started writing his memoir *Les Fils de la Nuit (Sons of the Night)*, finished in 1976 but published only thirty years later in 2006 – a racy document that captures, warts and all, life and love in the anarchist movement on the Aragon front. The book gives a unique insight into what the revolution meant on a day-to-day basis to the local people. An activist all his life, Antoine Gimenez died in Marseilles in 1982.

JOHN DOS PASSOS

THE VILLAGES ARE THE HEART OF SPAIN

from *Journeys between Wars*

Off the main road

First it was that the driver was late, then that he had to go to the garage to get a mechanic to tinker with the gasoline pump, then that he had to go somewhere else to wait in line for gasoline; and so, in pacing round the hotel, in running up and down stairs, in scraps of conversation in the lobby, the Madrid morning dribbled numbly away in delay after delay. At last we were off. As we passed the Cibeles fountain two shells burst far up the sunny Castillana. Stonedust mixed with pale smoke of high explosives suddenly blurred the ranks of budding trees, under which a few men and women were strolling because it was Sunday and because they were in the habit of strolling there on Sunday. The shells burst too far away for us to see if anyone were hit. Our driver speeded up a little. We passed the arch of Carlos Third and the now closed café under the trees opposite the postoffice where the last time I was in Madrid I used to sit late in the summer evenings chatting with friends, some of whom are only very recently dead. As we got past the controlposts and sentries beyond the bullring, the grim exhilaration of the besieged city began to drop away from us, and we bowled pleasantly along the Guadalajara road in the spring sunlight.

In a little stone town in a valley full of poplars we went to visit the doctor in charge of the medical work for the Jarama front. He was a small dark brighteyed young man, a C.P. member, I imagine; he had the look of a man who had entirely forgotten that he had a life of his own. Evidently for months there had been nothing he thought of, all day and every day, but his work. He took us to one of his base hospitals, recently installed in a group of old buildings, part of which had once been a parochial school. He apologized for it; they had only been in there two weeks, if we came two weeks later we'd see an improvement. We ate lunch there with him, then he promptly forgot us. In spite of the rain that came on, we could see him walking up and down the stony court inside the hospital gate with one member of his staff after another talking earnestly to them. He never took his eyes off whoever he was talking to, as if he were trying to hypnotize them with his own untired energy. Meanwhile we tried to stimulate our driver, a singularly spineless young man in a black C.N.T. tunic, the son of a winegrower in Alcazar de San Juan, to fix the gasoline pump on the miserable little Citroën sedan we had been assigned to. At last the doctor remembered us again and our driver had gotten the pump into such a state that the motor wouldn't even start, he offered to take us to the village to which we were bound, as he had to go out that way to pick a site for a new basehospital. We set out in his Ford, that felt like a racingcar after the feeble little spluttering Citroën.

Rain was falling chilly over the lichengreen stone towns and the tawny hills misted over with the fiery green of new wheat. Under the rain and the low indigo sky, the road wound up and down among the great bare folds of the upland country. At last late in the afternoon we came to a square building of light-brown stone in a valley beside a clear stream and a milldam set about with poplars. The building had been a monastery long ago and the broad valley lands had belonged to the monks. As we got out of the car larks rose singing out of the stubby fields. The building was a magnificent square of sober seventeenthcentury work. In the last few years it had been used as a huntingclub, but since July none of the members of the club had been seen in those parts. A family of country people from Pozorubio had moved out there to escape the airraids and to do some planting. They invited us in with grave Castilian hospitality and in a dark stone room we stood about the embers of a fire with them, drinking their stout darkred wine and eating their deliciously sweet fresh bread.

With his glass in his hand and his mouth full of bread the doctor lectured them about the war, and the need to destroy the Fascists and to produce as much food as possible. Wheat and potatoes, he said, were as important as machinegun bullets in war.

'I am an illiterate and I know more about driving a mule than international politics. That is all my parents taught me,' the tall dark thinfaced man who was the head of the family answered gravely. 'But even I can understand that.'

'But it's so terrible, gentlemen,' the woman broke in.

'There are no more gentlemen or masters here,' said the man harshly. 'These are comrades.'

'How soon will it be stopped? It can't last all summer, can it?' asked the woman without paying attention to the man. Tears came into her eyes.

'The war will stop when the Fascists are driven out of Spain,' said the doctor.

Then he explained how the country people must tell everybody in the village to send to Madrid to the Department of Agriculture for free seed potatoes and that they must use the milldam to irrigate the fields. Then we gravely wished them good health and went out to the car and were off into the rainy night again.

Village bakery

We stopped at their village, Pozorubio, to load up on bread. We went into the bakery through a dimly lit stone doorway. The baker was at the front, so the women and young boys of the family were doing the baking. The bread had just come out of the oven. 'Yes, you can buy as much as you want,' the women said. 'We'd have bread for Madrid if they'd come and get it. Here at least we have plenty of bread.' We stood around for a while talking in the dry dim room looking into the fire that glowed under the ovens.

As we got back into the car with our arms piled high with the big flat so sweet loaves the doctor was saying bitterly, 'And in Madrid they

are hungry for bread; it's the fault of the lack of transport and gasoline…
we must organize our transport.'Then he snapped at his Belgian chauffeur, 'We must get back to headquarters fast, fast.'You could see that he
was blaming himself for the relaxed moment he'd spent in the warm
sweetsmelling bakery. As the car lurched over the ruts of the road across
the hills furry black in the rainy night there went along with us in the
smell of the bread something of the peaceful cosiness of the village, and
country people eating their suppers in the dim roomy stone houses and
the sharp-smelling herbs in the fires and the brown faces looking out
from the shelter of doorways at the bright stripes of the rain in the street
and the gleam of the cobbles and the sturdy figures of countrywomen
under their shawls.

Socialist construction
Fuentedueña is a village of several hundred houses in the province of
Madrid. It stands on a shelf above the Tagus at the point where the direct
road to Valencia from Madrid dips down into the river's broad terraced
valley. Above it on the hill still tower the crumbling brick and adobe
walls of a castle of Moorish work where some feudal lord once sat and
controlled the trail and the rivercrossing. Along the wide well-paved
macadam road there are a few wineshops and the barracks of the Civil
Guard. The minute you step off the road you are back in the age of
packmules and twowheeled carts. It's a poor village and it has the air of
having always been a poor village; only a few of the houses on the oblong
main square, with their wide doors that open into pleasant green courts,
have the stone shields of hidalgos on their peeling stucco façades. The
townhall is only a couple of offices, and on the wall the telephone that
links the village to Madrid. Since July, '36, the real center of the town
has been on another street, in the house once occupied by the pharma-
cist, who seems to have been considered hostile, because he is there no
more, in an office where the members of the socialista (U.G.T.) Casa del
Pueblo meet. Their president is now mayor and their policies are dominant in the village. The only opposition is the C.N.T. syndicalist local
which in Fuentedueña, so the socialistas claim and I think in this case
justly, is made up of small storekeepers and excommissionmerchants,

and not working farmers at all. According to the mayor they all wear the swastika under their shirts. Their side of the story, needless to say, is somewhat different.

At the time of the military revolt in July the land of Fuentedueña was held by about ten families, some of them the descendants, I suppose, of the hidalgos who put their shields on their houses on the main square. Some of them were shot, others managed to get away. The Casa del Pueblo formed a collective out of their lands. Meanwhile other lands were taken over by the C.N.T. local. Fuentedueña's main cash crop is wine; the stocks in the three or four bodegas constituted the town's capital. The Casa del Pueblo, having the majority of the working farmers, took over the municipal government and it was decided to farm the lands of the village in common. For the present it was decided that every workingman should be paid five pesetas for every day he worked and have a right to a daily litre of wine and a certain amount of firewood. The mayor and the secretary and treasurer and the treasurer and the muledrivers and the blacksmith, every man who worked was paid the same. The carpenters and masons and other skilled artisans who had been making seven pesetas a day consented, gladly they said, to taking the same pay as the rest. Later, the master mason told me, they'd raise everybody's pay to seven pesetas or higher; after all wine was a valuable crop and with no parasites to feed there would be plenty for all. Women and boys were paid three fifty. The committees of the U.G.T. and the C.N.T. decided every day where their members were to work. Housing was roughly distributed according to the sizes of the families. There was not much difficulty about that because since the Fascist airraids began people preferred to live in the cavehouses along the edges of the hill than in the big rubble and stucco houses with courts and corrals in the center of town, especially since one of them had been destroyed by a bomb. These cavehouses, where in peacetime only the poorest people lived, are not such bad dwellings as they sound. They are cut out of the hard clay and chalky rock of the terraced hillsides facing the river. They have usually several rooms, each with a large coneshaped chimney for light and to carry off the smoke of the fire, and a porch onto which narrow windows open. They are whitewashed and often remarkably clean and neat. Before the civil war the housedwellers looked down on the cavedwellers; but now the caves seem to have definite social standing.

The village produces much wine but little oil, so one of the first things the collective did was to arrange to barter their wine for oil with a village that produced more oil than it needed. Several people told me proudly that they'd improved the quality of their wine since they had taken the bodegas over from the businessmen who had the habit of watering the wine before they sold it and were ruining the reputation of their vintages. Other local industries taken over by the collective are the bakery and a lime kiln, where three or four men worked intermittently, getting the stone from a quarry immediately back of the town and burning it in two small adobe ovens; and the making of fibre baskets and harness which people make from a tough grass they collect from the hills round about. This is a sparetime occupation for periods of bad weather. After wine the crops are wheat, and a few olives.

The irrigation project seemed to loom larger than the war in the minds of the mayor and his councillors. Down in the comparatively rich bottomland along the Tagus the collective had taken over a piece that they were planning to irrigate for truck gardens. They had spent thirteen thousand pesetas of their capital in Madrid to buy pumping machinery and cement. A large gang of men was working over there every day to get the ditches dug and the pump installed that was going to put the river water on the land before the hot dry summer weather began. Others were planting seed potatoes. An old man and his son had charge of a seedbed where they were raising onions and lettuce and tomatoes and peppers and artichokes for planting out. Later they would sow melons, corn and cabbage. For the first time the village was going to raise its own green vegetables. Up to now everything of that sort had had to be imported from the outside. Only a few of the richer landowners had had irrigated patches of fruits and vegetables for their own use. This was the first real reform the collective had undertaken and everybody felt very good about it, so good that they almost forgot the hollow popping beyond the hills that they could hear from the Jarama River front fifteen miles away, and the truckloads of soldiers and munitions going through the village up the road to Madrid and the fear they felt whenever they saw an airplane in the sky. Is it ours or is it theirs?

Outside of the irrigated bottomlands and the dryfarming uplands the collective owned a considerable number of mules, a few horses and cows, a flock of sheep and a flock of goats. Most of the burros were owned by individuals, as were a good many sheep and goats that were taken out to pasture every day by the village shepherds under a communal arrangement as old as the oldest stone walls. Occasional fishing in the river is more of an entertainment than part of the town economy. On our walks back and forth to the new pumping station the mayor used to point out various men and boys sitting along the river-bank with fishingpoles. All members of the C.N.T., he'd say maliciously. You'd never find a socialista going out fishing when there was still spring plowing to be done. 'We've cleaned out the Fascists and the priests,' one of the men who was walking with us said grimly. 'Now we must clean out the loafers.' 'Yes,' said the mayor. 'One of these days it will come to a fight.'

Cooperative fishing village

In San Pol, so the secretary of the agricultural cooperative told me with considerable pride, they hadn't killed anybody. He was a small, school-teacherylooking man in a worn dark business suit. He had a gentle playful way of talking and intermingled his harsh Spanish with English and French words. San Pol is a very small fishingvillage on the Catalan coast perhaps thirty miles northeast of Barcelona. It's made up of several short streets of pale blue and yellow and whitewashed houses climbing up the hills of an irregular steep little valley full of umbrellapines. The fishingboats are drawn up on the shingly beach in a row along the double track of the railway to France.

Behind the railway is a string of grotesque villas owned by Barcelona businessmen of moderate means. Most of the villas are closed. A couple have been expropriated by the municipality, one for a cooperative retail store, and another, which had just been very handsomely done over with a blue and white tile decoration, to house a municipal poolparlor and gymnasium, public baths and showers, a huge airy cooperative barbershop and, upstairs, a public library and readingroom. On the top of the hill behind the town a big estate has been turned into a municipal chickenfarm.

The morning I arrived the towncouncil had finally decided to take over the wholesale marketing of fish, buying the catch from the fishermen and selling it in Barcelona. The middleman who had handled the local fish on a commission basis was still in business; we saw him there, a big domineering pearshaped man with a brown sash holding up his baggy corduroys, superintending the salting of sardines in a barrel. 'He's a Fascist,' the secretary of the cooperative said, 'but we won't bother him. He won't be able to compete with us anyway because we'll pay a higher price.'

He took me to see a little colony of refugee children from Madrid living in a beautiful house overlooking the sea with a rich garden behind it. They were a lively and sunburned bunch of kids under the charge of a young man and his wife who were also attending to their schooling. As we were walking back down the steep flowerlined street (yes, the flowers had been an idea of the socialista municipality, the secretary said, smiling) it came on to rain. We passed a stout man in black puffing with flushed face up the hill under a green umbrella. 'He's the priest,' said the secretary. 'He doesn't bother anybody. He takes no part in politics.' I said that in most towns I'd been in a priest wouldn't dare show his face. 'Here we were never believers,' said the secretary, 'so we don't feel that hatred. We have several refugee priests in town. They haven't made any trouble yet.'

He took me to a fine building on the waterfront that had been a beach café and danceplace that had failed. Part of it had been done over into a little theatre. 'We won a prize at the Catalonia drama festival last year, though we're a very small town. There's a great deal of enthusiasm for amateur plays here.' We had lunch with various local officials in the rooms of the choral society in a little diningroom overlooking the sea. Far out on the horizon we could see the smoke of the inevitable nonintervention warship.

And a fine lunch it was. Everything except the wine and the coffee had been grown within the town limits. San Pol had some wine, they

---

said apologetically, but it wasn't very good. First we had broadbeans in oliveoil. Then a magnificent dish of fresh sardines. My friends explained that the fishing had been remarkably good this year, and that fish were selling at war prices, so that everybody in town had money in his pocket. The sardine fishing was mostly done at night with floating nets. The boats had motors and great batteries of acetylene lights to attract the fish to the surface. After the sardines we had roast chicken from the village chickenfarm, with new potatoes and lettuce. Outside of fish they explained new potatoes were their main cash crop. They sold them in England, marketing them through a cooperative. My friend the secretary had been in England that winter to make new arrangements. The cooperative was a number of years old and a member of the Catalan alliance of cooperatives. Of course now since the movement they were more important than ever. 'If only the Fascists would let us alone.' 'And the anarchists,' somebody added... 'We could be very happy in San Pol.'

We drove out of town in the pouring rain. As the road wound up the hill we got a last look at the neat streets of different colored stucco houses and the terraced gardens and the blue and white and blue and green fishingboats with their clustered lights sticking out above their sterns, like insect eyes, drawn up in a row along the shingle beach.

The defeated

Barcelona. The headquarters of the P.O.U.M. It's late at night in a large bare office furnished with odds and ends of old furniture. At a big battered fakegothic desk out of somebody's library a man sits at the telephone. I sit in a mangy overstuffed armchair. On the settee opposite me sits a man who used to be editor of a radical publishing house in Madrid. We talk in a desultory way about old times in Madrid, about the course of the war. They are telling me about the change that has come over the population of Barcelona since the great explosion of revolutionary feeling that followed the attempted military coup d'état and swept the Fascists out of Catalonia in July. They said Barcelona was settling down, getting bourgeoise again. 'You can even see it in people's dress,' said the man at the telephone, laughing. 'Now we're beginning to wear collars and ties again but even a couple of months ago everybody was wearing the most extraordinary costumes… you'd see people on the street wearing feathers.'

The man at the telephone was wellbuilt and healthylooking; he had a ready childish laugh that showed a set of solid white teeth. From time to time as we were talking the telephone would ring and he would listen attentively with a serious face. Then he'd answer with a few words too rapid for me to catch and would hang up the receiver with a shrug of the shoulders and come smiling back into the conversation again.

When he saw that I was beginning to frame a question he said, 'It's the villages… They want to know what to do.' 'About Valencia taking over the police services?' He nodded. 'Take a car and drive through the suburbs of Barcelona, you'll see that all the villages are barricaded…' Then he laughed. 'But maybe you had better not.' 'He'd be all right,' said the other man. 'They have great respect for foreign journalists.' 'Is it an organized movement?' 'It's complicated… in Bellver our people want to know whether to move against the anarchists. In some other places they are with them… You know Spain.'

It was time for me to push on. I shook hands with Andrés Nin and with a young Englishman who also is dead now, and went out into the rainy night. Since then Nin has been killed and his party suppressed. The papers have not told us what has happened in the villages. Perhaps these men already knew they were doomed. There was no air of victory about them.

Over the short wave

The syndicalist paper had just been installed in a repaired building where there had once been a convent. The new rotary presses were not quite in order yet and the partitions were unfinished between the offices in the editorial department. They took me into a little room where they were transmitting news and comment to the syndicalist paper in the fishingtown of Gijon in Asturias on the north coast, clear on the other side of Franco's territory. A man was reading an editorial. As the rotund phrases (which perhaps fitted in well enough with the American scheme of things for me to accept) went lilting through the silence, I couldn't help thinking of the rainy night and the workingmen on guard with machineguns and rifles at sandbag posts on the roads into villages, and the hopes of new life and liberty and the political phrases, confused, contradictory pounding in their ears; and then the front, the towns crowded with troops and the advanced posts and trenches and the solitude between; and beyond, the old life, the titled officers in fancy uniforms, the bishops and priests, the pious ladies in black silk with their rosaries, the Arab Moors and the dark Berbers getting their revenge four hundred and fifty years late for the loss of their civilization, and the profiteers and wop businessmen and squareheaded German travelling salesmen; and beyond again the outposts and the Basque countrypeople praying to God in their hillside trenches and the Asturian miners with their sticks of dynamite in their belts and longshoremen and fishermen of the coast towns waiting for hopeful news; and another little office like this where the editors crowded round the receiving set that except for blockaderunners is their only contact with the outside world. How can they win, I was thinking? How can the new world full of confusion and crosspurposes and illusions and dazzled by the mirage of idealistic phrases win against the iron combination of men accustomed to run things who have only one idea binding them together, to hold on to what they've got.

There was a sudden rumble in the distance. The man who was reading stopped. Everybody craned their necks to listen. There it was again. 'No, it's not firing, it's thunder,' everybody laughed with relief. They turned on the receiver again. The voice from Gijon came feebly in a stutter of static. They must repeat the editorial. Static. Black rain was lashing against the window. While the operator tinkered with the adjustments the distant voice from Gijon was lost in sharp crashes of static.

Antibes, May, 1937

⌐

Author of the *U.S.A.* trilogy, **John Dos Passos** was born in Chicago in 1896. Spain was the foreign country that meant the most to him. His writings about the country are contained in *Rosinante to the Road Again*, written in 1922, and *Journeys between Wars*, written in 1938, the book which includes his experiences of the Civil War. Writing from an anarchist perspective, Dos Passos was most interested in conveying the grassroots revolution that had started in the countryside. Much has been written about the bitter dispute between Dos Passos and Hemingway during the Civil War. Central to this fight was what had happened to Dos Passos' close friend José Robles. Hemingway accepted the Communist Party line that Robles had been outed as a Fascist spy and shot; for Dos Passos this was yet another example of Stalinist smear tactics. The attempt to find the truth about the Robles affair was important but it also stood for a fundamental political disagreement that was being fought out between communists and anarchists – which should come first: winning the war or making the revolution? Given that the Communist Party controlled access to the arms of the Soviet Union, it is not surprising that their view prevailed. Dos Passos left Spain disillusioned about the possibility of revolutionary change and began a rightward political journey that ended with his campaigning in the 1960s for Republican US presidential candidates Barry Goldwater and Richard Nixon. He died in Baltimore in 1970.

ANA MARÍA MATUTE

THE MASTER

from *El Arrepentido*

translated by Nick Caistor

O
UT OF HIS SMALL WINDOW he could see the Palace roof, covered
in green lichen, one of the stone escutcheons, and the balcony
that was occasionally opened by Gracián the caretaker's wife, to air the
rooms. Through the open balcony he could make out a big, dark painting
that from looking at it so often began to take on the dimensions of a
revelation. Years earlier, the canvas had enchanted him; it almost dazzled
him from its glittering shadow. Over time, the enchantment and amazement had faded: all that was left was the habit. Something fixed and
unavoidable, something to be looked at time and again, whenever the
caretaker's wife pushed back the balcony shutters. The painting showed
a man, with one hand raised. His pale features, black eyes and long hair
had slowly revealed themselves to his avid gaze. He knew them by heart.
The raised hand did not threaten, or seek to pacify. It was more as if it
was calling for something. Passively but insistently. A call of before and
after, an obscure summons that sent a shudder through him. Sometimes
he dreamed of it. He had never been in the Palace, because Gracián was
a sour individual who was difficult to approach. He preferred not to
ask any favours of him. And yet he would have liked to see the painting
close up.

Sometimes he would go down to the river to watch the water flow.
And without knowing why, that feeling bore some relation to the sight

of that painting. It was when the cold weather began, on the verge of autumn, that he used to go down to the river bank outside the village to watch the river flowing between the reeds and yellow broom.

He lived at the end of what was known as Calle de los Pobres. His possessions consisted of a black trunk with iron straps, a few books and some clothes. He had a tie knotted round the black iron bars of his bed. At the outset – a long time ago – he used to wear it on Sundays to go to mass. That seemed like the dim and distant past. Now the tie hung there like a rag, dangling from the foot of the bed. Like the dog at the feet of Beau Geste: the one who wanted to imitate the death of Viking warriors… (Ah, the days when he used to read *Beau Geste*; what a rotten world. 'Godmother, can I read this book?' He would tiptoe into the Great Godmother's library. The Great Godmother was scrawny; her money was magnanimous. He was the protected, favoured one, the ever so grateful washerwoman's son. 'The page-boy', he thought as he pulled on his boots, eyes half-closed, the eyelids still puffy from his hangover, staring at the rag dangling from the foot of the bed. Everything now was from another time, dangling like the grubby tie.

He was young when he arrived in the village, and very good. At least, that's what he heard the old women say:

'That new schoolmaster, what a good thing he is! His hair always combed, and wearing those smart little shoes all day long. Goodness, such extravagance! But of course, he means well.'

Not now. Now he had acquired a bad reputation. He knew they had asked for another master, to try to replace him. But they had to put up with him, because nobody wanted to come to this stinking corner of the world, unless it was as a punishment, or a naive youngster still full of faith and 'meaning well'. Not even the Duke went there; the Palace was rotting and falling to pieces, with that big painting inside, and the raised hand calling. He himself came there twenty-something years earlier, full of belief. He believed for example that he was put on this earth for self-denial and to do something. To redeem something, possibly. To defend some lost cause, perhaps. Instead of the tie knotted round the bars, he had his diploma on the wall above the trunk.

Now he had acquired a bad reputation. But sometimes he ran up the hill like a madman, to listen to the wind. He remembered when he was a boy and listened with a shiver to trains whistling in the distance.

That morning it was raining, and a patch of grey sky entered the tiny window. 'If only the wind could get in…' But the wind wandered down by the river to escape as well. And he meanwhile went on treading the earth, round and round, in his boots with holes in. Sometimes he scratched marks on the wall. What were they? Hours? Days? Glasses? Evil thoughts? 'We have no idea how change occurs. No-one knows how they change, how they grow, grow old, how they become another, distant person. Change is as slow as water dripping on a rock and eventually making a hole in it.' Time, cursed filthy time had done this to him.

'This? What's so bad about this?' he sniggered. He always got up late, didn't bother about anything or anybody. He didn't concern himself either with the school or the children. He did thrash them. He took pleasure in that, a substitute perhaps for other unattainable pleasures.

He no longer read the newspaper. Politics, events, the times in which he lived, were all one to him. Not so in the past. In the past, he had been an enthusiastic defender of men.

'What men?'

Possibly of men like him now. But no, he didn't see any dignity in himself. Dignity was a word as empty as all the others. When he drank anisette – he didn't like wine, he couldn't take wine – the world changed around him. Around him, even if it didn't change inside him. White clouds you walked on like cotton wool, treading on dead children who were only children because of their size. 'I came here thinking I'd find children, but there were only the larvae of men, evil larvae, weary and disillusioned before they reached the age of reason.'

He was on his way to the inn, and said out loud:

'The age of reason? What reason? Ha ha ha.'

That 'ha ha ha' came out slowly, with no hint of joy. It was things like that which led the old women who watched him pass by to shake their heads, look at him askance, and say:

'Crazy, off his head!' Wrapped in their foul-smelling black weeds. The same old women who had thought he was 'a good thing'. No, these were different ones, but identical to those who by now must be rotting with earth between their teeth.

Nowadays he didn't even notice their foul smell, that had once offended him so much.

'It used to offend me? Offences? What on earth are they...?'

He turned the street corner. A gaggle of barefoot boys flooded over him like a tidal wave. They were very small, about five or six years old, and almost knocked him off his feet. They often waited at street corners to push and jostle him. Then they would run off, laughing and calling him names he didn't understand. A light rain was falling, and the mud had stained their dry, stick-like little legs and slipped through their thin fingers when they raised them to their mouths to hide their laughter.

Stumbling, he shouted insults at them, then continued on his way for the first glass of the morning.

From the open door of the inn he could see the bulls roaming loose in the meadow. The rain made their black backs shine like the shells of enormous beetles. It looked as if four white crescent moons were charging the leaden sky. Beyond the grass, the earth was turning red. The month of great heat would soon be upon them, when all the blades of grass, all the cool greenery would be scorched; the bulls would raise the dust under their feet, charge the sun. That was how it always was. The boy looking after them was lying flat on the stone wall, like a frog. He couldn't understand how the boy could lie there like that without losing his balance, just like another stone.

The inn smelled of fresh wine. He hated that smell. Without a word, the inn-keeper served him a glass of anisette and a doughnut. He knew his habits. He dunked the cake in the drink, nibbling it like a mouse.

'Don Valeriano,' said the inn-keeper all of a sudden, 'what do you reckon to all this?'

He was holding out the newspaper, but the master swatted it away like a swarm of flies. The printed letters he had once cared so much about were now like flies to him.

He discovered a bat on the whitewashed wall above the inn door. It looked as if it was stuck there, with its wings spread.

'Lad!' he called the boy washing glasses in a bucket. A boy whose right eye was completely white, like a small, strange moon. His rough hands, with stubby wart-covered fingers, were streaming with cruelty. He raised his head, smiling, and dried the sweat from his brow with his fore-arm. The soapy water trickled up as far as his elbow.

'There's the devil for you, lad.'

The boy climbed on to the table. A short while later he climbed down, the two tips of the bat's wings dangling between his fingers like a handkerchief.

Before crucifying the creature like a condemned man, they made it smoke a little. One puff for the boy, another for him, another for the bat.

This was how most of the morning was spent, until he left to eat the pigswill his landlady Mariana cooked for him. It was the holidays.

2

The month of heat was already halfway through. The summer, dust, flies, thirst were racing towards them.

They came from the nearby village; and the men from this village went on to the next one. So they linked up in a chain.

He was lying on his bed and at first wasn't aware of anything. It was three in the afternoon, and he was dozing. He could hear the buzzing of mosquitoes over the water in the tank. He knew how they glinted in the sun like a swarm of silvery dust. It was then he heard the first cries, followed by a heavy silence. He lay without moving, feeling the heat on every pore of his skin. His long, white and hairy legs disgusted him. He had the withered, damp body of someone who flees the sun. He detested it, the implacable ruler over everything at that hour of the day. He heard the bulls bellowing and the clatter of their hooves as they fled up the street. Something was happening. Quickly pulling on his trousers, he walked barefoot to the adjacent room. Mariana had just mopped the floor, and the soles of his feet left marks on the red bricks like blotting paper. The old green shutter he himself had bought to protect himself from the hateful light was still down. A dancing, reverberating white glare shone through the slats. A blindness of whitewash and fire, a mortal glow. Covering his face in his hands, he felt his soft, stubbly cheeks, his eye sockets, his eyelids. Even so, the light reached him, he could sense it on the tips of his hands like a vapour, seeping in through all the cracks. Sweat soaked his brow, arms and neck. He could feel it making his clothes stick to his stomach, his thighs. The bellowing of the bulls faded in the distance, while on Calle de los Pobres he heard footsteps coming closer, and beneath his window came the shout:

'Ay de mi, ay de mi, ay de mi...'

He yanked open the shutter. It was like a dream, or rather, like wakening from a prolonged, strange dream. The sun's fierce glare overwhelmed his eyes. He sensed rather than saw the mayor's wife running down the street. The memory of the inn-keeper's newspaper struck him like a blow. He felt empty, as if all of him had become one huge expectation.

'Mariana,' he called out calmly. Then he saw her. She was in a corner, trembling, her face unusually white.

'It's broken out...' she said.

'What? What's broken out...?'

'The revolution...'

'And that woman shouting in the street? What's wrong with her?'

'They're looking for her husband... they're after him with sickles...'

'Ah, so that bastard has hidden, has he?'

Why was he insulting the mayor? All of a sudden he was filled with anger. Because the bellowing of the tame bulls, the lean, black shiny bulls charging the sky in the afternoon was inside him now; and all at once he was wide-awake, as if on a huge untidy bed, his filthy rented camp bed; on all the filthy earth he trod. And he didn't even know how he had changed, how he had become a rag like the threadbare tie knotted at the foot of his bed. He had changed little by little since the first day he arrived here, hair neatly combed and wearing his smart shoes from morning till night, striding round the village, explaining that the earth seemed to be eternally and pointlessly chasing the sun, trying to explain that the earth was round, slightly flattened at the poles, that we were nothing more than a dust particle spinning and spinning aimlessly around other particles of dust, like the silvery mosquitoes above the water tank. Trying to tell them that just as we looked at the mosquitoes as they pursued one another over the water, so an infinite number of balls of dust were looking at us as well; trying to explain that everything was an orgy of dust and fire. Ah, and Mathematics, and Time. And mankind, children, dogs were all embraced by his pity; but now he did not even have pity on himself; there was no room for it in all this dust. He no longer heard the bulls. The heart does not alter in a day, or even day by day. It is one particle of dust after another, dust where ambition, desire, lack of interest and interest, egoism all find themselves buried; and love too in the end. Was he once the boy who tiptoed in to his Great Godmother to ask if he could read *Beau Geste*? What are beautiful gestures? (As he was intelligent and hard-working, the Great Godmother paid for his studies. She paid for his studies and haggled over his pairs of shoes, his food, his suits: she denied him any amusements, leisure time, sleep, love. Later...) But there is no later. Life is one long elongated second filled with disgust and boredom, in which time is nothing more than an accumulation of emptiness and silence; and children's backs are like the feeble wings of a fallen bird; there's no room for the weight of the earth, hunger, solitude: none of it fits on to a child's back.

Now, without knowing how, or why, anger filled him. Although he had no idea how, the anger was within him.

3

They arrived in a van they had seized from the grain wholesaler. Some of them carried weapons: a rifle, a shotgun, an ancient pistol. The others were carrying pitchforks, scythes, sickles, knives, axes. All those peaceful tools being brandished against hunger and humiliation. Against thirst and all the meekness shown over the years; all of a sudden they were sharpened, threatening. El Chato, El Rubio and Berenguela's three young boys appeared, like rats who had been cowering in the darkness. They joined the newcomers, and their scythes, pitchforks and sickles also glittered like gold in the sun.

They couldn't find the mayor or the priest.

'The doctor's mother helped them escape on a straw wagon,' said two of the women who were on their way to plough, babies strapped to their backs.

The Duke's palace was closed up, as ever. They slit the caretaker Gracián's throat with a sickle, and strode over his body. He lay there outside the door with its big rose-shaped iron studs, as if he had collapsed on his own silence. His blood congealed in the sun, a prey to the flies' gluttony. A strange breeze had blown up that dried the sweat. Everybody in the village was curious to discover the inside of the Palace. The Duke only went there once on a hunting expedition; and Gracián would never let anyone in, not even for a quick glimpse.

Part of the Palace was visible from Mariana's window. The shutter was finally raised, without fear of the sun. To his surprise, he stood facing it, only too aware of his soft, white flesh, his wrinkles, the lines beneath his eyes, the black, moist down on his legs. The sun inundated him cruelly, with a stab of sharp, uneasy pain. He stared at the Palace. Its sloping green roofs rose proudly above the low clay tiles of Calle de los Pobres, its stone escutcheons stained by swallows' droppings, the balcony with the painting and its iron bars. He stood motionless at the window, like a statue of salt, while the armed men swarmed up Calle de los Pobres, and saw him. He heard their footsteps on the stairs, but didn't even turn round until they called out to him.

The leader of the mob lived three villages further up. The schoolmaster knew him from having seen him occasionally at the market. He sold leather harnesses. His name was Gregorio, and he had two grenades in his belt, as well as the only rifle. He must have taken it from one of the Civil Guards they had killed at dawn that day.

He pointed to him and asked:

'What about him?'

'Him? Who knows?' replied El Chato, shrugging his shoulders. He suddenly remembered El Chato as a boy. Still full of good intentions, he had told El Chato back then: 'The sun and the earth...' bah! Now here he was, with the same widely-spaced, staring eyes full of pained suspicion.

He stepped towards them, feeling beneath the soles of his feet the floor that was hot now, but still slippery from the water. He faced them with the same doleful courage that he had confronted the sun, and said, beating his chest:

'Me? You really want to know how I live?'

And like a boil that has been growing for a long, long time, it was as though his tongue finally burst:

'Me? If you want to know how I live, let me tell you: in hunger and misery. Hunger, misery, and thirst, and humiliation, and all the injustice of this earth. That's how I live. And it burns deep inside from breathing it in for so long... Do you hear me, big man? Hunger and misery my whole life through! Giving everything in return for this...'

He flung open the small door to his bedroom, and they could see the black iron bedstead, the dirty, crumpled sheet, the straw mattress. The trunk, the peeling wall, the sad naked bulb dangling from a wire covered in flies.

'For this: for that stinking bed, a plate of food at that table at mid-day, and another at night-time, my whole life through... Do you see that trunk? It's full of knowledge. The knowledge I devoured at the cost of my dignity... that's right, in exchange for my dignity, all that knowledge. And now... this.'

Gregorio was staring at him open-mouthed. El Chato explained, with another shrug:

'He's the schoolmaster, you see...'

'Oh, alright then,' said Gregorio, as if relieved. Dropping the rifle on to the table, he poured himself some wine. Wiping his mouth with the back of his hand, he said:

'So you know about reading and writing... Good, I need people like you.'

'And I,' he replied, in a hoarse, almost inaudible voice: 'I also need: people like you.'

4

They went after all those who, without him knowing or even suspecting it, he had engraved on the darkness of his immense thirst, his failure. He was the one who uncovered the priest's hiding place, and the mayor's. He knew in which hayloft, which corner they would be. A sharp lucidity led him on to places the others had not even imagined.

'What doesn't this fellow know...?' asked El Chato with surprise.

Gregorio wondered the same that night:

'How much do you know, mister?'

Then a muffled peace fell on the village. Only the anger, the setting fire to the church and the mayor's hayloft stayed in the memory. They were finally inside the Palace, in the Yellow Room, with the big balcony open on to the night. On the table, the Duke's wines and wine-glasses. And the pale July night turning pink beyond the roofs, down by the church. There was no sound from the bulls anywhere. They had been dispersed, and the boy looking after them was below, drinking with El Chato and Berenguela's boys. The others were doing the rounds of the houses, one by one. A big bonfire outside the Palace gates was consuming paintings and objects, male and female saints, books and clothing.

He was talking to Gregorio, even though Gregorio did not understand him. Gregorio was staring at him as he drank his wine. Looking and listening, trying hard to understand. It had been such a long time since he had talked to anyone!

'I was taken in as a child, my studies were paid for... in exchange for living like a slave, to be the old woman's plaything, do you hear? Turning me into a miserable dummy, for that swine of a woman...'

The nauseating memory of the Great Godmother's parchment-like skin came back to him, and her mansion that was similar to the Palace, with the same smell of mould and wet dust. Her clinging caresses, her alcoholic breath, the pearls on her wrinkled bosom.

'Aha, so you paid the price, did you? She used you as...' said Gregorio with a dark laugh, winking his right eye.

'That was what I had to pay. Do you understand, Gregorio? But I escaped all that, I wanted to make everything better, to make sure what was happening to me wouldn't happen to any other young boy. I slipped through her fingers and started to fight alone, with a faith... with a faith that...'

His ideas came back to him, fresh and new. His desire for revenge, but a revenge without violence, a reasoned, constructive revenge:

'So that it wouldn't happen to any other young boy... But what has happened to me here? I don't know. I don't know, Gregorio.'

All at once he was overwhelmed by an immense weariness:

'I'm as rotten as a dead man.'

And yet a day, an hour had arrived. Dust and fire spinning and spinning around dust and fire. Outside, the Duke's books and saints were burning. And there, on the wall above them, was the enchanting canvas. He lifted his gaze to it once more. The painting seemed to fill the whole room. 'Perhaps if I had owned a painting like that… or had painted it… perhaps things would have been different,' he told himself.

'Now everything is going to change,' said Gregorio. 'Aren't you drinking?'

He was thirsty. He didn't usually drink wine, but this was different. Suddenly everything was different. 'Perhaps I was afraid of wine…'

At that moment El Chato came in and said:

'It's time for this one,' pointing to the painting.

'No, not that one,' he said.

'Why not?'

'Because no. Just because.'

El Chato came up to him:

'Are you a church-goer then? You never went there!'

'I've got nothing to do with the church, but don't touch that painting.'

Gregorio stood up, curious. He bent over the small gilt plaque on the frame, reading it awkwardly. Then he burst out laughing:

'You don't want it touched because it's called THE MASTER?'

Without knowing how, an image flashed through his mind of a big Cross that was taken out whenever there was a drought, swaying from side to side above the fields. A man with gaping wounds, covered in blood. And the old women's chants: 'Oh sweet master, have pity…' He was a horrible sight, with his blood and wounds. But that wasn't the reason. Even though it was written there – as he knew very well, from staring at it so often through the window – even though it said: THE MASTER.

He shuddered the way he did when he went down to the river and the wind blew. And the man in the portrait was there as well; so big, so utterly alone, with his raised hand. His pale, narrow face, his long black hair, those dark eyes that always, always followed him wherever he hid...

'Because you're a master too?' laughed Gregorio, pouring himself more of the Duke's wine. He thought: 'Master? Master of what?'

Then he saw the pair of them. The two of them: El Chato and Gregorio, staring at him like larvae over in the damp school. With exactly the same expression in their eyes as when he told them: 'The earth revolves around the sun...' Oh, the mockery. Those incredulous peasant eyes, the utter pointlessness of words. I NEED PEOPLE LIKE YOU. He had been dreaming the whole day, the whole day.

'Give me some anisette: isn't there any?'

No, there wasn't any. Only wine. El Chato took out his knife and slashed the portrait from top to bottom.

As calmly as when he laughed without a hint of joy: 'Ha ha ha'; just as calmly he picked up Gregorio's rifle and fired at El Chato's stomach. El Chato's mouth gaped, and he fell slowly to his knees, staring and staring at him. Gregorio leapt like a snake. He stopped him, pointing the gun at him. And once again the two men's eyes stared at him: one pair closing in death; the other pair flooded with amazement, anger, fear. He cried out:

'Don't you understand? Don't you understand a thing?'

Gregorio's hand moved: perhaps he was trying to reach one of the grenades he was so childishly exhibiting. (Like the schoolboys with their cans of lizards, tadpoles, sloes; like schoolboys who understand nothing, who are weary before their time, and don't want to know anything about the sun and the earth, the stars and fog, the weather, or mathematics; like the boys who crucify the devil in bats, and throw stones at their schoolmaster, hidden behind the brambles; like those boys who lay traps and trip people up, and scoff and laugh, and moan when they are caned; and burn time, life, the whole of man, all hope...) Just like them, there in front of him once more were the burning eyes, the look of blank amazement that was born of another, vaster and interminable amazement he could not grasp. He said:

'Here's one for you too, and you can thank me for it.'

He shot at Gregorio not once but twice, three times. Then he threw away the rifle, went down the stairs and out of the back door into the countryside. With a loud, solitary cry he escaped, he fled and fled. Just as he had wanted to flee for almost twenty-five years.

5

He roamed the countryside for two days like a wolf, eating blackberries and wild strawberries, hiding in the bats' caves, near the ravine. From there he could hear the bulls again as they splashed in the water and on the pebbles. The bulls who had escaped, fearful of the church on fire, their bearings lost.

On the third day he saw the trucks arriving. This was the other side, the new ones. The revolution announced by Mariana had been snuffed out by these others.

He came back down into the village slowly, the sun blinding him. He was unshaven, and had the smell of death in his nostrils. Almost as soon as he reached the square, opposite the Palace, he saw them with their military jackets and tall boots, their black pistols. The old women who had once said: 'How well-combed his hair is, and he wears shoes all day', the ones who used to say 'crazy, off his head!' now pointed him out again. They had dragged out the swollen bodies of the mayor and the priest like two sacks of potatoes. And the black, scaly fingers of the old women pointed at him and Berenguela's young boys:

'Murderers! Murderers!'

Just as he was, with three days' beard and shirt open over his chest, they arrested him.

'Let me get something,' he asked them. They let him go into Mariana's house, keeping a gun on him. He went up to the bed, unknotted the tie from the bars, and put it on. When the truck pulled away, with his hands fastened behind his back, he had his eyes closed.

They lined the three Berenguela boys up on the river bank. He was the last. The air was warm, fragrant. The youngest of Berenguela's sons, just turned sixteen, shouted at him:

'Traitor!'

(Somewhere there was the man with his hand raised, calling out. A man with his hand raised, slashed from top to bottom by the clumsy knife of a boy, of an incomplete human larva; a grain of dust pursuing a ball of dust, a ball of dust pursuing a ball of fire.) The hot July sun carried the echo of the shots into the distance. He rolled down the bank towards the water. And he suddenly knew that always, always, denied any other love, he loved the river, with its reeds and its yellow broom, its round, smooth pebbles, its poplar trees. The river where upstream the frightened, tame bulls were splashing, still bellowing. He knew he loved it and that was why he rolled down towards it and began to stare at the water, as he stared at it on certain evenings in his life, when the cold weather was beginning.

～

Born in Barcelona in 1926, **Ana María Matute** was sent at the age of four to live with her grandparents in the mountain town of Mansilla de la Sierra. The mountain people that she grew up with feature constantly in her fiction. In the 'posguerra' (post-war) period, her writing attracted the attention of Franco's censors, who forced her, on many occasions, to make changes to her writings. As she said 'They called me irreverent, immoral, they twisted everything.' Matute's best-known novels are the trilogy The Awakening, Soldiers Cry in the Night and The Trap, which traces the history of a girl from the beginning of the Civil War to the 1960s. Matute believed that the post-war period was crucial in forming the literature of her generation:

The 'dazed children' as I call my generation, grew up into discontented adolescents who rebelled against all forms of mysticism and myth and refused to identify with a world governed by rewards and punishment, by good and bad men. The wolf was beginning to emerge from his sheep's clothing.

Winner of the Cervantes Prize in 2010, Matute died in Barcelona in 2014. This story is from her 1961 collection El Arrepentido.

GEORGE ORWELL

TWO MEMORIES

from 'Looking Back on the Spanish War'

Two memories, the first not proving anything in particular, the second, I think, giving one a certain insight into the atmosphere of a revolutionary period.

Early one morning another man and I had gone out to snipe at the Fascists in the trenches outside Huesca. Their line and ours here lay three hundred yards apart, at which range our aged rifles would not shoot accurately, but by sneaking out to a spot about a hundred yards from the Fascist trench you might, if you were lucky, get a shot at someone through a gap in the parapet. Unfortunately the ground between was a flat beetfield with no cover except a few ditches, and it was necessary to go out while it was still dark and return soon after dawn, before the light became too good. This time no Fascists appeared, and we stayed too long and were caught by the dawn. We were in a ditch, but behind us were two hundred yards of flat ground with hardly enough cover for a rabbit. We were still trying to nerve ourselves to make a dash for it when there was an uproar and a blowing of whistles in the Fascist trench. Some of our aeroplanes were coming over. At this moment a man, presumably carrying a message to an officer, jumped out of the trench and ran along the top of the parapet in full view. He was half-dressed and was holding up his trousers with both hands as he ran. I refrained from shooting at him. It is true that I am a poor shot and unlikely to hit a running man at a hundred yards, and also that I was thinking chiefly about getting back to our trench while the Fascists had their attention fixed on the aeroplanes. Still, I did not shoot partly because of that detail about the trousers. I had come here to shoot at 'Fascists'; but a man who is holding up his trousers isn't a 'Fascist', he is visibly a fellow creature, similar to yourself, and you don't feel like shooting at him.

What does this incident demonstrate? Nothing very much, because it is the kind of thing that happens all the time in all wars. The other is different. I don't suppose that in telling it I can make it moving to you who read it, but I ask you to believe that it is moving to me, as an incident characteristic of the moral atmosphere of a particular moment in time.

One of the recruits who joined us while I was at the barracks was a wild-looking boy from the back streets of Barcelona. He was ragged and barefooted. He was also extremely dark (Arab blood, I dare say), and made gestures you do not usually see a European make; one in particular – the arm outstretched, the palm vertical – was a gesture characteristic of Indians. One day a bundle of cigars, which you could still buy dirt cheap at that time, was stolen out of my bunk. Rather foolishly I reported this to the officer, and one of the scallywags I have already mentioned promptly came forward and said quite untruly that twenty-five pesetas had been stolen from his bunk. For some reason the officer instantly decided that the brown-faced boy must be the thief. They were very hard on stealing in the militia, and in theory people could be shot for it. The wretched boy allowed himself to be led off to the guardroom to be searched. What most struck me was that he barely attempted to protest his innocence. In the fatalism of his attitude you could see the desperate poverty in which he had been bred. The officer ordered him to take his clothes off. With a humility which was horrible to me he stripped himself naked, and his clothes were searched. Of course neither the cigars nor the money were there; in fact he had not stolen them. What was most painful of all was that he seemed no less ashamed after his innocence had been established. That night I took him to the pictures and gave him brandy and chocolate. But that too was horrible – I mean the attempt to wipe out an injury with money. For a few minutes I had half believed him to be a thief, and that could not be wiped out.

Well, a few weeks later, at the front, I had trouble with one of the men in my section. By this time I was a '*cabo*', or corporal, in command of twelve men. It was static warfare, horribly cold, and the chief job was getting sentries to stay awake and at their posts. One day a man suddenly refused to go to a certain post, which he said, quite truly, was exposed to enemy fire. He was a feeble creature, and I seized hold of him and began to drag him towards his post. This roused the feelings of the others against me, for Spaniards, I think, resent being touched more than we do. Instantly I was surrounded by a ring of shouting men: 'Fascist! Fascist! Let that man go! This isn't a bourgeois army. Fascist!' etc., etc. As best I could in my bad Spanish I shouted back that orders had got to be obeyed, and the row developed into one of those enormous arguments by means of which discipline is gradually hammered out in revolutionary armies. Some said I was right, others said I was wrong. But the point is that the one who took my side the most warmly of all was the brown-faced boy. As soon as he saw what was happening he sprang into the ring and began passionately defending me. With his strange, wild, Indian gesture he kept exclaiming, 'He's the best corporal we've got!' (*¡No hay cabo como el!*). Later on he applied for leave to exchange into my section.

Why is this incident touching to me? Because in any normal circumstances it would have been impossible for good feelings ever to be re-established between this boy and myself. The implied accusation of theft would not have been made any better, probably somewhat worse, by my efforts to make amends. One of the effects of safe and civilised life is an immense over-sensitiveness which makes all the primary emotions seem somewhat disgusting. Generosity is as painful as meanness, gratitude as hateful as ingratitude. But in Spain in 1936 we were not living in a normal time. It was a time when generous feelings and gestures were easier than they ordinarily are. I could relate a dozen similar incidents, not really communicable but bound up in my own mind with the special atmosphere of the time, the shabby clothes and the gay-coloured revolutionary posters, the universal use of the word 'comrade', the anti-Fascist ballads printed on flimsy paper and sold for a penny, the phrases like 'international proletarian solidarity', pathetically repeated by ignorant men who believed them to mean something. Could you feel friendly towards somebody, and stick up for him in a quarrel, after you had been ignominiously searched in his presence for property you were supposed to have stolen from him? No, you couldn't; but you might if you had both been through some emotionally widening experience. That is one of the by-products of revolution, though in this case it was only the beginnings of a revolution, and obviously foredoomed to failure.

George Orwell was born Eric Arthur Blair in Bengal in 1903. *Homage to Catalonia*, his book about his experiences during the Spanish Civil War, is a classic. Orwell went to Spain a man of the left: he went to fight fascism. But in Spain, he found that to do this was far from straightforward. Political infighting between the communists, the anarchists and the POUM made cooperation on the front difficult and in the cities created an explosive situation that erupted in the 1937 May Days of Barcelona. The victory of the communists in the fighting led to the dispersal and outlawing of the POUM, mass arrests of workers by the Republican government and the dissolution of the agricultural collectives of Aragon; voluntary militias were absorbed into the regular army of the Republic. As a supporter and member of the POUM, Orwell was clearly living on borrowed time and, with his wife, escaped to France in June 1937. The warrant for his arrest in Spain stated that he was wanted for 'rabid Trotskyism'. In *Homage to Catalonia*, Orwell wrote of these days: 'No one who was in Barcelona then, or for months later, will forget the horrible atmosphere produced by fear, suspicion, hatred, censored newspapers, crammed jails, enormous food queues and prowling gangs of armed men.' Orwell's writing on the Civil War is an attempt to convey what it was like for individuals. Orwell said that all he could write about was what he and other eyewitnesses saw in those heroic days. As more and more documents of the time become available, the accuracy of his testimony is confirmed. Orwell died in London in 1950.

JOAN SALES

'ACCURSED BOURGEOISIE, YOU SHALL ATONE FOR YOUR CRIMES!'

from *Uncertain Glory*

translated by Peter Bush

17 May

How mysterious that so many people cannot see mystery anywhere: I mean the incredulity of people whose starting point is the belief that nobody can believe. We should really pity them like those plain witless children one ought to love but can't…

Luckily, that's not by any means true of my father. He believes: he perhaps never grasps what, but he does believe. Else how do you explain his life? *La barrinada*… do you remember how we distributed it on the streets? We never sold a single copy.

That hapless weekly still appears every Thursday, now with articles against the 'cannibals disguised as anarchists', the 'hyenas who dishonour the most humane of social philosophies'. Hyenas are one of his obsessions, though I don't think he has the faintest idea what a hyena looks like. I don't believe he could tell an owl from a magpie, and apart from pine trees – which anyone can identify – I suspect he couldn't name any species of tree. My poor dad, who was born and has lived in the heart of Barcelona and whose only excursions have been occasional Sunday trips to Les Planes with its ocean of greasy paper and empty sardine tins.

He must be thinking of Les Planes when he writes his articles on Nature in *La barrinada*: wondrous Nature would cure the world's ills if she were only allowed to work unfettered. His beloved paper would reduce the whole of medicine to lemon, garlic and onion: he's almost a vegetarian, and if he doesn't agree with nudists it's because, in spite of everything, he still clings to vestiges of a sense of the ridiculous.

How can a person as harmless as my father arouse so much hatred in other anarchists? I don't know if you heard about it – some dailies covered the story but I'm not sure they reach the front – but supporters of *La Soli* attacked the editorial offices of *La barrinada*, that is, our flat on carrer de l'Hospital, a few weeks ago, long before the events earlier this month, and threw off the balcony a pile of back copies – unsold issues – that we kept in the lumber room.* Luckily the police arrived before they could do worse damage. The government even advised my father and his friends to arm themselves, avoid being caught off guard, and be ready to repel fresh attacks. 'The only arms I need are ideas' was all he would say.

A few weeks after you and Lluís went to the front a taxi brought him home one day with his face covered in blood. It gave me a fright but fortunately it wasn't serious. That great lifelong friend of his, Cosme, had brought him in the taxi – you may remember that short plump fellow with a pock-marked face, a turner by trade, who often came to our clandestine meetings. Cosme in fact supports the C.N.T. but is a close friend of my father's and he told me what happened while I washed Father's face with hydrogen peroxide: 'Just imagine, Trini,' Cosme said. 'A train of anarchist volunteers was leaving the estació de França for Madrid and my grandson was one of them – that's why I was in the station. The place was packed, what with people leaving and those who'd come to bid them farewell. All of a sudden we heard this bawling: "What are you doing, you wretches? Where are you going? You want to impose your ideas with guns? Have you let them militarise you? What happened to our principles that you always supported?" They weren't far off lynching

---

* *La Soli: Solidaridad Obrera*, the newspaper of the Confederación Nacional del Trabajo, C.N.T., the main anarcho-syndicalist union.

him as an agent provocateur! Lucky I spotted him! It was your father, old Milmany – who else could it be? It was one hell of a struggle to drag him away: he was refusing to come. I imagine he didn't recognise me, he was so overexcited. As I dragged him out of the station by the arm he was still bellowing: "You're off to defend Madrid? That octopus sucking our blood?"'

Father said nothing as I washed the cuts on his face. Luckily they were only scratches inflicted by a handful of women who'd grabbed him. Cosme talked and talked: 'I love your father, Trini. How can I not love him when we've always been friends? I love him more than he knows but it's sometimes very hard to keep faith with him. If volunteers don't go to the front, if we don't wage war with machine guns and cannons, the fascists will win and we'll be done for.' 'Yes,' I said, 'it's hard to see how any ideas can ever triumph if they reject any kind of organised strength.' I immediately regretted saying that: my father looked at me so sadly; he'd not said a word till then. 'Trini, everybody is a pacifist in peacetime.' He kept looking at me. 'Cosme was too, and now… you've heard him. The point is to be one always, in times of peace and times of war, whatever the situation. If not, it would mean nothing; there'd be no point in calling oneself a pacifist.'

Father stayed with me a few hours, during which I discovered that Llibert was climbing the greasy pole. 'He's got an office like a minister's,' he told me, 'with twenty typists and countless employees jumping to obey his orders. He has a cream limousine with a uniformed chauffeur who opens the door for him, standing to attention and saluting. It's a requisitioned vehicle, naturally; it must have been the Marquis de Marianao's, and I expect they requisitioned car and chauffeur alongside everything else.'

'Has Llibert no shame?' I asked.

'One day he wanted to show off and drive me home and I was the one who died of shame when I saw how our neighbours on carrer de l'Hospital who know me well were looking at me: they were amazed to see me in a vast vehicle that was so silent, creamy and shiny! And when his repulsive flunkey opened the door, stood to attention and saluted us militarily… I wanted the earth to open and swallow me up! If Llibert hasn't gone to the front like your man,' he added, 'don't think it's because he's keeping faith with the pacifist principles I inculcated in you from childhood – not at all! Later I'll tell you about his wall posters. If he hasn't gone to the front it's because he thinks he's more useful in the rearguard: to believe him, he is absolutely indispensable in Barcelona, he is irreplaceable because thanks to him, as he readily tells you, we are winning the war. We are winning the war, he says, thanks to the propaganda battle...'

In effect, they had made my brother something like the executive director of War Propaganda. It turns out that he was the one who plastered – and still does – the city walls with those justly famous posters: 'Make tanks, make tanks, make tanks, it's the vehicle of victory!' or else 'Barbers, break those chains!'* And so many others, half in Catalan and half in Castilian, respecting the two joint official languages, which would make us split our sides if Barcelona were in the mood.

One of these posters makes me want to vomit whenever I see it: it shows a wounded soldier dragging himself along the ground and making one last mighty effort to lift his head and point a finger: 'And what did you do for victory?' This is the offering from my brother and the other people safely ensconced in the Propaganda department offices! Posters encouraging others to go to the front are his speciality. There's also the enigmatic variety, abstract posters where you can only see blotches of colour, and amid the crazy chiaroscuro mess of light and shade it says: 'Liberatories of prostitution'. I've never met anyone who understands what that one's all about. At the other extreme there's a very specific one: a hen on a balcony accompanied by a slogan: 'The battle for eggs'. Apparently the idea is to suggest that if each citizen of Barcelona were to keep a hen on the balcony, nobody would go hungry. As if hens don't need grain to lay eggs! As if poor hens live on fresh air!

It seems all this is the work of Llibert, or at least so says his father. He's not only involved in poster production. His hyper-activity encompasses

---

* The barbers – and bakers – of Barcelona were organized in anarchist unions. The reference to chains also harks back to the early-nineteenth-century cry of '*Vivan las cadenas!*' of the clerical-led anti-liberal crowds who wanted to keep their chains.

broad and complex fields: the man is a walking encyclopaedia! He is behind various newspapers in Catalan and Castilian, all encouraging people to go to the front; he gives talks on the radio in a quivering tone that gives me the shivers, all to the same end; he contracts foreign lecturers to give similar talks – world famous celebrities nobody has heard of – and organises performances of 'theatre for the masses'…

This 'theatre for the masses' deserves special mention. According to Llibert, proletarian theatre must be performed by the masses. From what I've heard – I've never set foot inside – the masses fill the stage while the theatre remains empty, since nobody ever goes. This is the reverse of what used to happen when there were few actors – hardly any – and the theatre was packed from the stalls to the gods. Apparently that was *bourgeois* theatre.

Llibert's stirring dynamism and boldness aren't at all challenged by the difficulties of organising an equally proletarian opera season. He has requisitioned the Liceu and all they put on is proletarian opera. I don't know where my beloved brother found the libretti and music for the operas he stages, because I've not set foot there either, but a friend of mine from the science faculty, Maria Engràcia Bosch, was intrigued enough to go. She's a person I meet up with now and then and she tells me about what's happening in Barcelona: if it weren't for her, I'd never have found out. We met at the faculty years ago and although she's quite a bit older than me and was in her final year when I was only beginning, we felt close because we're from the same neighbourhood: she lives off carrer de Sant Pau.

I bumped into her not long ago on the Rambla and she invited me to a cup of malt in a café: 'I've things to tell you,' said Maria Engràcia Bosch. And she told me that as she often walked past the Liceu, that's on the corner of Sant Pau and very close to her house, she was intrigued by the proletarian opera they were advertising and one evening couldn't resist the temptation to go – I should add that the price of tickets to the Liceu is now within anyone's reach. She was one of the six who made up the audience that evening, and to compensate maybe two hundred people were on stage: 'Opera for the masses, right! Where on earth did your brother get the score and libretto? An unbelievably awful tearjerker about a people's uprising! The exploited masses come and go on stage, exit to the right, walk back on from the left, singing incantations to the future with their fists held high. From the rather nebulous plot you gathered that one of the exploited proletarians, the youngest in fact and a tenor, was practising free love and caught a bad dose of gonorrhoea – one for the history books! He separates out from the masses and staggers to the front of the stage. There is a deafening drumroll and the masses sink into a highly tragic silence whilst the tenor threatens the six members of the audience with a grand flourish of his arm and blasts out the first line of an aria full of pathos: "Accursed bourgeoisie, you shall atone for your crimes!"'

I couldn't believe it but Maria Engràcia Bosch had seen it with her own eyes and heard it with her own ears.

After this proletarian opera, what could one say of my darling brother Llibert that wouldn't pale in comparison? People who have been to his office tell me he gives all and sundry a big welcoming hug, calls everyone 'companion' and is ultra friendly, that his every pore breathes out success, victory, dynamism, smarminess and efficiency; he is organisation, efficiency and audacity personified; he is the provident hand for all those seeking a 'helping hand' or a 'voucher'.

He brings one of Uncle Eusebi's sayings to mind: 'By dint of revolving around others, we end up believing that others revolve around ourselves.' My brother had always wanted the entire world to revolve around him. When we were kids we crossed the courtyard of the Hospital of the Holy Cross four times a day going to and from our street to carrer del Carme, and the lay school where Mother and Father taught. He'd sometimes stop in front of the 'little pen' which is what we called the morgue; it looked out onto a side street that crossed Carme and a grille was all that separated it from passers-by. I had to hang on to the bars and stand on tiptoe to see the corpses. As they were laid out facing the grille, feet were what we saw best – yellow, filthy feet. Those feet were so sad! 'Here's the end that awaits us all,' was Llibert's invariable comment, 'if we don't look after number one!' I must have been six or seven and he eleven or twelve. In my eyes he was already a 'grown-up' who knew everything, the secrets of life and death, and I'd listen to him like an oracle. So a way existed to avoid ending up displaying one's filthy feet to the people walking from carrer de l'Hospital to carrer del Carme. I thought when I was Llibert's age I'd see it as clearly as he did.

One morning we found the traffic had ground to a halt: a funeral cortège, the like of which I've not seen since, was coming from Bethlehem parish church; six huge horses caparisoned in black velvet were pulling a black and gold open carriage that contained a coffin resembling a chest made of silver and gold; men on foot, in breeches and wearing white wigs and black dalmatics escorted the carriage; behind came fifty or sixty priests intoning dirges for the dead and in their wake a band of gentlemen in frock coats and top hats. 'Here's a fellow who looked after number one,' said Llibert. 'Who?' I asked. 'The men in wigs?' 'No, love, they're only the flunkeys.'

They've yet to give him a state funeral, but it will happen! Don't you find it incredible that people can envy a corpse? Anyway, he's already got a uniformed chauffeur opening the door to his cream limousine.

Perhaps you think I'm grousing too much, given that he's my own brother, but I was really incensed by one barbed comment of his. I'd muttered something about his cream car and uniformed chauffeur and he roared back at me in a rage: 'Yes, of course, you've got it all sewn up: a young guy from a rich family and an orphan to boot. I must look out for myself – it's every man for himself, you know – I can't go dowry hunting!'

I'd never thought anyone anywhere could interpret my relationship with Lluís in such a tawdry way.

Luckily, I've got a good supply of potatoes in the pantry and don't need to ask him for vouchers, which I've had to do occasionally, because I can't let Ramonet go without his ration of bread and potatoes. I feel so angry with Llibert. I could ask him for another voucher but I've taken a firm decision not to ask him for anything at all unless it's vital – I mean vital for the boy. I'll get by on my own as long as I can. I found a tenant farmer in Castellví de Rosanes by the name of Bepo who had potatoes to sell: he played hard to get and only wanted banknotes 'with serial numbers'. I can't tell the difference: those in the know hoard them, so none are in circulation. I'd not thought to bring silverware or anything similar, which was what Bepo wanted in place of banknotes 'with serial numbers'. We finally did a deal: almost the whole of Lluís' monthly pay for a sack of potatoes!

The worst was to come: I had to transport it. Bepo refused to organise that or even carry it from his farm to the station; he didn't want any complications, didn't want to be caught as a black marketeer since the punishment is now so draconian. The maid had stayed at home with the boy; perhaps I should have brought them with me so she could help carry the sack, but then Ramonet would have been a constant nuisance... Finally another fistful of notes helped decide Bepo to carry it to the railway station on his donkey: not all the way to the station – that was under police watch – but nearby. From then on I was on my own.

It was so heavy! That sack of potatoes landed me in bed for four days.

There is a heavy police presence in the Barcelona stations so you have to throw whatever you have out of the compartment window before reaching Sants station, and when the train begins to slow you jump out after your sacks. I confess that the trains reduce speed so much to help our feats that the acrobatics aren't especially remarkable: the train drivers themselves are into wholesale black marketeering. The spectacle of so many people jumping out of a moving train might even be a pretty sight if it weren't all so painful.

Once in Sants, the last act in the drama began: how to get the sack home. If you are really lucky you find a taxi, but it's more likely you'll have to carry it yourself – on your back and dragging it. There's always the danger the Supplies police will confiscate it or people hungrier than you will steal it. And, my God, there's no shortage of the latter. You can always see skeletal old men and women on wasteland searching through the rubbish accumulating there because it's hardly ever removed nowadays... I was exhausted when I got home and my aching back made me see every star in the sky and more besides. At least such episodes have the virtue of showing that people do sometimes help each other out of the benign understanding that comes from being in the same wretched boat. When I still had two kilometres to walk and couldn't take another step, two soldiers, who told me they were on leave in Barcelona, offered to carry the sack; they did it so disinterestedly that they didn't even want to tell me their names. All I know is that they came from Mollerussa. Would you believe it? Before their providential appearance, while I was walking with the sack on my back my thoughts were of Jesus walking along the Street of Bitterness with the Cross! It's always a consolation to think of someone who's had an even worse time: what you call a strange form of consolation.

Thanks to God, we got home and now have potatoes in the pantry once again. I'm back here and looking at the lime tree humbly doing its duty, which can't be as easy as we who aren't trees think it is. How comforting to have a house, a bolthole where one can curl up in the middle of the hostile, incomprehensible world that surrounds us! How happy the three of us – Lluís, Ramonet and I – could have been before the war if it hadn't been for Lluís' bad moods… He hasn't a clue about one obvious fact: we were happy, or could have been if he'd wanted. For him, having this large house and collecting the dividends from the factory was as natural as breathing: it never occurred to him that the majority of people have nothing apart from the clothes they stand in. I sometimes think Lluís would love me more if he were poor; I mean then he would at least be aware of his love for me. Because he *does* love me: the problem is he doesn't realise he does. If he were really, really poor, he would discover what a boon it is to have a quiet corner in the world with a table, two beds and three chairs – and a wife and son. In the end, we need so little to be happy: a little love is the secret, that's all there is to it. A little love for what you already have, and it's as if you have everything you could ever want! I am sure I could be poor and happy if Lluís loved me. I'm not at all like my brother Llibert… And that's where I find selfish consolation, the only silver lining in this never-ending war: the hope that with all these deprivations Lluís will come to appreciate his home and his family. We were once caught in a storm on an excursion of ours. There was a woodcutters' cabin nearby. We went in and lit a fire. It was lovely! Even Lluís said so: 'It's so pleasant to listen to the rain when you're in the dry, even if it's only a cabin.' We could be so happy in a cabin if we loved each other, so happy listening to the rain in the humblest of shelters! But he never stayed home, except on the evenings when you visited; you'd have thought the chairs were pricking his behind. He always seemed restless and unsatisfied: he expects more from life than it, poor thing, can ever give. He'll feel miserable until he realises that the best thing in life is that cup of herbal tea by the fireside drunk in the company of his loved one while out in the garden the wind is scattering the dead leaves. Uncle Eusebi used to say: 'Lluís is always looking but he never sees a thing.' When it comes to me, I think he's forever oblivious!

⌇

Joan Sales was born in Barcelona in 1912. At the beginning of the war, Sales, an early supporter of the Catalan republic, trained in its School for Officers and was posted to the anarchist Durruti Column which had just killed all its officers for attempting to turn it into a regular army unit! Sales survived this posting and was then sent to the Aragon front with the 30th Division. His war experiences are the subject of his wonderful novel, *Uncertain Glory*, which begins with the rise of Catalan anarchism from 1909. In exile in France, then in the Dominican Republic, then in Mexico, Sales kept Catalan culture alive, publishing the literary journal *Quaderns de l'exili*. In 1948, he returned to Catalonia to set up a publishing house, the Club Editor, which published the best of Catalan writing, including Mercè Rodoreda and Llorenç Villalonga. *Uncertain Glory* was published complete only in 1971. It is a laconic master-piece that covers the war from the bottom up. A great writer and promoter of Catalan culture, Sales died in Barcelona in 1983.

LEONARDO SCIASCIA

'TODAY SPAIN, TOMORROW THE WORLD'

from *Antimony*

translated by N. S. Thompson

THE FIRST TIME I WENT from my home town to Palermo I was ten years old. I was with my father and we were going to see off a brother of his who was leaving for America. It was my first train journey, and the train, the railwaymen, the stations and the countryside were all a wonderful novelty for me; there and back, I did the journey standing up, looking out of the window. It was then I had the idea that I would be a railwayman when I grew up: getting off the train a moment before it stopped, blowing the whistle, shouting out the name of the station, then remounting with a sure-footed leap as the train was pulling out. At a certain point in the journey, the railwayman shouted, 'Change for Aragona!' Those who were not going to Girgenti got out, loaded with suitcases and bundles, to get onto another train that was waiting. In the game I later played with the other boys in the district, I kept that cry for myself; it was like the voice of destiny itself, which had some men born to live to the east of Aragona, and others to the west, although I could not say exactly what fascination the cry had for me then. I remember the town of Aragona as it appears from the train, a few minutes before it arrives at the station. It seems to rotate on a pivot, doing a half turn around the large mansion which dominates the town, with the bare countryside below. It is only a few kilometres from my town, but I have never been to Aragona – I only have an image of it from the train.

In the Aragon of Spain, a region which has many towns like the Aragona in the province of Girgenti, I remembered that far-off journey and the game I played afterwards with the other boys, and that cry always came floating across my mind, 'Change for Aragona', just like a tune or the words of a song spring to mind, and develop and come in variations for days. I thought, 'Change, my life is changing trains... or, I'm about to get on the train of death... Change for Aragona... change here... change here...' and the thought became a musical obsession. I believe in the mystery of words, I believe that words can become life, or destiny, in the same way that they can become beauty.

So many people study, go to university and become good doctors, engineers and lawyers, or become civil servants, M.P.s and government ministers: and I would like to ask these people, 'Do you know what the war in Spain was? Do you know what it really was? Because if you don't, you won't ever understand what's happening under your own noses, you won't understand Fascism, Communism, religion or mankind, you won't ever understand anything about anything, because all the world's mistakes and its hopes were concentrated in that war, like a lens concentrates the sun's rays, causing fire, and Spain was lit by all the world's hopes and its mistakes, and the same fire's splitting the world today.'

When I went to Spain, I was barely literate, I could just about read the newspaper, the *History of the Royal Families of France* and write a letter home. When I came back, it seemed as if I could read the most difficult things a man could think and write about. And I know why Fascism is not dying, and I am sure I have met all the things which should die with its death, and I know what will have to die in me and in all other men so that Fascism will die out for ever.

'*Hoy España, mañana el mundo*', said Hitler from the propaganda postcards the Republicans dropped: they pictured him with an arm outstretched over Spain, with squadrons of aircraft appearing to drop from his gesture, and a wreath of weeping children's faces over the Spanish earth. 'Today Spain, tomorrow the world', said Hitler, and I felt they were not words invented by the propaganda machine, the whole world *would* become Spain; breaking the bank there would not mean that the game was all over. No one, except for Mussolini, wanted to play all his cards there. The Germans were testing their new, accurate instruments of war, while Italy was throwing in everything: new fighter planes and old Austrian cannon, tanks good enough for the regimental review and machine-guns from 1914, and the poor soldiers with their footcloths, puttees, and the grey-green uniforms that became as hard as a crust in the rain: the wretched unemployed of the Two Sicilies. And the best of it was that not even the Francoist Spanish were grateful for all our efforts, they had even made a joke of our initials, *Corpo Truppe Volontarie* [Volunteer Corps] with the phrase *Cuando te vas?* which means 'When are you leaving?', as if we were in Spain simply to annoy them. I would like to have seen them get by alone, all those priests, country gentlemen, pious women, young men of the parish club, career officers and the few thousand *carabineros* and Civil Guard – I would like to have seen them against the peasants and miners, against the Red hate of the Spanish poor. Or perhaps it was humiliating and shameful for them to have us see that misery and that blood, like being forced to have your friends see how poor you are at home and how mad your family is: there was all of Spain's irrational pride in that wish to have us leave. There were even those with Franco who secretly felt unhappy and anxious about what they saw happening on their side, it was not merely a few who said, 'If only José were here, everything would be different.' Without José Antonio they were not convinced by the general's revolt: '*no es justo que el conde Romanones poséa todas las tierras de Guadalajara*', and they were sadly certain that Franco would not take a hectare of land off Romanones. They felt shame at tearing Spain apart with foreign weapons and soldiers, with the Germans crushing whole cities with bombs just like someone out on a walk might squash an anthill, and with the Moors – led by the Spanish – coming to avenge themselves, after centuries, on the sons of that Christian Spain that had expelled them. When the prostitutes and bourgeois gentlemen of a captured city watched the Moors march past and applauded, '*Moros, moritos*', I could read the mortification and hate in the faces of some of the Spanish soldiers. As far as we Italians were concerned, the fact that we accused them of putting too many people up against the wall – and it seems our commanding officers were continually protesting about it – provoked antagonism in those who wanted the firing squads, and shame in those who did not, and so there was not a single Spaniard who was not upset by our presence.

All these feelings and reactions became intensified at Zaragoza, perhaps because of the prostitutes and next to a woman, prostitute or not, a man wants to be himself, and then there was the wine, that moment of truth that wine gives before the glass that makes you drunk. And in Zaragoza there were Moors and Germans, *requetés* and Falangists, Aragonese and Andalucians, and among the Italians too there was the dyed-in-the-wool Fascist from the north, who had enrolled to come and give the anti-Fascists in Spain a good hiding, who regarded the Sicilian unemployed in the same way that the Castilian soldier regarded the Moors. So with wine inside him and a woman by his side, everyone was either at his best or his worst.

I would say that the least peasant in my home district, the most 'benighted', as we say, that is, the most ignorant, the one most cut off from a knowledge of the world, if he had been brought to the Aragon front and had been told to find out which side people like himself were on and go to them, he would have made for the Republican trenches without hesitation, because for the most part, on our side, the country-side remained uncultivated, while on the Republican side the peasants worked away even under shell fire. As far as I can gather, the Republi-cans had divided the land up among the peasants and, seeing that the young ones were fighting the war, the old had attached themselves to their piece of land with so much fury that not even the shelling and the thought that the cultivated land might become disfigured with trenches from one moment to the next, could keep them away from it. Looking from a hill with binoculars on clear mornings, you could see the peas-ants beyond the Republican lines, with their black trousers, bluish shirts and straw hats, guiding the plough which a pair of mules, or a single mule, was pulling behind it. The ploughs were made in the shape of a cross, with a ploughshare no bigger than an axehead – the same that the peasants in my area still use – which makes a furrow like a mere scratch, barely turning over the dry crust of the earth. Ventura had a pair of binoculars, and I loved to watch the ploughing, when I could forget the war and feel as if I were in the countryside around my home town. It is a beautiful countryside in autumn: the whirr of partridges suddenly rising up, the slight mist from which the earth emerges, brown and blue. Aragon is a land of hills, the mist gets trapped between them and they become more beautiful in the mist and sunshine; not that it is a really beautiful landscape, which seems beautiful straightaway to everybody, it is beautiful in a special way, you would need to be born there to realize its beauty and love it.

The front was a zig-zag line, like the braid on a general's peaked cap. There had been no great movements from the start of the war, even the business of Belchite had not brought about anything new. There were actions which were like a fracas in hell, which seemed as if they would drag the front so much further forward, or even backwards, up to the houses of Zaragoza, but it all ended in nothing. We went to take possession of trenches that had belonged to the Reds the day before, or else the Reds would come and occupy ours, and then, again, we would go back to the trenches of the day before. Ventura liked this kind of exchange because he found American books and newspapers in the Republican trenches and he was in love with anything that came from America.

～

Born in Racalmuto, Sicily, in 1921, **Leonardo Sciascia** was one of the outstanding 20th-century Italian writers. A man of the left, his political views were greatly influenced by the Spanish Civil War, which Sciascia saw as a crucial moment in the fight against Fascism. In 'Antinomy', one of the four novellas that make up *Sicilian Uncles*, he writes about the Italian soldiers sent by Mussolini to fight with the Rebels. Peasants and workers, they were surprised to find that they ended up fighting for the landowners and the Church – their enemies in Italy. In the Civil War, Sciascia also saw the support for Franco of organized crime, which in Sicily took the form of the Mafia, a malignant force he fought in his political life and writings. In 1979, Sciascia was elected to the Italian Chamber of Deputies, where he remained until 1983. His time as a deputy was taken up by the Commission of Inquiry into the kidnapping and assassination of Aldo Moro, a former prime minister, by the Brigate Rosse (Red Brigades). The assassination is the subject of his 1978 novel, *The Moro Affair*. Sciascia's novels are elegant page-turners that entertain as they unravel the mechanism of power in our societies. He died in 1989 in Palermo.

JEAN-PAUL SARTRE

THE WALL

translated by Lloyd Alexander

T HEY PUSHED US INTO a big white room and I began to blink because the light hurt my eyes. Then I saw a table and four men behind the table, civilians, looking over the papers. They had bunched another group of prisoners in the back and we had to cross the whole room to join them. There were several I knew and some others who must have been foreigners. The two in front of me were blond with round skulls; they looked alike. I suppose they were French. The smaller one kept hitching up his pants; nerves.

It lasted about three hours; I was dizzy and my head was empty; but the room was well heated and I found that pleasant enough: for the past 24 hours we hadn't stopped shivering. The guards brought the prisoners up to the table, one after the other. The four men asked each one his name and occupation. Most of the time they didn't go any further – or they would simply ask a question here and there: 'Did you have anything to do with the sabotage of munitions?' Or 'Where were you the morning of the 9th and what were you doing?' They didn't listen to the answers or at least didn't seem to. They were quiet for a moment and then looking straight in front of them began to write. They asked Tom if it were true he was in the International Brigade; Tom couldn't tell them otherwise because of the papers they found in his coat. They didn't ask Juan anything but they wrote for a long time after he told them his name.

'My brother José is the anarchist,' Juan said, 'you know he isn't here any more. I don't belong to any party, I never had anything to do with politics.'

They didn't answer. Juan went on, 'I haven't done anything. I don't want to pay for somebody else.'

His lips trembled. A guard shut him up and took him away. It was my turn.

'Your name is Pablo Ibbieta?'

'Yes.'

The man looked at the papers and asked me, 'Where's Ramon Gris?'

'I don't know.'

'You hid him in your house from the 6th to the 19th.'

'No.'

They wrote for a minute and then the guards took me out. In the corridor Tom and Juan were waiting between two guards. We started walking. Tom asked one of the guards, 'So?'

'So what?' the guard said.

'Was that the cross-examination or the sentence?'

'Sentence,' the guard said.

'What are they going to do with us?'

The guard answered dryly, 'Sentence will be read in your cell.'

As a matter of fact, our cell was one of the hospital cellars. It was terrifically cold there because of the drafts. We shivered all night and it wasn't much better during the day. I had spent the previous five days in a cell in a monastery, a sort of hole in the wall that must have dated from the middle ages: since there were a lot of prisoners and not much room, they locked us up anywhere. I didn't miss my cell; I hadn't suffered too much from the cold but I was alone; after a long time it gets irritating. In the cellar I had company. Juan hardly ever spoke: he was afraid and he was too young to have anything to say. But Tom was a good talker and he knew Spanish well.

There was a bench in the cellar and four mats. When they took us back we sat and waited in silence. After a long moment, Tom said, 'We're screwed.'

'I think so too,' I said, 'but I don't think they'll do anything to the kid.'

'They don't have a thing against him,' said Tom. 'He's the brother of a militiaman and that's all.'

I looked at Juan: he didn't seem to hear. Tom went on, 'You know what they do in Saragossa? They lay the men down on the road and run over them with trucks. A Moroccan deserter told us that. They said it was to save ammunition.'

'It doesn't save gas,' I said.

I was annoyed at Tom: he shouldn't have said that.

'Then there's officers walking along the road,' he went on, 'supervising it all. They stick their hands in their pockets and smoke cigarettes. You think they finish off the guys? Hell no. They let them scream. Sometimes for an hour. The Moroccan said he damned near puked the first time.'

'I don't believe they'll do that here,' I said. 'Unless they're really short on ammunition.'

Day was coming in through four airholes and a round opening they had made in the ceiling on the left, and you could see the sky through it. Through this hole, usually closed by a trap, they unloaded coal into the cellar. Just below the hole there was a big pile of coal dust; it had been used to heat the hospital but since the beginning of the war the patients were evacuated and the coal stayed there, unused; sometimes it even got rained on because they had forgotten to close the trap.

Tom began to shiver. 'Good Jesus Christ, I'm cold,' he said. 'Here it goes again.'

He got up and began to do exercises. At each movement his shirt opened on his chest, white and hairy. He lay on his back, raised his legs in the air and bicycled. I saw his great rump trembling. Tom was husky but he had too much fat. I thought how rifle bullets or the sharp points of bayonets would soon be sunk into this mass of tender flesh as in a lump of butter. It wouldn't have made me feel like that if he'd been thin.

I wasn't exactly cold, but I couldn't feel my arms and shoulders any more. Sometimes I had the impression I was missing something and began to look around for my coat and then suddenly remembered they hadn't given me a coat. It was rather uncomfortable. They took our clothes and gave them to their soldiers leaving us only our shirts – and those canvas pants that hospital patients wear in the middle of summer. After a while Tom got up and sat next to me, breathing heavily.

'Warmer?'

'Good Christ, no. But I'm out of wind.'

Around eight o'clock in the evening a major came in with two falangistas. He had a sheet of paper in his hand. He asked the guard, 'What are the names of those three?'

'Steinbock, Ibbieta and Mirbal,' the guard said.

The major put on his eyeglasses and scanned the list: 'Steinbock... Steinbock... oh yes... you are sentenced to death. You will be shot tomorrow morning.' He went on looking. 'The other two as well.'

'That's not possible,' Juan said. 'Not me.'

The major looked at him amazed. 'What's your name?'

'Juan Mirbal,' he said.

'Well, your name is there,' said the major. 'You're sentenced.'

'I didn't do anything,' Juan said.

The major shrugged his shoulders and turned to Tom and me.

'You're Basque?'

'Nobody is Basque.'

He looked annoyed. 'They told me there were three Basques. I'm not going to waste my time running after them. Then naturally you don't want a priest?'

We didn't even answer.

He said, 'A Belgian doctor is coming shortly. He is authorized to spend the night with you.' He made a military salute and left.

'What did I tell you,' Tom said. 'We get it.'

'Yes,' I said, 'it's a rotten deal for the kid.'

I said that to be decent but I didn't like the kid. His face was too thin and fear and suffering had disfigured it, twisting all his features. Three days before he was a smart sort of kid, not too bad; but now he looked like an old fairy and I thought how he'd never be young again, even if they were to let him go. It wouldn't have been too hard to have a little pity for him but pity disgusts me, or rather it horrifies me. He hadn't said anything more but he had turned grey; his face and hands were both grey. He sat down again and looked at the ground with round eyes. Tom was good hearted, he wanted to take his arm, but the kid tore himself away violently and made a face.

'Let him alone,' I said in a low voice, 'you can see he's going to blubber.'

Tom obeyed regretfully; he would have liked to comfort the kid, it would have passed his time and he wouldn't have been tempted to think about himself. But it annoyed me: I'd never thought about death because I never had any reason to, but now the reason was here and there was nothing to do but think about it.

Tom began to talk. 'So you think you've knocked guys off, do you?' he asked me. I didn't answer. He began explaining to me that he had knocked off six since the beginning of August; he didn't realize the situation and I could tell he didn't want to realize it. I hadn't quite realized it myself, I wondered if it hurt much, I thought of bullets, I imagined their burning hail through my body. All that was beside the real question; but I was calm: we had all night to understand. After a while Tom stopped talking and I watched him out of the corner of my eye; I saw he too had turned grey and he looked rotten; I told myself 'Now it starts.' It was almost dark, a dim glow filtered through the airholes and the pile of coal and made a big stain beneath the spot of sky; I could already see a star through the hole in the ceiling: the night would be pure and icy.

The door opened and two guards came in, followed by a blond man in a tan uniform. He saluted us. 'I am the doctor,' he said. 'I have authorization to help you in these trying hours.'

He had an agreeable and distinguished voice. I said, 'What do you want here?'

'I am at your disposal. I shall do all I can to make your last moments less difficult.'

'What did you come here for? There are others, the hospital's full of them.'

'I was sent here,' he answered with a vague look. 'Ah! Would you like to smoke?' he added hurriedly. 'I have cigarettes and even cigars.'

He offered us English cigarettes and puros, but we refused. I looked him in the eyes and he seemed irritated. I said to him, 'You aren't here on an errand of mercy. Besides, I know you. I saw you with the fascists in the barracks yard the day I was arrested.'

I was going to continue, but something surprising suddenly happened to me; the presence of this doctor no longer interested me. Generally when I'm on somebody I don't let go. But the desire to talk left me completely; I shrugged and turned my eyes away. A little later I raised my head; he was watching me curiously. The guards were sitting on a mat. Pedro, the tall thin one, was twiddling his thumbs, the other shook his head from time to time to keep from falling asleep.

'Do you want a light?' Pedro suddenly asked the doctor. The other nodded 'Yes': I think he was about as smart as a log, but he surely wasn't bad. Looking in his cold blue eyes it seemed to me that his only sin was lack of imagination. Pedro went out and came back with an oil lamp which he set on the corner of the bench. It gave a bad light but it was better than nothing: they had left us in the dark the night before. For a long time I watched the circle of light the lamp made on the ceiling. I was fascinated. Then suddenly I woke up, the circle of light disappeared and I felt myself crushed under an enormous weight. It was not the thought of death, or fear; it was nameless. My cheeks burned and my head ached.

I shook myself and looked at my two friends. Tom had hidden his face in his hands. I could only see the fat white nape of his neck. Little Juan was the worst, his mouth was open and his nostrils trembled. The doctor went to him and put his hand on his shoulder to comfort him: but his eyes stayed cold. Then I saw the Belgian's hand drop stealthily along Juan's arm, down to the wrist. Juan paid no attention. The Belgian took his wrist between three fingers, distractedly, at the same time drawing back a little and turning his back to me. But I leaned backward and saw him take a watch from his pocket and look at it for a moment, never letting go of the wrist. After a minute he let the hand fall inert and went and leaned his back against the wall, then, as if he suddenly remembered something very important which had to be jotted down on the spot, he took a notebook from his pocket and wrote a few lines.

'Bastard,' I thought angrily, 'let him come and take my pulse. I'll shove my fist in his rotten face.'

He didn't come but I felt him watching me. I raised my head and returned his look. Impersonally, he said to me, 'Doesn't it seem cold to you here?' He looked cold, he was blue.

'I'm not cold,' I told him.

He never took his hard eyes off me. Suddenly I understood and my hands went to my face: I was drenched in sweat. In this cellar, in the midst of winter, in the midst of drafts, I was sweating. I ran my hands through my hair, gummed together with perspiration; at the same time I saw my shirt was damp and sticking to my skin: I had been dripping for an hour and hadn't felt it. But that swine of a Belgian hadn't missed a thing; he had seen the drops rolling down my cheeks and thought: this is the manifestation of an almost pathological state of terror; and he had felt normal and proud of being alive because he was cold. I wanted to stand up and smash his face but no sooner had I made the slightest gesture than my rage and shame were wiped out; I fell back on the bench with indifference.

I satisfied myself by rubbing my neck with my handkerchief because now I felt the sweat dropping from my hair onto my neck and it was unpleasant. I soon gave up rubbing, it was useless; my handkerchief was already soaked and I was still sweating. My buttocks were sweating too and my damp trousers were glued to the bench.

Suddenly Juan spoke. 'You're a doctor?'

'Yes,' the Belgian said.

'Does it hurt… very long?'

'Huh? When…? Oh, no,' the Belgian said paternally. 'Not at all. It's over quickly.' He acted as though he were calming a cash customer.

'But I… they told me… sometimes they have to fire twice.'

'Sometimes,' the Belgian said, nodding. 'It may happen that the first volley reaches no vital organs.'

'Then they have to reload their rifles and aim all over again?' He thought for a moment and then added hoarsely, 'That takes time!'

He had a terrible fear of suffering, it was all he thought about: it was his age. I never thought much about it and it wasn't fear of suffering that made me sweat.

I got up and walked to the pile of coal dust. Tom jumped up and threw me a hateful look: I had annoyed him because my shoes squeaked. I wondered if my face looked as frightened as his: I saw he was sweating too. The sky was superb, no light filtered into the dark corner and I had only to raise my head to see the Big Dipper. But it wasn't like it had been: the night before I could see a great piece of sky from my monastery cell and each hour of the day brought me a different memory. Morning, when the sky was a hard, light blue, I thought of beaches on the Atlantic; at noon I saw the sun and I remembered a bar in Seville where I drank manzanilla and ate olives and anchovies; afternoons I was in the shade and I thought of the deep shadow which spreads over half a bull-ring leaving the other half shimmering in sunlight; it was really hard to see the whole world reflected in the sky like that. But now I could watch the sky as much as I pleased, it no longer evoked anything in me. I liked that better. I came back and sat near Tom. A long moment passed.

Tom began speaking in a low voice. He had to talk, without that he wouldn't have been able to recognize himself in his own mind. I thought he was talking to me but he wasn't looking at me. He was undoubtedly afraid to see me as I was, grey and sweating: we were alike and worse than mirrors of each other. He watched the Belgian, the living.

'Do you understand?' he said. 'I don't understand.'

I began to speak in a low voice too. I watched the Belgian. 'Why? What's the matter?'

'Something is going to happen to us that I can't understand.'

There was a strange smell about Tom. It seemed to me I was more sensitive than usual to odors. I grinned. 'You'll understand in a while.'

'It isn't clear,' he said obstinately. 'I want to be brave but first I have to know… Listen, they're going to take us into the courtyard. Good. They're going to stand up in front of us. How many?'

'I don't know. Five or eight. Not more.'

'All right. There'll be eight. Someone'll holler "aim!" and I'll see eight rifles looking at me. I'll think how I'd like to get inside the wall, I'll push against it with my back… with every ounce of strength I have, but the wall will stay, like in a nightmare. I can imagine all that. If you only knew how well I can imagine it.'

'All right, all right!' I said. 'I can imagine it too.'

'It must hurt like hell. You know, they aim at the eyes and mouth to disfigure you,' he added mechanically. 'I can feel the wounds already; I've had pains in my head and in my neck for the past hour. Not real pains. Worse. This is what I'm going to feel tomorrow morning. And then what?'

I well understood what he meant but I didn't want to act as if I did. I had pains too, pains in my body like a crowd of tiny scars. I couldn't get used to it. But I was like him, I attached no importance to it. 'After,' I said, 'you'll be pushing up daisies.'

He began to talk to himself: he never stopped watching the Belgian. The Belgian didn't seem to be listening. I knew what he had come to do; he wasn't interested in what we thought; he came to watch our bodies, bodies dying in agony while yet alive.

'It's like a nightmare,' Tom was saying. 'You want to think something, you always have the impression that it's all right, that you're going to understand and then it slips, it escapes you and fades away. I tell myself there will be nothing afterwards. But I don't understand what it means. Sometimes I almost can… and then it fades away and I start thinking about the pains again, bullets, explosions. I'm a materialist, I swear it to you; I'm not going crazy. But something's the matter. I see my corpse; that's not hard but I'm the one who sees it, with my eyes. I've got to think… think that I won't see anything any more and the world will go on for the others. We aren't made to think that, Pablo. Believe me: I've already stayed up a whole night waiting for something. But this isn't the same: this will creep up behind us, Pablo, and we won't be able to prepare for it.'

'Shut up,' I said. 'Do you want me to call a priest?'

He didn't answer. I had already noticed he had the tendency to act like a prophet and call me Pablo, speaking in a toneless voice. I didn't like that: but it seems all the Irish are that way. I had the vague impression he smelled of urine. Fundamentally, I hadn't much sympathy for Tom and I didn't see why, under the pretext of dying together, I should have any more. It would have been different with some others. With Ramon Gris, for example. But I felt alone between Tom and Juan. I liked that better, anyhow: with Ramon I might have been more deeply moved. But I was terribly hard just then and I wanted to stay hard.

He kept on chewing his words, with something like distraction. He certainly talked to keep himself from thinking. He smelled of urine like an old prostate case. Naturally, I agreed with him, I could have said everything he said: it isn't natural to die. And since I was going to die, nothing seemed natural to me, not this pile of coal dust, or the bench, or Pedro's ugly face. Only it didn't please me to think the same things as Tom. And I knew that, all through the night, every five minutes, we would keep on thinking things at the same time. I looked at him sideways and for the first time he seemed strange to me: he wore death on his face. My pride was wounded: for the past 24 hours I had lived next to Tom, I had listened to him, I had spoken to him and I knew we had nothing in common. And now we looked as much alike as twin brothers, simply because we were going to die together. Tom took my hand without looking at me.

'Pablo, I wonder... I wonder if it's really true that everything ends.'

I took my hand away and said, 'Look between your feet, you pig.'

There was a big puddle between his feet and drops fell from his pants-leg.

'What is it?' he asked, frightened.

'You're pissing in your pants,' I told him.

'It isn't true,' he said furiously. 'I'm not pissing. I don't feel anything.'

The Belgian approached us. He asked with false solicitude, 'Do you feel ill?'

Tom did not answer. The Belgian looked at the puddle and said nothing.

'I don't know what it is,' Tom said ferociously. 'But I'm not afraid. I swear I'm not afraid.'

The Belgian did not answer. Tom got up and went to piss in a corner. He came back buttoning his fly, and sat down without a word. The Belgian was taking notes.

All three of us watched him because he was alive. He had the motions of a living human being, the cares of a living human being; he shivered in the cellar the way the living are supposed to shiver; he had an obedient, well-fed body. The rest of us hardly felt ours – not in the same way anyhow. I wanted to feel my pants between my legs but I didn't dare; I watched the Belgian, balancing on his legs, master of his muscles, someone who could think about tomorrow. There we were, three bloodless shadows; we watched him and we sucked his life like vampires.

Finally he went over to little Juan. Did he want to feel his neck for some professional motive or was he obeying an impulse of charity? If he was acting by charity it was the only time during the whole night.

He caressed Juan's head and neck. The kid let himself be handled, his eyes never leaving him, then suddenly, he seized the hand and looked at it strangely. He held the Belgian's hand between his own two hands and there was nothing pleasant about them, two grey pincers gripping this fat and reddish hand. I suspected what was going to happen and Tom must have suspected it too: but the Belgian didn't see a thing, he smiled paternally. After a moment the kid brought the fat red hand to his mouth and tried to bite it. The Belgian pulled away quickly and stumbled back against the wall. For a second he looked at us with horror, he must have suddenly understood that we were not men like him. I began to laugh and one of the guards jumped up. The other was asleep, his wide-open eyes were blank.

I felt relaxed and over-excited at the same time. I didn't want to think any more about what would happen at dawn, at death. It made no sense. I only found words or emptiness. But as soon as I tried to think of anything else I saw rifle barrels pointing at me. Perhaps I lived through my execution twenty times; once I even thought it was for good: I must have slept a minute. They were dragging me to the wall and I was struggling; I was asking for mercy. I woke up with a start and looked at the Belgian: I was afraid I might have cried out in my sleep. But he was stroking his moustache, he hadn't noticed anything. If I had wanted to, I think I could have slept a while; I had been awake for 48 hours. I was at the end of my rope. But I didn't want to lose two hours of life: they would come to wake me up at dawn, I would follow them, stupefied with sleep and I would have croaked without so much as an 'Oof!'; I didn't want that, I didn't want to die like an animal, I wanted to understand. Then I was afraid of having nightmares. I got up, walked back and forth, and, to change my ideas, I began to think about my past life. A crowd of memories came back to me pell-mell. There were good and bad ones – or at least I called them that before. There were faces and incidents. I saw the face of a little novillero who was gored in Valencia during the Feria, the face of one of my uncles, the face of Ramon Gris. I remembered my whole life: how I was out of work for three months in 1926, how I almost starved to death. I remembered a night I spent on a bench in Granada: I hadn't eaten for three days. I was angry, I didn't want to die. That made me smile. How madly I ran after happiness, after women, after liberty. Why? I wanted to free Spain, I admired Pi y Margall, I joined the anarchist movement, I spoke in public meetings: I took everything as seriously as if I were immortal.

At that moment I felt that I had my whole life in front of me and I thought, 'It's a damned lie.' It was worth nothing because it was finished. I wondered how I'd been able to walk, to laugh with the girls: I wouldn't have moved so much as my little finger if I had only imagined I would die like this. My life was in front of me, shut, closed, like a bag and yet everything inside of it was unfinished. For an instant I tried to judge it. I wanted to tell myself, this is a beautiful life. But I couldn't pass judgment on it; it was only a sketch; I had spent my time counterfeiting eternity, I had understood nothing. I missed nothing: there were so many things I could have missed, the taste of manzanilla or the baths I took in summer in a little creek near Cadiz; but death had disenchanted everything.

The Belgian suddenly had a bright idea. 'My friends,' he told us, 'I will undertake – if the military administration will allow it – to send a message for you, a souvenir to those who love you…'

Tom mumbled, 'I don't have anybody.'

I said nothing. Tom waited an instant then looked at me with curiosity. 'You don't have anything to say to Concha?'

'No.'

I hated this tender complicity: it was my own fault, I had talked about Concha the night before, I should have controlled myself. I was with her for a year. Last night I would have given an arm to see her again for five minutes. That was why I talked about her, it was stronger than

I was. Now I had no more desire to see her, I had nothing more to say to her. I would not even have wanted to hold her in my arms: my body filled me with horror because it was grey and sweating – and I wasn't sure that her body didn't fill me with horror. Concha would cry when she found out I was dead, she would have no taste for life for months afterward. But I was still the one who was going to die. I thought of her soft, beautiful eyes. When she looked at me something passed from her to me. But I knew it was over: if she looked at me now the look would stay in her eyes, it wouldn't reach me. I was alone.

Tom was alone too but not in the same way. Sitting cross-legged, he had begun to stare at the bench with a sort of smile, he looked amazed. He put out his hand and touched the wood cautiously as if he were afraid of breaking something, then drew back his hand quickly and shuddered. If I had been Tom I wouldn't have amused myself by touching the bench; this was some more Irish nonsense, but I too found that objects had a funny look: they were more obliterated, less dense than usual. It was enough for me to look at the bench, the lamp, the pile of coal dust, to feel that I was going to die. Naturally I couldn't think clearly about my death but I saw it everywhere, on things, in the way things fell back and kept their distance, discreetly, as people who speak quietly at the bedside of a dying man. It was his death which Tom had just touched on the bench.

In the state I was in, if someone had come and told me I could go home quietly, that they would leave me my life whole, it would have left me cold: several hours or several years of waiting is all the same when you have lost the illusion of being eternal. I clung to nothing, in a way I was calm. But it was a horrible calm – because of my body; my body, I saw with its eyes, I heard with its ears, but it was no longer me; it sweated and trembled by itself and I didn't recognize it any more. I had to touch it and look at it to find out what was happening, as if it were the body of someone else. At times I could still feel it, I felt sinkings, and fallings, as when you're in a plane taking a nose dive, or I felt my heart beating. But that didn't reassure me. Everything that came from my body was all cockeyed. Most of the time it was quiet and I felt no more than a sort of weight, a filthy presence against me; I had the impression of being tied to an enormous vermin. Once I felt my pants and I felt they were damp; I didn't know whether it was sweat or urine, but I went to piss on the coal pile as a precaution.

The Belgian took out his watch, looked at it. He said, 'It is three-thirty.'

Bastard! He must have done it on purpose. Tom jumped; he hadn't noticed time was running out; night surrounded us like a shapeless, somber mass, I couldn't even remember that it had begun.

Little Juan began to cry. He wrung his hands, pleaded, 'I don't want to die. I don't want to die.'

He ran across the whole cellar waving his arms in the air then fell sobbing on one of the mats. Tom watched him with mournful eyes, without the slightest desire to console him. Because it wasn't worth the trouble: the kid made more noise than we did, but he was less touched: he was like a sick man who defends himself against illness by fever. It's much more serious when there isn't any fever.

He wept: I could clearly see he was pitying himself; he wasn't thinking about death. For one second, one single second, I wanted to weep myself, to weep with pity for myself. But the opposite happened: I glanced at the kid, I saw his thin sobbing shoulders and felt inhuman: I could pity neither the others nor myself. I said to myself, 'I want to die cleanly.'

Tom had gotten up, he placed himself just under the round opening and began to watch for daylight. I was determined to die cleanly and I only thought of that. But ever since the doctor told us the time, I felt time flying, flowing away drop by drop.

It was still dark when I heard Tom's voice: 'Do you hear them?'

Men were marching in the courtyard.

'Yes.'

'What the hell are they doing? They can't shoot in the dark.'

After a while we heard no more. I said to Tom, 'It's day.'

Pedro got up, yawning, and came to blow out the lamp. He said to his buddy, 'Cold as hell.'

The cellar was all grey. We heard shots in the distance.

'It's starting,' I told Tom. 'They must do it in the court in the rear.'

Tom asked the doctor for a cigarette. I didn't want one; I didn't want cigarettes or alcohol. From that moment on they didn't stop firing.

'Do you realize what's happening?' Tom said.

He wanted to add something but kept quiet, watching the door. The door opened and a lieutenant came in with four soldiers. Tom dropped his cigarette.

'Steinbock?'

Tom didn't answer. Pedro pointed him out.

'Juan Mirbal?'

'On the mat.'

'Get up,' the lieutenant said.

Juan did not move. Two soldiers took him under the arms and set him on his feet. But he fell as soon as they released him.

The soldiers hesitated.

'He's not the first sick one,' said the lieutenant. 'You two carry him; they'll fix it up down there.'

He turned to Tom. 'Let's go.'

Tom went out between two soldiers. Two others followed, carrying the kid by the armpits. He hadn't fainted; his eyes were wide open and tears ran down his cheeks. When I wanted to go out the lieutenant stopped me.

'You Ibbieta?'

'Yes.'

'You wait here; they'll come for you later.'

They left. The Belgian and the two jailers left too, I was alone. I did not understand what was happening to me but I would have liked it better if they had gotten it over with right away. I heard shots at almost regular intervals; I shook with each one of them. I wanted to scream and tear out my hair. But I gritted my teeth and pushed my hands in my pockets because I wanted to stay clean.

After an hour they came to get me and led me to the first floor, to a small room that smelt of cigars and where the heat was stifling. There were two officers sitting smoking in the armchairs, papers on their knees.

'You're Ibbieta?'

'Yes.'

'Where is Ramon Gris?'

'I don't know.'

The one questioning me was short and fat. His eyes were hard behind his glasses. He said to me, 'Come here.'

I went to him. He got up and took my arms, staring at me with a look that should have pushed me into the earth. At the same time he pinched my biceps with all his might. It wasn't to hurt me, it was only a game: he wanted to dominate me. He also thought he had to blow his stinking breath square in my face. We stayed for a moment like that, and I almost felt like laughing. It takes a lot to intimidate a man who is going to die; it didn't work. He pushed me back violently and sat down again. He said, 'It's his life against yours. You can have yours if you tell us where he is.'

These men dolled up with their riding crops and boots were still going to die. A little later than I, but not too much. They busied themselves looking for names in their crumpled papers, they ran after other men to imprison or suppress them; they had opinions on the future of Spain and on other subjects. Their little activities seemed shocking and burlesqued to me; I couldn't put myself in their place, I thought they were insane. The little man was still looking at me, whipping his boots with the riding crop. All his gestures were calculated to give him the look of a live and ferocious beast.

'So? You understand?'

'I don't know where Gris is,' I answered. 'I thought he was in Madrid.'

The other officer raised his pale hand indolently. This indolence was also calculated. I saw through all their little schemes and I was stupefied to find there were men who amused themselves that way.

'You have a quarter of an hour to think it over,' he said slowly. 'Take him to the laundry, bring him back in fifteen minutes. If he still refuses he will be executed on the spot.'

They knew what they were doing: I had passed the night in waiting; then they had made me wait an hour in the cellar while they shot Tom and Juan and now they were locking me up in the laundry; they must have prepared their game the night before. They told themselves that nerves eventually wear out and they hoped to get me that way.

They were badly mistaken. In the laundry I sat on a stool because

I felt very weak and I began to think. But not about their proposition. Of course I knew where Gris was; he was hiding with his cousins, four kilometers from the city. I also knew that I would not reveal his hiding place unless they tortured me (but they didn't seem to be thinking about that). All that was perfectly regulated, definite and in no way interested me. Only I would have liked to understand the reasons for my conduct. I would rather die than give up Gris. Why? I didn't like Ramon Gris any more. My friendship for him had died a little while before dawn at the same time as my love for Concha, at the same time as my desire to live. Undoubtedly I thought highly of him: he was tough. But it was not for this reason that I consented to die in his place; his life had no more value than mine; no life had value. They were going to slap a man up against a wall and shoot at him till he died, whether it was I or Gris or somebody else made no difference. I knew he was more useful than I to the cause of Spain but I thought to hell with Spain and anarchy; nothing was important. Yet I was there, I could save my skin and give up Gris and I refused to do it. I found that somehow comic; it was obstinacy. I thought, 'I must be stubborn!' And a droll sort of gaiety spread over me.

They came for me and brought me back to the two officers. A rat ran out from under my feet and that amused me. I turned to one of the falangistas and said, 'Did you see the rat?'

He didn't answer. He was very sober, he took himself seriously. I wanted to laugh but I held myself back because I was afraid that once I got started I wouldn't be able to stop. The falangista had a moustache. I said to him again, 'You ought to shave off your moustache, idiot.' I thought it funny that he would let the hairs of his living being invade his face. He kicked me without great conviction and I kept quiet.

'Well,' said the fat officer, 'have you thought about it?'

I looked at them with curiosity, as insects of a very rare species. I told them, 'I know where he is. He is hidden in the cemetery. In a vault or in the gravediggers' shack.'

It was a farce. I wanted to see them stand up, buckle their belts and give orders busily.

They jumped to their feet. 'Let's go. Moles, go get fifteen men from Lieutenant Lopez. You,' the fat man said, 'I'll let you off if you're telling the truth, but it'll cost you plenty if you're making monkeys out of us.'

They left in a great clatter and I waited peacefully under the guard of falangistas. From time to time I smiled, thinking about the spectacle they would make. I felt stunned and malicious. I imagined them lifting up tombstones, opening the doors of the vaults one by one. I represented this situation to myself as if I had been someone else: this prisoner obstinately playing the hero, these grim falangistas with their moustaches and their men in uniform running among the graves; it was irresistibly funny. After half an hour the little fat man came back alone. I thought he had come to give the orders to execute me. The others must have stayed in the cemetery.

The officer looked at me. He didn't look at all sheepish. 'Take him into the big courtyard with the others,' he said. 'After the military operations a regular court will decide what happens to him.'

'Then they're not... not going to shoot me...?'

'Not now, anyway. What happens afterwards is none of my business.'

I still didn't understand. I asked, 'But why...?'

He shrugged his shoulders without answering and the soldiers took me away. In the big courtyard there were about a hundred prisoners, women, children and a few old men. I began walking around the central grass-plot, I was stupefied. At noon they let us eat in the mess hall. Two or three people questioned me. I must have known them, but I didn't answer: I didn't even know where I was.

Around evening they pushed about ten new prisoners into the court. I recognized Garcia, the baker. He said, 'What damned luck you have! I didn't think I'd see you alive.'

'They sentenced me to death,' I said, 'and then they changed their minds. I don't know why.'

'They arrested me at two o'clock,' Garcia said.

'Why?' Garcia had nothing to do with politics.

'I don't know,' he said. 'They arrest everybody who doesn't think the way they do.' He lowered his voice. 'They got Gris.'

I began to tremble. 'When?'

'This morning. He messed it up. He left his cousin's on Tuesday because they had an argument. There were plenty of people to hide him but he didn't want to owe anything to anybody. He said, "I'd go and hide in Ibbieta's place, but they got him, so I'll go hide in the cemetery."'

'In the cemetery?'

'Yes. What a fool. Of course they went by there this morning, that was sure to happen. They found him in the gravediggers' shack. He shot at them and they got him.'

'In the cemetery!'

Everything began to spin and I found myself sitting on the ground: I laughed so hard I cried.

⌇

Jean-Paul Sartre was born in Paris in 1905. It was as a student at the Ecole Normale that, in 1929, he met Simone de Beauvoir. They visited Spain in 1932 as tourists – in love with the country but unaware of the momentous political events (including a military coup!) going on around them. At that time, they rejected commitment: for both of them, the priority was to write and to be an intellectual. The Spanish Civil War forced them to reconsider these priorities; it was a crucial moment in the intellectual life of the time. It made Sartre and De Beauvoir realize that political events demanded a public show of commitment, action and support. Written in 1939, 'The Wall' contains in a fictional form many of the themes that were to become central to Sartre and De Beauvoir's existentialism; freedom of will, the priority of existence over essence and the notion of the absurd. In the story, Pablo's solution of his dilemma has had a fatal result very different from the expected outcome. He sees that he is responsible for the death of Ramon Gris: it is so absurd that all he can do is laugh. Over time, Sartre refined his philosophy in works like *Being and Nothingness*, but 'The Wall' remains an early, succinct exposition of these ideas – and an easier read! In 1964, Sartre was awarded the Nobel Prize for Literature but declined it, saying that 'a writer should not allow himself to be turned into an institution'. He died in Paris in 1980. His funeral was attended by 50,000 Parisians, who mourned a man for whom remaining silent was not an option.

MANUEL RIVAS

BUTTERFLY'S TONGUE

from *Vermeer's Milkmaid: And Other Stories*

translated by Margaret Jull Costa

To Chabela

'Hello, Sparrow. I'm hoping this year we'll finally get to see the butterfly's tongue.'

The teacher had been waiting for some time for those in state education to send him a microscope. He talked to us children so much about how that apparatus made minute, invisible things bigger that we ended up really seeing them, as if his enthusiastic words had the effect of powerful lenses.

'The butterfly's tongue is a coiled tube like the spring of a clock. If a flower attracts the butterfly, it unrolls its tongue and begins to suck from the calyx. When you place a moist finger in a jar of sugar, can you not already feel the sweetness in your mouth, as if the tip of your finger belonged to your tongue? Well, the butterfly's tongue is no different.'

After that, we were all envious of butterflies. How wonderful. To fly about the world, dressed up as if for a party, stopping off at flowers like taverns with barrels full of syrup.

I loved that teacher very much. To begin with, my parents couldn't believe it. I mean they couldn't understand why I loved my teacher. When I was only little, school represented a terrible threat. A word brandished in the air like a rod of willow.

'You'll see soon enough when you go to school!'

Two of my uncles, like many other young men, had emigrated to America to avoid being called up for the war in Morocco. Well, I dreamt of going to America as well just to avoid being sent to school. In fact, there were stories of children who took to the hills in order to escape that punishment. They would turn up after two or three days, stiff with cold and speechless, like deserters from Barranco del Lobo.

I was almost six and everyone called me Sparrow. Other children of my age were already working. But my father was a tailor and had neither lands nor livestock. He would rather I were far away and not creating mischief in his small workshop. So it was that I spent a large part of the day running about the park, and it was Cordeiro, the collector of litter and dry leaves, who gave me the nickname. 'You look like a sparrow.'

I don't think I ever ran as much as in that summer before starting school. I ran like a madman and sometimes I would go for miles beyond the limits of the park, my eyes fixed on the summit of Mount Sinai, fondly imagining that some day I would sprout wings and reach as far as Buenos Aires. But I never got past that magical mountain.

'You'll see soon enough when you go to school!'

My father would recount as a torment, as if he were having his tonsils torn out by hand, the way in which the teacher would try to correct their pronunciation of the letters g and j. 'Each morning, we had to repeat the following sentence: *Los pájaros de Guadalajara tienen la garganta llena de trigo.* We took many beatings for the sake of Juadalagara!' If what he really wanted was to frighten me, he succeeded. The night before, I couldn't sleep. Huddled up in bed, I listened to the wall clock in the sitting room with the anguish of a condemned man. The day arrived with the clarity of a butcher's apron. I wouldn't have been lying if I'd told my parents I was sick.

Fear, like a mouse, gnawed at my insides.

And I wet myself. I didn't wet myself in bed, but at school.

I remember it very well. So many years have gone by and still I can feel a warm, shameful trickle running down my legs. I was seated at the desk at the back, half crouching in the hope that no one would realize that I existed, until I was able to leave and start flying about the park.

'You, young sir, stand up!'

Fate always lets you know when it's coming. I raised my eyes and saw with horror that the order was meant for me. That teacher, who was as ugly as a bug, was pointing at me with his ruler. It was a small ruler, made of wood, but it looked like the lance of Abd al-Krim.

'What is your name?'

'Sparrow.'

All the children burst out laughing. I felt as if I were being whacked on the ears with tins.

'Sparrow?'

I couldn't remember anything. Not even my name. Everything I had been up until then had disappeared from my head. My parents were two hazy figures fading from my mind. I looked towards the large window, anxiously searching for the trees of the park.

It was then that I wet myself.

When the other children realized, their laughter increased, echoing like the crack of a whip.

I took to my heels. I began to run like a madman with wings. I ran and I ran the way you only run in dreams, when the Bogeyman's coming to get you. I was convinced that this was what the teacher was doing. Coming to get me. I could feel his breath and that of all the children on the back of my neck, like a pack of hounds on the trail of a fox. But when I got as far as the bandstand and looked back, I saw that no one had followed me and I was alone with my fear, drenched in sweat and pee. The bandstand was empty. No one seemed to notice me, but I had the sensation that the whole town was pretending, that dozens of censorious eyes were peeping through the curtains, and that it would not take long for the rumours to reach my parents' ears. My legs decided for me. They walked towards the Sinai with a determination hitherto undetected. This time, I would arrive in Coruña and embark as a stowaway on one of those ships whose destination is Buenos Aires.

The sea was not visible from the summit of the Sinai, but another, even taller mountain, with rocks cut out like the towers of an inaccessible fort. Looking back on it, I feel a mixture of surprise and wistfulness at what I was capable of doing that day. On my own, at the summit, seated in a stone armchair, beneath the stars, while the members of the search party with their lamps moved about the valley below like glow-worms. My name crossed the night mounted on the back of the dogs' howling. I was not scared. It was as if I had gone beyond fear. So I did not cry, nor did I offer any resistance, when the robust shadow of Cordeiro came to my side. He wrapped me in his jacket and held me in his arms. 'It's all right, Sparrow, everything's over.'

I slept like a saint that night, lying close to my mother. No one had told me off. My father had remained in the kitchen, smoking in silence, his elbows on the oilcloth covering the table, the butts piled up in the scallop shell ashtray, just as had happened when my grandmother died.

I had the sensation that my mother had not let go of my hand all night. Still not letting go, as if handling a Moses basket, she took me back to school. And on this occasion, with a calm heart, I managed to get a look at the teacher for the first time. He had the face of a toad.

The toad was smiling. He pinched my cheek with affection. 'I like that name, Sparrow.' And that pinch wounded me like an after-dinner sweet. But the most incredible thing was when, surrounded by absolute silence, he led me by the hand to his table and sat me down in his chair. He remained standing, picked up a book and said,

'We have a new classmate today. This is a joy for all of us and we're going to welcome him with a round of applause.' I thought that I was going to wet my trousers again, but all I felt was a moistness in my eyes. 'Good, and now, let us begin with a poem. Whose turn is it? Romualdo? Come, Romualdo, come forward. Now, remember, slowly and in a loud voice.'

Romualdo's shorts looked ridiculous on him. His legs were very long and dark, the knees criss-crossed with wounds.

A cold and dark afternoon...

'One moment, Romualdo, what is it you are going to read?'
'A poem, sir.'
'And what is the title?'
'*Childhood Memory*. By Antonio Machado.'

'Very good, Romualdo, carry on. Slowly and in a loud voice. Don't forget the punctuation.'

The boy named Romualdo, whom I knew from carting sacks of pine cones like other children from Altamira, hawked like an old smoker of cut tobacco and read with an incredible, splendid voice, which seemed to have come straight out of the radio set of Manolo Suárez, the emigrant who had returned from Montevideo.

A cold and dark afternoon
in winter. The schoolboys
study. Monotony
of rain behind the glass.
This is the class. A poster
shows Cain in flight,
and Abel dead,
next to a crimson stain...

'Very good. What does "monotony of rain" mean, Romualdo?' asked the teacher.

'That it never rains but it pours, Don Gregorio.'

'Did you pray?' Mum asked, while ironing the clothes that my father had sewn during the day. The pot on the stove with the dinner gave off a bitter smell of turnip greens.

'We did,' I said, not very sure. 'Something to do with Cain and Abel.'

'That's good,' said Mum. 'I don't know why they call that new teacher an atheist.'

'What's an atheist?'

'Someone who says that God does not exist.' Mum gestured with distaste and energetically ironed out the wrinkles in a pair of trousers.

'Is Dad an atheist?'

Mum put the iron down and stared at me.

'What makes you think your father's an atheist? How can you even think to ask such a stupid question?'

I had often heard my father blaspheming against God. All the men did it. When something was going badly, they would spit on the ground and take God's name in vain. They would say two things: 'God damn it!' and 'To hell with it!' It seemed to me that only women really believed in God.

'And the Devil? Does the Devil exist?'

'Of course!'

The boiling made the lid of the pot dance. From that mutant mouth emerged puffs of steam and gobs of foam and greens. A moth fluttered about the light bulb in the ceiling hanging from intertwined wires. Mum was moody, the way she always was when she had to iron. Her face would tense up when she was creasing the trouser legs. But she spoke now in a soft and slightly sad tone, as if she were referring to a waif.

'The Devil was an angel who turned bad.'

The moth beat against the bulb, which swung from side to side, throwing the shadows into disarray.

'The teacher said today that the butterfly has a tongue, a very long, thin tongue that it carries around rolled up like the spring of a clock. He's going to show it to us with an apparatus they've to send him from Madrid. Isn't it amazing that the butterfly should have a tongue?'

'If he says so, it must be true. There are lots of things that seem amazing, but are true. Did you like school?'

'A lot. He doesn't hit us either. The teacher doesn't hit.'

No, Don Gregorio the teacher did not hit. On the contrary, he almost always smiled with his toad's face. When there was a fight in the playground, he would call the children to him, 'Anyone would think you were rams,' and make them shake hands. Then he would sit them down at the same desk. This is how I made my best friend, Dombodán, who was big, kind and clumsy. There was another boy, Eladio, who had a mole on his cheek, which I would have smacked with great pleasure, but never did for fear that the teacher would have told me to shake his hand and moved me from next to Dombodán. The way Don Gregorio would show that he was really angry was by silence.

'If you won't be quiet, then I shall have to be quiet.'

And he would walk towards the window with a distant look, his gaze fixed on the Sinai. It was a prolonged, unsettling silence that was as if he had deserted us in a strange country. I soon felt that the teacher's silence was the worst punishment imaginable. Because everything he touched was an engaging story. The story might begin with a piece of paper, having visited the Amazon and the systole and diastole of the heart. Everything fitted, made sense. Grass, sheep, wool, my cold. When the teacher turned to the map of the world, we were as absorbed as if the screen at the Rex Cinema had lit up. We felt fear with the Indians when they heard the neighing of horses and the report of an arquebus for the first time. We rode on the back of the elephants that took Hannibal of Carthage across the snowy Alps, on his way to Rome. We fought with sticks and stones at Ponte Sampaio against Napoleon's troops. But it wasn't all wars. We made sickles and ploughshares in the smithies of O Incio. We wrote love songs in Provence and on the sea of Vigo. We built the Pórtico da Gloria. We planted the potatoes that had come from America. And to America we emigrated at the time of the potato blight.

'Potatoes came from America,' I said to my mother at lunch, when she placed the dish in front of me.

'What do you mean, from America! There've always been potatoes,' she pronounced.

'No. Before, people ate chestnuts. And maize came from America too.' It was the first time that I had the clear impression that, thanks to the teacher, I knew important things about our world that they, my parents, did not know.

But the most fascinating moments at school were when the teacher talked about insects. Water spiders invented the submarine. Ants cultivated mushrooms and looked after cattle that produced milk with sugar. There was a bird in Australia that painted its nest in colours with a kind of oil it made using pigments from plants. I shall never forget. It was called the bowerbird. The male would put an orchid in the new nest to attract the female.

My interest was such that I became supplier of insects to Don Gregorio and he accepted me as his best pupil. There were Saturdays and holidays he would stop by my house and we would go off on an outing together. We would scan the banks of the river, heathland and woods, and climb up Mount Sinai. Each of these trips was like a journey of discovery for me. We always came back with a treasure. A mantis. A dragonfly. A stag beetle. And a different butterfly each time, though I only remember the name of one that the teacher called an Iris, which shone beautifully when it alighted on the mud or manure.

On our return, we would sing along the paths like two old friends. On Mondays, at school, the teacher would say, 'And now let us talk about Sparrow's bugs.'

My parents considered the teacher's attentions an honour. On the days we went out, my mother would prepare a picnic for the two of us. 'There's no need, madam, I've already eaten,' Don Gregorio would insist. But afterwards he would say, 'Thank you, madam, the picnic was exquisite.'

'I'm quite sure he suffers hardships,' my mother would say at night.

'Teachers don't earn what they should,' my father would declare with heartfelt solemnity. 'They are the lights of the Republic.'

'The Republic, the Republic! We'll soon see where the Republic ends up!'

My father was a Republican. My mother was not. I mean that my mother went to Mass every day and the Republicans appeared as the enemies of the Church. They tried not to argue in front of me, but at times I overheard them.

'What have you got against Azaña? That's the priest putting ideas into your head.'

'I go to Mass to pray,' my mother said.

'You do, but the priest doesn't.'

Once, when Don Gregorio came to pick me up to go looking for butterflies, my father said to him that, if he didn't mind, he'd like to take his measurements for a suit.

'A suit?'

'Don Gregorio, please do not take offence. I should like to repay you in some way. And the one thing I know how to do is make suits.'

The teacher looked around in embarrassment.

'This is my trade,' said my father with a smile.

'I have a great deal of respect for people's trades,' said the teacher finally.

Don Gregorio wore that suit for a year and was wearing it on that day in July 1936 when he passed me in the park, on his way to the town hall.

'Hello, Sparrow. Maybe this year we'll get to see the butterfly's tongue at last.'

Something strange was happening. Everyone seemed to be in a hurry, but they did not move. Those looking ahead turned around. Those looking to the right turned to the left. Cordeiro, the collector of litter and dry leaves, was seated on a bench, near the bandstand. I had never seen Cordeiro seated on a bench. He looked upwards, shielding his face with his hand. When Cordeiro looked like this and the birds went quiet, it meant that there was a storm on the way.

I heard the bang of a solitary motorbike. It was a guard with a flag tied to the back seat. He passed in front of the town hall and looked over at the men chatting uneasily in the porch. He shouted, 'Long live Spain!' And accelerated away again, leaving a series of explosions in his wake.

Mothers started calling out for their children. At home, my grand-mother seemed to have died again. My father piled up butts in the ashtray and my mother wept and did things that made no sense, such as turning on the tap and washing the clean dishes and putting the dirty ones away.

There was a knock at the door and my parents stared at the handle apprehensively. It was Amelia, the neighbour, who worked in the house of Suárez, the emigrant.

'Do you know what's happening? In Coruña, the military have declared a state of war. They're firing shots against the civilian government.'

'Heaven help us!' My mother crossed herself.

'And here,' continued Amelia in a low voice, as if the walls had ears, 'apparently the mayor called the chief of police, but he said to say that he was sick.'

The following day, I was not allowed on to the street. I watched at the window and all the passers-by looked like shrivelled up shadows to me, as if suddenly winter had fallen and the wind had swept the sparrows from the park like dry leaves.

Troops arrived from the capital and occupied the town hall. Mum went out to attend Mass and came back looking pale and saddened, as if she had grown old in half an hour.

'Terrible things are happening, Ramón,' I heard her saying, between sobs, to my father. He had aged too. Worse still. He seemed to have lost his will. He had sunk into a chair and not moved. He was not talking. He did not want to eat.

'We have to burn the things that might compromise you, Ramón. The newspapers, books. Everything.'

It was my mother who took the initiative during those days. One morning, she made my father dress up and took him with her to Mass. On their return, she said to me, 'Come, Moncho, you've to come with us to the park.' She brought me my best clothes and, as she helped me to do up my tie, she said to me in a very serious voice, 'Remember this, Moncho. Daddy was not a Republican. Daddy was not friends with the mayor. Daddy did not say bad things about the priests. And most important of all, Moncho, Daddy did not give the teacher a suit.'

'He did give him a suit.'

'No, Moncho. He did not. Have you understood? He did not give him a suit.'

'No, Mummy, he did not give him a suit.'

There were a lot of people in the park, all in their Sunday best. Some groups had come down from the villages as well, women dressed in mourning, old countrymen in hats and waistcoats, children with a frightened air about them, preceded by men in blue shirts, with pistols strapped to their waist. Two lines of soldiers cleared a path from the steps of the town hall to some lorries with trailers fitted with awnings, like the ones used to transport the cattle to market. But in the park there was not the hustle and bustle of markets, but a grave silence, like that of Holy Week. People did not greet each other. They didn't even seem to recognize one another. All their attention was directed towards the front of the town hall.

A guard half opened the door and ran his eyes over the assembled throng. Then he opened it completely and gestured with his arm. From the dark mouth of the building, escorted by other guards, emerged the prisoners, their hands and their feet tied, roped in a silent line to each other. Some of their names I did not know, but I knew all their faces. The mayor, the trade unionists, the Athenaeum's librarian Resplandor Obreiro, Charlie, who sang with the Sun and Life Orchestra, the stone-mason they called Hercules, Dombodán's father… And at the end of the line, hunched up and ugly as a toad, the teacher.

We heard some orders and isolated shouts that echoed around the park like bangers. There was a crescendo of murmurs coming from the crowd, that finally reiterated those insults.

'Traitors! Criminals! Reds!'

'Shout as well, Ramón, for the love of God, shout!' My mother held my father by the arm, as if she were using all her strength to stop him from fainting. 'Let them see you shouting, Ramón, let them see you shouting!'

And then I heard my father whisper, 'Traitors!' And then, as his voice grew stronger, 'Criminals! Reds!' He let go of my mother's arm and drew nearer to the line of soldiers, his gaze fixed furiously on the teacher. 'Murderer! Anarchist! Monster!'

Mum was trying now to hold him back and pulled on his jacket discreetly. But he was beside himself. 'Bastard! Son of a bitch!' I'd never heard him aim those words at anyone, not even the referee at the football ground. 'It's not his mother's fault, eh, Moncho? Remember that.' But he was turning now towards me, urging me on with this mad look, his eyes brimming with tears and blood. 'You shout as well, Monchiño, you shout as well!'

When the lorries drove off with the prisoners, I was one of the children who ran after them throwing stones. I desperately searched for the face of the teacher to call him a traitor and a criminal. But the convoy by now was a cloud of dust in the distance, as I stood in the park, with clenched fists, capable only of murmuring with rage, 'Toad! Bowerbird! Iris!'

The Galician writer **Manuel Rivas** was born in La Coruña in 1957. A campaigning journalist, Rivas is a founding member of Greenpeace Spain and was centrally involved in the protests against the Prestige oil spill caused by the sinking of a tanker off the coast of Galicia in 2002. Rivas, who writes in Galician, has been very important in championing Galician literature and making its stars like the poet Rosalia de Castro known internationally. Many of his fictions have been filmed, including *Butterfly's Tongue*, the film of which was directed by José Luis Cuerda. Both book and film are a brilliant portrayal of everyday cowardice and the ease with which people can be made to conform. Subsequent books, *The Carpenter's Pencil* and *Books Burn Badly*, have established Rivas as one of Spain's most important writers.

FRANCISCO GARCÍA PAVÓN

IN WHICH ARE EXPLAINED THE ROMANCES OF JOSÉ REQUINTO AND NICOLÁS NICOLAVICH WITH LA SAGRARIO AND LA PEPA RESPECTIVELY, BOTH YOUNG WOMEN FROM PUERTA DEL SEGURA, JAÉN PROVINCE

from *Los Liberales*

translated by Nick Caistor

IN THE 1935 GRAPE HARVEST, either because more strangers came than ever or because the crop wasn't very abundant, a lot of people who usually arrived from Andalusia to pick grapes ended up without work. You could see them in the town square, sitting on the edge of the pavements or forming circles while they waited for the landowner to come and employ them in their vineyard. When carts or lorries went by full of companions who had been luckier, they waved to them sadly. They all came from the provinces of Córdoba and Jaén, especially from Puerta del Segura and Bujalance. Spurred on by hunger, they walked all the way to the flatlands of La Mancha looking for work. Emaciated and prematurely aged, men in faded smocks smoked green tobacco and looked warily around them. Sallow women in brightly-coloured clothes who ate over-ripe melons. They smelled of sour sweat. Their leathery flesh spoke of a centuries-old hunger. At night you could see them clustered in corners. They slept in a heap, all piled together. They left their children with relatives or neighbours in their villages and until they found someone to take them on, dragged all their possessions around town.

It so happened that in September at one of those dusks that are as dark as wine, granddad came home with a radiant young girl, with a splendid body and childish gestures, who was dressed in old rags and wore a pair of tattered rope sandals.

When she arrived we were sitting out in the factory's big courtyard, by the little garden, enjoying the cool evening air. We all fell silent and looked at this fresh young woman accompanying granddad. Flustered, she stood there in the dark twilight, clutching her little bundle.

'Here's a servant for us, Emilia,' said granddad. 'Her name is Sagrario and she comes from La Puerta. She wants to stay and live here.'

We all stared in surprise at her buxom charms, so unusual in the 'strangers', who were mostly thin, downtrodden-looking.

'Tomorrow you can buy her a pinafore,' granddad continued, still staring at her.

Grandma, who never dared question her husband's decisions, asked La Sagrario what seemed like a simple question:

'Are you pleased that you're staying with us?'

La Sagrario's only reply was to burst into tears. Grandma looked at her husband inquisitively.

'Damn it, what's wrong, girl?'

For a while all we could hear were her sobs. Finally she said, still sobbing:

'I want to be with my Pepa.'

She explained that 'her Pepa' was from the same village and that they had been lifelong friends, and she had come to the failed grape harvest with her.

Grandma said she only needed one maid. Auntie also chipped in to say we didn't need anyone else.

'What's "her Pepa" like?' the two women asked granddad.

'Dunno. I didn't notice.'

'She didn't want me to be left without a job,' said La Sagrario, still sobbing her heart out. 'She vanished when the master came over to talk to me… my Pepa is very good.'

That was how things stood when mama appeared through the shadows of the big courtyard, with her sick woman's stumbling gait. She had come from her sister Paulina's house, just opposite.

She sat down, tired as always, and took my hand. I can remember the pale gleam from her big blue eyes. Her pulled-back dark hair. Her small hands.

When they explained what was going on, she glanced at La Sagrario, who was still recovering, clutching her bundle, and raised her arms in the kind gesture she always had for those who were humble and tender-hearted like her.

'And now there's the problem of "her Pepa"…' grandma said, imitating the newcomer's voice.

Mama smiled and said it would be a godsend if this Pepa were good because she was really upset as our own maid had just announced she was off to the grape harvest the following Monday.

'So it's La Pepa then,' said granddad, who seemed determined to keep La Sagrario.

'Will your Pepa want to stay here?' mama asked Sagrario.

'Yes, señora…' she replied, suddenly all smiles. 'You'll see. She's really good. And she has a way with her.'

'So where is La Pepa now?'

'Over there, where I was, in a corner of Los Portales.'

'Well then,' said granddad, 'tell her to come and live here until Monday when your girl leaves.'

'Is that alright, señora?' Sagrario asked mama with child-like joy.

'Yes of course, my girl.'

'Come on, leave your bundle here and let's go and fetch La Pepa,' said granddad, delighted everything was settled.

The two of them scurried off to the corner of the arcade where La Pepa had been left on her own.

La Pepa had a pretty face and a pleasant character. A bit silly and clumsy in her movements. A lackadaisical sort, with a very measured way of speaking, and slow gestures. She made a big impression, even if she was so leisurely in her ways. When she finished eating, she used to lay her hands across her stomach and declare to whoever was with her:

Aha, now we've eaten
Everything's fine.
May God give health
To us and our masters…
Let them get caught in brambles
So they can't get out
And we can't get in.

The winsome manner in which she acted and talked made her something of a joker.

Often when we went to grandma's after supper or she came to us, La Sagrario and La Pepa would go out for a stroll together, sharing stories about where they were from and the friends they had there.

And La Pepa used to say:

'Señora, all the men round here are so soft; but anyhow if one of them showed an interest…'

Mama took to her at once, and spent a long time listening to her gentle grace and wit.

'Señora, why do we like men if they're so ugly and have so much hair?'

She told us tales of gypsies and olive harvesters, who apparently ate something called 'gachamiga'.

La Sagrario, who was younger than her, used to listen fascinated and made amused comments about everything. She giggled with the high-pitched laugh of a happy child. La Pepa on the other hand laughed more with her face and eyes than with her mouth.

A few months after her arrival, La Sagrario found a very small, really small suitor called Pepe Requinto.

'My goodness, what have I done to have such a little small man fall for me?'

'Child,' La Pepa would tell her, 'hang on to him until you find someone bigger, half a loaf is better than none.'

'But he doesn't even come up to my shoulder... he's thin as a scalpel... ha ha ha!'

'Child, don't be so hard on poor Pepito Requinto. As if size had anything to do with marriage.'

'Ah, Pepa! On our wedding night it'll be like I'm breast-feeding him.'

The following year, when war came, the two girls were already well accustomed to life in La Mancha and to all our customs. La Sagrario was officially engaged to Requinto.

'Pepa my dear, I'm so sorry you don't have a boyfriend though you're so beautiful!'

'Don't you worry about me, there's one on the way.'

Requinto took to walking out with both of them, making incredible attempts to look taller.

'Listen, Requinto, I'm not leaving my Pepa behind for anything. So until she's got a boyfriend, the three of us can go round together.'

Requinto muttered, knitted his brow and made timid allusions to the need for those in love to be alone.

Pepito Requinto had a battered old Ford he had put together with spare parts from all over. Sometimes to give himself airs he would turn up for La Sagrario in the car, which was such a disaster that not even the militiamen had impounded it for the war effort.

When he invited them out for a drive, they both refused. La Sagrario didn't want to give him the wrong impression and have him drive her to her perdition rather than to the castle at Peñarroya as he claimed. And La Pepa told him:

'It's not that I'm scared, Requinto, it's more that I'd be embarrassed to go round in a car like a lady.'

An airfield was built on the outskirts of town, on the far side of the park, and squadrons of twin-engined planes kept arriving to stop over or for training. For a long while the crews were Russian. They were usually tall, fair-haired, and wore leather flying jackets. They smiled at everybody and didn't speak a word of Spanish. They attracted attention, among other things, because they smoked cigarettes at the end of long cardboard holders.

A doctor living opposite us made friends with the first Russians who arrived, and it became a habit that any of them who were in town passed by his house at sunset. They played the piano in his yard, sang songs we thought were very sad, and drank squatting down until they fell over.

The children and maids who lived nearby used to gather in the doctor's gateway to watch the Russians dance, sing and drink. One evening we were with La Pepa in the doorway watching them having fun. They seemed happier than ever. They jumped high into the air. They sweated. The one playing the piano was going crazy. We didn't know, or I don't remember, why they were so happy.

During a pause in the dancing, a very tall, blond Russian who had been peering at us all evening took out a long box of chocolate bars and offered it to La Pepa with a smile, but without saying anything.

La Pepa went bright red and said:

'God go with you, my lad.'

He stood there like an idiot, staring at her. She lowered her eyes. As they remained like that for quite a while, everybody's gaze eventually focussed on this silent idyll.

Finally, still looking down, La Pepa slowly opened the box and offered the Russian and those of us with her a bar each. The Russian bowed as he accepted his. While La Pepa was handing out ours, he stared at her with his blue, metallic, slightly almond-shaped eyes. Then he took another bar from the box, gave her half to bite, and ate the other half himself. All this in the midst of a great silence. As the two of them were chewing on their halves, all the Russians looking on suddenly raised their glasses in the air. One of them brought a glass for La Pepa and another for his comrade; he said something out loud and they all drank, laughing and shouting loudly, apart from La Pepa, who looked startled. But her Russian gave her a gentle push, and she took a sip. Then the dancing and singing started up again. When it was La Pepa's friend's turn to dance, he did so without taking his eyes off her, as if he was dedicating all his bends and leaps to her.

In the days following that famous toast, the neighbourhood was kept entertained by the love affair between the Russian and La Pepa. And for her, that was a wonderful time: she went about her tasks in a daze or as if she could hear tender music in her heart.

'Oh, sweet Jesus,' she said the whole time.

Mama would watch her with those clear, caressing eyes of hers.

One stormy evening the two of them talked for a long while, sitting on the wicker armchairs we used in summer.

'Oh, sweet Jesus, señora. What are they going to say in La Puerta?'

I once saw mama stroke her hair.

At nightfall, when the Russians and the music master, who was a good friend of theirs and lived in the same hotel, arrived at the doctor's house, mama would let La Pepa come out with us to the corner café. The silly girl would wear a flower from mama's flower-bed in her hair, and stand there waiting in her white pinafore and red sandals.

'There's La Pepa waiting for her Russian,' the women would say from their doorways, windows and balconies.

The Russians would arrive in their leather jackets and carrying bottles, together with the music master, who knew how to say *tovarich*. When he saw La Pepa, the tall Russian with the blue-grey eyes would come forward with a broad smile on his face. He would give a deep bow and give her boxes of sweets or tablets of soap. And occasionally fabrics. Then they would stand staring at each other for ages, without a word. At most, he would say in a lilting voice: 'love… love'. Or: 'pretty girl… love.'

At this La Pepa would blush and give him the little flower from her hair. And the Russian would kiss it and put it in his big haversack. All the local kids and nannies would crowd round them, but they didn't seem to care.

'Sweet Jesus, señora, he's called Nicolás Nicolavich.'

'So what, Pepa?'

'Well, what does that Nicolavich mean?'

One evening, Nicolás insisted La Pepa enter the doctor's house, but she
didn't want to. She had felt too ashamed ever since the day of the toast.
The doctor's wife had to come out and convince her.

When we were in the courtyard, Nicolás Nicolavich called for
silence and then addressed everyone solemnly. He said a lot in Russian,
staring at La Pepa. Everyone applauded. Then a very small Russian who
looked like a Mongol from the comic books who acted as their interpreter translated what his comrade had said in a syrupy accent: '…that
Nicolás Nicolavich was pleased to inform everyone that he was going
to make la Pepa his "partner".' And that he was going to dedicate with
all his heart, or something similar, the dance he was about to perform.
And that he – the interpreter – especially wished to congratulate La
Pepa on having the good fortune to become part of 'the great Soviet
family'.

All we Spaniards applauded. The Russians came over one by one
to shake hands with La Pepa. Then Nicolás gave her two big kisses on
the cheeks. La Pepa received all this public declaration without moving,
although she had turned very pale, and was perspiring.

Nicolás Nicolavich gave another shout, and all of a sudden to the
sound of the piano played by someone called Kolsof, he started spinning
round on one leg.

We all clapped our hands in tune like the Russians did.

Drawn by this extraordinary celebration, a lot of people from the
nearby houses came to the gateway and surrounded La Pepa admiringly.
She was still rooted to the spot, breathing heavily through flared nostrils,
her hands folded across her chest like a mannequin.

The next day, La Pepa had a long discussion with La Sagrario and
Requinto. La Sagrario listened open-mouthed to everything her friend
was saying. Requinto looked on snootily. All of a sudden, La Sagrario
burst out laughing and slapped herself on the backside.

'Well, well, my dear Pepa… what are you going to do with a husband you don't understand? A Russian, by Jesus! Ay, Pepa my love, who would credit it?'

Requinto was blowing out clouds of cigarette smoke and looking very superior.

'Nobody knows where their destiny will take them,' he declared finally.

Possibly Requinto would himself have liked to be the protagonist of that famous love story. As we were to discover later on, he was someone with a great desire for fame and distinction.

'You're head over heels in love with him, aren't you, Pepa my love? And you not understanding a word: who would have thought it? Wait till they hear about it in La Puerta...'

Requinto must have been annoyed as well that La Pepa was more head over heels than his Sagrario.

When doña Nati learned from mama the direction Hispano-Russian affairs were taking, in the shape of their modest representatives Nicolás and Pepa, one evening as we were passing in front of her house on the way to granddad's factory, she appeared on her balcony and called us over.

An extremely long conversation ensued, in which naturally doña Nati was the main protagonist, since to begin with all La Pepa did was give a brief account of what she knew about the Russian and her love for him.

Doña Nati spoke her mind. She referred to the differences in climate, language, religion, customs, food and political systems between the two countries. On this last subject she made a real declaration of principle, explaining how she, who was nothing more than a liberal Republican, repudiated all kinds of dictatorship and state intervention. She further rejected any coercion of conscience and thought. She hated all militarism and the farce of a single party. And she could not fail to mention her doubts when it came to Communist theories of equality in economic and social matters. She thought that human beings ought to have complete freedom even when it came to being poor... and yet – and here she made a very theatrical gesture to emphasize the reasons she was about to give – she understood that true love was a sublime emotion capable of overcoming whatever differences might get in the way of normal relationships that were not fired by the divine temperature of passion. And that this – doña Nati still used many romantic turns of phrase – when it was both pure and strong, was sufficient to fuse two beings into one even if they were of very contrasting natures. And that she, La Pepa, would end up learning Russian without noticing it, as though it was knowledge spread by the heart and the bloodstream. As for the temperature, climate, customs and even the political regime, La Pepa would assimilate them all if her love for Nicolás was as intense and unstoppable as it appeared… and that, in conclusion and always taking into account the burning heat of her passion, doña Nati considered she was doing the right thing by marrying her Russian.

When she had finished her speech, La Pepa answered briefly as follows:

She loved Nicolás very much. It had come over her all of a sudden, like a fever she couldn't get rid of. She was sure he was a very good and loving man. She had nothing to lose in Spain. As for cold and hunger, until she arrived in our house she had not known what it meant to have a hot meal every day and to sleep in a bed with sheets. As for religion, the poor life she had led had not allowed her to consider the Spanish god with any great sympathy. And as for political ideas, she didn't understand about dictatorships and freedoms, but of course she thought it was splendid there were no rich and poor because we were all God's children, and she didn't see why some people had more than enough whereas others didn't even have bread to eat… And as an afterthought she added that she, who was destined to marry a half-starving labourer who would have no work for half the year, could never have dreamt of a husband who was not only a commissioned officer but an air force pilot…

Doña Nati listened calmly to La Pepa's defence, questioning some of her assertions with a doubtful gesture, but when she saw how determined she was, she decided not to make any further recommendations, congratulated her and wished her all the best.

The only thing she made La Pepa promise was that she would write with her impressions of Russia so that she could have direct information about that mysterious country.

La Pepa promised she would; doña Nati gave us both a kiss; the two women said farewell, and off we went.

Very early one morning, María la Foca appeared at our front door. She was a poor beggar woman – at that time helped by Red Aid – who traded in the cheapest flesh, was an expert in maids, and lustful old men. She came with a secret message for La Pepa.

She was stocky, her skin so dark it was almost black, with one wandering eye and the other tearing the whole time, and drooping Chinese moustaches. She was leaning on a pitchfork, her greasy grey hair straggling out from beneath the black kerchief she wore as a cap.

Winking her rheumy eye and gulping down her words, she told poor Pepa that the Russians were going home that evening without telling a soul… 'I'm warning you, my child, so you'll get a move on. You don't want that airman to leave you at the altar.'

When we got up that morning, mama found La Pepa on her bed in her room, howling softly to herself like a wounded animal.

Mama sat beside her and gave her encouragement and hope once she had learned that things between the two of them 'had not gone too far'.

'No, señora, no. Like two angels…'

When papa arrived and learned what was going on, he also reassured La Pepa. He told her he had the impression that as far as he could see, Nicolás wasn't going to play any dirty trick on her. La Pepa recovered a little and got up off her bed. Although she carried on with her sniffles, she set about her household chores as usual. Papa said that as soon as he had eaten he would go and visit our doctor neighbour to find out if it was true that the Russians were pulling out. But there was no need.

We were having dessert after lunch when there was a loud banging at the door. La Pepa went as stiff as if she had been punched in the chest. Then she went to open, visibly quaking.

The front door was flung wide open, and the afternoon sun came flooding in. We heard a few short words. Then in the doorway we heard the resolute footsteps of three Russians and the music master who knew how to say *tovarich*. Of course, one of them was Nicolás Nicolavich; another was a high-ranking officer with a fine uniform, and the third was the Mongol with the face out of a comic.

After nodding his head several times in greeting, the interpreter began to speak to papa, while the others, even the music master, remained motionless. Mama asked them to sit down, but they refused, saying they were in a great hurry.

The interpreter said that the squadron had received orders to return to its base in Russia that same day. That Nicolás was a perfect gentleman, and had asked the squadron leader for permission to take La Pepa with him, as he would probably never be returning to Spain. His superior had said it was essential La Pepa had papa's permission to leave, as he seemed to be her guardian or relative – they did not recognize the master–servant relation, which had been abolished in their country by the glorious 1917 revolution. And that the commander wanted papa to confirm his permission verbally and by signing the piece of paper they had placed on the table.

Papa told the interpreter that La Pepa was an adult and so was free to marry whomever she chose. That if she was in agreement he himself, aware of her feelings towards Nicolás Nicolavich, had no objection. So then, with great formality, the interpreter asked Pepa if she wanted to go to Russia with Nicolás that same evening, and there be joined to him in marriage according to the laws of that country. Without a moment's hesitation, La Pepa said she did. She put her hand on Nicolás' shoulder, and the pilot, still standing to attention, encircled her waist.

Papa was bold enough to say to Pepa that he assumed she had considered that she had never left Spain and was now going to discover a land that was different in every way.

The interpreter did not let him finish, interjecting with great pride that Pepa's destiny could not be rosier. She would be a Soviet citizen. The wife of a valiant officer in the USSR's air force… 'what you call here a real lady'.

Papa didn't pay much attention to this speech, but asked Pepa if her family knew anything about all this. She told him she only had one brother, and that she would write to him that afternoon to tell him about her journey.

Papa signed the paper written in Russian that he was told gave his authorization for Pepa to leave the country. It also had to be signed by the mayor, the town's military commander and I don't know who else. The Russians then bade papa and mama farewell, having agreed that Nicolás would come to fetch La Pepa two hours later, because at seven that evening the squadron would be taking off for its destination in Russia. La Pepa would be flying in the twin-engined plane that Nicolás piloted.

News got round, and people began arriving to say goodbye to Pepa. She was ready very quickly; the only luggage she took was a small painted cardboard suitcase. La Sagrario wept disconsolately.

'Ay, my Pepa!... my Pepa... in an aeroplane... To Russia!... How awful!... Ay, my Pepa, what good luck!'

That was how poor Sagrario went from lamentation to envy, with an inconsistency that was as infantile as it was amusing.

The silent Requinto, visibly upset, was smoking furiously.

'What luck, Pepa! The wife of a commissioned military.'

Pepe Requinto had not been called up because he wasn't tall enough. When he heard this he gave Sagrario a look of fury.

With a flower in her hair, La Pepa was smiling, still clutching her small suitcase.

Everybody had something to say, and they all congratulated her, although sometimes they added a word of warning.

'Russia! That must be further than France.'

'Be careful, my child,' Sister Mariana told her. 'They're all heretics there.'

'Who would have thought it, from grape-picker to pilot!'

Mama gave her a pair of antique ear-rings, and granddad and Lillo came with a big bouquet of flowers. La Pepa stroked our heads and said she would write.

It wasn't long before a car drew up outside our door. In came Nicolás wearing a leather overall and a balaclava. The music master was with him.

'My, my,' he said to La Pepa. 'You've become a real *tovarich*.'

Nicolás had a purple gabardine over his arm and was holding a little hat of the same colour. He offered them to La Pepa for the aeroplane. She tried them on at once.

'Ay, Pepa, aren't you beautiful!' said La Sagrario, stroking the fabric.

Requinto was staring at the ground, seething with indignation.

When she tried the clothes on, La Pepa was transformed. She looked like a real young lady. Nicolás gave her a gentle kiss on the forehead. Then he shook hands with everyone, smiling all the time and muttering a few words in Russian and Spanish. All we understood was 'adiós... adiós'.

La Pepa allowed everyone to embrace her, and gave mama lots and lots of kisses.

The music master presented her with a lined piece of paper he said was a pasadoble he had composed for the two of them, entitled 'The Russian Bride'.

Nicolás eventually took La Pepa in his arms, and led her out to the car.

There were more waved goodbyes as the car started up. Behind everyone else, granddad said:

'Damn it, damn it, who would have thought it...?'

Very early the next morning, we saw the extremely unusual sight of granddad sitting in our courtyard talking to mama. He looked indignant. He had his arms folded across his chest and was nodding his head a lot, lips pursed.

'That blasted girl.'

'I blame Requinto,' said mama.

I eventually gathered that earlier that morning there had been no sign of La Sagrario; her bed had not been slept in, and her clothes and suitcase were not in her room.

Granddad had reported her as missing, and it seemed enquiries were underway, although what had happened was plain for all to see.

Granddad was livid:

'After all we've done for that girl... Where can she have got to?'

After listening to him for a long while without saying a word, mama said, almost smiling:

'Requinto has eloped with her. No doubt about it.'

'The devil he has... so he's eloped with her. Why? Was anyone against them getting married?'

'He was jealous of the Russian.'

'You think so?'

'I'm sure of it.'

'I'll see about that.'

And granddad shot off to heaven knows where.

By mid-day everything had been cleared up. Some soldiers known as 'scouts' based here during the war had discovered Sagrario and Pepito Requinto at the inn in Argamasilla de Alba, six kilometres from our town. That was where the petrol in Requinto's battered Ford had run out.

They came home three days later, but didn't dare come to see my family. Granddad had to go and find them and take them in front of the judge to marry them.

Later he told his friends:

'Requinto's Ford was the only vehicle those damned militiamen should have requisitioned.'

He added:

'And that idiot Requinto is pleased as Punch with his adventure. As if he had taken her into the stratosphere.'

The story ended with a commentary by doña Nati about Sagrario and La Pepa:

'It was God's will that their lives ran in parallel.'

⤻

Francisco García Pavón was born in 1919 in Tomelloso, a small town in the province of Ciudad Real in La Mancha. Pavón spent the war in his home town, a Republican stronghold. His stories of the period are collected in *Los*

Liberales (1965) and *Los Nacionales* (1977), which shine an acerbic, ironic light on both sides. García Pavón is best known for his novels set in Tomelloso that feature Plinio, the local head of police, who is equally at home solving a murder as the theft of a ham. A Spanish Maigret, Plinio was made into a very popular television series. Plinio's fame was a mixed blessing for Pavón, who failed to get for his literary fiction the success it deserved; he was always known as the man who invented Plinio and the founder of the crime novel in Spain. He died in Madrid in 1989. This story from *Los Liberales* is included in the excellent anthology of Civil War stories *Partes de Guerra*, edited by Ignacio Martínez de Pisón.

CURZIO MALAPARTE

THE TRAITOR

from Malaparte's journal, Paris, 1948

translated by Walter Murch

IN FEBRUARY 1942 during the siege of Leningrad I found myself attached to General Edqvist, the commander of a division of Finnish troops stationed near Lake Ladoga. One morning he asked me to pay him a visit.

We have just taken eighteen Spanish prisoners, he said.

Spanish? I said. *Now you're at war with Spain?*

I don't know anything about that, he said. *But I have eighteen prisoners who speak Spanish and claim they are Spanish, not Russian.*

Very strange.

We have to interrogate them. Of course, you speak Spanish.

No, actually I don't.

Well, you're Italian, so you're more Spanish than I am. Go interrogate them.

I did as I was told. I found the prisoners under guard in barracks. I asked whether they were Russian or Spanish. I spoke in Italian, slowly, and they answered in Spanish, slowly, and we understood each other perfectly.

We are soldiers in the Soviet army, but we are Spanish.

One of them went on to say that they were orphans of the Spanish Civil War; their parents had been killed in the bombardments and reprisals. One day they were all put on board a Soviet ship in Barcelona and sent to Russia, where they were fed and clothed, where they learned a trade, and where they eventually became soldiers in the Red Army.

But we are Spanish.

In fact, I remembered reading at the time that the Russians had evacuated thousands of Red Republican children to the USSR to save them from the bombardments and famine of the Spanish Civil War.

Are you members of the Communist Party? I asked.

Naturally.

Well, keep quiet about it. You've told me, and for the moment that's enough. Don't tell anyone else. Do you understand?

No, we don't understand.

That doesn't matter. If I stop to think about it, I don't understand it either. It's just that I think it would be better if you didn't tell anyone else you are members of the Communist Party.

No, we can't accept such a compromise. We were taught to tell the truth. There is nothing wrong about being Communist. We won't hide the fact that we are Communists.

All right, do as you wish. Meanwhile, you should know that the Finnish people are honest and humane, that among the men in the Finnish army there are many Communists but they are fighting against the Russians who invaded their country in 1939. So being Communist or not has no fundamental importance, that's what I want to say. But you understand me, I think.

No, we don't. We understand you are spouting propaganda, that's all.

No, that's not all. You should know that I will do everything possible to make sure you are not harmed. Do you understand?

Yes.

All right then. Goodbye. I will come and see you tomorrow.

I found General Edqvist and told him about my conversation.

What can we do? the general asked me. *You know, their situation is extremely precarious. They are Communists, Spanish volunteers in the Red Army. Of course they were children when they were evacuated, so they aren't responsible for the education they were given. If it were up to me, I would help them. But under the circumstances, the best thing would be for you to telegraph your friend de Foxá, the Spanish ambassador in Helsinki. Ask him to come at my request. I will turn the prisoners over to him and he can do what he wants with them.*

I sent a cable to de Foxá: *Have eighteen Spanish prisoners come quickly take them in consignment.*

Two days later, during a blizzard, de Foxá arrived in a sleigh, the temperature forty-two degrees below zero. He was half-dead with cold and lack of sleep. As soon as he saw me he shouted:

What do you think you're doing? Why did you telegraph me? What can I do with eighteen Spanish Red Army soldiers? Put them up at the embassy? Now I have to sort things out. You are a meddler.

And you are the Spanish ambassador.

Yes, but of Franco's Spain. And these kids are Communists. At any rate, I'll do what I can. But I would really like to know why you got mixed up with this.

He was furious. But de Foxá had a good heart, and I knew that he would do everything possible to help. He went to see the prisoners, and I tagged along.

I am the ambassador of Franco's Spain, de Foxá said to them. *I am Spanish, you are Spanish, I came to help. What can I do for you?*

For us? Nothing, said the prisoners. *We don't want to have anything to do with a representative of Franco's Spain.*

Do you think this is some kind of a joke? It took me two days and two nights to get here and now you're sending me away? Nevertheless, I'll do everything in my power to help you. Francisco Franco knows how to forgive.

Franco is our enemy. He killed our parents. We're just asking you to leave us alone.

De Foxá went to find General Edqvist.

They're stubborn, he said. *But I will do my duty anyway. I'll telegraph the ministry in Madrid for instructions, and then we'll do whatever Madrid says.*

The next day, de Foxá prepared to leave for Helsinki.

Mind your own business, you understand? he said, getting into his sleigh. *It's your fault that I'm in this jam, you hear me?*

Adiós, Agustin.

Adiós, Malaparte.

A few days later, one of the prisoners fell ill. The doctor said: *Inflammation of the lungs. Very dangerous.*

We have to let de Foxá know, said General Edqvist.

So I telegraphed de Foxá: *One prisoner sick, very serious, come quickly with medicine chocolate cigarettes.*

Two days later, de Foxá arrived in his sleigh. He was furious.

Now what have you done? he shouted as soon as he saw me. *Is it my fault that this kid got sick? What can I do? I am alone in Helsinki, you know, without an attaché – no assistants, nothing, I have to do everything myself. And you make me snowshoe around Finland in a blizzard, all because of your meddling.*

Listen, he's sick, he's dying, it's good that you're here. You represent Spain.

All right, all right, let's go and see him.

De Foxá had brought a huge amount of medicine, food, cigarettes, warm clothes. He really did things royally, my old pal Agustin.

The sick soldier recognized de Foxá, and even smiled. His comrades, though, stood back silent and hostile, staring at Agustin with disdain and hatred.

De Foxá stayed for two days, then he went back to Helsinki. Before getting in his sleigh, he said:

Malaparte, why do you keep getting mixed up with things that don't concern you? When will you learn to just leave me in peace? You aren't Spanish, you know. Leave me alone.

Adiós, Agustin.

Adiós, Malaparte.

Three days later, the soldier died of his inflammation. General Edqvist summoned me:

I could have him buried in the Finnish custom. But I think it would be better to let de Foxá know. After all, this soldier was Spanish. What do you think?

Yes, we should tell de Foxá. It would be the diplomatic thing to do.

And so I sent a telegram: *Soldier just died come quick need to bury.*

Two days later, de Foxá arrived. He was furious.

Will you stop harassing me? he shouted as soon as he saw me. *This is driving me crazy! Of course once you let me know that this kid is dead and has to be buried, it's impossible for me not to come. But what if you just hadn't told me? It's not as if my coming here is going to revive him.*

No, but you are Spain. We can't just bury him like a dog, in these woods, far from his country, from Spain. At least, with you here, everything is different, you know? It's as if all of Spain is here.

Naturally, said de Foxá. *That's why I came. But why do you get mixed up in these things? You are not Spanish, válgame Dios!*

He has to be buried properly, Agustin. That's why I contacted you.

Yes, I know, I know. Let's move on. Where is he?

We went to see the poor kid, who was laid out in the barracks surrounded by his comrades. They stared at de Foxá with a somber, almost menacing defiance.

We will bury him, said de Foxá, *according to Catholic ritual. Spaniards are Catholic. I want him to be buried like a true Spaniard, a good Spanish soldier.*

We will not allow that, said one of the prisoners. *Our comrade was an atheist, as are all of us. This must be honored. We will not permit him to be buried as a Catholic.*

I represent Spain, and the deceased was Spanish, a Spanish citizen. I will have him buried as a Catholic. Do you understand?

No, we don't.

I am the ambassador of Spain, and I will do my duty! If you don't understand me, I don't care.

And with that, de Foxá turned and went outside.

Agustin, my friend, I said, *General Edqvist is a gentleman. He wouldn't like it if you forced your opinions on a dead man. Finnish people are freethinkers, they will not understand your position. We have to find some compromise.*

Yes, but I am Franco's ambassador! I cannot bury a Spaniard without Catholic ritual. Mi Dios! Why didn't you just go ahead and bury him without me? You see what you've done, with your obsession for getting mixed up in things that don't concern you?

All right, don't worry, it will all turn out for the best.

We went to see the general.

Evidently, said the general, *if the deceased was a Communist, an atheist, as his comrades say and as I believe he was, it won't be possible to bury him as a Catholic. I am aware, however, that the ambassador represents Spain, and can't officiate at a burial without Catholic rites. What shall we do, I wonder?*

I suggested that we send for the only Catholic priest in Helsinki, an Italian. (There was also a Catholic bishop in Helsinki, from the Netherlands, but it was unthinkable to ask a bishop to come to the front.) So we telegraphed the priest, and two days later he arrived. He was from upper Lombardy – a highlander, very simple, direct, and pure. He grasped the situation immediately and set about arranging things for the best.

The burial took place the next day. In a clearing in the woods where the little cemetery was located, a grave had been blasted by dynamite out of the frozen earth. A group of Finnish soldiers was arranged along one side of the grave, and the flag of Franco's Spain had been placed at the bottom. The snow covering the ground nearby glowed softly in the milky daylight. The coffin was carried by four of the prisoners, followed in procession by Ambassador de Foxá, General Edqvist, myself, the Spanish prisoners, and finally by a few Finnish soldiers. The priest kept himself apart, about fifty feet away. His lips moved, reciting the prayers for the dead – but in silence, out of respect for the opinions of the deceased. When the coffin was lowered into the grave, the Finnish soldiers, all Protestants, discharged their rifles. General Edqvist and the Finnish officers and soldiers all saluted with elbows bent, as did I; Ambassador de Foxá saluted with his arm straight out, palm flat, in the Fascist manner; and the comrades of the deceased also held their arms straight out, but with fists closed.

The next day de Foxá prepared to leave. Before settling into his sleigh for the ride back, he took me aside and confided:

I want to thank you for all you've done. You've been very thoughtful and considerate. Excuse me if I was angry, but you know… You are always getting mixed up in things that don't concern you!

A few days passed. The prisoners waited for the response from Madrid, which did not come. General Edqvist grew increasingly nervous.

You know, he said, *I can't keep these men here much longer. A decision has to be made: either Spain takes them, or I send them to a concentration camp. Their situation is delicate. It is better to hold them here, but I can't keep them forever.*

Have a little patience. We will get a response.

The response arrived: *Only those prisoners who declare themselves to be Spanish, who recognize the government of Francisco Franco, and who express the desire to return to Spain, will be recognized as Spanish citizens.*

Go and explain the situation to them, said General Edqvist.

We do not recognize the government of Franco, the prisoners said, *and we do not want to return to Spain.*

I respect the firmness of your opinions, I said, *but you should appreciate how delicate your predicament is. If you admit to fighting as part of the Red Army, you will all be shot. The laws of war are the laws of war. So make it possible for me to help you. Consider this carefully. Basically, you are Spaniards. All the Republicans still in Spain have accepted the legitimacy of Franco. They lost the game, and their loyalty to their cause does not prevent them from realizing that Franco won. Do what the Republicans in Spain have done. Accept your defeat.*

There are no more Republicans in Spain. They have all been shot.

Where did you hear that story?

We read it in the Soviet newspapers. We will not recognize the Franco regime. We would rather be shot by the Finnish than by Franco.

Listen, I've had it with you, with Communist Spain, with Fascist Spain, with Russia! But I can't abandon you, I will not abandon you. I will do everything in my power to help. If you don't want to recognize the Franco regime, I will sign the declarations in your name. That will be perjury, but it will save your lives. Understand?

No. We will say that you forged our signatures. We just want you to leave us alone! Don't get involved in things that don't concern you. Are you Spanish? No. So why are you getting involved in this?

I am not Spanish, but I am a man, a Christian, and I will not abandon you. I repeat: let me help you. You will go back to Spain, and once you are there you will act like all the rest, like all the other Republicans who have accepted defeat. You are young, and I will not let you die.

Just leave us alone!

I went away, dispirited.

We have to tell de Foxá, General Edqvist said. *Telegraph him that he needs to come and settle this situation.*

I telegraphed de Foxá: *Prisoners refuse come quick persuade them.*

Two days later, de Foxá arrived. The north wind blew with unusual violence; de Foxá was covered with frost. As soon as he saw me, he shouted:

Again! Why telegraph me? What good did you think it would do? These kids won't listen to me. You don't know the Spanish. They are as stubborn as the mules of Toledo.

Go and talk to them, I said. *Perhaps…*

Yes, yes I know. That's why I came. But really, Malaparte…

He went to see the prisoners, and I accompanied him. They were resolute. De Foxá pleaded with them, cajoled them, threatened them. Nothing worked.

So we will be shot. And then? they said.

And then I will have you buried as Catholics! shouted de Foxá boiling with rage, tears in his eyes. Agustin was a good man, and he was suffering from this magnificent and terrible stubbornness.

You would not do that, said the prisoners. *Usted es un hombre honesto.* They were moved as well, in spite of themselves.

In turmoil, de Foxá prepared to leave. He urged General Edqvist to hold the prisoners a bit longer, and to do nothing without telling him. Once he was installed in his sleigh, he turned to me:

You see, Malaparte, it's your fault I am in such a state. I don't want to think of the fate of these poor kids. I admire them, I am proud of them – real Spaniards. Yes, they are real Spaniards, loyal and brave. You know...?

There were tears in his eyes, and his voice trembled.

We have to do whatever we can to save them. I am counting on you, he said.

I will do my best. I promise I won't let them die. Adiós, Agustin.

Adiós, Malaparte.

I went every day to talk to the prisoners, trying to persuade them, but it was hopeless.

Thank you, they would say, *but we are Communists, and will never recognize Franco.*

A few days later, General Edqvist called for me.

Go and see what is happening with the prisoners. They have almost killed one of their comrades. We don't know why.

I went to see the prisoners. One of them was sitting by himself in a corner of the room, covered with blood, guarded by a Finnish soldier armed with a *Suomi-konepistooli,* the famous Finnish submachine gun.

What have you done to this man?

He's a traitor, they answered. *Un traidor.*

Is this true? I said to the wounded man.

Yes. I am a traitor. I want to return to Spain. I can't take it any more. I don't want to die. I want to go back to Spain. I am Spanish. I want to go back to Spain.

He is a traitor! Un traidor! said his comrades, looking at him with stares full of hate.

I had *el traidor* placed by himself in another barrack, and telegraphed de Foxá: *One soldier wants to return to Spain come quick.* Two days later, de Foxá arrived. He was blinded by the snow; his face had been pelted by chunks of ice which the hooves of the horses had chipped from the frozen road.

What are you doing? Why do you keep meddling in things that don't concern you? When will you stop harassing me with this nonsense? Where is this soldier?

Over there, Agustin.

All right, let's go see him.

El traidor welcomed us in silence. He was a boy of about twenty, blond, with blue eyes, very pale. He was blond the way Spaniards are blond, he had blue eyes the way Spaniards are blue-eyed. He began to cry. He said: *I am a traitor. Yo un traidor. But I can't take it any more. I don't want to die. I want to go back to Spain.* He cried, and his eyes were full of fear, hope, supplication.

De Foxá was moved.

Stop crying, he said. *We will send you back to Spain. You will be welcomed there. You will be pardoned. It wasn't your fault if the Russians made you into a Communist. You were just a kid. Don't cry.*

I am a traitor, said the prisoner.

We are all traitors, de Foxá said brusquely, quietly.

The next day, de Foxá had him sign the declaration and prepared to leave. Before doing so, he went to see General Edqvist.

You are a gentleman, he said. *Give me your word that you will help the rest of these poor kids. They would rather die than renounce their beliefs.*

Yes, they are good kids, said General Edqvist. *I am a soldier, and I admire courage and loyalty even in our enemies. I give you my word. Besides, I agree with Marshal Mannerheim: they will be treated as prisoners of war. Don't worry, I will answer for their lives.*

De Foxá shook General Edqvist's hand in silence, choked by emotion. When he was settled in his sleigh, he smiled, finally:

At last, he said, *you are done annoying me. I'll telegraph Madrid, and as soon as I have an answer, we'll know where things stand. Thank you, Malaparte.*

Adiós, Agustin.

Adiós.

A few days later, the answer came from Madrid. The prisoner was taken to Helsinki, where Spanish officers were waiting for him. *El traidor* was flown to Berlin, and on from there to Spain. It was clear that the Spanish authorities wanted to make something out of this. The prisoner was overwhelmed with care and attention, and he took it all joyfully.

Two months later, I returned to Helsinki. It was spring. The trees were covered with a foam of tender green leaves, birds singing in their branches. I went to fetch de Foxá from his villa at Brunnsparken, and we strolled along the Esplanade, heading towards Kämp. The sea was so green it seemed also to be bursting with leaves, and the little island of Suomenlinna was white with the wings of seagulls.

And the prisoner, el traidor? Any news?

Again? shouted de Foxá. *Why do you keep meddling in this business?*

I did something to help save his life, I said.

De Foxá told me that *el traidor* had been warmly welcomed in Madrid. He was paraded around, and the people said: *See this handsome boy? He was a Communist, he fought with the Russians, he was taken prisoner on the Russian front. But he wanted to come home, to Spain. He has recognized Franco. He is a brave boy, a good Spaniard.*

He was taken to the cafés, the theaters, bullrings, stadiums, cinemas. But he said: *You think this is a café? You should see the cafés in Moscow.* And he laughed:

This is a theater? A cinema? You should see what they have in Moscow! And he laughed. They took him to the stadium. He shouted out:

This is a stadium? You should see the stadium in Kiev.

And he laughed. Everyone turned to look at him, and he shouted:

You think this is a stadium? The stadium in Kiev, now that's a stadium! And he laughed.

Do you understand now? said de Foxá. *Do you finally understand? It's your fault they were furious with me at the ministry. It's all your fault. That should teach you to meddle in things that don't concern you!*

But el traidor – what did they do with him?

What did you want them to do with him? Nothing! They didn't do anything with him, said Agustin with a strange voice. *Why are you always getting involved?*

Then he smiled: *Anyway, they buried him as a Catholic.*

∽

Curzio Malaparte was born Kurt Erich Suckert in Tuscany in 1898. Promoted to captain during the First World War, Malaparte joined the Partito Nazionale Fascista and took part in Mussolini's March on Rome in 1922. In 1926, encouraged by the idea of the Fascist New Man, he took the name Malaparte in homage to (Napoleon) Bonaparte. *Coup d'Etat: The Technique of Revolution*, a book published in 1931 that was critical of both Hitler and Mussolini, got Malaparte into trouble with the Fascist authorities and stripped of party membership. In 1941, he was sent to the Finnish and Russian fronts by *Corriere della Sera* to cover the war – his experiences in eastern Europe provide the material for his great war 'novel' *Kaputt*, a collection of journalism, *The Volga Rises in Europe*, and brilliant short stories that include 'The Traitor' ('*El Traidor*'). After the war, Malaparte moved to the left and joined the Italian Communist Party. An admirer of Chairman Mao, Malaparte fell ill on a visit to China in 1957. He died in Rome in 1958. His house, Casa Malaparte on the island of Capri, is the star of Godard's 1963 film *Contempt* (*Le Mépris*) – the modernist villa and Brigitte Bardot are a marriage made in heaven. 'The Traitor' is included in *The Bird that Swallowed Its Cage: The Selected Writings of Malaparte* adapted and translated by Walter Murch.

MERCÈ RODOREDA

MOVIE MATINÉE

translated by Peter Bush

SUNDAY, 2 JUNE. This afternoon Ramon and I went to the Rialto. By the time we were inside we'd already fallen out and while he was buying the tickets, I felt like crying. And it was all over something stupid, I know. This is how it all started. Yesterday I went to bed at one. I'd stayed awake until midnight because the electric blue thread had gone missing and without it I couldn't finish the smock. And mother was grumbling: 'You never remember where you leave things, just like your father,' making me feel even more upset. Father glared at her and went on squeezing the blackheads on his nose by the table, the hand mirror propped up against the bottle of wine. Finally I did find the thread and could finish the smock. However, I still had to iron my blouse and skirt. I was exhausted when I got into bed and thought about Ramon for a bit until I fell asleep. Today when he rang the bell after lunch, I was ready and dressed, with three roses in my hair into the bargain. He walked as if he was crazy and didn't give my blouse and skirt that had been such a bother to iron a single glance, he went over to my father, who was half-dozing in the rocking-chair, and told him: 'Figueres says better not to fill in any form: I'd been thinking they must have lied to you.' Father opened one eye, shut it straight away, and started rocking. But he carried on talking as if he didn't realize he was annoying father, harping on about how refugees had to do this and that and all the while

not a glance in my direction. In the end he said: 'Let's be off, Caterina.'
And he took my arm and we went out. I told him: 'You're another one
always saying things to upset him. You're a pain.' However, that was the
least of it. Halfway there we were walking and still not saying a word
when all of a sudden he let go of my arm. Oh, I immediately saw what
that was all about: Roser was approaching along the pavement, going
in the opposite direction. He's always telling me that he and Roser had
only had a bit of fun. Yes, right, a bit of fun. But he'd let go of my arm.
She walked by stiffly, not even looking our way. I told him, 'Anyone
would think she was your fiancée and not me.' (I've just noticed that
I've written this without a break, and my teacher always told me to start
a new paragraph now and then. But as I'm only writing this for myself,
it makes no odds.)

So I still felt like crying when he was buying the tickets, and the
cinema warning bell made me feel even sadder. I wanted to cry because
I love Ramon and I like him when he's got the scent of quinine he gets
when he's been to the barber for a haircut, even though I'd rather he
wore his longer and looked more like Tarzan. I'm sure I'll get married,
because I'm pretty, but it's *him* I want to marry. Mother always says he'll
end up in Guyana with all his black marketing. But he won't spend his
whole life doing that, and he says it means we can get married quicker.
And perhaps he's right.

We sat down without exchanging a word and the picture-house
reeked of Zotal disinfectant. First it was the news: a girl skating, then
a lot of bicycles, and after that four or five gentlemen sitting around a
table and then *he* started whistling and stamping his feet like a mad man.
The gentleman sitting in front turned round and they kept on arguing
until the news finished. Then they showed a cartoon that I didn't like at
all: there was a load of talking cows. In the interval we went to the bar to
drink a glass of Pampre d'Or and he met a friend there who asked him if
he had any packets of Camel and Nylon stockings and he said he would
next weekend because he'd be going to Le Havre. I really suffer when he
goes away because although I never say anything, I always think they'll
catch him and put him in handcuffs.

The black market was to blame for the fact we missed the start of the main film and when we went to take our seats, everybody grumbled because my wooden soles squeak a lot even if I walk very slowly. The characters in the film really were in love. I can see we don't love each other in the same way. There was a spy and a soldier and at the end they executed both of them. I think films are very nice because if the characters who are in love are unhappy you feel a bit sorry for them but you think it will all turn out fine; now when I'm in that state I *never* know if it will all turn out fine. And if, like today, there's an unhappy ending, everybody is sad and thinks: what a pity! On days when I'm feeling desperate, though nobody knows, it's much worse. And if they did, they'd all laugh. When it got to the saddest part, he put his arm round my shoulder and that's when we stopped being angry with each other. I said: 'Don't go to Le Havre this week.' And a lady behind went: 'Shush.'

I've just read everything I've just written and I can see it's not really what I wanted to say. I always have this problem: I describe things I think are important at the time and then realize they aren't. For example, the business about the blue thread I couldn't find last night. Then, anyone who read this diary would say I think Ramon doesn't love me when I believe he really does, even if it seems he's only got buying and selling rubbish on his mind. But even that's not what I really wanted to say. What I'd like to know how to say is the fact that, although I'm always sad, deep down I *am* happy. If anyone read that, they'd laugh like crazy. Yes, I know I'm a chump, and father always tells me he's a simple soul, and that's what makes me even sadder because I think we'll both end up a couple of miserable souls. But, you know…

⸺

Born in Barcelona in 1908, **Mercè Rodoreda**, a star of Catalan writing, is best know for her novel *In Diamond Square*, about a working-class woman surviving in Barcelona during the Civil War. The novel is an amazing collage of the everyday set against a backdrop of historical events that shaped the 20th century. Rodoreda said she based *In Diamond Square* on the story 'Movie

Matinée' included here. Although she refused the label feminist, Rodoreda has great empathy for the conditions in which women survived in wartime – like the photographer Gerda Taro, she sees what the male gaze neglects. In 1937, Rodoreda started to work for the autonomous government of Catalonia; it is said that at this time she had a relationship with Andrés Nin, Catalan intellectual and leader of the POUM. Nin was arrested in June 1937, tortured and executed under direct orders from Stalin. At the end of the war, Rodoreda went into exile, first in France and then in Switzerland. She returned to Catalonia in 1972 and died in Girona in 1983. She is now a Catalan national treasure with Barcelona enriched with libraries named after her and a sculpture in Diamond Square. 'Movie Matinée' is included in Rodoreda's collection *Vint-i-dos contes* published in 1958.

JUAN GOYTISOLO

THE EMPTY BLACK BAG

from *Forbidden Territory*

translated by Peter Bush

I REMEMBER MY MOTHER GOING ROUND the nearby farmhouses in search of food. During my father's illness, the factory committee paid his salary regularly; but the money was gradually losing its value and as the war advanced and the situation in the Republican camp got worse, the ancient barter economy reappeared. We would go with my mother and brothers and sister to visit Aunt Rosario's family in her flat in the main square in the village or we would walk round the outskirts, taking the road to Espinelves, the path to la Noguera, or one of the shortcuts that curled down to the hidden springs nearby. We often got together to play hide-and-seek with other children in the spacious garden of the Bioscas' villa or we would go to their house for a Charlie Chaplin film show from a Baby Pathé projector. I can remember a soirée of film and poetry when someone pathetically inspired declaimed poems by Gustavo Adolfo Bécquer. At home, I read the illustrated stories my mother gave me and I began to draw and write 'poetry' in an exercise book. My future career as a writer was thus inaugurated at the age of six: the lines poured out and, once adorned with my own scribbled illustrations, I was quick to show them to visitors with a precocious feeling of pride.

While I write these lines, I am trying to hold steady the few, faithful memories of my mother: the time she had an argument with father – I don't know why – and she wiped her nose with her handkerchief; the day I was feeling uncared for by her and I said that I would like to fall ill too, since she was entirely absorbed in caring for her husband, and, unable to restrain herself, she gave me the smack I deserved; the afternoon at my aunt and uncle's when I learned of the accident in which cousin Paco, Aunt María's son, had lost a leg, cut off by a tram while he was roller-skating: Aunt Rosario asked me to tell her only about 'some bad news,' without giving any specific detail what it was about and, while my mother got dressed and ran with me to her house, I selfishly enjoyed my momentary power over her gradually suggesting, in my own way, all I knew about the drama.

Until then the civil war and its disasters had distant, indirect repercussions on my awareness. The small colony of well-off Barcelona bourgeois lived in Viladrau provisionally on the margin of the conflict and maintained a public attitude of prudent neutrality. Only a few ironic comments – the obligatory reference to the fact that Bono, a well-known ladies' hairdresser who had also taken refuge in the village, was picked up weekly by an official car in order to do the hair and beautify the wives of government and *Generalitat* ministers – allowed one to read their real feelings. But, out of earshot of any indiscreet listeners, tongues would be unleashed. At night, we used to be visited by Lolita Soler, a woman in her forties, a gaunt spinster from a monarchist military family, who had lived the siege of Madrid before being evacuated to Catalonia to be stranded like us in that isolated mountain spot. Her bloodcurdling tales of murders, executions, deportations, heroic martyrdoms, recounted in whispers so that we children could not hear her, mingled with encouraging news of the other side's progress, which she apparently intercepted via a crystal radio on the Burgos wavelength. Her tribulations and adventures – which my family thought were exaggerated – aroused endless discussions in the dining room, which continued long after her departure. The precarious situation in which my grandparents lived, the helplessness of Aunt Consuelo, shut up with them in a flat on the Diagonal, the ever more frequent bombing of the city, intensified my mother's state of anxiety, and she was already overwhelmed by four children and a sick husband with no hope of a quick cure. In a letter, which my sister found years after, she told her parents of her fear and worry because of a lack of news after an air attack. Every two or three weeks she would get on the coach that took her to the railway station of Balenyà and, after spending the day with them and doing a little shopping, she would return to Viladrau at night. These ever so brief visits did not stop her worries, however, and after several months they became a kind of ritual.

On the morning of March 17, 1938, my mother started her journey as usual. She left home at daybreak and, although I know the tricks that memory and its fictitious re-creations play, I retain a clear memory of looking out my bedroom window while that woman, soon to become unfamiliar, walked with her coat, hat, and bag, toward the definitive absence from us and from herself: destruction, emptiness, nothing. It no doubt seems suspicious that I should wake up precisely on that day and that, forewarned of my mother's departure by her footsteps or the noise of the door, I should have got up to watch her leave. However, it is a real image and for some time it filled me with bitter remorse: I should have shouted to her, insisted that she give up the visit. It was probably the fruit of a later guilt mechanism: an indirect way of reproaching myself for my inertia, for not having warned her of the imminent danger, and for not attempting the gesture that, in my imagination, could have saved her.

My memory of the frustrated waiting for her to return – my father's growing anxiety, our comings and goings in search of news to our aunt and uncle's house or to the village coach stop – is much more reliable. Two days of tension, anticipatory anguish, unbearable silence, visits from our uncle and aunt, Lolita Soler's sobbing, a round of whispered conversation in my father's room until that sad St. Joseph's holiday when the three brothers and sister were brought together on the outside staircase that descended to the garden and Aunt Rosario, with occasional feeble interruptions from Lolita Soler, told us about the bombing, its victims, how she too had been caught, very seriously injured, leading us gradually, like that bull that has just been stabbed by the *torero* and is now pushed skilfully by his team onto its knees so that the fighter can finish it off with one quick thrust, to the moment when, her voice drowned in tears, ignoring the other woman's pious protests, she uttered the unutterable word, leaving us in a state of bewilderment not because of the grief immediately expressed in sobbing and wailing but rather the inability to take in the brutal truth, still untouched by the bare reality of the fact, and especially its definitive, irrevocable nature.

How her death happened, in exactly which place she fell, where she was taken to, at which moment and in what circumstances her parents recognized her is something that I have never known nor will I ever know. The unknown woman who disappeared suddenly from my life, did so discreetly, far from us, as if to temper delicately the effect that her departure would inevitably have, but thickening at the same time the shadows which would envelop her in the future and turn her into a stranger: the object of guesswork and conjectures, incomplete explanations, and doubtful, undemonstrable hypotheses. She had gone shopping in the center of the city and was caught there by the arrival of the airplanes, near where the Gran Vía crosses the Paseo de Gracia. She was a stranger, also, to those who, once the alert was over, picked up from the ground that woman who was already eternally young in the memory of all who knew her, the lady who, in her coat, hat, and high-heeled shoes, clung tightly to the bag where she kept the presents she had bought for her children, which the latter, days afterward, in suits dyed black as custom ruled, would receive, in silence, from the hands of Aunt Rosario: a romantic novel for Marta; tales of Doc Savage and the Shadow for José Agustín; a book of illustrated stories for me; some wooden dolls for Luis that would remain scattered round the attic without my brother ever touching them.

The empty black bag: all that remained of her. Her role in life, in our life, had finished abruptly before the end of the first act.

Only twenty years later – during the preparations for the editing of Rossif's film, Mourir à Madrid, *the day you and some French friends were viewing a series of Spanish and foreign news and documentary films on the civil war – did the horror that dominated her last moments impose its sharp outline on your consciousness. A weekly news film from the Republican government, in its denunciations of the enemy's aerial attacks on defenseless civilian populations, shows the results of the one suffered by Barcelona on that unforgettable seventeenth of March: alarm sirens, noisy explosions, scenes of panic, ruins, destruction, desolation, cartloads of corpses, hospital beds, wounded comforted by members of the government, an endless line of bodies laid out in the morgue. In the foreground the camera slowly pans the victims' faces and, soaked in cold sweat, you suddenly realize the harsh possibility that the face you fear may suddenly appear. Fortunately, the absent one, with a sense of elegance and modesty, hid in some way to spare you the traumatic, ill-timed reunion. But you were forced to rush from your seat, go to the bar, drink a glass of something, just the time necessary to hide your emotion from the rest and discuss the film with them as if nothing had happened.*

The bond linking that death and the meaning of the civil war would not be apparent to you until the day when, now interested in politics, you began to be fascinated in eye-witness accounts and books on the recent history of Spain. Your religious and family education in the forties had succeeded in breaking the link between the two events. On the one hand, after the collective rosary that followed supper, you quickly prayed in a mechanical, routine fashion three Lord's Prayers for the eternal rest of the absent one's soul; on the other hand, you accepted without any reservations whatsoever the official version of the conflict as rehearsed by radio, newspapers, teachers, relatives, and all around you: a crusade undertaken by healthy, patriotic men against a Republic stained by all kinds of crimes and abominations. The stark, undeniable reality that your mother had been the victim of your side's strategy of terror, a product of cold, hateful calculation, was ignored by your father and the rest of the family. The setbacks the former suffered – imprisonment, illness, widowhood – were, according to him, the work of a band of enemies generically labelled as 'reds.' Deprived of its context, clean and disinfected, your mother's death was thus transformed into a kind of abstraction that, although it exempted the real guilty ones from their responsibility, emphasized conversely for you the unreal confusion of their fate. Although the ease with which this whitewashing operation was carried out may seem suspicious, the closed, conservative circle in which you live, the silent complicity of your home, the difficulty in getting objective information, spotlights once more the uncritical acceptance of the facts. It was only at university, when you befriended a student with ideas hostile to the regime and, thanks to him, got to know the books that told the story of the civil war from an opposite point of view, that the bandage fell from your eyes. Imbued with crude but refreshing Marxist principles – hostile to the reactionary values of your class – you began to focus on the events you experienced marginally from childhood from a very different perspective: Franco's bombs – not the innate evil of the Republicans – were directly responsible for the break-up of your family.

To tell the truth – apart from that belated feeling of historical indignation – the early date of your mother's departure took from her exit any real degree of grief. What was snatched from you then would weigh heavily on your destiny, but the consequences of your orphanhood would only appear later: alienation from the father figure, insipid religiosity, lack of patriotism, an instinctive rejection of any kind of authority, all the elements and features that later would fix your character no doubt have a close relationship to that state. However, to the extent that the affection for your mother vanished with her, you can say quite rigorously that rather than her son, the son of a woman who is and always will be unknown to you, you are a son of the civil war, its Messianism, cruelty, and anger: of the unhappy accumulation of circumstances that brought into the open the real entrails of the country and filled you with a youthful desire to abandon it forever.

You remember now, in the light of what you have just written, the episode with the axe: the destructive rage that overpowered you one morning in Barcelona, a few months after the war, when you were wandering through the house along with Luis.

At the back of the garden, in the space between the garage and a room used as a junk room, there were two cubbyholes for storing wood and coal beneath the space under the staircase that led to the terrace on the first floor. The junk room was crammed with furniture belonging to the family, awaiting, you suppose, the probable move to Torrentbó. You can remember a number of sofas, armchairs, consoles, corner shelves covered in dust and cobwebs where you used to hide to play at ghosts, happy in the midst of that mixture of valuable objects and broken or useless bric-a-brac. This spot had been transformed into your favorite hiding place when you came back from school until the day when, out of temper or whim, you took the axe from the woodpile and with your brother's help proceeded to destroy its contents with ferocious enthusiasm.

Piece of furniture after piece of furniture, with no quarter given, you began to cut legs, arms, backs, chop tables, rip the stuffing out of chairs, break decorations, pull springs, bash chairs, possessed by a cheerful, absorbing sense of inspiration that you would not meet again, you think today, except in the act of creation, the exultant vandalism of adult writing: the pleasure of exorcising the symbols of a society, the conventions of a code suddenly perceived as an obstacle; an intense desire for vengeance against an ill-formed universe; the effusive, primeval impulse linked to the binomial of creation–discreation. What meaning can be given to this sudden, excited, enjoyable act of two brothers who were normally calm yet suddenly overtaken by a plan of destruction whose ultimate explanation was beyond them? A protest, accumulated rage, a desire to retaliate? Or boredom, pure lack of awareness, an attempt to imitate the grown-ups? The original cause of the scene, the swiftness and audacity of its execution, will always be an enigma impossible to resolve. You will then focus your memory on the image of those small boys who, with the blows of the axe, liberate in some way mysterious inner energy, perhaps the unconscious, secret desire to make their voices heard.

Juan Goytisolo, born in Barcelona in 1931, is one of Spain's best-known writers. A bitter opponent of Franco's regime, Goytisolo went into exile in France in 1956, vowing not to return until Franco's death – until which time his novels were banned in Spain. *Forbidden Territory*, his autobiography from which this extract is taken, is, in the words of the *TLS*, 'a moving and sympathetic portrait of how one courageous victim of the Franco régime fought his way out of a cultural and intellectual wasteland, educated himself, and went on to inflict a brilliant revenge on the social system which so isolated and insulted him'. Much of Goytisolo's writing, including the trilogy that comprises *Marks of Identity*, *Count Julian* and *Juan the Landless*, is a celebration of the Arab contribution to Spanish culture which, for Goytisolo, has never recovered from the expulsion of the Moors in 1492. A brilliant essayist and controversial journalist, Goytisolo has lived in Marrakesh for the last twenty years. He was awarded the Cervantes Prize in 2015.

GAMEL WOOLSEY

PUNCTUAL BOMBS

from *Death's Other Kingdom*

T HE IMPROVEMENT IN THE STATE OF THINGS seemed to be continuing, and we began to hope that some arrangement would be come to between the various parties. We even hoped that perhaps the military *coup* had not really come off after all, and also that the Government would be able to dominate the revolutionary forces which seemed to be coming to the front. After all there had been so many military *coups* in Spain and so many revolutions, and so few of them had come to anything. Our village continued perfectly quiet, and in Malaga everything appeared almost normal on the surface, but we began to hear sinister rumours of continual arrests and nightly murders by gangs in the city and also in some of the villages near us.

The Province of Malaga had practically become an independent state with almost the old limits of the Moorish Kingdom of Malaga. The little trains ran but they did not run very far, the posts arrived and went out, but they only went to a few places. Granada, Algeçiras, Cadiz, Seville had all become enemies and everyone thought in provinces – a Spanish habit at the best of times.

'Granada is attacking us,' people said. 'Seville is attacking us.' The capture of a town in the province of Granada was regarded as putting us one up on Granada. We had scored; and it was seriously suggested that the captured town should be incorporated in the Province of Malaga!

This extreme federalism was more important to most of the country people than the class-war aspects of the struggle which some of their leaders were emphasising. They had always thought of the Granadinos as foreigners anyway, and there was nothing very surprising about their turning into active enemies.

Some of the villagers of course were very class-war conscious, and there was one remark which was common at the time which used to annoy me more than I can say. To my irritated ears it used to seem to go on all the time like a sort of chorus, and it was always spoken with maddening self-complacency. It was: 'You can do nothing against the will of the people!' And I used to think that anyone silly enough to make such a remark at such a moment ought not to be allowed any exercise of the will at all. Another remark which was also common and annoyed me only slightly less, and was made with almost equal self-complacency was 'If all the Provinces did their part as *we* have done it would be all over now. But now they want *us* to help them with their work.' I used almost to join Maria in her snort of contempt when some villager who had taken no part in the struggle and had no intention of taking part in it unless it actually broke out in the street he lived in and forced itself in at his front door, used unctuously to produce this piece of wisdom again.

Still I can't help thinking that it was really to the credit of the Malagueñans·that they did not on the whole show any disposition for war. They were people of peace, and wanted to take as little part in this unnecessary struggle as possible. They never made any real attempt even to defend their city, which seems curious in Spain, the country of remarkable sieges. Malaga did not seem to us even at that time likely to be the scene of a second Numantia or Saragossa; and time was to prove that we were right.

But those appalling sieges for which Spain is famous, sieges which seemed designed to show how much human beings can force themselves to endure without even hope to aid them, have always taken place in the *north* of Spain. Numantia, Saragossa, Gerona, the Alcazar at Toledo and of course Madrid, in the present war, and a dozen other sieges which could be named all occurred in the north.

I don't mean to suggest that Andalucians can't be extremely brave: they have proved their bravery in every war they have taken part in. But that extraordinary tenacity of whole populations, that screwing your courage to the sticking point and never wavering again, those forlorn hopes which last not for an hour, but for months of taut agonising endurance, that gaunt stoical holding-out against all rhyme and reason, that sublime, or demoniac, stubborn, desperate insanity of courage seems only to exist in northern Spain out of all the countries in the world.

'The Insurgents can take Malaga any afternoon they feel like it,' I remember Gerald saying at about that time. 'But I don't believe they will take it now, because from a military point of view they ought to get on with their drive north. Malaga isn't of sufficient strategical importance for them to spare the men to take it.' Of course we didn't realise then how many Moors would be brought, much less that there would be foreign intervention on a great scale.

Poor Gerald had had only too much experience of wars, for he had gone to Belgium as a boy of nineteen in the spring of 1915, and not returned to England except for short periods of leave and longer periods spent in hospitals until the summer of 1918 when he finally ceased to be passed for active service at the age of twenty-three. As one of his reasons for living in Spain (besides trying to recover his health) had been that it had been neutral in the last war, and so was not connected in his mind with a period he so much disliked remembering, it seemed curiously hard luck that we should have chosen a house on the edge of an unsuspected volcano.

One hot day when things seemed particularly quiet we heard the really alarming news that several thousand Moors had been brought over.

'I'd bring over an army in canoes!' snorted an English naval officer we happened to meet at the club, in disgust at the inefficiency of the officerless Spanish Government Navy, which seemed usually to be tied up to the dock in Malaga at that time.

The poor old women who hung about the kitchen were dreadfully upset at the news about the Moors, and their chorus of 'Los Moros! Los Moros!' murmured on all day.

'Won't England help us against the Moors?' they used to ask pathetically. I don't think that they ever had the least idea of who was fighting
or why. They had heard of old wars against the Moors, and thought
that those evil days had returned. They had in any case no conception
of what the world consisted of. They lived in a medieval world – there
was Spain, or rather Malaga, and there was the sea, and they had heard
that there were lands beyond the sea; but what lands, or what they were
like, they did not know. When we told them that England was cold
and wet, they replied quite simply and understandingly 'Ah! you live in
high mountains, but there is no doubt plenty of wood to burn there.'
To explain why England was really cold and wet you would have had
to begin at the beginning and reform the school system of Spain sixty
years ago.

And so we could not easily explain why England would not help
them now 'against the Moors' – we were rich, we had plenty of battle-
ships, they had often seen vast grey boats flying the British flag coming
up from the Straits – it would cost us so little – they sighed – and we
sighed too over the impossibility of explaining to these poor creatures
suddenly waking up in the midst of a civil war, why it was that Spaniards
were killing one another.

But there were terrors even greater than the Moors coming for them.
One morning we were quietly sleeping under a grey sky, for it was early
morning and the blackness of the night was fading, when – CRASH! a large
bomb had fallen out of the grey air, and after it came the sharp rattle of
a machine-gun. We leaped from our beds before we even realised what
the dreadful noise was. The loud drone of the plane overhead warned us
that there was still danger about, and we rushed out, calling the servants
as we went, and met Pilar carrying the sleeping Mariquilla and hurrying
down the passage towards our room crying, 'Don Geraldo! Don Geraldo!
What has happened?' There was a second terrific crash as we met, and we
hurried her downstairs where we found Maria and Enrique who had run
in half-dressed from their cottage, and led them all into the big storeroom
where we hung the fruit. Its thick walls and the fact that it had only one
small high window and that its only door opened into a long passage
made it *seem* the safest place anyway.

There were two more terrific crashes, but the next sounded much further away. Maria muttered to herself, I don't know whether prayers or curses, Pilar quietly wept, rocking the sleepy, whimpering Mariquilla in her arms, Enrique as befits a man wrapped his coat stoically about his shoulders. Another crash was obviously at a considerable distance, and Gerald and I rushed up to the balcony to see what was happening.

A big silver-grey plane was hovering at a great height probably trying to hit the planes at the airfield. Artillery and machine-guns had begun to crash and rattle in Malaga. The louder crash of the bursting bombs came at intervals. They left tiny white puffs of smoke in the air as they fell (or were those from shells?). A fire blazed up suddenly near the sea – at the airport? But the planes had dropped all their bombs. Like silver flies they sailed away out to sea, towards Africa. Two little aeroplanes had got up from the field to pursue them, barking and coughing, obviously completely outclassed, but gamely willing to attack these deadly grey strangers. But the grey bombers out-flew them, grew tiny in the distance and disappeared, and the little coughing planes returned. Distant as we were they looked like noisy toys as they sailed in circles and finally settled down.

The next morning promptly at four, bombs again! as punctual and arousing as an alarm clock, and after that we were bombed almost daily for some time, generally in the early morning but sometimes later and occasionally in the afternoon; the night raids came later. After the first raid we all knew what to do, and were downstairs and gathered together in two minutes, but I refused to stay in the storeroom, it seemed to me to resemble a tomb too closely; I preferred the corner of the dining-room though it was obviously not so safe a place, as it had a large window on the patio, but I think we all had an irrational feeling that the bombs would come to the front door instead of the back. Anyway the servants either through that belief or through blind confidence in us joined us in the dining-room and left the safer *despensa* to the more timid of the villagers who came seeking refuge.

For after that first air raid the lower floor of the house was always crowded with refugees. Our big house seemed so much safer to them than their own poor little cottages that all our poor neighbours rushed in with their children at the first rumour that planes were coming, or at the sound of some shots in the distance, and many of them spent almost the entire day in our garden too frightened to go home except to get a little food ready. We had one very large room opening off the patio which we gave up to them completely, and a number of them brought their bedding and slept in it after the night raids began. But as the air raids continued a great many villagers became too frightened to stay in the village during the day, and every morning there was a pathetic stream of frightened people carrying their children and driving their goats, going off to the mountains. I can still see in my mind the touching little Swiss Family Robinson groups and hear their shrill frightened chatter, as they hurried by looking up at the sky as they went fearful of seeing planes approaching.

I found later that Pilar and I had received the same impression from the little groups going to the mountains: we wanted to go too. Not then, but if things got very much worse and if 'the Moors were coming'. We found each other out in this, and used to enjoy planning it all. We decided that we would try to buy a donkey to carry our food and blankets, and a couple of milk goats to take with us, we would grind the maize which we had just harvested to make corn meal mush of, and buy as much flour as we could, and we would take the chickens, but would have to eat them soon as we could not feed them. The chief problem was 'Piggy', Enrique's pig, who like all Spanish swine was practically a household pet – should we take him on the hoof or in the form of hams and sausages? He was still small, but could we find enough acorns to feed him during our Robinson Crusoe life among the cork oaks. I regretfully decided that Piggy probably ought to be turned into sausages.

For I was much attracted by the vision of our expedition to the woods and the wilds accompanied by Platera, two brown nanny goats and Piggy; led by tall, fair Don Geraldo springing actively up the mountain with the goats and followed by severe black-clothed Maria acting as rearguard and turning back to lay a final curse upon the wicked city. Pilar and I could not help feeling that even after Piggy was disposed of, Maria might turn out to be an insoluble difficulty; so we rather tended to leave her out of our dream of desert island life in the sierra.

But often later on when things began to get worse, I used to wander off in my mind to the mountains – I would be sitting by a stream under an ilex tree with Piggy eating up the acorns on the ground, and the donkey and the goats cropping the grey, sweet mountain herbs, while Don Geraldo leaped from rock to rock above us looking for dangers and Enrique gathered sticks for the little fire on which the corn meal was cooking in a black iron pot, and Pilar sang Mariquilla to sleep with a Christmas *copla*.

'The Virgin hung her washing
On the rosemary to dry,
All the birds were singing
And the river running by.'

Or I would imagine that we were just setting out, going further and further away from towns and men, weary and hungry, but climbing higher and higher into the clear, free, mountain air.

Air raids soon became almost a part of normal life. It is strange how quickly you become accustomed to them; and in a curious way when there was no air raid as sometimes happened I *missed* it. I was keyed up to expect it, and if it did not come I felt a sort of flatness. But our raids were not really bad ones, the bombs were usually small and we always felt that unless there was a direct hit on the house just above us, or unless we were hurt by flying splinters or glass, we were fairly safe indoors; and Gerald and I were fortunate in both being of rather philosophic temperament and inclined to feel the bombs probably were not going to hit us and if they were we could not help it – and of course Gerald had had so many worse times in the last war already.

When huge modern bombs are being used I know from experience in Malaga when they were trying to wreck the port with them, it is impossible to be philosophic. The noise and shock are appalling and the feeling that there is no defence anywhere, that whole houses will fall upon you, is horrible.

What I really minded most about the air raids in our village was the terror of the villagers. Our servants were very stoical, but some of the

women lost all control of themselves and sobbed and screamed hysteri-
cally, while the poor children, terrified by the behaviour of their parents
as much as by the unknown horror of the sky, shrieked and sobbed
convulsively. Something I felt then (and am ashamed to have felt) was
a physical repugnance towards these poor frightened creatures, towards
their lack of control which is always an ugly thing to see and to the
sharp fetid smell which fear produces. I felt all the time that my sensa-
tions were meanly fastidious just when I should have felt the strongest
solidarity with my fellow men. But I could not help that instinctive
distaste and withdrawal into myself when outwardly I was being kindest
and most reassuring. But there were times when the pain of these others
melted the thin icicle in my heart (we need no Snow Queen, any of us,
to put one there).

One day one of the village women was caught out of the village by
an air raid while she was taking some food to her husband at the airfield.
Her fear for herself alone in the fields with huge planes hovering overhead scattering death must have been very great, it must have seemed
like a horrible nightmare to her, but her fear for her children was much
greater, and she did not try to take cover, but ran all the way home to
them. They had already come in to us and were crying 'Oh! Mother!
Mother!' sure that she had been killed by the first explosions. When she
rushed in, not having found them at home and desperate with anxiety
and saw them sitting with me, she tried to take a few steps further to
reach them and fell in a fit at my feet. As I knelt on the floor beside her
while she foamed at the mouth and jerked and twisted in convulsions I
felt not the slightest trace of repulsion. She was among the poorest of the
women: she was dirty, emaciated, ugly, unkempt, ill-smelling – everything that man's inhumanity daily makes of man, except unloving or
unloved. But as I sat there holding the poor creature in my arms as she
gradually grew quieter and the fearful upturned eyes closed in uncon-
sciousness, while her daughter sat beside me embracing her mother and
sometimes kissing my helping hands, my mind held no tinge or taint of
distaste, I felt nothing but love – for them and for the millions like them,
the poor, the suffering, the burden bearers of this world.

One morning not long after the raids began we were awakened as usual by the crash of a bomb: it was just beginning to be light. The bombs seemed fairly distant, so we went up on the balcony to see what was happening. The planes were dropping incendiary bombs, trying to hit the petrol tanks and the standing planes at the airfield: they caught the dry grass where they fell and blazed with much white smoke. Presently black smoke poured up from the airfield, probably one of the standing planes had been hit. Gerald brought out his field-glasses.

'I hope Don Carlos is all right,' he said, and then a moment later 'My God! They've hit his house!' Don Carlos was a poor but aristocratic Spanish friend who lived on some land he farmed near the sea, which actually adjoined the airfield. Now his house was hidden by clouds of white smoke.

'Oh! the children!' I said. I imagined them burnt by the bombs, trapped in their rooms.

'We'd better go at once,' Gerald said. I seized a basket and put in bandages, iodine, and a bottle of brandy and Enrique said that he would come with us as we might need him, and we set off.

I have to confess (and I am again ashamed to confess it) that I enjoyed that walk. There was just enough feeling of danger in the air to give me a feeling of heightened life, of using some faculty that generally sleeps. Dawn was coming over the sea and we were walking towards the growing light. And we walked rapidly, seeming almost to fly as one sometimes walks in dreams.

A patrol hailed us and we stopped to explain where we were going. 'Two boys were killed at the San Fernando farm,' they told us. 'A bomb fell right on them as they were standing in the patio drinking some milk the farmer's wife had given them, the bomb fell and – nada—' They made a gesture of dispersal – *nothing*. They just happened to be there. It was chance – *and what of those six on whom the Tower of Siloam fell*, my mind asked, retreating from the thought of those too near, too recently shattered, bodies. Well, it will be *our mala sombra*, our ill-shade, if one of these bombs catches us and poor Enrique while we are rushing away across these early morning fields. And yet I could not repress that lift of excitement, of happiness, as if quicker, more ardent life were running through my veins, or as if I had been drinking some wine not meant for me but for creatures of more fiery birth.

I hate war, I have a perfect horror of it; and what little of it I saw in Spain confirmed me in my fear and hatred. And yet after that early morning walk across the fields I understood, better than Bertrand Russell could ever explain it, *Why Men Fight.*

And when we got near Don Carlos's house we saw that it was not on fire at all! Two incendiary bombs had fallen near it, one on an empty chicken house in the backyard and the other in some dry grass and both were still burning and sending off great clouds of white smoke. But the house itself was untouched and we could see figures moving calmly about. We went on anyway; we had other reasons besides the danger of bombs to make us anxious about Don Carlos and his family.

We crossed the main Algeçiras road and reached their gateway and Don Carlos and his family came to meet us full of surprise at seeing us there at five o'clock in the morning, and full of gratitude when they found out that we had come to rescue them, however unnecessarily. They were excited but not at all frightened. Don Carlos was tall and florid and slightly bald, and always somehow reminded me of a charming, aristocratic, Spanish Wilkins Micawber (if such a combination can be imagined!); he had spent a lifetime of difficulties but was always full of hope that something was 'just going to turn up'. He had been in Chile and Tierra del Fuego for years, where he was sheep farming, acting as consul for other South American countries, and in fact doing anything that 'turned up'. Don Carlos and his family particularly attracted me because they reminded me of my half-brother and his family who lived on the cotton plantation he had inherited from our father (where I was brought up) in a state of extraordinary happiness and improvidence, with half a dozen riding horses and no money to speak of.

Doña Maria Louisa, I might as well say without mincing words, was almost the nicest woman I ever knew anywhere. Tall, fair and handsome, a devoted wife, mother, daughter, friend, very kind, and courteous and friendly with rich man, poor man, beggar or thief. The whole family were gay and amusing, and Don Carlos had the Spanish genius for telling a story and for making gossip and personalities interesting and vivid, and somehow universal in their application. Their children were charming too; there were two nearly grown-up boys and two nearly grown-up girls and little Emilio who was only six.

'Have you been all right here?' we asked Don Carlos rather anxiously. He was unfortunate in having a famous name, though he had not inherited much besides, except this strip of land along the sea on which he had built a small house and a part share in the family house which we had bought from him and other members of the family. But a famous name at that period brought death to a great many harmless and innocent people. One of Don Carlos's nephews, a boy of eighteen, was taken away and shot because he had this too well-known name and because only a few weeks before he had got a small place as clerk in Malaga's principal industry which was managed and partly owned by a distant cousin. The cousin was shot as a matter of course after spending a few weeks in prison. He deserves to be remembered for he was a brave man. He was safe in hiding but gave himself up when some of the men under him were put in prison, and tried to take upon himself the entire responsibility for the conduct of the firm, which had been having trouble with strikers. But I'm afraid they were all shot anyway. I liked his last words, they were: 'Do you mind if I light a cigarette?' He lit it and took a few puffs and then gave the signal to fire, himself. Having a feeling even then that famous names were going to be a fatal possession in Malaga we were worried about the C— family (on both sides they had a great deal of English blood and used English names) even apart from their living so unfortunately close to the airfield.

'Come and stay with us,' we urged them.

'Seven of us!' said Maria Louisa, 'and we can't leave the chickens – but how good you are!'

'Do you really think you're safe?' we asked bluntly. 'What about your name?'

'Oh! but I've never done anything; I've been in South America half my life, and I've never taken any part in politics. Why should they do anything to me?' said Don Carlos. 'I'm a poor man too; the boys work as hard as peons, and we always get on well with the country people.'

We knew that that was true, but we were not thinking of the country people but of the gangs in Malaga.

'Well, come any time,' we said. 'We'll always be expecting you. And bring as much as you can in the car. Why not bring the best chickens (they had prize Rhode Island Reds). You could bring a lot of them, you know we've got that huge fowl-house with only a few old hens in it. Do come! Fill up the car and come on over this very morning.'

'The car!' Don Carlos began to laugh. 'Did you see the burnt remains of something along the road: that was the poor old Buick! The Anarchists came to get it. Well, you know what the poor old car was – Pepe and Carlete and I could just start it all working together. You had to know its ways. Of course the Anarchists couldn't start it at all. They cranked it and cranked it and pushed it down the road, and finally they got so angry they put a match to the petrol and Poof! there it is! Poor old thing, it was a pity.

'But they gave poor Maria Louisa and the children a dreadful fright when they came for it – two lorries full of pistoleros bristling with rifles and revolvers. All of them got out and came up to the door, poor Maria Louisa was sure that they had come for me. I was in Malaga. But no, everything was politeness, they only wanted the car, they were requisitioning all private cars. The children warned them what a dreadful old crock it was, but they would drag it off.'

As we stood in the garden saying goodbye, a constant stream of lorries and commandeered cars kept passing by. The house was only fifty yards from the main road: we did not like it at all.

'Do come to us,' we urged again as we went away. Doña Maria Louisa stood smiling and waving goodbye with the girls and little Emilio while Don Carlos and the boys walked to the road with us. What admirable things courage and self-control are, I thought, especially when combined with cheerfulness and good manners. For that smiling family we left behind must have realised even more clearly than we did, and felt – how much more poignantly – the loneliness and danger of their situation in that isolated house, too far for any help to reach them even if there were any help for them in those days, with the armed lorries rushing by and bombs falling out of the air above them.

⌇

Gamel Woolsey was born in South Carolina in 1895. She moved to New York in 1921 and there in 1927 met Llewelyn Cowper Powys, John's brother, with whom she began a love affair that lasted until Llewelyn's death in 1939. In order to be near Llewelyn, Gamel moved to Dorset, where she met Gerald Brenan, with whom she went to Spain in 1931. They lived in Gerald's house in Malaga through the beginning of the Civil War and on their return to London wrote their respective books: *The Spanish Labyrinth*, which focused on political and social issues, and *Death's Other Kingdom* (from which this extract is taken) on everyday domestic life. After the Second World War, Gerald Brenan and Gamel Woolsey returned to their house in Malaga. Gamel continued to write poetry (rejected for publication by T. S. Eliot) and translate Spanish literature, including Perez Galdos' wonderful novel *The Spendthrifts* (*La de Bringas*). Virtually unknown, she died in Malaga in 1968. Recent reprints of *Death's Other Kingdom* and her autobiographical novel *One Way of Love*, written in the 1930s but not published then because of the publisher's fear of obscenity, now make possible an appreciation of the work of this fine writer.

MEDARDO FRAILE

AN EPISODE FROM NATURAL HISTORY

from *Things Look Different in the Night*

translated by Margaret Jull Costa

I REMEMBER THE THICK LIPS, the hiccoughing laugh and the check scarf of that small, skinny boy with innocent eyes and a man's gruff voice, who, at only eleven, poor thing, was burdened with the name of Plácido Dornaleteche, and with whom, at that tender age, I was doubt-less unwittingly bound by the shared oddity of our names. We would leave school, go round the corner of Mártires de Alcalá and up Santa Cruz de Marcenado, but we took a very long time to reach the corner of Conde-Duque because we were talking and laughing so much, and when we did arrive, we would continue to stand there chatting, with neither ears nor time for clocks, until he crossed the road and walked along by the barracks to Leganitos, while I continued straight on and went in the street door of number four. We were studying for the first year of our *bachillerato* (a shrill word that set our teeth on edge) with names that were full of bounty and light, like Antonio Machado, Helena Gómez-Moreno and Julia or Carmen Burell, and others that were full of fear and foreboding, like that of the miserly-looking man, unshaven, grizzle-haired and wild-eyed, who was the author of at least one book on mathematics, ours, and who would occasionally spin the class globe and then gleefully, noisily spit on it. Like us, he had been weighed down as a child with a problematic name: Adoración Ruiz Tapiador.

I remember Plácido trying to instil in me the radiant hope of his beliefs or, rather, those of his older brother, whom I never met, but who apparently wore – for reasons I did not entirely understand – a blue shirt with red arrows embroidered on the breast pocket and who sang a song that my friend would perform with appropriately martial gestures, and of which I remember only – although possibly not exactly – the first two lines: 'Marching along the white road/comes a strong and gallant lad…' And he would ask if I knew Marx, Who? Carlos Marx, and I would say No, although he obviously didn't know him very well either, because he would say, oh, no matter, but what my brother and his comrades want, you see, is the nationalization of that Marx fellow's doctrine, he was Russian or something, an atheist and a good-for-nothing, but he had some useful ideas about bringing bosses and workers together and uniting them once and for all in fraternity and justice. Plácido was like a small, bright, whitewashed window, full of pots of geraniums, through which I could see Madrid and my mother and grandmother's village flooded with sunlight and happiness, so much so that my sheer impatience to see this change come about quite over-whelmed me with contentment, because in my mother's village, there were always a lot of men standing around in the square and in Madrid we were constantly seeing the riot police cordoning off fires or baton-charging students.

I was due to take my exams that year, 1935–1936, and in late March, we moved from no. 4 Santa Cruz de Marcenado to no. 9 Españoleto, and I doubtless gave Plácido Dornaleteche my new address, although I had never been to his house and knew only the name of the street.

On 18 July, the offended parties on both left and right decided to improve Spain by destroying it and plunged into a civil war with horrific massacres perpetrated by both sides, and we would-be high school grad-uates living in Madrid were unable to continue our studies until well into 1937. We had to stand in long queues in order to satisfy our hunger with lentils, sweet potatoes and sunflower seeds and make day-long walks to vegetable gardens outside the city and to nearby villages, only to return with a loaf of bread or three lettuces, but we boys took advan-tage of the barricades in the streets to hurl stones at the war and, each evening, the radio bulletin about the war wafted out through the open windows, seeming to spread and thicken the blood-dark twilight.

In 1937, our apartment filled up with evacuees: an elderly lady from my mother's village, a couple – friends of the family – and their three daughters, two of my father's sisters, Maria and Nazaria, along with their husbands and sons, three of whom were intermittently sent off to fight on the government fronts in Talavera, Brihuega, at the battle of Brunete and Casa de Campo in Madrid. There were only three of us, but we managed to squeeze another seventeen people into our apartment.

It must have been one day in January 1938 when I came back from school to be informed by my father's indolent new wife, whose usual indifference was made all the more exasperating by her inexactitudes and hesitations:

'A lady came with her son; she said he was a friend of yours.'

'Who?'

'Doleteche or Dorteche or something.'

'Do you mean Dornaleteche?'

'Yes, that sounds about right.'

'And?'

'Nothing. They just came to ask if we could help them.'

'Had something happened?'

'I don't know, she said a son or her husband had been killed, or both, I'm not sure.'

'Why didn't you ask?'

'Well, she was speaking really softly, almost crying, and because at that point, your Aunt María came out into the corridor and told them: "We don't want any fascists here!"'

'And what did they say?'

'What could they say? They left.'

I kept grimly pestering both my aunt and my stepmother all afternoon and learned that Plácido – who had probably been the one who had persuaded his mother to come and ask his old schoolfriend for help and who was normally a real chatterbox – didn't say a word; that neither of them was wearing black and that the mother, whom I had never met, had greying hair and was nothing but skin and bone. My Aunt María, who occasionally fancied herself as another La Pasionaria, claimed she had said what she said because her sons – your cousins, she screamed – were risking their lives at the front every day, but that didn't mean – she added illogically – that she wished my friend and his mother ill, because God and the Holy Virgin knew that all she wanted was for the fascists to be crushed once and for all and for the war to end.

The war ended a year later, and most of us adolescents, for a longer or shorter period, wore the blue shirt, which no longer meant the same as the blue shirt for which my friend's brother and possibly his father had died. For years, Spain's tattered skin was an altar besieged by many funerals, although beneath the black trousers and the blue shirts and the red berets there seethed fierce passions – fear, ambition, guilt, revenge – passions that you could feel incubating in the icy silence of those endless masses for the dead.

And, when our time came, most of us students did our training for military service in the University Militias, and it was in one of those long lines of tents, when a captain was doing the roll call, that I heard the name Plácido Dornaleteche, and, as soon as I could get away, I went to look for him, hoping we would be able to reminisce about those conversations in the street after school, our school being the Instituto Calderón de la Barca, a vast house that had originally belonged to the Jesuits until the republicans cleansed it by fire and changed it into a secular institution.

But he wasn't there. Or, rather, Plácido was there in his tent, sitting on his kit bag, but he barely responded to my words and barely looked at me. And it was then that I felt the enormity of that day – which, at only twelve years old, I could have done nothing to avoid – when he and his mother came to my apartment asking for help. His tent was only thirty or forty metres from mine, and we saw and passed each other several times, but we never again spoke. Years before we were born, our French teacher had written a line of verse, saying that one of the two Spains would freeze our hearts.*

---

*A famous line by the great poet Antonio Machado, who died shortly after crossing the French border, as he fled Franco's troops, along with his mother and his brother José and family. For a few years prior to the Civil War he taught French at the school mentioned in the story.

∽

Medardo Fraile was born in Madrid in 1925. He lived through the siege of Madrid during the Civil War and wrote about it in many short stories. With Francisco García Pavón and Ana María Matute (both featured in *!No Pasarán!*), he was central to the development of the short story in Spanish literature in the post-world-war period. He rewrote his stories many times over: ' The word which is not the exact and perfect word is the enemy of the short story'. Fraile read widely and his favourite writers included Katherine Mansfield and Carson McCullers. His style is understated and restrained – not interested in plot, he is masterful at capturing a moment. In 1964, Fraile moved to Scotland and taught Spanish at the University of Strathclyde. He was a popular figure in Scottish literary circles and was a great enthusiast of Scottish culture. His translations into Spanish include Stevenson's unfinished masterpiece *Weir of Hermiston*. Medardo Fraile died in Glasgow in 2013.

ESMOND ROMILLY

AT THE END OF THE ALPHABET

from *Boadilla*

M Y NEURALGIA WAS WORSE in the morning – it hurt to get up. Jeans told us we were all to get ready with rifles loaded. 'It's almost certain the attack'll be soon,' he said.

It was half-past seven. After waiting ten minutes we began to eat the rations they had brought up. 'You lie down there, quiet, boy,' said Joe. 'I'll see if I can get a spot of brandy we can fill up with.'

Food made me feel better, but I still blinked wearily – our trench seemed to have the appearance of a party the morning after. The little Austrian doctor came up to see if there were any cases for treatment. Jeans brought him along to our dug-out. The doctor gave me two aspirins which I swallowed with the brandy. Jeans asked me if I was all right, or if I wanted to go back. I was all right.

We could hear the rumble of tanks and lorries from the enemies' lines even more clearly than in the night. The big guns had started up on both sides, but that meant nothing much. At ten o'clock there was a nasty rush of short range rifle fire. I crept on my stomach back to our dug-out. We crouched down.

'Don't like those bullets, boy,' said Joe. 'You keep your head down. Did you see that one, slap into that tree there, might have got my fingers; sounds like something wrong this time of the morning.'

Jeans was walking along the ridge behind us with Walter and the doctor.

'That fellow's a bloomin' marvel; can't keep his head down. They'll get him one day.'

We heard shouting on our right, and I peered cautiously up to see what was happening. The doctor was bending down on his knees, someone was hit. Jock had a bullet through the side of his neck. When the strafing ceased a minute, two stretcher-bearers ran up from the valley behind and took him back.

I heard Babs say: 'I thought Jock was shamming at first. You know he's always up to that sort of thing, so when I saw him lying on the ground I didn't take any notice.'

Birch shouted: 'There's a fascist sniper on that first ridge there. They couldn't have got Jock otherwise.'

All of this is very clear. Jock being wounded, Jock being taken back, Birch talking about the sniper and cursing Sid. All these things belong to another existence – they happened before that orderly life of ours which I regarded as everlasting because it was so strongly present, before that finished.

This was a big attack. We had our positions; we were well entrenched; we knew where our lines were; we knew we were on one ridge, the enemy on another; we knew all about the whole point of the fascist attack – to cut the Escorial road and encircle Madrid to the north. So it ought to have been simple – something of which you can give a thrilling dramatic description. How we withstood the shells and the bombs and the swooping aeroplanes and the fire of machine-gun and rifle, how we held our positions against bombs and hand grenades, how we fixed our bayonets as they charged our lines, withdrew and disputed the ground, inch by inch, hand to hand... But that sort of thing only happens in fiction and journalism.

A few minutes after Jock went back, our dug-outs were crowded with Spaniards. I don't know how they got there, probably they came up from behind, then over the top. I don't know whether the bullets were still twanging through the branches when they arrived – I am sure we did not fire. Practically all that morning, we still had the command:

'Don't shoot. Patrol out.' The patrol had returned long ago, but we were good at obeying orders.

The Spaniards talked about tanks and about their bombs being no good. They crowded the dug-outs and the shallow communication trenches – there was no room to move. Joe and I had five in our dug-out. There is only one word for their state, they were scared stiff. Perhaps if we had understood them their fear would have communicated itself to us. It didn't. We cheered them up; we pointed out how good the trench was; we stammered slogans about camaradas; we offered them sardines. Joe and Birch were the best at this. After five minutes the men who had been forced in, quivering, at the pistol point, were pulling out red scarfs and handkerchiefs and shouting, '*Viva la Brigada Internationala!*'

'What's happening?' I shouted to Birch.

'It's obvious,' he shouted back, over the heads of five Spaniards (I was pleased and relieved, I knew Birch would know, would find it obvious). 'These chaps have all been in the trenches over the ridge on our right, towards Boadilla, God knows who's there now. Where's Jeans? We can't all stay here in this trench, a shell in here will blow us all out of it. Hi, Tich, you're in command now. Couldn't we get these chaps digging while there's time?'

'We'll have to wait till Jeans comes back with the orders.'

I slipped out and ran along the ridge to the left to see if the Germans in our zug and the other zugs further to the left were still there, and if there were any messages. The machine-gunners next to us were worried – there was no news. Then I saw Jeans panting up the ridge and I went back to see him.

'Thaelmann Battalion forward to the right!'

They were shuffling and scrambling along before we got the message. I shouted it back to the Germans on our left. 'Thaelmann, everyone!'

Joe shouted with me. Bullets were singing over the trench, but the fire was not very intense. Everyone was getting back from the dug-outs to the lower ground behind – the men in front seemed to be going along straight, parallel with the ridge. It looked like a disorganized retreat.

'We're going to advance,' I shouted to the Spaniards. Birch could speak Spanish better, he seized one of them by the shoulder to explain.

This one produced a pole with a black and red flag which he waved in the air, the rest grouped round him. The confusion was the beginning of the tragedy; some wanted to come with us in an attack, others thought we were retreating and leaving them to hold the position alone – they wanted to come with us too. As Joe and I scrambled off to catch up the rest of the English we turned back and shouted once again for the Germans to follow us. Some of the Spaniards came, but the whole of the first and second zugs on our left stayed in their trenches – they had received new orders. We ran along the edge of the ridge and I passed Aussie. He was sitting down pulling up his boots.

'Come on, Aussie,' Joe shouted. 'You'll miss this if you don't hurry!'

All the English were together – we were separated from the rest. Jeans was in front with Tich and Birch close behind him, Babs was close to Sid, then Joe and I, who had decided to keep together whatever happened, and Ray Cox behind us – we were a solid mass. I had no idea where we were going or what was happening. I don't think we went along for more than five minutes, just beyond the protection of the ridge to the right, when we had to stop and lie down on account of the hail of bullets that came over.

'I don't know where Oswald is,' I heard Jeans saying. 'He must be ahead of us somewhere, with a whole patrol. Where are the other zugs?'

All this is still quite clear – I can picture it today. We sat and lay on the grass slope, or crouched behind the trees; we talked about what was happening. It might have been a Group Meeting.

The bullets were getting unpleasant. They were coming from the ridge the Spaniards had evacuated – that must be it; if we kept behind the trees, we were safe. We returned the fire.

Then Tich and Birch were leaning over Jeans's body.

'We can't do anything,' I heard someone say, and then, 'We've got to get him out here, you pull his feet down, Lorrie, I'll get hold of the head.'

I sat up and saw Jeans's face under a pool of blood. They were trying to get his helmet off. 'Cut the strap, Lorrie, with your bayonet,' I heard. It was Tich, groping over to hold up the chin of the man lying still on the grass. 'That bullet must have come from the left, where our own trenches are; we're under cross fire.'

At this moment we all had to duck flat as another hurricane of lead came over.

When I looked up and spoke to Joe I turned my head. That was just incidental – it wasn't because he had not answered. Joe was kneeling on the grass, his gun pointed on to the ground through his hands. I could touch him with my arm. I tried not to look at his head – it was sunk forward on to his chest. I felt I was in the presence of something horrifying. I didn't think about where we were, or the bullets – I didn't think about Joe being dead – I just thought it was all wrong Joe's head being like that. I picked it up. Then there were more bullets, and I lay flat again – that was instinctive. Perhaps I was there three minutes.

Tich and Birch were still arguing about Jeans. I heard someone say, 'He's finished,' but all the time I was quite calm. I kept saying to myself, 'All right, Joe's killed, that's finished, absolutely settled, that's all right, Joe's killed, that's the end of that,' till the words screamed in my ears. All that is still clear. Afterwards it is not so plain.

Tich was shouting out: 'Get back, all of you, quick as you can,' and Ray was sitting in front of a tree firing when he crumpled up and collapsed. These are blurred images. Then my own name being called, 'Here, Romilly, here, quick, man, run all out,' and I rushed through a hail of bullets to a bank where Babs was lying. After that we were together all the time. I went on saying, 'I must find Walter and tell him Joe is dead.' We saw men pouring across the ridge behind us. We were safe where we were; and I climbed up a tree to see over the valley – it was better than the maddening suspense of waiting. Through the branches I saw silvery gleams moving up the track. I knew they were tanks, but it wasn't very real. And later on we ran back till we had to throw ourselves down on the grass and rest. All this is very blurred. Only Joe's head, slumped forward, was real, and Babs shouting to me to run quickly.

Then there were forty of us (this is only a number we thought of afterwards), Germans and Spaniards, mixed up together. We were firing all the time. I copied the others and fired in the same direction till the barrel was red-hot. And always, starting every few minutes, there was the deadly cross fire. But we were in woods now and the trees were thicker, and we would wait behind a thick one, then dodge back quickly to the next tree behind. There are some things which stand out clearer – the sun getting hotter, and stumbling over belts and coats and ammunition discarded in the retreat, and the lack of any feeling when someone fell, only the quick rush back to the next tree.

And then the blur was over, and everything was quiet all around, and we gathered together; and this time I counted and there were seventeen of us, and a few people were talking and arguing, but most were just resting. I didn't think about Joe then, I wanted to sleep and forget everything.

It was cooling and growing dark when we found the rest of our company – Aussie was there, and he told me, 'When I'd got my boots on, you were all gone, and the Spaniards only waited a couple of minutes and they were off. There's a lot of wounded men they left there in the trench. Next thing, I was standing down below when I saw them fellows come over the parapet – walking ever so steadily, and they were calling out, "Don't fire, comrades." So I hung around as I thought these were the same bunch – and I heard a lot of shooting going on, so I looked up again and I saw these fellows. I couldn't make out any sort of uniform or what they were, but they weren't Moors, I'll swear that, Spaniards they must have been, they were strolling along that trench with their guns on to the ground, firing – took no notice of anything, you know, just took it all calmly, finishing them off. There was a whole cluster of us down in the valley there, some of that bunch of anarchists were still hanging about and waiting around to see what was happening and old Harry was there, so we started letting 'em have it. Took 'em by surprise all right at first. There's one big fellow – I know I got him all right. Next moment all our bunch was gone, so I followed as quick as I could. It seemed all quiet, and someone shouted "*Alto! Alto!*" and I got behind a tree and saw two of these chaps calling out, so I put my gun up to fire and took a shot, but it didn't get him, and I took another, then he said comrades. But I knew they weren't our lot, they'd got a green uniform on and red caps like the Moors. So I took another shot and got one of 'em and the other one dashed off, and I didn't wait any longer. Then I came up with the Germans, and Sid was in their bunch and Birch, too. Sid was on the ground with a bullet in his stomach. He was dead – right dead – when

I got there, and one of the Germans told me he said to give his saluta-tions to the English comrades. I never saw Birch after that – I called out to him and he didn't hear, just went on you know, we were all firing, too, so it was the noise, and then I never saw him. Then Messer too. You know, when you passed me, Romilly, I was getting my boots on and I saw Messer then, he was getting a strap together on his pack, and that's all I saw of him.'

There were bombing-planes over us and shrapnel bursting behind – but all those were only incidents. At six o'clock the retreat stopped – Walter and Babs and the big fat English doctor, whom we had seen at Majadahonda, and who appeared without his coat, his arm grazed and bleeding, with a revolver in his hand, got most of the credit. The frantic rush from ridge to ridge, the frantic wild firing into the air, the frantic rush to go faster than those tanks was ended. Companies and groups and nationalities were all mixed up, but order ensued at last. I had a group of five Spaniards to command and place in positions on an advanced ridge, part of forty men whom Babs was given to cover the retreat of the main body while they re-organized and dug new trenches. There were incidents then – the sixty seconds when we saw a valley track filled with columns of men with brown skins and red caps, swinging along easily, carelessly, and we saw those ranks crumple up and scatter to the sides under our fire.

The battle went on three days. The enemy retreated finally till they occupied only our own original positions. The woods and slopes were covered with bodies and rifles and ammunition pouches. There were night patrols to recover rifles and ammunition and the bodies of our dead. None of the English could be found. But none of those last five days before we were relieved have much to do with this story.

The last chapter of our story was written on the day that Joe was killed. It was written when a dispirited little band gathered together that night – Babs and Aussie and I dug ourselves only a shallow protection – we had not much interest in parapets and firing positions. There was a thin, greasy soup and tepid cocoa. Walter took the roll-call of the 1st Company, Thaelmann Battalion, just before the midnight guard.

He called out each name and paused, till the suspense was unbearable.

Oswald and his patrol of fifteen men were every one of them missing – and we thought of the rifles pointed downwards in that trench and the bayonet slashes in the bodies of the men they brought back. The commander crossed their names all with the same word:

'*Gefallen.*'

From the 1st and 2nd Zugs, fifteen men called out the answer, '*Hier!*' Forty-three did not answer.

'Third Zug.' Three Germans answered '*Hier*' before he came to the English Group.

Addley – no answer, no information, '*gefallen*'.
Avener – killed,   '*gefallen*'.
Birch – no answer, believed killed,   '*gefallen*'.
Cox – killed,   '*gefallen*'.

The suspense was still there; we knew they were killed, but yet we did not believe it. It was as if this was their last chance to plead before the final death sentence of the word written against their names.

Gillan – wounded.
Gough – killed,   '*gefallen*'.
Jeans – killed,   '*gefallen*'.
Messer – no answer, missing,   '*gefallen*'.

There had been nothing to break the chain of those answers – we were all at the end of the alphabet.

Those last five days at the front were not so bad. We had enough to think about in the cold, miserable damp and in the fighting that went on. It was the relief, the return to the castle of El Pardo that was bad.[*] They talked about the action, about what ought to have been done, about the men who had been killed.

There were speeches when we said good-bye to return to Albacete,

---

[*] After 1939 the Madrid residence of General Franco.

Valencia, Barcelona and England. Commander Richard said: 'In the battles of the future, if we know that there are Englishmen on our left flank, or Englishmen on our right, then we shall know that we need give no thought nor worry to those positions.'*

We returned to England on January 3. Albacete was just the same, except that it was muddier and dirtier – and the troops now slept on the stone floors without mattresses. Here the first British battalion was being trained. It was part of the section of a thousand Englishmen who, in February, were to hold the most vital positions near the Valencia road under twelve days of the biggest artillery bombardment of the war, then counter-attack and make Madrid's road safe for months – perhaps for good. I might have gone back and joined those men, who are the real heroes of the Spanish struggle. But I did not go. I got married and lived happily instead.

Yet more and more I see that those three months were not just an adventure, an interlude. The mark which they left is something that does not diminish but grows with time. When we were all together at the castle of El Pardo there was a kind of faith which made us feel that we could not ever be destroyed. But seven of those men – including Joe – were killed at Boadilla. They were killed, and forgotten, because they were only important for a day. Then there were other fighters, other martyrs, other sympathies.

There is something frightening, something shocking about the way the world does not stop because those men are dead. Over all this war there is that feeling. It is not something which is specifically due to the fact that one is seeing the struggle of a race of people one loves, that one's friends are fighting, or have died – it is a feeling of the vast-ness of the thing which has caught up so many separate entities and individualities.

I am not a pacifist, though I wish it were possible to lead one's life without the intrusion of this ugly monster of force and killing – war

---

*Colonel 'Richard' was a German communist named Staimer. He survived both the Civil War and the world war to become police chief in East Germany.

– and its preparation. And it is not with the happiness of the convinced communist, but reluctantly that I realize that there will never be peace or any of the things I like and want, until that mixture of profit-seeking, self-interest, cheap emotion and organized brutality which is called fascism has been fought and destroyed for ever.

〜

Esmond Romilly was born in Herefordshire in 1918. He became a rebel at his public school, Wellington College, from which he ran away to work in a communist bookshop in London. At the outbreak of the Civil War, Romilly cycled to Marseille and, from there, went by boat to Valencia to join up with the International Brigades. After minimal training in Albacete, Romilly was sent to the front at Boadilla to fight Franco's troops attempting to take Madrid. *Boadilla* is the account of this fighting which ended in the decimation of his unit, the Thaelmann Battalion. It is a moving book that brilliantly captures the chaos of battle. Suffering from dysentery, Romilly returned to England, where he married Jessica Mitford, like him a class traitor. *Boadilla* was written in 1937 when the couple were on honeymoon in Bayonne after having been expelled from Bilbao, where Romilly had been sent to cover the Civil War for the *News Chronicle*. They returned to England and became active in the fight against Mosley's British Union of Fascists. In 1939, Romilly and Mitford went to the United States to seek their fortune. At the outbreak of the Second World War, Romilly went to Canada and joined the Royal Canadian Air Force. He was killed in November 1941 in a bombing raid over Germany. He was twenty-three.

DULCE CHACÓN

THE MISSING TOE

from *The Sleeping Voice*

translated by Nick Caistor

A S USUAL, ACTIVITY in number two block began early. The prisoners were roused at seven in the morning. This was Christmas Day, visiting day. They were all forced to hear mass, as on every holy day, but only a handful of the women took communion. All the others stayed standing throughout the ceremony in protest. They held their heads high as the priest cursed them in his sermon:

'You are dross, and that is why you are here. And if you don't know that word, I'll tell you what dross means. Shit, that's what it means.'

Furious, Tomasa called a meeting straight after mass. She proposed they all go on hunger strike until the priest apologised for his insult.

'More hunger?'

It was Reme who spoke. She looked desperately over at Hortensia, as though asking her for help, asking for bread.

'Not more hunger, for the love of God.'

A few of the women supported the idea of the strike, but Hortensia interrupted them:

'We have to survive, comrades. That's our only obligation, to survive.'

'Survive, survive, what's so important about that?'

'So we can tell the story, Tomasa.'

'What about our dignity? Is someone going to tell the story of how we lost our dignity?'

'We haven't lost it.'

'No, we've only lost the war, haven't we? That's what you all think, isn't it? That we've lost the war.'

'We'll only have lost it when we die, but we're not going to give them that satisfaction. No more craziness. If we resist, we win.'

Further voices joined in, some in favour, others against the possibility of a hunger strike; and the word dignity drowned out that of 'craziness'. Then Elvira came running into the shower room:

'Watch out, Little Miss Poison's coming!'

The women who had towels wrapped them round their hair or slung them over their shoulders. Those with no towels pretended they were drying their hands on their skirts. The meeting was over. Little Miss Poison appeared at the door, with Mercedes by her side. She was carrying a Baby Jesus. Mercedes turned the key and pushed the door open, let her superior enter and followed her in. She locked the door behind them, hung the key from her belt, and pushed in a hairpin that was sticking up out of her chignon.

'Line up!'

It was not time for their roll-call. But none of the prisoners asked why they were being made to get into line. Mercedes clapped her hands three times and they obeyed.

Sister María de los Serafines lifted up the Baby Jesus crowned with a gilt crown, put one hand under his plump crossed legs, and offered the statue's foot to the first prisoner:

'Religious devotion is part of your re-education. You refused to take communion, although this is Christ's birthday. You will all kiss his foot. All those who do not do so will have their visits cancelled this afternoon.'

One by one, the prisoners bent and kissed the proffered foot of the Christ-child. Little Miss Poison deliberately held it level with her stomach so they would have to bow their heads. After each kiss, Mercedes dried the cardboard foot with a piece of starched linen.

'Now you, Tomasa.'

As the nun came close, Tomasa stared straight at her, her mouth twisted in fury. After a few seconds, Little Miss Poison grabbed her head and pushed it down towards the statue. Tomasa yielded, brought her mouth close to the tiny foot, and then, instead of kissing it, opened her mouth wide.

A crack resounded through the silence of the block.

A crack.

And then a smiling mouth, gripping a toe between its teeth.

A shout:

'Communist swine!'

The shout came from Sister María de los Serafines.

Mercedes rushed to cover the amputated toe with her starched cloth, as if trying to staunch the flow of blood. The nun shouted again:

'Communist swine!'

And punched Tomasa in the mouth with her clenched fist.

The white flurry of her habit's wide sleeves as she assaults a face which has not lost its smile.

The punch was so hard the sacrilegious prisoner spat out the toe, and Baby Jesus' extremity flew through the air.

The foot-kissing session is over. Sister María de los Serafines orders them to find the missing toe. The prisoners break ranks, trying hard not to laugh. Elvira can feel two tears rolling down her cheeks, and Hortensia raises her hands to her belly and exclaims:

'Oh dear mother of mine, dear heart!'

In order not to laugh, the prisoners search for the toe without looking at each other. They cannot look at Tomasa.

'Here it is!'

Reme has found God's toe and hands it over to the nun.

Tomasa's lip has started to bleed. Sister María de los Serafines pushes her towards Mercedes.

'Get this sacrilegious creature out of my sight!'

Then she lifts the tiny toe to the tiny foot to see if she can cure the wound. Yes, she'll be able to stick it back on. She looks at it in ecstasy. A teardrop wells up in the corner of her eye. She'll be able to stick it back, although the join will look like a tiny scar.

The inmates of block number two will be able to laugh when they are getting ready to go out to the visiting-room. When the bustle of activity and the anticipation of seeing their families helps them forget the sad sight of Tomasa trying to keep her balance as she was pushed roughly out of the room to face her punishment. They can laugh when they forget how sorry they felt to see her walking away buttoning up Elvira's mother's dress. It is only as the prisoners are preparing to meet their relatives that they can laugh. And it is Reme who makes them do so. Like all the women, she is pinching her cheeks to give them a bit of colour so her face will look healthier – a little less haggard and starving – and she says:

'Now they'll know they are telling the truth when they say we Communists eat young babies. What a stupid cunt that woman is.'

Reme bursts out laughing. Elvira is next, as she asks Hortensia:

'Did you see Little Miss Poison's face?'

'She looked incredible! I thought she was going to have a fit!'

All the built-up tension is released as the women who have got visitors are helped by those who haven't.

'Here, Reme, wear this red scarf, it makes your face look prettier.'

Reme uses saliva to wash her hands: the water was cut off much earlier. As she washes, she thinks of Benjamín. She shouldn't have asked him to bring soap at his last visit. Soap is hard to find. She shouldn't have asked him for that, and still less for the little wicker chair. Poor Benjamín, she shouldn't have asked him for anything. He always brings her what he can. Reme smiles thinking of her grandson, whom she is going to see for the first time this afternoon. Her son's son, born in León barely six months earlier.

Hortensia is more excited than usual, and can't imagine why. She had been making two plaits, the way Felipe likes her, when a woman from Salamanca who was brought into the prison a few days earlier came up to her. All they knew about this small, energetic woman who entered number two block without a trace of fear in her eyes was that she was accused of collaborating with bandits. Some of the women thought she must be a guerrilla fighter, but in fact she was a member of the Communist Party leadership in Salamanca.

'My name is Sole.'

After telling Hortensia her name, she explains that she is a midwife, and that her daughter has sent her a message:

'She says I'm to stay next to you, that we're to go out to the visiting-room together. She says it's very important for us to stick together.'

'Why?'

'She didn't say.'

And Elvira sings, more cheerful than ever, while she is tying a piece of string in her pony-tail, just how Paulino likes it. She still can't get rid of the last of her fever, but today she's glad of it, because that way her grandfather will see colour in her cheeks.

Elvira has no idea that in a few minutes she is going to see her brother Paulino. Paulino does not know it either.

Paulino is already on his way to Ventas prison with Felipe.

Dulce Chacón war born in Zafra in Extremadura in 1954. Her father, the mayor of Zafra, was a supporter of Franco who loved literature. After Franco's death in 1975, the democratic government passed, as part of the Amnesty Law, the Pact of Forgetting – an attempt to forget the past and concentrate on the future. For writers like Chacón this attempt at forced collective amnesia was unacceptable. The research for *The Sleeping Voice* took her all over Spain to interview survivors of Franco's rule. For her, the women she interviewed were 'the silenced voices, the figures in shadow… who lost so much and then had no right to complain'. *The Sleeping Voice* is set in the Prisión de Ventas, a well-known prison during the Civil War. It is a book in which the political views of the women are paramount. Chacón wrote the book out of 'a personal necessity dating back a long way, to dig out the history of Spain that I hadn't been taught: a censored and silenced history'. A moving book shot through with dark humour, *The Sleeping Voice* won the Spanish Book of the Year Award in 2002. Dulce Chacón died in Madrid in 2003.

VICTOR SERGE

'SPEAK PLAINLY, YOU KNOW ME'

from *The Case of Comrade Tulayev*

translated by Willard R. Trask

AT FIVE THOUSAND FEET, in a sky that was pure light, the most sun-drenched catastrophe in history was no longer visible. The Civil War vanished at just the altitude at which the bomber pilots prepared to fight. The ground was like a map – so rich in colour, so full of geological, vegetable, marine, and human life that, looking at it, Kondratiev felt a sort of intoxication. When at last, flying over the forest of Lithuania, an undulating, dark mossiness which struck him as looking pre-human, he saw the Soviet countryside, so different from all others because of the uniform colouring of the vast kolkhoze fields, a definite anxiety pierced him to the marrow. He pitied the thatched roofs, humble as old women, assembled here and there in the hollows of almost black ploughlands, beside gloomy rivers. (Doubtless at bottom he pitied himself.)

The situation in Spain must have appeared so serious that the Chief received him on the day he arrived. Kondratiev waited only a few moments in the spacious ante-room, from whose huge windows, which flooded the room with white light, he could see a Moscow boulevard, trams, a double row of trees, people, windows, roofs, a building in course of demolition, the green domes of a spared church... 'Go in, please...' A white room, bare as a cold sky, high-ceilinged, with no decoration except a portrait of Vladimir Ilich, larger than life, wearing a cap, hands in his pockets, standing in the Kremlin courtyard. The room was so huge that at first Kondratiev thought it empty; but behind the table at the far end of it, in the whitest, most desert, most solitary corner of that closed and naked solitude, someone rose, laid down a fountain pen, emerged from emptiness; someone crossed the carpet, which was the pale grey of shadowed snow, someone came to Kondratiev holding out both hands, someone, He, the Chief, the comrade of earlier days – was it real?

'Glad to see you, Ivan, how are you?'

Reality triumphed over the stunning effect of reality. Kondratiev pressed the two hands which were held out to him, held them, and real warm tears gathered under his eyelids, only to dry instantly, his throat contracted. The thunderbolt of a great joy electrified him:

'And you, Yossif?... You... How glad I am to see you... How young you still are...'

The short greying hair still bristled vigorously; the broad, low, deeply lined forehead, the small russet eyes, the stiff moustache, still held such a compact charge of life that the flesh-and-blood man shouldered away the image presented by his innumerable portraits. He smiled, and there were smiling lines around his nose, under his eyes, he emanated a reassuring warmth – would he be as warm and kind as he looked? But how was it that all the mysterious dramas, the trials, the terrible sentences pondered in the Political Bureau had not exhausted him more?

'You too, Vania,' he said (yes – it was the old voice). 'You've stood up well, you haven't aged much.'

They looked at each other, relaxed. How many years, old man! Prague, London, Cracow years ago, that little room in Cracow where we argued so fiercely all one evening about the expropriations in the Caucasus; then we went and drank good beer in a *Keller*, with Romanesque vaulting, under a monastery... The processions in 'seventeen, the congresses, the Polish campaign, the hotels in the little towns we captured, where fleas devoured our exhausted revolutionary councils. Their common memories came back in such a crowd that not one became dominant: all were present, but silently and unobtrusively, re-creating a friendship beyond expression, a friendship which had never known words. The Chief reached into the pocket of his tunic for his pipe. Together they walked across the carpet, towards the tall bay windows at the farther end of the room, through the whiteness...

'Well, Vania, what's the situation now, down there? Speak plainly, you know me.'

'The situation,' Kondratiev began with a discouraged look and that gesture of the hands which seems to let something drop, 'the situation...'

The Chief seemed not to have heard this beginning. His head bowed, his fingers tamping tobacco into the bowl of his short pipe, he went on:

'You know, brother, veterans like you, members of the old Party, must tell me the whole truth... the whole truth. Otherwise, who can I get it from? I need it, I sometimes feel myself stifling. Everyone lies and lies and lies! From top to bottom they all lie, it's diabolical... Nause-ating... I live on the summit of an edifice of lies – do you know that? The statistics lie, of course. They are the sum total of the stupidities of the little officials at the base, the intrigues of the middle stratum of administrators, the imaginings, the servility, the sabotage, the immense stupidity of our directing cadres... When they bring me those extracts of mathematics, I sometimes have to hold myself down to keep from saying, Cholera! The plans lie, because nine times out of ten they are based on false data; the Plan executives lie because they haven't the courage to say what they can do and what they can't do; the most expert economists lie because they live in the moon, they're lunatics, I tell you! And then I feel like asking people why, even if they say nothing, their eyes lie. Do you know what I mean?'

Was he finding excuses for himself? He lighted his pipe furiously, put his hands in his pockets, squared his head and shoulders, stood firmly on the carpet in the harsh light. Kondratiev looked at him, studying him sympathetically, yet with a certain basic suspicion, considering. Should he risk it? He risked an unemphatic:

'Isn't it a little your own fault?'

The Chief shook his head; the minute wrinkles of a warm smile flickered about his nose, under his eyes...

'I'd like to see you in my place, old man – yes, that's something I'd like to see. Old Russia is a swamp – the farther you go, the more the ground gives, you sink in just when you least expect to... And then, the human rubbish!... To remake the hopeless human animal will take centuries. I haven't got centuries to work with, not I... Well, what's the latest news?'

'It's execrable. Three fronts barely holding out – a push, and collapse... They haven't even dug trenches in front of essential positions...'

'Why?'

'Lack of spades, bread, plans, officers, discipline, ammunition, of...'

'I see. Like the beginning of 'eighteen with us, eh?'

'Yes... On the surface... But without the Party, without Lenin' – Kondratiev hesitated for a fraction of a second, but it must have been perceptible – 'without you... And it's not a beginning, it's an end – *the end.*'

'The experts have prophesied it – three to five weeks, don't they say?'

'It can last a long time, like a man taking a long time to die. It can be over to-morrow.'

'I need,' said the Chief, 'to keep the resistance going for a few weeks.'

Kondratiev did not answer. He thought: 'That is cruel. What's the use?'

The Chief seemed to divine his thought:

'We are certainly worth that,' he resumed. 'And now: Our Sormovo tanks?'

'Nothing to boast about. Armour plate passable...' Kondratiev remembered that the builders had been shot for sabotage, and felt a momentary embarrassment. 'Motors inadequate. Breakdowns in combat as high as thirty-five per cent...'

'Is that in your written report?'

'Yes.' Embarrassment. Kondratiev was thinking that he had laid the foundation for another trial, that his 'thirty-five per cent' would burn in phosphorescent characters in brains exhausted by night-long interrogations. He resumed:

'In point of defectiveness, the human *matériel* is the worst...'

'So I've been told. What is your explanation?'

'Perfectly simple. We fought, you and I, under other conditions. The machine pulverizes man. You know I am not a coward. Well, I wanted to see – I got into one of those machines, a No. 4, with three first-class men, a Catalan Anarchist…'

'…a Trotskyist, of course…'

The Chief had spoken with a smile, out of a cloud of smoke; his russet eyes twinkled through almost closed lids.

'Very likely – I didn't have time to go into it… You wouldn't have either… Two olive-skinned peasants, Andalusians, wonderful marksmen, like our Siberians or Letts used to be… Well, there we are, rolling along an excellent road, I try but can't imagine what it would be like if we were on bad terrain… There are four of us inside there, dripping sweat from head to foot, stifling, in the darkness, the noise, the stench of gasoline, we want to vomit, we're cut off from the world, if only it were over! There was panic in our guts, we weren't fighters any longer, we were poor half-crazed beasts squeezed together in a black, suffocating box… Instead of feeling protected and powerful, you feel reduced to nothing…'

'The remedy?'

'Better planned machines, special units, trained units. Just what we have not had in Spain.'

'Our planes?'

'Good, except for the old models… It was a mistake to unload so many old models on them…' The Chief gave a decided nod of approval. 'Our B104 is inferior to the Messerschmitt, outclassed in speed.'

'The maker was sabotaging.'

Kondratiev hesitated before answering, for he had thought a great deal on the subject, convinced that the disappearance of the Aviation Experiment Centre's best engineers had unquestionably resulted in poorer quality products.

'Perhaps not… Perhaps it is only that German technique is still superior…'

The Chief said:

'He was sabotaging. It has been proved. He confessed it.'

The word *confessed* produced a distinct feeling of discomfort between them. The Chief felt it so clearly that he turned away, went to the table for a map of the Spanish fronts, and began asking detailed

questions which could not really have been of any significance to him.
At the point which things had reached, what could it matter to him
whether Madrid's University City was more or less well supplied with
artillery? On the other hand, he did not discuss the shipping of the
gold reserves, probably having been already informed of it by special
messenger. Kondratiev passed over the subject. The Chief made no reference to the changes in personnel suggested in Kondratiev's report... On
a clock in the faraway bay window, Kondratiev read that the audience
had already lasted more than an hour. The Chief walked up and down,
he had tea brought, answered a secretary, '*Not until I call you...*' What was
he expecting? Kondratiev became tensely expectant too. The Chief, his
hands in his pockets, took him to the bay window from which there was
a view of the roofs of Moscow. There was only a pane of glass between
them and the city, the pale sky.

'And here at home, in this magnificent and heart-rending Moscow,
what is not going right, do you think? What isn't gelling? Eh?'

'But you just said it, brother. Everyone lies and lies and lies. Servility,
in short. Whence, a lack of oxygen. How build Socialism without
oxygen?'

'Hmm... And is that all, in your opinion?'

Kondratiev saw himself driven to the wall. Should he speak? Should
he risk it? Should he wriggle out of it like a coward? The tension in him
prevented him from reading the Chief's face clearly, though it was only
two feet away. Despite himself he was very direct, and therefore very
clumsy. In a voice that was emphatic though he tried to make it casual:

'The older generation is getting scarce...'

The Chief put aside the outrageous allusion, pretending not to
notice it:

'On the other hand, the younger generation is rising. Energetic,
practical, American style... It's time the older generation had a rest...'

'May they rest with the saints' – the words of the Chant for the Dead
in the liturgy...

Tensely, Kondratiev changed his tack:

'Yes, the younger generation, of course... Our youth is our pride...'
('My voice rings false, now I'm lying too...')

The Chief smiled curiously, as if he were laughing at someone who was not present. And then, in the most natural tone:

'Do you think I have many faults, Ivan?'

They were alone in the harsh white light, with the whole city before them, though not a sound from it reached them. In a sort of spacious courtyard below and some distance away, between a squat church with dilapidated towers and a little red-brick wall, Georgian horsemen were at sabre practice, galloping from one end of the courtyard to the other; about half-way they stooped almost to the ground to impale a piece of white cloth on their sabres...

'It is not for me to judge you,' said Kondratiev uncomfortably. 'You are the Party.' He observed that the phrase was well received. 'Me, I'm only an old militant' – with a sadness that had a shade of irony – 'one of those who need a rest...'

The Chief waited like an impartial judge or an indifferent criminal. Impersonal, as real as things.

'I think,' said Kondratiev, 'that you were wrong in "liquidating" Nicolai Ivanovich.'

Liquidating: the old word that, out of both shame and cynicism, was used under the Red terror for 'execute.' The Chief took it without flinching, his face stone.

'He was a traitor. He admitted it. Perhaps you don't believe it?'

Silence. Whiteness.

'It is hard to believe.'

The Chief twisted his face into a mocking smile. His shoulders hunched massively, his brow darkened, his voice became thick.

'Certainly... We have had too many traitors... conscious or unconscious... no time to go into the psychology of it... I'm no novelist.' A pause. 'I'll wipe out every one of them, tirelessly, mercilessly, down even to the least of the least... It is hard, but it must be... Every one of them... There is the country, the future. I do what must be done. Like a machine.'

Nothing to answer? – or to cry out? Kondratiev was on the point of crying out. But the Chief did not give him time. He returned to a conversational tone:

'And in Spain – are the Trotskyists still intriguing?'

'Not to the extent that some fools insist. By the way, I want to talk to you about a matter that is of no great importance but which may have repercussions… Our people are doing some stupid and dangerous things…'

In a few sentences Kondratiev set forth the case of Stefan Stern. He tried to divine whether the Chief had already been told of it. Natural and impenetrable, the Chief listened attentively, made a note of the name, Stefan Stern, as if it were new to him. Was it really new to him?

'Right – I'll look into it… But about the Tulayev case, you are wrong. It was a plot.'

'Ah!'

'Perhaps, after all, it was a plot…' Kondratiev's mind gave a halting assent… 'How accommodating I'm being – the devil take me!'

'May I ask a question, Yossif?'

'Of course.'

The Chief's russet eyes still had their friendly look.

'Is the Political Bureau dissatisfied with me?'

That really meant: 'Are you dissatisfied with me, now that I have spoken to you freely?'

'What answer can I give you?' said the Chief slowly. 'I do not know. The course of events is unsatisfactory, there is no doubt of that – but there was not much you could do about it. You were in Barcelona only a few days, so responsibility does not extend far… When everything is going to the dogs, we have no one to congratulate, eh? Ha-ha.'

He gave a little guttural laugh, which broke off abruptly.

'And now what shall we do with you? What work do you want? Would you like to go to China? We have fine little armies there, a trifle infected with certain diseases…' He gave himself time to think. 'But probably you've had enough of war?'

'I've had enough of it, brother. No, thank you – so far as China is concerned, spare me that, please. Always blood, blood – I am sick of it…'

Precisely the words he ought not to have spoken, the words that had been in his throat since the first minute of their meeting, the weightiest words in their secret dialogue.

'I see,' said the Chief, and suddenly the bright daylight became sinister. 'Well, what then? A job in production? In the diplomatic corps? I'll think about it.'

They crossed the carpet diagonally. Sleepwalkers. The Chief took Ivan Kondratiev's hand.

'I have enjoyed seeing you again, Ivan.'

Sincere. That spark deep in the eyes, that concentrated face – the ageing of a strong man living without trust, without happiness, without human contacts, in a laboratory solitude… He went on:

'Take a rest, old man. Have yourself looked after. At our age, after our lives, it has to be done. You're right, the older generation is getting scarce.'

'Do you remember when we hunted wild ducks on the tundra?'

'Everything, everything, old man, I remember everything. Go and take a rest in the Caucasus. But I'll give you a piece of advice for down there: let the sanatoriums look out for themselves, and you go climb as many mountain trails as you can. That's what I'd like to do myself.'

Here there began, within them and between them, a secret dialogue, which they both followed by divination, distinctly: 'Why don't *you* go?' Kondratiev suggested. 'It would do you so much good, brother.' – 'Tempting, those out-of-the-way trails,' mocked the Chief. 'So I'll be found one day with my head bashed in? I'm not such a fool as that – I'm still needed…' – 'I pity you, Yossif, you are the most threatened, the most captive of us all…' – 'I don't want to be pitied. I forbid you to pity me. You are nothing, I am the Chief.' They spoke none of these words: they heard them, uttered them, only in a double *tête-à-tête* – together corporeally and also together, incorporeally, one within the other.

'Good-bye.'

'Good-bye.'

Half-way across the huge ante-room Kondratiev encountered a short man with shell-rimmed glasses, a thick, curving nose, and a heavy brief case which almost dragged along the carpet: the new Prosecutor of the Supreme Tribunal, Rachevsky. He was going in the opposite direction. They exchanged reticent greetings.

Born in Brussels in 1890 to anti-Czarist Russian exiles, **Victor Serge** was directly involved in the major political conflicts of the first half of the 20th century. In 1913, he was sentenced in France to five years in prison for his alleged involvement in the robberies of the anarchist Bonnot Gang. Released from prison in 1917, Serge went to Russia to support the revolutionary move-ment. An early supporter of the Bolsheviks, Serge worked, after the Revolution, for the Comintern. The harsh repression by the government of the Kronstadt Uprising in 1921 confirmed Serge's doubts about the 'democratic deficit' of the new regime, and from 1923 he was a member of the Left Opposition led by Trotsky. Expelled from the Communist Party in 1928, Serge was sent into internal exile and forced to leave the Soviet Union in 1936. He went to Paris, where he was the Paris correspondent of the POUM. When the Germans occupied Paris in 1940, Serge escaped south. He was able to sail on the last ship out of Marseille (André Breton and Claude Lévi-Strauss were also on board) and arrived in 1942 in Mexico City after having been imprisoned in Martinique and the Dominican Republic on the way! A firm friend of the many Republicans in exile in Mexico, Serge died in Mexico City in 1947 – without a nationality, he was buried as 'a Spanish Republican'.

Throughout this tumultuous life, Serge wrote an amazing amount: non-fiction books on the political events he witnessed, poems and a series of seven 'witness-novels'. In the prefatory note to *The Case of Comrade Tulayev*, from which this extract is taken, Serge writes: 'This novel belongs entirely to the domain of literary fiction. The truth created by the novelist cannot be confounded, in any degree whatever, with the truth of the historian or the chronicler.'

PIERRE HERBART

MY GODS ABANDONED

from La Ligne de Force

translated by Nick Caistor

O N MY RETURN FROM THE USSR I was very depressed. Nobody aban-
dons their gods without anguish. I had decided to break with the
Party. But there was the war in Spain. We thought the USSR was helping
the Republicans. I managed to persuade Gide to wait for Malraux's
judgment before he published the book he had written in such haste.
Before leaving for Spain (Malraux was in Albacete), I went to see Aragon.
There was already a rumour going round Paris that Gide was preparing
a 'bomb'. Of course, Aragon knew more about it than anyone. I told him
– which was true – that I was hoping to bring back evidence from Spain
that would convince Gide to postpone the publication of his book until
much later. I boarded the plane with the proofs of *Return from the USSR*
in my pocket. In Barcelona, anarchist friends of mine outlined their situation. Hunted down by the GPU, their comrades were disappearing one
after another. Their bodies were discovered by the roadsides, a bullet
in the back of their heads. Soviet 'aid' consisted mainly of a vast police
operation against the 'dissidents'. In Albacete, Marty was doing the same
with the International Brigades. In the midst of all this turmoil, Malraux
was doing his best to provide the Republicans with an air force. I gave
him the famous proofs. The next day, he looked worried.

'You've got yourself into a fine mess,' he told me.

'Why's that?'

'Are you *absolutely* sure that Gide isn't going to publish the book while you're in Spain?'

I went pale. I wasn't sure of anything. Left to his own devices, Gide was capable of quickly forgetting his promise. I knew only too well how hard he found it to resist the temptation of the printed word.

'And even if he doesn't publish it,' Malraux went on, 'the simple fact of finding it on you…'

He didn't finish his sentence.

'I'll go to Madrid,' I told him, 'and show the proofs to Koltsov.'

Malraux remained thoughtful.

'That's perhaps the best option… better still would be for you to return to Paris straightaway.'

'No. I'm going to Madrid.'

'Fine. I'll come and see you in a few days.'

In Madrid, Koltsov put me up near him in the Russian embassy. I couldn't bring myself to broach the matter. I suddenly realized that Gide's book was a huge threat to him. He was the one responsible for organizing the trip to the USSR.

One morning I was in his office. I had promised myself I wouldn't leave without giving him the proofs that were weighing down my jacket pocket.

'Yes,' he said, pacing up and down the room as he usually did: 'Yes… our situation is… delicate. Comrade Stalin's orders are clear, and as ever, realistic: *stay out of range of the guns.*' He raised his forefinger. 'Do you understand? There's a nuance: we're here, and yet we're not here. The telephone you can see over there puts me in contact with Moscow; that other one, with Paris. When the one on the left rings, I know it's Aragon. On the right, it's… Do you understand? The vital thing is not to confuse them. But what on earth are you doing getting involved in all this? Do you want to fight?'

'Hmm. I'm not really sure. In general terms, it's not my kind of thing.'

'Ah! Dear Herbart, dear comrade Herbart, how I understand you! But you see, we're also fighting here, in this office. We'll fight side by side, in here!'

He pressed a buzzer.

'My militiaman comrade,' he said in his poor Spanish, 'please bring us some caviar and vodka. The comrade from France is famished.' Then, turning to me he said, his finger raised once more: '*Stay out of range of the guns*. Brilliant, eh? Blum is also staying out of range. The problem is, he's a bit too far away. That spoils the effect. Aha, it's ringing on the left. That will be Aragon, you'll see.'

He picked up the 'phone. 'Ah, good morning. Just imagine, I was convinced it would be you. So what's new?' A long silence, then his curt interjection: 'When?' Silence. 'Yes, he's here in my office.' I could hear interference on the line. 'Responsible? Why is he responsible?' Eventually: 'Yes, of course they were together. But even so, he didn't write the book. Oh well, thank you, thank you. I'll keep you informed.'

Koltsov turned towards me. His face was white as chalk.

'Gide has just published a book about his trip to the USSR. A terrible book.'

'Here are the proofs,' I told him.

That afternoon, Koltsov came looking for me in my room.

'I've read it,' he said. 'It may be less serious than I feared.'

'Why is that?'

'It is not dissidence; it's opposition. Gide is criticizing from the outside. You can't prohibit people from being outside the door. But if they cross the threshold and come into my office, for example, then you can't tolerate any hair-splitting.'

'I don't follow you,' I said.

'I don't either,' he said with a strained smile. 'I'm trying to see how I can limit the damage. It's going to create an incredible storm on that side,' he added, pointing to the right-hand telephone. 'Let's go out for a while, shall we? I need some air.'

'I can't go out. I haven't been given a safe-conduct yet. All I have is the document from the Spanish embassy in Paris. You know that's worthless.'

Koltsov seemed very interested.

'When did you request a safe-conduct? Who to? Our ambassador here?'

'Yes, I requested it three days ago, when I arrived.'

'Aha,' muttered Koltsov. 'And you still haven't received anything? Could they have… could someone have told them… anyway, it doesn't matter, you'll be safe with me. Let's go.'

The car, red flag fluttering, dropped us near Puerta del Sol. A wide, completely deserted avenue rose towards the sky, visible in the distance between rows of houses. We walked along the pavement. From time to time came the sound of gunfire. We were stopped several times by militiamen taking cover in corners.

'*Ambajada sovietica*,' Koltsov would say.

And they would let us through.

'This is the furthest we can go,' said Koltsov.

It was a barricade of sacks of earth, behind which soldiers kept watch, their rifles pointing at another barricade blocking the avenue a hundred metres further on. There was a special quality to the silence; the air seemed rarefied. The no man's land between the two barricades held an obsessive attraction for me. A bullet grazed the façade behind our heads.

'Let's go in,' said Koltsov.

'Go in where?' I wondered. Into the last house before the barricade. I could see all the ground floors formed a kind of corridor where the walls had been knocked through to allow passage from one to the next. The windows obscured with sacks in a feeble daylight. It was as if we were in a basement. It went on like that for fifty metres, through possibly ten houses. All the rooms were completely empty. At first glance nothing recalled their former use, but suddenly I could tell from my sense of smell that I was crossing a long chain of small shops. I slowed down, sniffing cautiously. Here, a shop selling rope sandals. There, a butcher's; further on, a bakery. Faint or strong smells wafted through the air. Occasionally I came to a halt, at a loss. 'Leather and furs,' I would decide. Or again: 'Oranges', 'Absinthe'. This corridor giving onto death if any exit door was pushed open seemed to offer the greatest protection in the city. The sound of the rare gunshots, muffled by the sandbags, came from a very distant, sham world. Real life was mysteriously hidden here in the memory of these old-fashioned smells.

'Here we are at the end of the night,' said Koltsov, thumping a wall. Other blows responded immediately from the other side of the wall, together with a burst of shouted insults. The Falangists were there, fifty centimetres from us. One of our militiamen shouted some insults in reply, and then started singing in a high, piercing, if slightly hoarse voice. He was a young boy, almost a child. As he sang, he closed his eyes and poured out notes with his head thrown back like a dog howling at the moon. When he fell quiet, a voice on the far side of the wall took up the same song, and our boy continued the minute he too fell silent.

Koltsov and I looked at each other in silence.

'By the way,' he said, 'I had to account for Gide's book to comrade X. (I didn't understand the name he said.) 'I'm sure he will want to question you.'

I was asleep some time around midnight when my door opened (I thought I had locked it). An extremely fat man with a pallid look came across to my bed. He grabbed a chair, sat on it, and began without so much as introducing himself:

'Comrade Herbart, I have read André Gide's anti-Soviet book closely... But you were sleeping, and I'm disturbing you... Wait, let's drink some champagne...'

He rang, and to my great surprise a servant appeared with a bottle of champagne and two glasses. The stranger carefully uncorked it, filled the glasses and said, raising his own:

'Here's to the health of the traitor André Gide... What, aren't you drinking?'

'I'm not thirsty,' I said.

'Perhaps you don't like my toast?'

'I don't like your toast.'

'Does it shock you?'

'It shocks me. André Gide didn't betray anything apart from his own bewilderment faced with certain contradictions that a non-Marxist mind finds it hard to resolve.'

'How well I talk,' I said to myself. 'The fact is, I'm not at all afraid.

I'm not frightened because I started thinking of N. and I don't care about anything.'

'Objectively…' my visitor began.

I cut him short.

'Yes, objectively, I know… But doubtless you wanted to ask me questions about the trip.'

'I'll ask whatever questions I like,' he replied curtly.

I was filled with rage, one of those overwhelming rages that immediately boils over.

'Comrade,' I shouted, sitting up in my bed. 'It will soon be one in the morning. I am tired. I won't answer a single question tonight.'

To show I was serious, I covered my head with the blanket. Some time later, I risked leaving my refuge. I was alone. I jumped out of bed, ran to the door and shot the bolt. I was about to get back into bed when I came up short, the blood freezing in my veins. My revolver which, as I did every night, I had left on my bedside table, was no longer there. 'That's bad,' I grunted. I fell asleep immediately like a brute.

The next morning I kicked up a big fuss about my revolver. 'There are Francoist spies even in the embassy,' I complained.

Koltsov was listening to me curiously.

'And when will I get my safe-conduct?'

'You're nervous,' Koltsov observed. 'Just wait calmly…'

The fat man from the night before came in and handed Koltsov a piece of paper without a word. I noticed that the stranger had his hair plastered down on his forehead. When he had read what was written on the paper, Koltsov looked enquiringly at the fat man, who merely touched his cap a couple of times. I don't know why, but this silent scene filled me with unease (probably also because the obese gentleman, when he caught my eye, stared vacantly at me as if he had never seen me before).

The next night, Madrid was bombed.

I had put in my Quiès ear-plugs. When I opened my eyes, I was astonished to see three men waving their arms about inside my room. A bomb had gone off on my balcony. The window frame had been blown in and was lying on my bed. There was a delicate halo of broken glass all round my head. I had not heard a thing. I took out my ear-plugs, and the film suddenly became a talkie. Stalenkov (let's call him that) was shrieking at me:

'You left your light on… as a signal to the enemy!'

'If the Francoist airmen are so accurate with their bombs, the Republic's had it,' I replied.

The fat man's two acolytes were picking up the shards of glass on my sheets with their fingers.

'Get up!' they ordered me. 'We'll find you another room.'

I got dressed. The fat man was staring out of the window. For a split second I hoped he would take another step forward and fall from the fourth floor, as the balcony balustrade had been torn away by the bomb.

'Something is burning,' he said. He turned towards me: 'Would you like to go and see the fire?'

That suited me fine. What was burning was a covered market. The pavements all round it were packed with armed militiamen who were arguing furiously with murderous-looking civilians. They all claimed the market had not been hit by a bomb. Spies had taken advantage of the air-raid to set the place on fire. One woman was shouting: 'They want us to starve!' Stalenkov, his men and I spoke French to each other. I caught some of the crowd looking at me menacingly. All of a sudden we were confronted by militiamen.

'*Ambajada sovietica*,' said Stalenkov. But this time the password didn't work. With deliberate slowness, the fat man took out his wallet and produced a document.

'*Ambajada sovietica*,' he repeated, pointing to his two companions.

'What about this one?' said the militiamen.

Stalenkov glanced casually in my direction, shrugged his shoulders, and left without responding. The barrel of a sub-machine gun was jabbed into my ribs. The angry crowd closed in around me. 'This time I'm done for,' I told myself. 'They're in such a state they're either going to shoot me or let the crowd tear me to pieces.' It was the fact that the militiamen were so small that saved me. I could see over their heads. A few feet away I saw the poet José Bergamín also watching the fire.

'What's happening to you?' he shouted. Then, to the militiamen: 'For goodness' sake, let him go!'

The threats changed to applause. I was quaking with fear and horror.

'Could you take me back to the Soviet embassy?' I asked Bergamín.

When he saw me, Koltsov's face brightened. The fat man and his henchmen did not react.

'What's this then?' said Koltsov. 'You get lost now like Tom Thumb, do you?'

'People lose me like Tom Thumb,' I corrected him.

Koltsov had a bed made up for me on his couch. He had to lend me a pair of pyjamas, because my things had disappeared, and my suitcase had apparently 'gone astray'.

One sleeps wonderfully after a real fright. But when I woke up I didn't feel so triumphant. I was cornered like a rat. How was I to escape? 'Telephone Paris,' I told myself. 'They might be embarrassed if people find out I'm their guest at the embassy.' I picked up the left-hand telephone. 'There's no point calling home,' I calculated. 'Nobody will be there.'

'What number?' asked the girl on the switchboard in Paris.

'Littré 13–31,' I told her.

That was Malraux's number. 'Please god let Clara be in, let Clara be in…' I begged. Koltsov came into the office.

'Is that you, Clara?' I said. 'I wanted to ask you to call my wife to re-assure her. Tell her I've been taken in by the Russian embassy. Yes, I'm living there. I saw André last week. He's fine. So please call my wife straightaway.'

Koltsov was standing in front of his desk, tidying some papers.

'…I wanted them to know in Paris that I'm safe, staying here with you,' I said.

Koltsov nodded.

'Clara Malraux is a very good comrade,' he said.

That afternoon, Malraux swept in. I suspect he made the journey from Albacete to Madrid just to find out what had become of me. I managed to get him on his own.

'I'm taking you with me,' he declared once I had explained everything to him. And to Koltsov: 'Herbart is wasting his time here. Send him to Barcelona; I'll find a plane for him in Albacete.'

Koltsov leapt at this chance to get rid of me. In all seriousness, he drew up a list of comrades I must see in Catalonia, wrote letters of introduction, added lots of official stamps.

'We need you to carry out an investigation into the state of mind of the anarcho-syndicalist groups,' he insisted. 'And you'll bring back the results. So I'll see you soon. Or rather, I won't. I will probably be recalled to Moscow.' He shook my hand. 'Farewell. I'll send your greetings to Maria.'

I knew I would never see him again.

When I landed at Le Bourget, I jumped into a taxi that took me straight to Aragon's. I'm sure he remembers that visit. As for Gide, he welcomed me with open arms.

'My *Return from the USSR* is the talk of the town.'

'You almost got me shot.'

'Don't be ridiculous! Look my dear man, *since you're here*, admit that what I did was for the best. And believe me, I thought and thought about it.'

'Jef Last is still in Madrid,' I said in a worried tone.

'He's writing me such wonderful letters! I wonder whether we shouldn't publish a small collection.'

'For goodness' sake, at least wait until he authorizes it.'

'I can assure you, those letters deserve to be published.'

'But Jef doesn't deserve a bullet to the back of the head. When will you understand…'

'My dear friend, not another word. I have a very firm opinion about all that. I have still to formulate it precisely. Meanwhile therefore I prefer not to talk about it. You must admit though that as far as *Return from the USSR* is concerned, I was right not to give in to any pressure, even from you, and to publish without backing down. Just look at these press cuttings. (He lowered his voice.) My wife is worried, you know. She is afraid of violence, an attack… But I'm not frightened. Fear is an emotion that is foreign to me. Except for once, in Italy, when my window flew open in the middle of the night. It was the wind.'

↜

Born in Dunkirk in 1903, **Pierre Herbart** fought in the French army in Morocco in 1923. His experiences in Africa made him a committed opponent of colonialism and he joined the French Communist Party in 1933. He went to the USSR with André Gide in 1936. On his return from the Soviet Union, Herbart set off to Spain with the manuscript of Gide's *Return from the USSR*, one of the first publications by a fellow traveller to criticize post-revolutionary Russia. While Herbart was in Spain asking Malraux's advice about publication, Gide published the incendiary manuscript in Paris. These events among others are narrated with brittle humour in Herbart's autobiography, *La Ligne de Force*. Herbart played a key role in the Resistance in Brittany and under the name General Le Vigan was in charge of the liberation of Rennes. He was sent to cover the situation in Algeria for the daily *France-Soir*, and his 1947 articles were among the first to warn of impending unrest in North Africa. An iconoclast, who never refrained from attacking the powers that be, Herbart died in total poverty in Grasse in 1974.

ALBERTO MÉNDEZ

SECOND DEFEAT:
1940 OR MANUSCRIPT
FOUND IN OBLIVION

from *Blind Sunflowers*

translated by Nick Caistor

THIS TEXT WAS FOUND in a cabin in the mountains of Somiedo, on the borders of Asturias and León. Also discovered were the skeleton of an adult male and an infant's surprisingly well-conserved naked body, laid on some cloth sacks stretched out over a palliasse. They were covered in a wolf skin and the fleece of a mountain goat, as well as wild boar fur and dried moss. The two bodies lay side-by-side, and were wrapped in a white bedspread, 'as if in a nest', according to the official report. The bedspread was as clean as the rest of the room was dirty, foul-smelling and wretched. The dried but still stinking remains of a cow missing its head and one hoof were also found. In 1952, while I was searching for other documents in the Civil Guard General Archive, I came across a yellow envelope with the letters NN (no name) written on it. The envelope contained an oilskin notebook, consisting of a few ruled pages. The contents were written in a neat, flowing hand. On the first pages, the handwriting is large, but it grows progressively smaller, as if the writer had more to write about than would fit into the book. Comments apparently added later are occasionally scribbled in the margins. This is obvious not only because of the handwriting (which as I said becomes progressively smaller) but also because they clearly reflect very different states of mind. I have nevertheless included these comments on the corresponding pages.

A shepherd came across the notebook on a stool, under a heavy stone that could not have been put there by accident. A leather satchel, an axe, a bed-frame with no mattress and two pottery bowls on the cold hearth were the only other items listed in the civil guardsman's report. A simple black dress was hanging from the ceiling. There were no other signs of life, although the report states (and this is what encouraged me to read the notebook) that a phrase had been scrawled on the cabin wall: 'Infamous flock of nocturnal birds.'

The text of the notebook is as follows:

Page 1
Elena died giving birth. I was unable to keep her on this side of life. To my surprise though, the boy is alive.

There he is, unravelled, shivering, lying on a clean cloth alongside his dead mother. I have no idea what to do. I don't dare touch him. I think I am going to let him die with his mother. She will know how to look after an infant's soul. She will teach him to laugh, if there is a place for souls to laugh. We will not get over the mountains to France. Without Elena I have no wish to reach the end of the journey. Without Elena there is no way through.

How does one correct the mistake of being alive? I've seen so many dead people, but I haven't learned how one dies!

Page 2
It's not right that death should come so soon, when life itself has had no time to begin.

I've left everything as it was. Nobody will be able to say I interfered. The mother dead, the child restlessly alive, and me paralysed by fear. The colour of flight is grey; the sound of defeat is sadness.

At this point there is a poem that has been crossed out. Only a few words are legible: 'vigorous', 'no light' (or 'my light', it is not clear which) and 'to forget the explosion'. In the margin, in smaller handwriting: 'Is this child the cause of death, or its fruit?'

Page 3

I want to leave everything written down in order to make it clear to whoever finds us that they are also to blame, unless they are victims too. Whoever reads this, please scatter our remains out on the hills. Elena could go no further, and the boy and I want to stay beside her. I am guilty only of having allowed what happened to happen. I had not learned how to avoid grief, and now grief has chopped Elena from me with its scythe. I only know how to write and tell stories. Nobody has taught me how to talk to myself, or to protect life from death. I write because I don't want to remember how to pray or to curse.

How can such a beautiful story end on a mountain racked by the wind? It's only October, but up here every night autumn becomes winter.

The child cried all day, with surprising strength. He has forced me to think of him, even though all I do is stare at Elena dead beside me, and have paid him no attention the whole morning. I now realise I have not shed a single tear over her, probably because the child's sobbing is more than enough. And it's necessary. I would never have managed to cry so helplessly; I would never have succeeded in screaming so angrily. Tears have been shed over Elena's dead body without any effort on my part. How is it possible for someone to shed tears and fade away at the same time? Now it seems as though the boy has lost consciousness. I went over to look at him. He's still breathing, although it felt to me as though his skeleton had somehow been removed.

Page 4

I've been studying Elena's chalky face. She is not as waxily pallid as she was when she died. It's as though all the colour has drained from her. Perhaps death is transparent. And frozen. For the first few hours, I felt the need to keep her hand in mine, but little by little the sense of her fingers caressing me faded, and I was afraid this would be the memory of her that remained engraved on my unrequited skin. I haven't touched her for several hours, and am no longer capable of lying down beside her. The boy is, though. He's curled up against his mother. For a moment I thought he was trying to bring some warmth back to the lifeless body that was his shelter through all the droning numbness of war.

Yes. We've lost a war, and to allow ourselves to be caught by the Fascists would be akin to handing them another victory. Elena wanted to follow me, but now we know we made the wrong decision. I'd like to think it was the most generous mistake imaginable.

We should have listened to her parents. I beg their forgiveness for having allowed Elena to come with me when I fled.

Stay here, it's not you they're after, I told her. I'll follow you. They'll kill me. I'm dying. We talked of death in order to take a chance with life. But we were wrong. We should never have started out on such an endless journey with her eight months pregnant. The child will not survive, and I'll let myself fall onto the grass. The snow will come and bury me, and later out of my eye sockets will grow flowers that will enrage those who preferred death to poetry.

Miguel, your prophecy will come true!

Where can you be now, Miguel, why aren't you here to comfort me? I would gladly sacrifice eternity to hear your liquid verses just once more, your level voice, your friendly advice. Perhaps all this pain will make a poet of me, Miguel, perhaps you won't have to be so kind in your appreciation of me? Do you remember, you used to call me the proletarian archer? Elena loved you for that, and loves you even after her death, I'm sure.

Page 5

Would Elena have preferred me to disentangle the child from the placenta, to tie his umbilical with one of my bootlaces, to seek to humble the victors with the seed of revenge? I don't think she would have wanted a defeated child. I don't want a son born of flight. My son does not want a life born of death. Or does he?

If the God I have heard about were a good God, he would allow us to choose our past, but neither Elena nor her son will be able to go back along the path that has brought us to this cabin that will be their burial place.

At first light, sleep overcame me, and I dozed off leaning on the table. I was awakened by the boy's sobs: they sounded less vigorous, more ailing. His anger yesterday left me indifferent, but today's lament has touched me. I don't know whether it was because I was dazed from sleep and cold, or because after three days without food I'm also beginning to feel weak, but the fact is that without realising it I found myself giving him the tip of a rag dipped in diluted milk. At first he did not seem to know if he should live or simply allow himself to become part of my plan, but after a while he began to suck on the liquid. He was sick, but then went on sucking greedily. Life seems determined to win out.

I think it was a mistake to pick him up. I think it was a mistake to distance him from death for even an instant, but the warmth of my body and the food he managed to take in have sent him into a fitful but deep sleep.

Page 6

I used some sacks of hay to make him a cosy cradle. I covered him with the crocheted bedspread Elena's grandmother made. Elena insisted on bringing it with her, as if all her past were bundled up in it. It's no longer as comforting as it was when the three of us fled, but it warms the child up. Perhaps it still bears traces of his mother's smell.

I must confess I find the contrast between life and death unbearable.

To see the two of them in the same bed, flat on their backs, with Elena completely gone and him still so undefined was like drawing a line between what's true and what's false. All at once death was death, nothing more, stripped of the body's innocence, of life's animal nature. By the end of three days, a dead body is a mineral without the moisture of breath or the fragility of flowers. It isn't even a defenceless object. It's not something that could feel under attack, and yet it crouches there as though trying to hide. By the end of three days, a dead body is nothing more than solitude. It doesn't even have the gift of sadness. The boy's umbilical cord is drying out. He's still crying.

Around this passage there is a faint drawing in which one can make out a shooting star, or the childish representation of a comet, which is crashing into a tearful, waning moon.

Page 7

I haven't eaten. I still have some dry bread and tins of fish that we brought with us on our escape. The boy has had some more diluted milk. It seems to fill him up. Today I'll bury his mother under the oak tree. I don't have the strength to milk the cows, but they are becoming ill and their lowing also serves to take my mind off Elena. I'd like someone to come up from the valley and round up the cattle so I don't have to decide whether to feed myself or let myself roll down the slope to death. But in these fearful times, even cattle have to fend for themselves. Until winter arrives, they will be unaware of the existence of wolves, cold, and the natural order of things. As it stands, they and I are facing the same fate. If nobody comes, the four or five of them that need to be milked will die. How could the person looking after them have vanished, just like that? But that is of no importance in such bleak times as these. Anyway, while I make my mind up, I'll need milk for the boy.

It's raining. So much the better; no one will dare make the trip up to the cabin in such unsettled weather. I've managed to catch two of the cows. One of them has mastitis. I'll have to kill her to stop her suffering. Today the child ate three times.

Page 8

Today I buried Elena under a beech tree. It's less robust than the oak. The sound of the earth falling on her mingled with the smell of her decomposing body. I was reduced to such bitter tears that for a moment I felt sure I was going to die too. But dying is not contagious. Defeat is. And I feel I am transmitting that particular epidemic. Wherever I go there will be the stench of defeat. Defeat killed Elena, and it will be the death of my son, whom I have not yet named. I lost a war and Elena, whom nobody could ever have considered an enemy, has died defeated. My son, our son, who is not even aware he was conceived with the flames of fear all around him, will die, mortally wounded by defeat.

I placed a big white stone on her grave. I didn't write her name on it, because I know that if any angels still exist, they will recognise Elena's kindly soul among a whole host of other kindly souls.

I'm trying to recall some of Garcilaso's verses to recite over your tomb, Elena, but I no longer have any recollection of them. How did they go?

There are several failed attempts to write the poem, all of them crossed out. The only lines that are legible are the following:

> Take these tears which on ground so bare
> I shed today as so often in the past
> although they may not help you there,
> until that dark and eternal night
> closes these eyes that saw you last
> and brings me new and brighter sight.

Page 9

I don't know why I'm writing this notebook. And yet I'm glad I brought it with me. If I had someone to talk to, I probably would not write it; I derive a certain morbid pleasure when I think that somebody will read it after they have found my dead son and me. I've put a stone marker on Elena's grave so that the sense of remorse will be threefold, even though the time for pity is past. It's very cold now. Soon it will start to snow, and then all the paths up to the cabin will be cut off. I'll have the whole winter to decide what death we are to die from. Yes, I think the time for pity has gone.

Page 10

In the margin are several roughly-drawn faces, obviously meant to be portraits. Three of them show the face of a child, and two that of a woman — the same woman in both cases. There are sketches of old people, both men and women, some of them wearing berets, others with scarves tied round their necks. There's also a dog, pictured complete. Underneath all these drawings is the phrase: What graves are you lying in now?

The sick cow lows plaintively. Its milk has dried up. I don't dare kill her yet because I need snowdrifts to build up for me to keep the carcass in. There is plenty of firewood, and I'll try to feed the other one by digging out grass from under the snow. What worries me most is this pencil. It's the only one I have, and I want to be able to write everything so that whoever finds us in spring knows how we met our death.

Written in capitals as if in a printed book, the following phrase: I AM A POET WITH NO VERSES.

Page 11

Today it snowed all day. These mountains must be where all winters have their home.

The boy is still alive. The snow round the cabin is like a shroud. The dead cow provides us with meat: I keep some of it smoked, and the rest has been frozen by this early winter weather. Fortunately we get plenty of milk from the living cow, which is now inside the cabin with us. It helps to keep us warm. The sweet potatoes we stole as we went through Perlunes keep perfectly, buried in the snow. To judge by the greedy way he drinks the soup I make, the boy seems to like them. What's surprising is the way he is beginning to fill the space. I can remember when he was an intruder in the cabin, something that should not have been there. Now the entire hut revolves around him. On the few days when there is sun, our bed reflects the light like a mirror, and the silence piles up around the noises the boy is constantly making, either because he is crying, or is taken by surprise by his bare leg waving in mid-air, or the sight of the withered, weary cow that has replaced a hearth to warm our family. His gentle, rhythmic breathing helps ward off the loneliness which without him would vanquish me.

Page 12

I found a mountain goat half-eaten by wolves. There was a lot of meat left on it, so today we will eat the remains. I've made a very mild soup from its bones and innards which the boy seems to keep down well.

At this point there is a significant change in the handwriting. Although it is still very neat and tidy, it seems to be written in more haste. Or perhaps less steadily. Probably some length of time has elapsed.

Would my parents recognise me if they saw me? I can't see myself, but I imagine I am filthy and humiliated. I am yet another product of the war they tried to ignore but which flooded their stables, their starving cattle, their sparse crops with fear. I remember the poor, silent village of ours that closed its eyes to everything apart from fear. I remember how it shut its eyes when they killed Don Servando, my teacher, when they burned all his books and exiled all the poets whose work he knew by heart.

I've lost. But I could have won. Will someone else take my place? I'm going to tell my son, who is gazing at me as though he understands, that I would not have left my enemies to flee with nothing, I would not have condemned anyone for being a poet. I threw myself into battle armed only with paper and pencil, and words gushed out of me that brought comfort to the wounded. But the comfort I gave also created bloodthirsty generals who were the reason for the wounded. Wounded, generals, generals, wounded. And there was I, stuck in the middle with my poetry. Their accomplice. And then there were the dead.

Page 13
Here there is a sentence crossed out which is illegible. The text on this page is placed around the outline of an infant's hand. Presumably he used his child's hand as a stencil. He wrote on it:

Time has passed. I have no idea how many days because they are all the same, but what most surprises me is how the boy grows. When I reread this notebook, I realise I no longer feel the same. And if I lose my anger, what is there left? The winter is a closed box which stores up all the snowstorms. These mountains still seem like the place where winter spends the winter. My sadness has also frozen with the cold. All I have left is the fear that used to make me so afraid. I'm afraid the boy might fall ill, afraid the cow will die because I can barely feed her by digging up roots or giving her the few shoots of grass still growing when the snow came. I'm afraid of falling ill myself. I'm afraid someone will discover we are up here on the mountain. I'm afraid of so much fear. But the boy is unaware of all of this. Elena!

At night, the wind howls round the mountain with an almost human moan. It's as if it were trying to show me and the child how humans should grieve. Fortunately, the cabin is strong enough to withstand all the storms.

Page 14

Today I killed a wolf! Four of them came sneaking round the cabin. At first I was frightened, because their hunger gives them an almost human ferocity. But then I thought they might be able to provide us with food. When the biggest wolf came scratching at the door, I carefully opened it wide enough for him to poke his head in, then I quickly trapped his neck in the door's edge. A single blow from the axe was enough. I hit him so hard his appetite spilled out with his blood. I'll eat its flesh, and the entrails will provide the boy with nourishment. That is good, but the bad thing is I have smelled blood once more, I have heard again the sounds of death, and seen the colour of victims.

On this page there is a drawing which shows a boy riding on a wolf; both of them are smiling and seem to be flying through the air above a field full of flowers.

Page 15

A wolf told a boy that with his tender flesh
He could survive the winter.
The boy told the wolf to eat only one leg
Because he was so young and tiny
That he needed the wolf to be nice and plump
Ready for the moment when
Even one-legged, he would need some roasted
Wolf to dine on.

They stared at each other, sniffed one another and felt so bad
That they would have to harm each other
They agreed to repeat the scene
Without resorting to the deceit
That for two people who love each other to survive
They always have to admit

That whatever their feelings, one must live
And the other one die.

And as a corollary:

The pair of them perished of hunger.

Underneath these lines there is a musical scale and some notes, although these do not correspond to anything that resembles real music. Several experts have tried to decipher this supposed tune, but to no avail.

Page 16

The snow keeps coming down. I feel so weak it's harder and harder for me to chop firewood to heat the cabin where the cow, the boy and I live. All three of us are losing strength. Yet the boy, whom I still have not given a name, is surprisingly lively. He makes noises in his throat when he's awake that sound like gurgling. On the one hand, I like it that he's not asleep, because his total dependence on me makes me feel important in a way that no one except Elena has ever done before. On the other, his eyes are so huge in his eye sockets and his cheeks so sunken that I can see his skull. He is so skinny! The cow is too, but she still gives enough milk for the boy and me. I am emaciated too, and frozen stiff.

I have no idea what month we are in. Could it be Christmas already?

Today I followed an animal's tracks and went down the mountain in the direction of Sotre. In the valley bottom I saw some woodcutters. I felt a familiar, solid fear grip me. Nowadays I am proud of my fear, because at the end of this monstrous war I have seen too many people die thanks to their courage. If we stay up here, the cow, the boy and I will die. If we go down into the valley, the cow, the boy and I will die.

Page 17

I've thought a lot about it, but I don't want to give them the final satisfaction of victory. It may be right and proper for me to die, since I was nothing more than a bad poet who sang of life in trenches where death ruled the roost. But for the boy to die is nothing more than necessity.

Who is going to tell him about the colour of his mother's hair, about her smile, the graceful way she glided through the air as though trying not to disturb it? Who is going to beg for forgiveness for having conceived him? And if I do survive, what am I going to tell him about me? That Caviedes is a village perched on a mountain that smells of the sea and firewood, that I had a teacher who could recite Góngora and Machado from memory, a father and mother who were unable to keep me on the farm, that I have no idea what I was looking for when I went to Madrid in the midst of the war… a balladeer dodging bullets? That's right, my son! I wanted to be a balladeer dodging bullets!

Now I'm your gravedigger!

This last phrase is underlined with a thick, heavy line, so firmly drawn it has torn the paper of the black oilskin notebook.

Page 18
I can no longer provide food for the cow, and the cow can no longer provide food for the boy. I scrape about under the snow searching for grass shoots, but they are increasingly rare and straggly. Among the roots of the frozen hazel trees I found some kind of bulbs. I use them to make a paste that is completely tasteless but which, when boiled and mashed, I offer to the cow and the boy. I don't know if it is of any use as food, but I am giving him my saliva, and he is surviving. Even though he is very weak, he is already trying to stir, but he doesn't have the strength. He bends backwards, supporting himself on his head and feet. He quickly collapses. If I could, I would go down into the valley and beg for food, but it's impossible now to get out of these mountains. I was born in a village where it never snows, and nobody taught me how to cope with this silent, endless snow. Whenever I stray further than usual from the cabin I find myself buried up to the waist, and it takes me an age to free myself from this white trap. What little the wolves left of the dead cow is so hard by now I can't even shave off any bits with the axe. Fortunately, the carcass is covered with snow, because yesterday I tried to dig it out to find lean meat

Page 19

among its remains and I discovered a beast, half torn flesh and half skeleton, which stretched out its neck as though trying desperately to escape. The cow's few remaining ribs form a kind of bowl that looks as if it should contain its soul. But the soul has also been devoured by the wolves. And by me. And the boy.

Here there is a drawing meant to show a stylised cow's head, elongated like an arrow, flying through the air. Underneath is the phrase: Where can cows' heaven be?

I ought to kill the other cow while she still has some meat on her. But I have no way of keeping it fresh. If I leave the meat out in the snowdrifts, the prowling wolves would only sniff it out. I keep the inside of the cabin warm enough that what's left of her would soon go off. I wonder if the cow thinks I am saving her from the wolves, or does she know that it is the wolves that are saving her from my axe? Perhaps she knows the truth, and that is why she no longer gives milk.

There follow several pages, nine in total, which must have been torn out together, because the tear is exactly the same in all of them. It has been carefully done: there are no jagged edges. In the numbering that follows, we have not taken into account the sheets missing from the notebook.

Page 20

The boy is ill. He hardly moves. I've killed the cow, and am giving him her blood, but he can barely swallow any. I've boiled her meat and bones to make a thick, dark broth. I'm giving it to him diluted in snow water. Yet again, everything smells of death.

He's very hot. I'm writing with him asleep on my lap. How much I love him! I sang him a sad song by Federico:

The tears of a skull
Awaiting a golden kiss.
(Outside, dark wind

And muddied stars).

I can't remember any more which poems I used to recite for the soldiers. When you are hungry, the first thing that dies is memory. I can't write a single verse, and yet my mind is full of a thousand lullabies for my son. They all start the same way: Elena!

Today I kissed him. For the first time. I had not used my lips for so long I had forgotten about them. What must he have felt when he first came into contact with their cold touch? It's terrible, but by now he must be three or four months old, and until today nobody had ever kissed him. He and I know how, without a kiss, time stretches out interminably, and now it seems as if there's not enough of it left for us to be able to catch up. Fear, cold, hunger, rage and loneliness drive out tenderness. Like a crow it only comes back when it scents love and death. Now it is back, but it's confused. It can smell both things. Can tenderness be white and black? Elena, what colour was your tenderness? I no longer remember. I don't even know if what I feel is sorrow. But I kissed the boy without trying to take your place.

Page 21

There's a smell of something rotten. Yet all I remember is the scent of wild fennel.

In large, very large letters, the remainder of the page is covered with the words 'OH, WITHOUT YOU THERE IS NOTHING' *written in an unsteady hand.*

Page 22

I couldn't find my pencil (or what's left of it) so was unable to write for several days. That is silence too, that is being gagged. Today, when I discovered the stub again under a pile of firewood, I felt I had rediscovered the gift of speech. I don't know what I feel until I write it down. It must be my rural education. Today I spent a long time up on a leafless tree trunk trying to spot the tracks of an animal that could provide us with food. All I saw was an uninterrupted white expanse stretching to the horizon. A stubborn, freezing wind swept across the snowy waste, its howling only reinforcing the silence. While I was up there watching, I felt something I could not identify, something that might have been good or bad. Now I've found my pencil, I know what it was: solitude.

I have the feeling that everything will come to an end once I come to the end of this notebook. That is why I only write in it occasionally. My pencil must also have lost the war. I think the very last word it will write will be 'melancholy'.

Page 23
The boy has died. I have decided to call him Rafael after my father. I did not have enough warmth to keep him alive. He learned from his mother how to die without any fuss, and this morning simply did not respond to my words of encouragement.

The rest of the page, written in an almost beautiful handwriting that is much more carefully done than anything up to this point, repeats over and over Rafael, Rafael, Rafael, *a total of sixty-three times. The R of Rafael is always a vertical flourish interlaced with a big round circle that starts on the left, rises above the vertical line, and comes back to the vertical more or less in the middle, only to part from it again, like a starched petticoat that tails away at the bottom. It is both English and gothic at the same time.*

Page 24
The word Rafael *is repeated a further sixty-two times.*

Page 25
The word Rafael *again, in the same handwriting, but much smaller: one hundred and nineteen times.*

Page 26
This is no longer written with the same pencil, which has probably run out. Instead the author has used a piece of charcoal or something similar. The words are hard to make out because, after they were written, he obviously drew his hand across the page in an attempt to rub them out. Bearing this in mind, we think

we have faithfully transcribed what was written: 'Infamous flock of nocturnal birds'.

EDITOR'S NOTE: *In the year 1954 I visited a village in the province of Santander called Caviedes. It is perched on a mountain top and smells of the nearby sea, although this cannot be seen because the houses all overlook an inland valley. I asked around, and was told that the local schoolteacher, known as Don Servando, was shot as a Republican in 1937, and that his best pupil, who had a boundless love of poetry, had fled aged sixteen to the loyalist zone in order to join the army which lost the war. Neither his parents, who were called Rafael and Felisa and died at the end of the war, nor anyone else in the village ever heard from him again. People thought he was crazy because he was always writing and reciting poems. His name was Eulalio Ceballos Suárez. If he was the author of this notebook, he must have been eighteen when he wrote it. I personally think that is too young for so much suffering.*

~

Alberto Méndez was born in Madrid in 1941. Published in 2004, the year of his death, the short story collection *Blind Sunflowers* is his only book. The organizing theme of the book is defeat – not defeat on a grand scale but defeat as it affected everyday lives on both sides of the war. Like Cercas' *Soldiers of Salamis*, Méndez's work is part of the process of rediscovering the grassroots history of the Civil War. It is a process that seeks to disprove the view propagated by Franco and the Nationalist movement that 'There were no victims, only heroes; no dead people, only those who had fallen in the name of Spain'. The stories of *Blind Sunflowers* are part of a wider process to give back a history to the many unidentified and lost dead. Méndez died in Madrid in 2004.

ARTURO BAREA

THIS WAR IS A LESSON

from *The Clash*, part 3 of *The Forging of a Rebel*

translated by Ilsa Barea

THE DEADLY CLOUD HAD LIFTED. The anti–climax made us laugh. It was no longer likely that the police would be used to get rid of Ilsa. I had lodged a sharp complaint against the denouncers, not sparing the man whom I suspected behind the move. At lunch, while we were sitting in amity with the police agents, I had seen George Gordon's face flushed and twitching. A couple of days later he made a movement as though to greet us, but we overlooked it.

I wanted to be merry. I took Ilsa round the corner to the Andalusian bar, Villa Rosa, where the old waiter Manolo greeted me as a lost son, examined her thoughtfully, and then told her that I was a rake, but not a genuine rake, and that she was the right woman to cope with me; drank a little glass of Manzanilla with us, tremulously, because the war had made him very old. He did not get enough food. When I let him have some tins given us by a friend in the International Brigades, he was so humbly grateful that I could have cried. In the evening we went to Serafín's and plunged into the warm welcome of the cronies. Torres, Luisa, and her husband came gabbling with pleasure. They thought that our troubles were over and that soon we would do work in Madrid again.

But Agustín, who had staunchly visited us every day, though it could do him no good with his boss Rosario, told me bluntly that we ought to leave Madrid. As long as we stayed on, certain people would resent our very existence. Intrigues might not always go through official channels, and we could not walk about for good with a bodyguard. Moreover, I was going crazy, in his opinion.

I felt in my bones that he was right. But I was not yet ready to leave Madrid. I was tied to it with hurting, quivering nerve-strings. I was writing a story about Angel. If they did not let me broadcast any more, I had to talk through print. I believe that I could do it. My very first story (The story of the militiaman who made a fly his pet) had been printed, incongruously enough, in the *Daily Express*, and the fee had overwhelmed me, accustomed as I was to the rates of pay of Spanish journalism. I realized that the story had been published mainly because Delmer had liked it and provided a witty headline and caption such as: 'This story was written under shellfire by the Madrid Censor – who lost his inhibitions about writing by censoring our dispatches.' All the same, my first piece of simple story-telling had gone out to people who, perhaps, would through it get a glimpse of the mind of that poor brute, the Miliciano. I wanted to go on; but what I had to say had its roots in Madrid. I would not let them drive me away, and I could not go before I had cleared the red fog of anger out of my brain. It swept me, together with the relief that she was alive and with me, every time I watched Ilsa. All my submerged violence rose when I saw her still bound to her rack, still lashed by the ugliness of the thing which people of her own creed were inflicting on her, and still quiet.

The man who helped me then, as he had helped me through the evil weeks that went before, was a Catholic priest, and of all those I met in our war he commands my deepest respect and love: Don Leocadio Lobo.

I do not remember how we first came to talk to each other. Father Lobo, too, lived in the Hotel Victoria, and soon after we had moved in he became a regular guest at our table, together with Armando. The mutual confidence between him and Ilsa was instantaneous and strong; I felt at once the great attraction of a man who had suffered and still believed in human beings with a great and simple faith. He knew, because I said so, that I did not consider myself a Catholic any more, and he knew that I was divorced, living in what his Church called 'sin' with Ilsa and intending to marry her as soon as she had her divorce. I did not spare him violent outbursts against the political clergy in league with the 'powers of darkness,' and against the stultifying orthodoxy I had come to hate in my schooldays. Nothing of all this seemed to impress him or to affect his attitude to us, which was that of a candid, detached friend.

He wore no cassock but a somewhat shiny dark suit. His strong, regular features would have made him an attractive man, had they not been deeply furrowed by his thought and struggle; his face had a stamp of inwardness which set him apart even in his frequent moments of expansion. He was one of those people who make you feel that they only say what is their own truth and do not make themselves accomplices of what they believe to be a lie. He seemed to me to be a reincarnation of Father Joaquín, the Basque priest who had been the best friend of my boyhood. Curiously enough the origins of both were alike. Father Lobo, like Father Joaquín, was the son of simple country folk, of a mother who had borne many children and worked tirelessly all her life. He, too, had been sent to the seminary with the help of the local gentry because he had been a bright boy at school, and because his parents were glad to see him escape from grinding poverty. He, too, had left the seminary not with the ambition of becoming a prelate, but with that of being a Christian priest at the side of those who were hungry and thirsty for bread and justice.

His history was well known in Madrid. Instead of staying in a smart, influential parish, he chose a parish of poor workers, rich in blasphemies and rebellion. They did not blaspheme less for his sake, but they loved him because he belonged to the people. At the outbreak of the rebellion he had taken the side of the people, the side of the Republican Government, and he had continued in his ministry. During the wildest days of August and September he went out at night to hear the Confession of whoever demanded it, and to give Communion. The only concession he made to circumstances was that he doffed his cassock so as not to provoke rows. There was a famous story that one night two Anarchist Milicianos called at the house where he was staying, with their rifles cocked and a car waiting at the door. They asked for the priest who was living there. His hosts denied that there was one. They insisted, and Father Lobo came out of his room. 'Yes, there is a priest, and it's me. What's up?'

'All right, come along with us, but put one of those Hosts of yours in your pocket.'

His friends implored him not to go; they told the Anarchists that Lobo's loyalty was vouched for by the Republican Government, that they simply would not allow him to leave, that they would rather call in the police. In the end, one of the Anarchists stamped on the floor and shouted:

'Oh hell, nothing will happen to him! If you must know, the old woman, my mother, is dying and doesn't want to go to the other world without confessing to one of these buzzards. It's a disgrace for me, but what else could I do but fetch him?'

And Father Lobo went out in the Anarchists' car, into one of those gray dawns when people were being shot against the wall.

Later on he went for a month to live with the militiamen in the front line. He came back exhausted and deeply shaken. In my hearing he rarely spoke of his experiences in the trenches. But one night he explained: 'What brutes – God help us – what brutes, but what men!'

He had to fight his own bitter mental struggle. The deepest hurt to him was not the fury vented against churches and priests by maddened, hate-filled, brutalized people, but his knowledge of the guilt of his own caste, the clergy, in the existence of that brutality, and in the abject ignorance and misery at the root of it. It must have been infinitely hard for him to know that princes of his Church were doing their level best to keep his people subjected, that they were blessing the arms of the generals and overlords, and the guns that shelled Madrid.

The Government had given him a task in the Ministry of Justice which was anything but simple: he had come to Madrid to investigate cases of hardship among the clergy, and he had to face the fact that some of the priests whose killing by the 'Reds' had been heralded and duly exploited came out of their hiding, safe and sound, and demanded help.

I needed a man to whom I could speak out of the depth of my mind. Don Leocadio was most human and understanding. I knew that he would not answer my outcry with admonitions or canting consolation. So I poured out all the turgid thoughts which clogged my brain. I spoke to him of the terrible law which made us hurt others without wanting to hurt them. There was my marriage and its end; I had hurt the woman with whom I did not share my real life and I had hurt our children because I hated living together with their mother. I inflicted the final pain when I had found my wife, Ilsa. I told him that Ilsa and I belonged together, complementing each other, without superiority of one over the other, without knowing why, without wanting to know, because it was the simple truth of our lives. But this new life which we could neither reject nor escape meant pain, because we could not be happy together without causing pain to others.

I spoke to him of the war, loathsome because it set men of the same people against each other, a war of two Cains. A war in which priests had been shot on the outskirts of Madrid and other priests were setting the seal of their blessing on the shooting of poor laborers, brothers of Don Leocadio's own father. Millions like myself who loved their people and its earth were destroying, or helping to destroy, that earth and their own people. And yet, none of us had the right to remain indifferent or neutral.

I had believed, I still believe, in a new free Spain of free people. I had wanted it to come without bloodshed, by work and good will. What could we do if this hope, this future was being destroyed? We had to fight for it. Had we to kill others? I knew that the majority of those who were fighting with arms in hand, killing or dying, did not think about it, but were driven by the forces unleashed or by their blind faith. But I was forced to think, for me this killing was a sharp and bitter pain which I could not forget. When I heard the battle noise I saw only dead Spaniards on both sides. Whom should I hate? Oh yes, Franco and Juán March and their generals and puppets and wirepullers, the privileged people over there. But when I would rather hate that God who gave them the callousness which made them kill, and who punished me with the torture of hating any killing and who let women and children first suffer from rickets and starvation wages, and then from bombs and shells. We were caught in a monstrous mechanism, crushed under the wheels.

And if we rebelled, all the violence and all the ugliness was turned against us, driving us to violence.

It sounded in my ears as though I had thought and said the same things as a boy. I excited myself to a fever, talking on and on in rage, protest, and pain. Father Lobo listened patiently, only saying sometimes: 'Now slowly, wait.' Then he talked to me for days. It may be that the answers I gave myself in the quiet hours on the balcony, while I stared at the Church of San Sebastian cut in two by a bomb, were fused in my memory with the words Father Lobo said to me. It may be that insensibly I made him into the other 'I' of that endless inner dialogue. But this is how I remember what he said:

'Who are you? What gives you the right to set yourself up as a universal judge? You only want to justify your own fear and cowardice. You are good, but you want everybody else to be good too, so that being good doesn't cost you any trouble and is a pleasure. You haven't the courage to preach what you believe in the middle of the street, because then you would be shot. And as a justification for your fear you put all the fault on to the others. You think you're decent and clean-minded and you try to tell me and yourself that you are, and that whatever happens to the others is their fault, and whatever pain happens to you as well. That's a lie. It is your fault.

'You've united yourself with this woman, with Ilsa, against everything and everybody. You go with her through the streets and call her your wife. And everybody can see that it's true, that you are in love with each other and that together you are complete. None of us would dare to call Ilsa your mistress because we all see that she is your wife. It is true that you and she have done harm to others, to the people who belong to you, and it is right that you should feel pain for it. But do you realize that you have scattered a good seed as well? Do you realize that hundreds of people who had despaired of finding what is called Love now look at you and learn to believe that it exists and is true, and that they may hope?

'And this war, you say it's loathsome and useless. I don't. It is a terrible, barbarous war with countless innocent victims. But you haven't lived in the trenches like me. This war is a lesson. It has torn Spain out of her paralysis, it has torn the people out of their houses where they were being turned into mummies. In our trenches illiterates are learning to read and even to speak, and they learn what brotherhood among men means. They see that there exists a better world and life, which they must conquer, and they learn too, that they must conquer it not with the rifle but with their will. They kill Fascists, but they learn the lesson that you win wars not by killing, but by convincing people. We may lose this war – but we shall have won it. They, too, will learn that they may rule us, but not convince us. Even if we are defeated, we will be stronger at the end of this than ever we were because the will has come alive.

'We all have our work to do, so do yours instead of talking about the world which doesn't follow you. Suffer pain and sorrow and stick it out, but don't shut yourself up and run round in circles within yourself. Talk and write down what you think you know, what you have seen and thought, tell it honestly and speak the truth. Don't produce programs which you don't believe in, and don't lie. Say what you have thought and seen, and let the others hear and read you, so that they are driven to tell their truth, too. And then you'll lose that pain of yours.'

In the clear, chill nights of October it seemed to me sometimes as though I were conquering my fear and cowardice, but I found it very hard to write down what I thought. It is still difficult. I found out, however, that I could write honestly and with truth of what I had seen, and that I had seen much. Father Lobo exclaimed when he saw one of my stories: 'What a barbarian you are! But go on, it's good for you and us.'

One evening he knocked at our door and invited us to go with him to see a surprise. In his small room was one of his brothers, a quiet workman, and farm labourer from his village. I knew that his people brought him wine for Mass and wine for his table whenever they could, and I thought he wanted to invite us to a glass of red wine. But he took me into his bathroom. An enormous turkey was standing awkwardly on the tiles, hypnotized by the electric light. When the countryman had gone, we spoke of those simple people who brought him the best thing they had, not caring whether it was absurd or not to dump a live turkey in the bathroom of a city hotel.

'It isn't easy for us to understand them,' Father Lobo said. 'If you do, it's a basis for art like Breughel's or like Lorca's. Yes Lorca's. Listen.' He took the slim war edition of the *Romancero Gitano* and started reading:

And I took her down to the river,
Thinking she was a maiden,
But she had a husband...

He read on with his strong, manly voice, not slurring over the words of naked physical love, only saying: 'This is barbarian, but it's tremendous.' And he seemed to me more of a man, and more of a priest of men and God, than ever.

In the worst weeks, when it took some courage to be seen with us, he spent long hours at our table, aware that he gave us moral support. He knew more about the background of our tangled story than we ourselves, but he never gave away what he had heard from others. Yet I did not dream of doubting his word when, after the campaign had passed its peak, he suddenly said: 'Now listen to the truth, Ilsa. They don't want you here. You know too many people and you put others in the shade. You know too much and you are too intelligent. We aren't used to intelligent women yet. You can't help being what you are, so you must go, and you must go away with Arturo because he needs you and you belong together. In Madrid you cannot do any good any more, except by keeping quiet as you do. But that won't be enough for you, you will want to work. So go away.'

'Yes, I know,' she said. 'The only thing I can do for Spain now is not to let people outside turn my case into a weapon against the Communists – not because I love the Communist Party, for I don't, even when I work with Communists, but because it would at the same time be a weapon against our Spain and against Madrid. That's why I can't move a finger for myself, and even have to ask my friends not to make a fuss. It's funny. The only thing I can do is to do nothing.'

She said it very dryly. Father Lobo looked at her and answered: 'You must forgive us. We are in your debt.'

Thus Father Lobo convinced us that we had to leave Madrid. When I accepted it, I wanted it to be done quickly so as not to feel it too much. It was a gray, foggy November day, Agustín and Torres saw us off. The Shock Police lorry, with hard loose boards for benches, rattled through the suburbs. There were few shells that morning.

Father Lobo had sent us to his mother in a village near Alicante. In his letter he had asked her to help me, his friend, and my wife Ilsa; he did not want to bewilder his mother, he said, and he had put down the essential truth. When I stood before the stout old woman with gray hair who could not read – her husband deciphered her son's letter for her – and looked into her plain, lined face, I realized gratefully Don Leocadio's faith in us. His mother was a very good woman.

Arturo Barea was born in Badajoz in 1897. At the start of the Civil War, he organized office workers in a Republican volunteer military unit La Pluma ('The Pen'). His knowledge of French and English were ideal qualifications for his job as censor at the Foreign Ministry's press office, where he met Ilsa Kulcsar, who later became his second wife and the translator of his writings into English. He kept the job as censor until rumours of Ilsa's Trotskyist sympathies forced the couple to go into exile in February 1938, first to Paris, then to England. The rumours stemmed from the fact that Arturo and Ilsa wanted to be more flexible in allowing foreign reporters to report bad news – this went against the Communist Party line. From 1939 until his death in 1957, Barea worked for the Latin American section of the BBC's World Service. During this time, he made over eight hundred fifteen-minute broadcasts under the pseudonym 'Juan de Castilla' – these broadcasts often came top of the station's listener poll. Barea, who found the pub the ideal place to discover English habits, even learnt the locals' way of dealing with the weather:

> What I am quite proud of is the fact that I have now mastered the rules of the game played each morning when people meet in the street: 'Lovely morning, Sir.'

'Very nice day, isn't it?'

At the beginning I tried earnestly to say that it looked like rain when it did. But after having heard many times a reproachful: 'Oh, don't say that, Sir,' I understand that here I have come across a national complex. Now I answer always: 'Yes, indeed, a very nice day,' even if the shower already hangs over our heads. After all, these are still 'nice' peaceful days which I, the refugee, can appreciate more than others.

Arturo Barea is buried in the churchyard of Faringdon near Oxford, where he lived for the last ten years of his life.

BERNARDO ATXAGA

MARKS

from *De Gernika a Guernica*

translated by Margaret Jull Costa

I N A SMALL MUSEUM IN MILAN, there is a rock known as *il masso di Borno*. It isn't just any rock. It's full of striations, lines and marks made by some sharp implement, marks that are sometimes straight, sometimes slightly curved, and there are spiral shapes too, like suns or asterisks; marks that form what we would now call geometric designs.

A plaque on the base on which the rock sits explains that it remained buried until 1956, the year in which it was uncovered by a flood and the subsequent shifting of the soil; it explains, too, that its abstract decoration dates back seven thousand years. Archeologists believe that, at that moment in prehistory, five thousand years before the birth of Christ, a few human beings chose to leave those marks on that rock, a message capable of reaching us across seventy centuries.

We cannot decipher the message in all its detail, because we lack the necessary references which, in cave paintings, point to a particular event or speak of the hunt for bison or the death of a warrior. All we can say about *il masso di Borno* is that the striations, lines and marks express a primordial, elemental message, saying basically: 'We were here. Once we, too, were alive.'

It must have been more than a mere need to scribble, more than a mere impulse. One has only to look at the precise way the marks were made, the care taken to make the resulting design attractive and enduring. These are not chance incisions in clay blocks or sandstone. These are deep marks made on a very large, hard rock. There is no doubt about it, the people who made those marks did so for a reason. They wanted their striations, lines and marks to have meaning and to carry a message. Seven thousand years later, we cannot understand precisely what they meant to say, apart, as I say, from that elemental message: 'We were here. Once we, too, were alive.'

The message is far from straightforward. If we accept that the marks were made on purpose, we must assume that already, seven thousand years ago, those people understood about death or – which comes to the same thing – had grasped the idea that life is the most valuable thing there is, life as life, the simple acts of breathing, eating, thinking, drawing, sleeping, singing.

This is not an exaggerated assumption to make. We know that they buried their dead – an unequivocal sign of their awareness of death – and constructed tombs and cromlechs, like those that can still be seen today in Carnac and in many places in the Basque Country. From the chronicles left by those who had dealings with primitive peoples similar to those who lived seven thousand years ago, we do know something of their feelings about death. As Cabeza de Vaca wrote in the sixteenth century about the indigenous peoples of North America: 'These people love their children and treat them better than anyone else in the world, and when someone's child dies, the parents and the relatives and all the village mourn them for a whole year, and each morning, before dawn, the parents begin to weep, and the whole village follows suit...' They were perhaps, as Cabeza de Vaca himself says, 'crude people, lacking reason', but they knew about the elemental, basic values.

Nor would it be any exaggeration to speak of our ancient ancestors' sensitivity to beauty, the sensitivity shown by the people who made those marks on *il masso di Borno* and by their predecessors, men and women living fifteen, thirty or even a hundred thousand years ago. The proof of this is that shells have been found in the caves they lived in, the shells of molluscs with no food value, like those of the colourful Nassa reticulata. Even clearer proof can be found in the rock paintings of bison and horses in the caves of Altamira, Lascaux, Pimiango or Santimamiñé.

A parenthesis: I once visited one of those Cantabrian caves – Santi-mamiñé, on the outskirts of Gernika – and there I met the painter José Luis Zumeta, and, rather childishly, I began asking myself if they were so very different, the painter standing before me and the Neolithic creator of the horses and bison on the cave walls. I soon gave up, because the differences were innumerable, and I began thinking, instead, about possible similarities. I came to no firm conclusion about that either, until we left and Zumeta said: 'Right, I'm off back to my studio to see if I can get some work done.' At the time, he was working on a version of Picasso's *Guernica*, and was in a hurry to get on. It occurred to me then that what they did have in common, the present-day painter and the painter living seven thousand, thirty thousand or a hundred thousand years ago, was that strong desire to draw, to paint. In fact, in our own age, the connection has grown even stronger, ever since the avant-garde artists of the twentieth century taught young painters to appreciate primitive art.

We are not so very far from those people living seven thousand years ago. Many of our experiences are similar. Raise your hand anyone who has never made a mark on a wall. Many years ago, in a barracks in Hoyo de Manzanares, I did just that.

It was a very isolated barracks, about one square kilometre in extent, with a central building that had doubled as the Nazi headquarters in *The Dirty Dozen*. The sentry boxes looked across at the bare slopes of the mountain, and doing guard duty there was no joke, especially in winter, when the temperatures often plummeted to twenty degrees below zero. The worst thing, though, wasn't the cold or the howling of the dogs that prowled round the barracks, but the feeling that our lives were not our own, that – to give just one example – they depended less on us and more on the whim of some jumped-up student promoted to the rank of temporary second lieutenant. It was a situation wholly inimical to poetry or any kind of creative writing because, if I may put it like this, we were not inhabited by the Word, but by anger and a loathing for all the manipulative authority figures above us. Sometimes, though, we did manage to shake off that mood and fly a little higher; then we would get out a knife or some other sharp implement and carve something on the wall of the sentry box or of the barracks itself. Our mark would remain there for those who came after, leaving a message: 'We were here too. Once we, too, were alive.'

That was in the winter of 1974. Less than a year later, in that same barracks, Baena Alonso, Sánchez Bravo and García Sanz were all shot. In another barracks, Otaegi was shot, and in Barcelona, Paredes Manot. As we know, they were the last prisoners to be shot under Franco.

...from the rock to the tree

From the rock to the tree, from *il masso di Borno* to the forests of California or Nevada, whose trees bear carvings made by the shepherds who lived there, utterly alone, with only their sheep and their dogs for company, and visited only by coyotes.

There are hundreds of such carvings in the forests of California and Nevada. Many of them represent the house where the shepherd was born, the house in Vizcaya or Navarra that he left behind, others show women who were not quite as remote as that house where they were born, women from some roadside club or brothel in Stockton or Fresno. There are also names and dates on the white bark of the aspens: 'Jean Saroiberry, 1912'; 'Pierre S, 14-VIII-1931'; 'Miguel García, 1935'.

By carving their names and adding a date, by being more explicit than the men and women of seven thousand years ago, the shepherds were giving a more specific meaning to their marks. Initially, these were simply an affirmation of the fact that they were alive, an expression in which the negative – nostalgia for home, the lack of a wife – mingled with the positive – 'I can at least give expression to those feelings'; but when we look at them thirty or forty years on, the messages have a more dramatic quality, because they speak of people who are no longer here. Walking among those carvings, we inevitably feel that we are in a gallery of epitaphs.

In one such 'gallery', in a forest in the Peavine Mountains, I met a young man who had returned to America with the sole object of visiting the carving made by his father in 1957, a few years before he vanished in a snowstorm. 'I had to do it,' he told me, 'because when he died, I was still a child, and afterwards, we went back to Vizcaya, and I forgot all about our life here. Now that I've seen his tree, though, I feel at peace. I've put a cross by the tree too, so now the tree is complete.' I asked him if he had found it hard to find the tree, and he told me that a shepherd who came from the same Basque village as his father and who still lived in Nevada, had drawn him a map.

On the way back, he continued talking about his father as if we really had visited a cemetery and were on our way home for a comforting bowl of soup. When we reached the car park and he opened the door to his car, I saw on the seat a tape by Paco Ibañez. 'Ah, yes,' he said, seeing that I had noticed, 'I was listening to him on the way here. I really love those songs, especially Jorge Manrique's poem on the death of his father. "And even though his life was lost," he quoted, "'his memory brings us sweet consolation.'" Those lines summed up the conversation we had just had.

And yet — and now I begin a darker parenthesis — not all deaths are like those of the shepherd in the Peavine Mountains or like the one mourned by Jorge Manrique, deaths whose pain diminishes over time and that leave a scar, a mark on our memory. There are other deaths that, far from fading over time, never stop hurting.

Popular stories passed on by word of mouth are also marks, words that stand out on the linguistic surface like the lines and asterisks on the surface of that rock, and they often refer to such enduring deaths. They speak of 'lost souls' who cannot rest because they left some important matter unresolved. Like the Flying Dutchman, or Mateo Txistu, a priest who, just as he was about to consecrate the host, left the church to go off with his dogs to hunt a hare; an irredeemable sin that doomed him to keep on hunting for ever, never to rest again, always whistling to his dogs, his whistles blending in with the whistling wind. Or perhaps like the farmer who, in a village in Guipúzcoa, during the Civil War, betrayed one of his neighbours and thus condemned him to death; perhaps he will never rest either. Years after the event, sensing that his final hour was near, he asked the priest to go to the dead man's widow and beg her forgiveness, 'Otherwise,' they say he said, 'I will end up in hell.' But the widow told the priest to tell the traitor to talk to God about it, not her, because He was wiser and knew the human heart better than anyone.

I remember that, as children, we never went anywhere near the house of that repentant traitor. People said you could still hear agonizing cries issuing from it, saying *barkaidan, mesedez*, 'please, forgive me'.

There are, however, other still more sinister stories or marks, for not all criminals are like the farmer who took literally what his religion had taught him and lived in mortal fear of hell. On the contrary, most belong to the line of Cain and, like him, never acknowledge their crime. They say and go on saying: 'Am I my brother's keeper?' Or they say, even more wickedly than Cain: 'I'm not the murderer. The real murderer was Abel.' Or they say: 'So what if it was a murder. He deserved to die.' Poets like Jorge Manrique are not equipped to speak of such crimes; for that we need poets who are more like prophets. Like Celso Emilio Ferreiro, who walked to a mountain in Galicia to visit the place where, in 1936, hundreds of people had been killed, and there he recited: 'Here in this mountainous place, innocent people were sacrificed. Few now remember that holocaust, but we will not forget it as long as we live. Each year we come here to curse the murderers.'

The marks on the tree or on the rock, the ones that say 'once we, too, were alive', last over time; no one erases them and they can be visited fifty or a hundred years later, like those carvings left by the shepherds; even seven thousand years later, like those on *il masso di Borno*. But the marks that say 'they were killed here' are harder to find. They rarely last. And when they do, it's always down to the efforts of people who, despite all, know what truly matters, know the importance of death. That is what happened in the Guipúzcoan village of Andoain and what happened in the valley of Valdediós, near Oviedo.

In Andoain, Franco's so-called 'nationalists' shot a man they had taken prisoner near a farm called Asu. It happened on 16 August 1936. His bones were found and his story reconstructed thanks to a farm labourer who remembered the mark left by his own father: 'My father and I used to come to this field to mow,' he explained years later. 'And he used to say to me: "Be careful, because there's a dead man buried over there." We always put the hay rick beside the man who had been shot.'

The place was eventually excavated and the bones taken to the cemetery. Then an investigation was made into what exactly had happened, and the message of that mark became clearer still. Now it says:

'They killed him here, in this field near Andoain. There was no trial, they didn't even bother taking him to prison. When he realised what awaited him, he wrote a letter to his family, who lived in Bordeaux; but he couldn't give it to the owner of the farm, because the lieutenant in charge of the batallion took the letter from him and tore it up. The lieutenant warned him, moreover, that he would have no cross or epitaph, so that no one would ever know what had become of him. The people on the farm were watching, though, and finally, after nearly seventy years, they were able to give him a decent burial.'

A grave without a name and a criminal getting off scot-free and whom no one can now identify. All we know about that lieutenant is that he belonged to a batallion of *requetés* – Carlist militiamen – the kind who always had the name of Christ on their lips.

And from Andoain to Oviedo, where, during the Civil War, a particularly cruel crime was committed. It happened in the monastery of Valdediós, which, at the time, was being used as a psychiatric hospital. Nationalist soldiers from the Arapiles batallion arrived and shot most of the people working there: thirteen women and five men, to judge by the remains retrieved from the mass grave. This is how the British writer Justin Webster described it in the first Spanish edition of *Granta* magazine:

'It was an exceptional case, even bearing in mind the exceptional brutality of the war in Asturias. The fighting had stopped there. The victims were not just civilians, but nurses, mainly women. They clearly assumed they would be safe from any reprisals, otherwise they would have left. Two of them were little more than girls. They were all executed without trial, at night, and buried in a makeshift, shallow grave. Their murderers were members of the regular army, not crazed fanatics.'

Justin Webster managed to speak to a woman, who had lived next door to the hospital, and who, in 1937, was nine years old. At first, she refused to talk to him, because she had received two phone calls, both asking the same question: 'How much have those bastards paid you to say where the dead are buried?' In the end, she agreed to speak to him, on condition that he didn't use her real name.

'Concepción Moslares and Ángeles García, both from Oviedo, were working on the day and night shifts respectively,' writes Justin Webster. 'Nati remembers how, on that night, she was in bed, about to go to sleep, when she heard shots, the instantly recognisable rat-a-tat-tat of the machine gun coming from somewhere in the village below. No one went outside.

'At first light, her father went down the hill to see what had happened. He found only dead bodies buried in a grave so shallow that human hands and hair were still visible. Nati's father remembered seeing the fair hair of Lucía, a beautiful nineteen-year-old girl who worked in the kitchen. The soldiers had already left.'

With the help of several men sent by the landowner, Nati's father covered up the scantily buried bodies, placing stones on the grave so that the dogs would not continue to gnaw at the corpses. Years later, the new owner of the land finished the job, filling up the grave with heavy, clayey soil and creating a path that went around it, 'so that the cows don't trample over the dead', he said.

It has often been said that humanity, civilisation, began at the point when the men and women of seven thousand, fifteen thousand or thirty thousand years ago decided to begin burying their dead, creating a 'marked place', for example, the dolmen at Locmariaquer, near Carnac. The family who owned Asu farm and the people who worked the land in Valdediós felt exactly the same, which is why they took pains to make those graves decent and to separate them off, thus saving them from the dogs and from being forgotten.

The burial of the dead is a threshold. Outside that threshold, there is nothing, just a zone bereft of humanity. Unfortunately for Lucía and the other people shot on the night of 25–26 October 1937, that was the true homeland of the commanders of the Arapiles battalion.

...and from landscape to skin

I was on holiday in Hondarribia – or as it was known then, in the mid-1960s, Fuenterrabia – and one of my cousins asked me to go with him to the harbour where his father, my uncle, was mending the engine on a boat. It was a hot day and, when we arrived, all the fishermen were bustling about barechested and in shorts. My uncle was too. I noticed a strange mark on his skin, which looked like a piece of whitish rope that ran from his right shoulder to just below his knee. In a low voice as if he didn't want to be heard, my cousin explained that this was a scar dating from his father's days as a soldier in the Civil War. A German plane had machine-gunned him on 26 April near Gernika.

In fairy tales, a mark on the skin is almost always a good sign, for it offers proof that the hero, though apparently only a woodcutter's son, is really a prince. This was not the case here. The scars were a bitter memory for my uncle and, as he himself told us that night, the sight of them in the mirror always filled him with gloom. The world was full of murderers. The pilot of the Heinkel 51 who had, in the literal sense of the word, hunted him down, was clearly one of them. He kept coming back again and again to the field where my uncle was trying to hide, until he had shot him and left him for dead. My uncle thought the pilot would give up and go on his way, but no. 'He wanted another trophy,' he said. 'He flew so low that I could see him clearly. He was wearing a kind of red jumpsuit.'

I think that, by then, in the early 1960s, I'd already heard about the war, thanks to a teacher, who used to get very upset whenever he found us playing at 'war', and would tell us how horrible real wars were, but I had no idea about what had happened in Gernika. I did recall a story my mother told us about her experiences in the shelters in Eibar and Bilbao, and how she saw the chemist Boneta burst into hysterical laughter when, on emerging from one of those shelters, he saw that his house and his pharmacy had been destroyed by the bombs dropped by the planes, and how, two hours later, she saw that same man sobbing like a child because he had lost everything; and once, at a swimming pool, I was approached by a woman who wanted to tell me that her father had died during the bombing of Durango while he was attending mass. But not a word about Gernika. I hadn't even seen a reproduction of Picasso's painting.

Other marks

In August 1936, the nationalist troops are leaving Asu farm and walking down the streets of Andoain, and a boy is watching anxiously. The soldiers are behaving not like disciplined soldiers, but like vandals, breaking down the doors of houses and stealing anything they find there: some are looking for jewellery, others for furniture or clothes. From one of the houses in the square they take – at this point, the boy changes windows so as to see better – a particularly fine wardrobe with an oval mirror; the mirror gleams in the sunlight. For some reason, the soldiers deposit it in the middle of the square, and there it stays for hours, losing its glitter as the light fades, until night falls. The boy can see nothing now, but from his room, with the window still open, he hears the sound of guns: rapid fire followed by individual shots. 'They're shooting people,' his mother tells him, coming into the room and closing the window. 'Then giving them the coup de grace.' The following morning, the window is still closed, but he can hear perfectly clearly what the soldiers out in the square are shouting: '¡Viva Cristo Rey! Long live Christ the King!' He gets up and goes over to the window to look out: the wardrobe is still there, but it has been totally destroyed. The sun is again beating down, but the mirror no longer glitters.

The years pass, and the boy, who has grown up now and works in a factory, decides to take a chance and leave some record of what happened. He can't do what the people at Asu farm did – he doesn't know where the shots came from, nor where the victims were buried – so he decides to compose a kind of traditional ballad and tell what he saw and knew: '*Ate guztik ireki burdin handiz jota, zerbait dagon lekura atzaparrak bota; ez da bekaturikan, ez zaio inporta, Kristoren izenian eginda dagota. Nahigabeturik daukat gaur nire bihotza, ezin ahazturik nago tiro haien hotsa, hemezortzi gizoni eman heriotza…*' (They broke down the doors with iron bars, grabbing anything that took their fancy, it's not a sin, it doesn't matter, it's all done in the name of Christ. My heart today is sad, I cannot forget that I heard those shots, they killed eighteen men…') Later in the song, he lists all the names of the eighteen men who were shot, as well as the names of some of the village's *señoritos*, the young gentlemen from wealthy families who, it was thought, had collaborated with the murderers.

The tune, the easy rhymes – typical of this kind of mark, the equivalents of the lines and asterisks carved on the rock – continued to broadcast that story for a good long time. I heard the song, shortly after returning from my holiday in Hondarribia, sung by a boy who worked at the same factory as the composer, and it impressed me even more than my uncle's scars, because I didn't know then how common such executions and criminal acts were, nor about the existence of mass graves like the ones visited by Celso Emilio Ferreiro.

A parenthesis. In the newspaper *El País*, dated 4 November 2006, I read these words spoken by a man from Fuenteguinaldo, in the province of Salamanca:

'Apparently, the Falangists asked the priest to draw up a list of all the reds and atheists in the village. On 7 October 1936, they went from house to house looking for them. At nine o'clock at night, they were taken to the prison in Ciudad Rodrigo, and at four o'clock in the morning, were told they were being released, but, at the door of the prison, a truck was waiting and, instead of taking them home, it brought them here to be killed.'

By now, the only surprising thing is how long it has taken for these facts to come to light: seventy years. A whole lifetime.

Another parenthesis, an anecdote. Towards the end of 1981, when I was living in a village in Castille with fewer than two hundred inhabitants, I became friendly with a young socialist who was a local councillor. When I met him one day, he was looking positively distraught. He had just found out that in February of that year, on the night Colonel Tejero burst into Parliament and the tanks came out onto the streets, the local priest had gone straight to the nearest military barracks intending to hand in a list of local men who should be arrested; my friend's name was at the top of the list.

Bernardo Atxaga was born Josebia Irazu Garmendia in Asteasu in the Basque Country in 1951. He is the region's best-known writer and his works – including *Obabakoak* and *The Lone Man* – have been translated the world over. Atxaga himself translates his works into Spanish. This extract is taken from his book *De Gernika a Guernica*, first published in Basque in 2007. Modelled on Picasso's painting of 'Gernika', the book is structured in a sequence that follows the destruction of the town by German and Italian bombers. Its powerful argument is that it can take a very long time for the crimes of the past to surface and their surfacing requires the efforts of those who know 'the importance of death'. Only now is the precise, planned nature of the destruction of the town becoming known – from the choice of a market day (Monday) to the waves of bombing sequenced to inflict the maximum number of casualties. Finally, the last remaining eyewitnesses are coming forward to break the silence, a silence first imposed by Franco, who banned the Basque language and claimed that it was retreating Republicans who had destroyed the town!

JAVIER CERCAS

'THERE'S NOBODY OVER HERE!'

from *Soldiers of Salamis*

translated by Anne McLean

A T DUSK ON THE 29TH, Sánchez Mazas, Pascual and his cellmates are taken to the roof of the monastery, a place they've never been before and where they are assembled with other prisoners, 500 in total, maybe more. Pascual knows some of them – Pedro Bosch Labrús, Viscount Bosch Labrús and airforce captain Emilio Leucona – but barely manages to exchange a few words with them before a Carabinero immediately orders silence and begins to read out a list of names. Because the hope of a prisoner swap comes to mind again, as soon as he hears the name of someone he knows Pascual desires heart and soul to be included in the list, but, without any precise reason for this shift in opinion, by the time the Carabinero pronounces his name – shortly after that of Sánchez Mazas and immediately following Bosch Labrús – he has already regretted formulating this wish. The twenty-five men who have been named, among whom are all of Sánchez Mazas and Pascual's cellmates except Fernando de Marimón, are taken to a cell on the first floor where there are only a few desks pushed against the crumbling walls and a blackboard with patriotic historical dates scribbled in chalk. The door closes behind them and an ominous silence falls, soon broken by someone declaring that they are about to be exchanged and who manages to distract the anguish of a few of them with the discussion of a conjecture that fades away after a while to make room for unanimous pessimism. Sitting at a desk at one end of the cell, before the evening meal Father Guiu hears the confession of some of the prisoners, and then prepares communion. No one sleeps that night: lit by a grey stony light that comes in through the window, giving their faces a hint of their future cadaverous appearance (although as time passes the grey thickens and the darkness becomes real), the prisoners stay awake listening through the wall to noises in the corridor or seeking illusory comfort in memories or in a last conversation. Sánchez Mazas and Pascual are stretched out on the floor, leaning their backs against the cold wall, their legs covered by one insufficient blanket; neither of them will remember exactly what they talked about during that scant night, but both will recall the long silences punctuating their secret meeting, the whispers of their companions and the sound of their sleepless coughing, the rain falling, indifferent, assiduous, black and freezing on the paving stones in the courtyard and the cypresses in the garden; and it keeps falling until dawn of 30 January slowly changes the darkness of the windows for the sickly whitish, ghostly colour that stains the atmosphere in the cell like a premonition at the moment the jailer orders them out.

No one has slept, everyone seems to have been awaiting that moment and, as if drawn by the urgency of resolving the uncertainty, obey with somnambulant diligence and gather in the courtyard with another similar-sized group of prisoners, to bring the number to fifty. They wait a few minutes, docile, silent and soaked, under a fine rain and a sky thick with clouds, and finally a young man appears in whose indistinct features Sánchez Mazas recognizes the indistinct features of the warden of the *Uruguay*. He tells them they are going to be put to work at an aviation camp under construction in Banyoles and orders them to form into ten lines, five deep; while obeying, unthinkingly taking the first place on the right in the second line, Sánchez Mazas feels his heart bolt: in the grip of panic, he realizes the aviation camp can only be an excuse – senseless to build one with the Nationalist troops launching a definitive offensive a few kilometres away. He begins to walk at the head of the group, unhinged and shaking, unable to think clearly, absurdly searching the blank faces of the armed soldiers lining the road for a sign or a glimmer of hope, trying in vain to convince himself that at the end of that journey what awaited him was something other than death. Beside him, or behind him, someone is trying to justify or explain something he doesn't hear or doesn't understand, because every step he takes absorbs all his attention, as if it might be his last; beside him or behind him, the sickly legs of José María Poblador say, Enough, and the prisoner collapses in a puddle and is helped up and dragged back to the monastery by two soldiers. A hundred and fifty metres on from this, the group turns left, leaves the road and goes up into the forest along a path of chalky soil that opens out into a clearing: a wide expanse surrounded by pine trees. From out of the woods booms a military voice ordering them to halt and face left. Terror seizes the group, which stops in its tracks; almost all its members automatically turn to the left, but dread confuses the instinct of others who, like Captain Gabriel Martín Morito, turn to the right. For an instant, which feels eternal, Sánchez Mazas thinks he's going to die. He thinks the bullets that are going to kill him will come from behind his back, which is where the commanding voice had come from, and that, before he dies from bullets hitting him, they'll have to hit the four men lined up behind him. He thinks he's not going to die, that he's going to escape. He thinks that he can't escape to the back because the shots will come from there; nor to his left, because he'd run back out to the road and the soldiers; nor ahead, because he'd have to jump over a wall of eight utterly terrified men. But (he thinks) he can escape towards the right, where no more than six or seven metres away a dense thicket of pines and undergrowth holds a promise of hiding. To the right, he thinks. And he thinks: Now or never. At that moment several machine guns stationed behind the group, exactly where the commander's voice had come from, begin to sweep the clearing; trying to protect themselves, the prisoners instinctively seek the ground. By then Sánchez Mazas has reached the thicket, he runs between pines that scratch his face with the pitiless clatter of the machine guns still ringing in his ears, finally trips providentially and is flung, rolling over mud and wet leaves, into the ravine at the edge of the plateau, landing in a swampy ditch at the mouth of a stream. Because he rightly imagines that his pursuers imagine him trying to get as far away from them as possible, he decides to shelter there, relatively close to the clearing – cringing, panting, soaking wet and with his heart pounding in his throat, covering himself as best he can with leaves and mud and pine boughs, hearing his unfortunate companions receiving *coups de grâce* – and then the barking of the dogs and the shouts of the Carabineros urging the soldiers to find the fugitive or fugitives (because Sánchez Mazas doesn't yet know that, infected by his irrational impulse to abscond, Pascual has also managed to escape the massacre). For a length of time he has no idea whether to measure in minutes or hours, while he scratches ceaselessly at the ground to cover himself in mud till his fingernails are bleeding and hopes that the incessant rain will prevent the dogs from finding his trail, Sánchez Mazas keeps hearing shouts and barks and shots, until at some moment he senses something shift behind him and urgently turns around, cringing like a cornered rat.

Then he sees him. He's standing beside the ditch, tall and burly and silhouetted against the dark green of the pines and the dark blue of the clouds, panting a little, his large hands grasping the slanted rifle and the field uniform with all its buckles, threadbare from exposure. Prey to the aberrant resignation of one who knows his time has come, through his thick glasses blurred by the rain, Sánchez Mazas looks at the soldier who is going to kill him or hand him over – a young man, his hair plastered to his skull by the rain, his eyes maybe grey, his cheeks gaunt and cheek-bones prominent – and remembers him or thinks he remembers him from among the ragged soldiers who guarded them in the monastery. He recognizes him or thinks he recognizes him, but takes no comfort from the idea that it's going to be him and not a SIM agent who redeems him from the endless agony of fear, and it humiliates him like an injury added to all the injuries of these years on the run not to have died with his cellmates or not to have known how to die in an open field in broad daylight and fighting with a courage he lacked, instead of dying now and there, muddy and alone and shaking with dread and shame in an undignified hole in the ground. So, his mind raving and confused, Rafael Sánchez Mazas – exquisite poet, fascist ideologue, Franco's future minister – awaits the shot that will finish him off. But the shot doesn't come, and Sánchez Mazas, as if he were already dead and from death remembering this scene from a dream, watches guilelessly as the soldier slowly advances towards the edge of the ditch in the unceasing rain and the threatening sound of soldiers and Carabineros, just steps away, the rifle pointing at him unostentatiously, the gesture more inquisitive than tense, like a novice hunter about to identify his first prey, and just as the soldier gets to the edge of the ditch the vegetal noise of the rain is pierced by a nearby shout:

'Is anyone there?'

The soldier is looking at him; Sánchez Mazas is looking at the soldier, but his weak eyes don't understand what they see: beneath the sodden hair and wide forehead and eyebrows covered in raindrops the soldier's look doesn't express compassion or hatred, or even disdain, but a kind of secret or unfathomable joy, something verging on cruelty, something that resists reason, but nor is it instinct, something that remains there with the same blind stubbornness with which blood persists in its course and the earth in its immovable orbit and all beings in their obstinate condition of being, something that eludes words the way the water in the stream eludes stone, because words are only made for saying to each other, for saying the sayable, when the sayable is everything except what rules us or makes us live or matters or what we are or what this anonymous defeated soldier is, who now looks at this man whose body almost blends in with the earth and the brown water in the ditch, and who calls out loudly without taking his eyes off him:

'There's nobody over here!'

Then he turns and walks away.

For nine days and nights of the brutal winter of 1939 Rafael Sánchez Mazas wandered through the region of Banyoles trying to cross the lines of the Republican army in retreat and pass over into the Nationalist zone. Many times he thought he wasn't going to make it; alone, no other resources than his will to survive, unable to get his bearings in unfamiliar territory of wild, dense woods, weakened to the point of exhaustion from walking, by the cold, hunger and three uninterrupted years of captivity, many times he had to stop to gather his strength in order not to let himself just give up. The first three days were terrible.

He slept during the day and walked at night, avoiding the exposure of the roads and villages, begging for food and shelter at farms, and though he prudently dared not reveal his true identity at any of them, but rather introduced himself as a lost Republican soldier, and though almost everyone he asked gave him something to eat, let him rest awhile and gave him directions without asking questions, fear kept anyone from offering him protection. At dawn on the fourth day, after more than three hours wandering through dark forest, Sánchez Mazas made out a farm in the distance. Less by rational decision than out of utter fatigue, he collapsed onto a bed of pine needles and remained there, his eyes closed, barely sensing the sound of his own breathing and the smell of the dew-soaked earth. He had eaten nothing since the morning before, he was exhausted and felt ill, because not a single muscle in his body didn't ache. Until then the miracle of having survived the firing squad and the hope of encountering the Nationalists had given him a perseverance and a fortitude he'd thought lost; now he realized that his energy was running out and that, unless another miracle occurred or someone helped him, his adventure would very soon be at an end. After a while, when he felt a little restored and the sun shining through the foliage had instilled in him a scrap of optimism, he gathered all his strength, stood up and started walking towards the farm.

Maria Ferré would never forget the radiant February dawn she first set eyes on Rafael Sánchez Mazas. Her parents were out in the field and she was getting ready to feed the cows when a man appeared in the yard – tall, famished and spectral, with his twisted spectacles and many days' growth of beard, in his sheepskin jacket and trousers full of holes, and covered in mud and weeds – and asked her for a piece of bread. Maria wasn't scared. She'd just turned twenty-six and she was a dark blonde, illiterate, hard-working girl for whom the war was nothing more than a confusing background noise to the letters her brother sent home from the front, and a meaningless whirlwind that two years earlier had taken the life of a boy from Palol de Revardit she'd once dreamed of marrying. During this time her family hadn't been hungry or frightened, because the farm lands they cultivated and the cows, pigs and hens sheltering in the stables were enough, more than enough, to feed them, and because, although Mas Borrell, their house, was located halfway between Palol de Revardit and Cornellà de Terri, the abuses of the days of revolution didn't reach them and the disorder of the retreat brought them only the odd lost, disarmed soldier who, more frightened than threatening, asked for something to eat or stole a hen. It's possible that at first Sánchez Mazas was to Maria Ferré just another of the many deserters who roamed the area during those days, and that's why she wasn't scared, but she always maintained that as soon as she saw his pitiful figure outlined against the ground of the path that ran past the yard, she recognized beneath the ravages of three days' exposure to the elements the unmistakable bearing of a gentleman. Whether that's true or not, Maria gave the man the same kind treatment she'd given countless other fugitives.

'I don't have any bread,' she told him. 'But I could heat something up for you.'

Undone by gratitude, Sánchez Mazas followed her into the kitchen and, while Maria heated up the previous night's saucepan – where, in a rich, brown broth, floated lentils and big chunks of bacon, sausage and chorizo along with potatoes and vegetables – he sat down on a bench, enjoying the nearness of the fire and the joyful promise of hot food, took off his soaking shoes and socks, and suddenly noticed a terrible ache in his feet and an infinite tiredness in his bony shoulders. Maria handed him a clean rag and some clogs, and out of the corner of her eye watched him dry his neck, his face, his hair, as well as his feet and ankles, while watching the flames dance amid the logs with staring, slightly glazed eyes, and when she handed him the food she saw him devour it with a hunger of many days, in silence and scarcely forgoing the manners of a man raised among linen tablecloths and silver cutlery, which, more out of his courteous instincts than his recently acquired habit of fear, made him set the spoon and pewter plate down by the fire and stand up when Maria's parents burst into the half-light of the kitchen and stood, looking at him, with a bovine mixture of passivity and suspicion. Perhaps mistakenly thinking their guest didn't understand Catalan, Maria told her father in Catalan what had happened; he asked Sánchez Mazas to finish his meal and, without taking his eyes off him, put his farming tools down beside a stone bench, washed his hands in a basin and came over to the fire. As he sensed the father approach, Sánchez Mazas scraped the plate clean. His hunger calmed, he'd reached a decision: he realized that, if he didn't reveal his true identity, he wouldn't have the slightest chance of being offered shelter there either, and he also realized that the hypothetical risk of denunciation was preferable to the real risk of starving or freezing to death.

'My name is Rafael Sánchez Mazas and I am the most senior living leader of the Falange in Spain,' he finally said to the man who listened without looking at him.

~

Born in Ibahernando in 1962, **Javier Cercas** is one of a generation of Spanish writers whose writings mix fact and fiction in an attempt to uncover the 'historical memory' of the Civil War. His book *Soldiers of Salamis* is both about what happened to the Falange leader Rafael Sánchez Mazas, who escaped execution at the end of the war, and a reflection on the nature of historical explanation.

Cercas' generation grew up with parents who were reluctant to talk or write about the Civil War; they wanted to spare their children its burden. As is often the case, the children rebelled and enquired.

In 2000, the sociologist Emilio Silva-Barrera created the Association for the Recovery of Historical Memory as part of an attempt to find out what had happened to his grandfather, shot by Franco's army in 1936. This grassroots movement now involves local people throughout Spain. However, its progress has been hampered by the refusal of the government to provide funds. Cercas' later works, *The Anatomy of a Moment* and *Outlaws*, continue in this rich vein of mixing fact and fiction. In 2003, *Soldiers of Salamis* was made into a fine feature film directed by David Trueba.

MAX AUB

JANUARY WITHOUT NAME

translated by Peter Bush

In defeat they carry off victory

Cervantes

26 January 1939

Men have always been ones for walking, that's why they have legs, though I've only just discovered air is what moves them along. They only have one small ear either side of their head, which is enough for them to run at the slightest sound; they can never stay still, or see beyond the ends of their noses, and are crazy about one thing: speed; not satisfied with wheels, they want wings. They prefer to ignore that once born, they grow roots, even if they don't want them, that subterfuges, dodges, ruses or wiles are futile: it's the sap, not the flesh that counts.

I was born standing. I was always tall, bigger than my age warranted; I was born somewhere in the 1880s and, as is only right, I've gradually broadened my trunk and my landscape. Figueras has gained in extension what I've gained in perspective; when it thought it had fenced me in, I beat it on high. Labourers built their encampments with their sweat and time following the lie of the land, imagining they laid bricks the way they wanted. Many years ago I even managed to see San Martín, and when they constructed three-storey flats in the Rambla to shut off my horizons, from the city-gates I already had sight of Perelada.

In my youth I saw the playboys drive the first cars past my feet. Nothing ever shocks me, I always was a bit of a know-all: I am what I am, and so what? They covered the sewers, erected telephone posts, eternal landmarks to our greatness; reapers of corn became lads who pumped petrol.

One pruning followed another: men can try to belittle our lives, it makes no odds, we're stronger, they're afraid of the elements and hence die, naked, they're like flowers, but then they put clothes on! A wretched bunch. As they're rootless, they cut back the world to sustain themselves. The wind is what counts, and they just don't want to know. They insist on extracting seed from barren heaths, timber – life that is our death – from thicketed peaks. Foul-smelling jack-the-lads, they only live to spin yarns, call it wild oats to show off, but hide when doing so, I know because I see them; hagglers, braggarts, ass-lickers who the moment it drizzles, scurry like hens or invent umbrellas; or even turn vegetarian as if it were any use eating things one's not made of: let them eat meat, and leave us in peace, or, if they wish, keep planting saplings in the twenty-foot, even if that only means soldiers shaft strumpets as the sun goes down, or the branches dip in the irrigation channels, but don't let them maim us with their machetes year after year, telling us it's all for our own good… I'm way off pole; back on track; the castle escarpments haven't changed, they green in spring-time, as they should: a castle is a serious business. The road's sopping, sinking and silting up with the rain; when it's a heatwave, it sprinkles dust over the fields; they tarmacked it and it loves to parade; it should stick to milestones.

Round and about, the plain disappears in the distance: one way is Llansá, and the other the sea and opposite the sun's early-morning gate, behind the hills hiding it from my view, Rosas. The Pyrenees are my north, and proud it's so; they do their duty by the snow when it's due.

They praise my memory, I know all about Napoleon from the stories people tell, and about the Carlists from my family, a great number of which they turned to ash, as their hosts suffered from the cold. Men take a long while to grow and, in any case, never move beyond the stunted stage.

(Perhaps men are wretched because they never stand still, though much more is gone with the wind.)

Last night a boy died by my foot; he died a sapling and his mother carried him on the road to France, thinking he'll come back to life. I don't believe in miracles. Nor do I understand why children die: dying is about drying up. Men know that only too well, and admit as much. One can also rot to death, from the worms gnawing one's guts. Men die ravaged on the outside, faces devoured by blood and bandages, by pus, mange, lice and pain. From what I heard last night, hunger kills too. What's hunger? The land provides all our needs. 'Yes, whatever you want,' said one. 'But the day before yesterday, I don't remember if it was Tuesday or Wednesday, whatever, they called my home. It was two a.m. The sirens had wailed; a clear night, searchlights, the whole malarkey. You know, it was to deliver a child. Off I went, scared of the ack-ack guns, and unable to light the torch with a brand-new battery Vicente had brought me from Perpignan. The child was still-born: his mother's lack of nourishment. A neighbour helped me. "Now come and have a look at mine," she says, when we've cleaned up. I curse all the way, the alarm's over and the electricity comes back. Naturally, the famous child-birth took place by the light of candles they'd had to requisition from the whole staircase and a nearby bomb-shelter; can you imagine? The lobby was a room to pay respects; each neighbour came for their candle and ask after the woman who'd given birth. It was like a movie, kid. I heard nobody say: "Good, it's better that way." No, they all said: "A pity, there'll always be a next time." The mother was desperate. And then I go upstairs with her neighbour and look at her child, a one-year old. "This boy's dying." We give him a warm bath and an injection of camphor oil: "I knew as much," the mother rasps, "he didn't eat." And that was that. Not a single cry of protest; not one complaint. What a people! My God, what a people!'

Men haven't a clue what it's like to have birds on your fingers; men and animals are like rocks, the wind doesn't move them, they take refuge from hurricanes and cyclones, they've not the roots to withstand them, they're pure stalk, they only grow outwards, if they grow inwards, it's invisible, and I believe what I see: and that's how I tell it. Men give you an idea of what makes a passing phenomenon: they're like storms or better, as they like to say, they are tormented. In their view, the seasons don't exist and it's irrelevant whether it's spring or autumn; life doesn't spring from man but from his surroundings, they're merely mirrors to the world and defend themselves against their inferiority, invent dreams, would-be seed-corn, flints sparking on the air: for starters, they can't tell a beech-tree from a lime, a banana-tree from a chestnut, let alone a cherry from an orange tree. The human condition is a sorry affair; if they want to make their mark, they must die in the attempt; blood is a shocking sort of sap, and men always seem to be spurting forth; they only know how to bear fruit in pain, and as for blossoming like flowers, they should be so lucky. Don't you go comparing a hen with an almond tree.

27

'Did you ever think we might lose?'

'I don' think note. I can't think note. I'd chuck it all in but I ain't got note to chuck in.'

A world passes down this road with ears, and without a tongue, and has emerged out of nothing, swept along on a southern breeze that bottles it up in Figueras; the road to la Junquera is like a funnel. Suntraps have become garages. The city is brimming with cars and trucks, a stream of black blood bubbling from a hundred wounds night-time has inflicted. A half-dead world walking on two legs as if it had but one, a world that only knows how to walk yet knows that walking solves nothing, walking simply to prove to itself that it's still alive. They flee their shadows not realising that night alone can solve that problem, they walk and light bonfires when darkness falls; their shadows are reborn with fire. The world has aged in forty-eight hours. A very, very old man comes by, in mourning, like all old Spaniards. Mourning becomes winter. One woman says: 'Look at him, so old and scared of death.' They walk. The first brightness of day blows up from the sea. The road is full of trucks, customs police, soldiers, cars, assault guards, old people, torn newspapers, old people, petrol tankers, three cannons abandoned to my right, children, soldiers, mules, old people, wounded, cars, wounded, women, children, wounded, old people. Opposite me, a woman crouches by a fence crying, showing her legs in cinnamon-coloured stockings, and, around the top, thighs the colour of almond blossom, weeping her heart out. Nobody stops, everyone with their tiny stretch of the road on their shoulder.

'The government's to blame.'

'The communists are to blame.'

'The CNT is to blame.'

'The republic is to blame.'

One child is alone, with an umbrella.

'Where's your mother?'

'In France.'

'Where's your father?'

'Dead.'

He's by himself, still as a small island, in the thick of it, creating eddies.

People come, go, walk, pass by, move, stretch, peer, slip, wear out, wither, age, die. By dint of all that walking, everything comes to an end. Women are more burdened than men; nobody helps anyone. The soldiers, guns adrift, seem determined, but don't know why.

'So, where are you from?'

'From near Bilbao. Wi'd been in Barcelona fer a year with an 'ouse an' all. An' all bought fer new, near El Siglo. Bedspreads, crockery, the lot. An' wi've left the lot. Now it's git on the road agen. It's disgustin'. The Catalans are to blame.'

He stops, gasps, switches the bags strapped to the right of his waist to the other side.

'Disgustin'. An' there ain't no help from a soul, not a soul.'

A voice: 'Would you like them to take in their carriage.'

'Yer *all* cowards. If I could, if I could...'

There are thousands of carts; the horses manage, effortlessly, the weight isn't much, the bulk is: the burden of the people fleeing is large, but not heavy. Mattresses take up space, cages are mostly air, rabbits and hens need space to move. Wooden beds act as sides for the carts; pots and pans travel in big vegetable baskets. They're not covered waggons rolling across the plains, they're rural carts with broad metal rimmed wheels and screeching axles that have never left the farm. The bags of goods underneath hang over the sides like big bladders; a cart transforms into a swaying bunch of fruit; a rope or lone animal pulls it along, snout down, mane and coat caked in filth, withers and flanks scratched, hocks bleeding, fetlocks and hoofs like clods of earth. When the road jams up, stopping brings no respite, is only cause for impatience; jerky movements bite into backsides, send everything flying. Then some animal lifts its head and looks, collar tinkling: the heavens in its eyes. There's no space on the cart for anyone, lest an old woman has turned into a black, prostrate item; neither reins nor straps guide the beast, nor a bit pulled right or left, the crowds carry it along; each cart is a world with its satellites in tow on their way to the French frontier. Every burden is different; no cart is like another, but they *are* all the same.

A plane takes off from San Martín's field.

A soldier: 'One of ours.'

A one-armed man: 'We called *La Gloriosa* the Invisible Air-force.'

A woman is pulling two boys along, a black scarf on her head, an enormous sack above that, each boy's carrying his sack on his back.

'What's the point of fighting anymore? Can't they see we've lost? What's the point? So more can die?'

And she walks on.

One man: 'Who told you to come? Stay here.'

The woman can't turn her head, presses her parched lips together, and walks on.

Thousands cloaking the road, with their coarse blankets, except those on crutches, or those huge, wire-covered artefacts, arms on their backs.

'Hey, where you going, Eiffel Tower?'

More lame than one-armed, and more one-armed than wounded in the head. I've seen one-legged children on crutches, it's an unpleasant sight. A grey-haired, skinny-faced paraplegic is being pushed along in an old wheel chair, under a bonnet; he clutches a piece of pink oilskin to his knees, in case it rains.

Cars stop, move ten metres, stop, jam the road, people in the distance bunch together.

A guard, with his rifle: 'This is what they want, but they won't get their way.'

Horse-faced, a week-old beard, messy hair, hat on the slant, black-ened teeth. A girl speaks to him.

"'Ow on earth could this 'appen? What went wrong?'

'What went wrong? Well, do you reckon they're throwing out crusts? Or what? More artillery, then tanks, and more and more planes. It's appalling, and don't those damn planes shit death.'

Someone else joins in.

'The worst are the mortars; for every one we've got, they've a hundred. If you decide to shoot, they fry you alive; you end up not shooting.'

The girl: 'An' changing sides.'

The guard grips his gun with both hands: 'Just repeat that.'

The girl: 'An' changing sides.'

'And what about you?'

She shrugs her shoulders and keeps on walking. The other man says: 'They ran us ragged. It's a miracle we got out.'

And joins the previous fellow.

A water tanker overtakes against the flow, they look at it in surprise. Shout at it.

'They've disembarked in Rosas.'

'Lies. I've just come from there,' comes a reply in Catalan.

Blasting its klaxon it clears a path through to the control post. The men's faces are serious, wrinkles furrowed deep by the dust. You have no idea what a human face is like. I agree there's nothing like it. Every-thing's boxed into such a small space: fire, land and water, all that they're made of, giving them an unmistakable air.

A black car, republican flag flapping, judders along, adding to the racket, trying to overtake everyone else. Its irritable klaxon ratchets up the hue-and-cry: the

'Kid.'

'Luis.'

'Pepe.'

'Come on.'

'Hurry up,' that one doesn't hear because they're making one hell of a human furore that rises to the surface like birds swift of wing. A customs policeman goes over to that headstrong car, then moves away respectfully and addresses those forming a wall, explains things I don't catch. An assault guard intervenes.

'Not even Christ will get through.'

'But...'

'Not even God. If we're goin' to be stuck 'ere, then every sod is goin' to be stuck with us.'

The fellow shouting is sallow-featured, with greasy ear-locks. People stand still or twitch like a mangy tail. The guard is angry, releases the catch on his gun.

'I said no one is gettin' through, if I'm not. Either the control post lets me through, or if they catch me, they catch the lot of us.'

He's sweating.

'Not even God is gettin' through, and if anyone tries it, I'll shoot.'

Get through, get through, get through... A voice: 'The control post is only carrying out orders.'

'What bloody orders? They must be customs police. Anyone who tries it on is a dead duck, I swear to God.'

As he sees he's losing ground, that people reckon he's crazy, he shouts: 'The government made a run for it tonight.'

A plumpish young man interjects.

'That's not true, they're in a meeting in the castle.'

'And what do *you* know about the price of eggs?'

Vayo gets out of the car.

'What's the problem?'

'Nobody's gettin' through if I'm not.'

'And where are you going?'

'To join my company.'

And where might that be?'

'I don't know.'

A group grabs the young fellow and shoves him aside: 'It's the minister.'

'So fuckin' what?'

'He's going to La Agullana, to his ministry, and then he'll come back.'

'Nobody's gettin' past!'

But he slumps down on the slope, feet in the muddy ditch, eyes dead tired, chin sunk into his chest, hand gripping his musket. The minister gets back into his car and drives through.

I've never seen so many people together, so many old folk or so many dressed in black. A woman with a blanket keeps repeating: 'My papers are all in order, my papers are all in order…'

A uniformed man stops a car, brandishing a pistol.

'Official Mission.'

Another: 'French Embassy.'

Another: 'Cuban Embassy.'

Finally, he climbs on to the running board of another 'Official Mission'. The road is jet black at twilight, as if night arises there, they walk past, brushing my foot, thousands in flight, a line that's not aligned, some helping, and others brusquely rejecting appeals for help. Masses of wounded.

'The major came to tell us: "We can't guarantee the evacuation of the hospital, all those who can go under their own steam should leave."'

'I've come from Vallarca. How about you?'

'I don't know.'

Some can't take anymore, some say as much, one lies down.

'If I'm going to die, this place is as good as any.'

All this hubbub:

'When?'

'What?'

'Luis, is it very far?'

'Luis.'

'Rafael.'

'José.'

'Come here.'

'Get a move on.'

'Luis.'

'Luis.'

And kids bawling, vehicles hooting and changing gear, others starting up. Now it starts to drizzle. Two people are walking along under the same blanket.

'Azaña is to blame.'

'Like fuck he is.'

An old man is pushing a covered cart, feels tired and stops; a child pushes it, he can't manage more than five metres; his mother takes over, thirty metres further on granddad pushes it again. A soldier's carrying a barren sheep over his shoulder.

A woman: 'They're probably not as bad as they make out.'

And walks on. Things gradually lose their colour. Night falls fast, as if it's been snuffed out. I can feel my branches. It rains, then starts raining again. Cars honk like crazy, switch on their headlights, off, then on again, to see through the drizzle and not crash; mark out a path, then collide. More wounded. Where are they going? They're running away. Why? They're running away. I pity them at times like this. Yes, men are so pitiful, they're so stupid. A tree will always be a tree and a man, even though he'd like to, will never come up to our shins. The night sparks bonfires along the road to France, like fire-flies. It's cold. The wind blows explosions our way, but the night keeps its secrets.

28

The women are dressed in black as if they were in mourning, though their baggage is swathed in coloured headscarves; their blankets are grey with three white stripes. Few wear shoes: jute espadrilles and sandals. Among the colours returning with the early morning, the most visible, the brightest are bandages and plaster casts.

'They were coming along the coast.'

'Machine-gunned down, then more fucking machine-guns. Eighty killed in front of me.'

'What about the wounded?'

'As if we didn't have enough already!'

Back to yesterday. An old man walks along, doubled over two walking-sticks, his filthy head and broad-brimmed hat shaking between the two, it's grey and green it's so old and seen so much water; underneath a black kerchief, knotted the Aragonese way, encircles his baldpate. He mutters: 'I ain't sayin' this for thee, or me. The lousy bastard came and took 'im away. Thee 'eard aright; what else can I say if misself don' know 'ow? It took 'im away.'

A loud-mouthed braggart is pissing on my feet, as he buttons up his flies, he asks the centurion in a kidding tone: 'Where you off to, gran'dad?'

The man stops, raises his head, looks at the fool: 'To the knacker's yard, mate.'

And shuffles on.

The men always walk with heads bowed, and never look up; they only think of us if it's sunny or raining, or they're looking for shelter, like right now. Two wounded adolescents lean against me, the colour gone from their cheeks, unshaven.

'I'm from Andújar. What about yersself?'

'From Saragossa.'

It's the first time I've seen people walking under the rain. I've always seen them running or stopping to wait for it to clear up, like the two sticking to me at this minute.

'No, I din't belong to any party, or even the union. I'm sixteen, or do I look over eighteen? Mi brothers did. Two of them. They wen' after them straight off, but they escaped to France, wen' through Navarra. I expect they wen' back to Barcelona; they'll still be aroun' there. I ain't 'eard a word. They din't wan' to execute me: only brand me. Yes, 'ere on my fore'ead, see a cross. The one who did it, din't know 'ow, that much were bleedin' obvious. Another guy, who were there, 'ands on 'ips, looked at 'im an' said: "Come on, mate." An' put the iron in the red-hot stove. It weren't 'alf a big room in an old 'ouse, near La Seo. Yer could 'ear the river.'

'The Ebro.'

'Of course. That guy came for me, and when 'e were within firin' range, I kicked him in the goolies, if yer'll forgive mi French. 'E reared up like a wild animal, but 'e din't 'it me. I din't want anyone brandin' me for all the tea in China. "Right!" 'e said, "so we're a little bolshie, are we? So we're tryin' it on big time, well you just see." An' 'e insulted me an' were rude about my mother. Yer know… An' gave the order for them to put me in the truck, an' then I stopped thinkin' about 'er, till days later. Nobody 'ad to tell me what that meant. But right then I couldn 'ave cared less. Later, it were different. I waited two 'ours an' could only think about mi mother. Finally they threw me in the truck. As it were last minute, I weren't on the list and they din't tie me up. There were eleven of us. They drove us to the cemetery, I worked that out straight away. It were a pitch-black night. Nobody said a sausage. When we got there, the gate were open. Don' yer know the cemetery in Saragossa? It don' matter. They took us roun' the back. The truck stopped an' they asked the fellow next to the driver: "How many yer got?" "Ten an' a bonus." I were that bonus. I knew they was goin' to shoot me, yet I couldn't really believe it were 'appenin'. I felt bad I din't know any of the people that were with me. As you couldn't see a thing, they put the lorry that 'ad brought us behin' them that was goin' to execute us. That way we could see our shadows and the fascists' as well. They stood us with our backs to them. Perhaps they was ashamed to look us in the face, or din't 'ave 'an'kerchiefs to blin'fold us, though I reckon they've never blin'folded a soul. An' why would they? It were a stone wall, an' were pitted with grey and black marks, and little 'oles, all crumblin'. The ground were soft as putty. They shot without warnin'. No bullet 'it me, I fell down with the others, in all that blood. They must 'ave reckoned I were dead an' as it were night-time they din't bury us, they'd be leavin' that for the mornin'. When they'd gone, I escaped. Dead lucky, weren't I? They'd be really pissed off the next day when they wen' to bury me. I wen' to Huesca. Before all that business, I weren't so sure. Now I know the fascists is a load of crooks. If I could… There's so many rifles here… When I see what's 'appenin', I want to die of rage. I'd rather die than become a fascist. They wen' to bury me an' din't find me.'

The young lad laughs.

'Then they executed mi mother an' mi four brothers. That's what fascism is and note else.'

A stretch of bright sky peeps up towards the north.

'First they woul'n't believe me when I reached our side. Where Ortiz was. They wounded me four days after. Then I were in Barcelona, an' then in Madrid. I didn't have much luck, I were wounded three times.'

'Were you in the CNT?'

'I was. I'm a communist now. It's better. They take more notice.'

'Where're you from?'

'From Arenys. They told us to leave. But we will win. We 'ave to. We 'ave no choice. We must win. *Must*. I always thinks about the look on their faces when they wen' to bury me an' din't find me. They must 'ave counted the bodies several times. They'd not put much effort into catchin' me, an' now they can take a runnnin' jump. It's 'ardly rainin' now. Time to go?'

The man talking – a feverish glint in his eye – lifts his arm inside a fantastic hodge-podge of wire and bandages; his companion is limping, the toes on his left foot pointing at the sky.

Nobody else is talking. Their voices lost to their eyes. They're walking. The women's hips have broadened, dragging behind them memories, baggage, children, and these years.

'They beat him to death in the village barracks. Yes, in '34. This lad's from Sograndio as well.'

The road jams up, people ebb, their path, a canal eddying towards death, a reservoir, a dam; the crowds flow over the sides, horns blow any air they can catch, but the wind erases them. It's stopped raining, is completely grey.

'Can't we go now?'

'What's happened?'

'Can't we go now?'

'What's up?'

The shouting goes hoarse, the joy's all gone.

They start to move off slowly, silently, crestfallen. It's jammed with packed cars, islands in a sea of people. They all stay quiet. Six or seven ambulances drive up, queue up, like everyone else.

'He hid in the village. They said he'd be all right. But the second he went into the street, they did him in. That's why I fled. I went via San Sebastián. That'll be a year ago by now.'

'Where's this lot going?'

'What do you expect, resistance has its limits.'

'And its frontiers.'

'You can joke. Death strikes every man-jack. Everyone has to keep going. If one fails, the whole thing falls apart. These people don't know what they want, but they know only too well what they do *not* want.

That's why they're fleeing. It's not that they're afraid, they simply don't want to be fascists. Do you understand? It's as clear as water: they don't want to be fascists.'

'What are they hoping to find in France?'

'They don't know. They don't want to be fascists and that's all there is to it.'

A woman approaches carrying a child in her arms; she sees they are better dressed and imagines they're men of learning, from the glow they give off. She hands them the kid: 'He's got a temperature, sir, he's got a temperature.'

One of the men touches the little boy.

'No, he hasn't. Come with me.'

By the time they turn round, the woman has vanished into the stream.

'Why don't you run after her?'

'He's dead.'

'But if they don't want to be fascists, why do they run away rather than putting up a fight?'

'They're more afraid of falling prisoner than dying.'

'A dead man – or woman – doesn't fall prisoner.'

'They don't always die. People will find it hard to explain why Catalonia was lost so quickly, and even harder when they discover that after he'd taken Tarragona, Franco didn't have to fire a single shot. It's what I told you: people haven't fled because they are cowards, it's fear, fear of falling prisoner, of becoming fascists. Fear of becoming fascists. If we discount – and that's saying something – their incredible material superiority, they only had to plant their flag on a peak for our people two or three kilometres away to retreat for fear of a rout. That's the word: rout, they routed us; that did us as much damage as the Fiat planes. It wasn't cowardice but fear. Lots of people can't fathom how some of our units were totally defeated one day and the next fought magnificently; it's simple, they felt supported by other forces, their flanks were covered. I don't think it's ever been any different when it's a real rout, they die rather than surrender. The reasons for our defeat are too complex to be put down to a single feeling, but lack of unity, in every sense, has been lethal.'

'And what about the vanguard?'

'They were the first to see the enemy flags.'

'And the first to join the rear. Right?'

'Stop being so very unfunny. I know I'm exaggerating but when it came to relying on last minute formations, it was too late. You only fight fear of being caught by the fascists shoulder to shoulder. When you see you've lost, you do what you can. What's amazing is that people don't blame the ones who are to blame, and that everybody knows who that might be if it's not themselves: the *compañero*; the communist, the non-communist; the anarchist, the non-anarchist, etc.'

'It's always easy to accuse someone who's near to hand.'

The raindrops, held back by us, plop as they fall on the loose earth, gravel or asphalt. The wind whips up, the clouds scurry; it reaches the sky. People dawdle, drag their feet; they are the counterpoint to the moaners and the horns. People have got into the habit of being slow, carry on as long as they can, don't seek explanations, are more silent and subdued, older and blacker than ever.

Sirens. Everyone hesitates for a second, then scatters frantically in every direction in small trickles cross-country or towards Figueras: the plight of refugees. Any cheer disappears. You hear any engines? Some old women have stretched out in ditches while, further up the road, people scamper towards open fields. Some use a dyke as a shield, soak their buttocks and more besides, some shelter against a wall, sit behind a tree, squat in a watercourse, think the plain will protect them, squeeze between ridges and riverbeds; many decide their lucky star will defend them and look up from the place they first scarpered to. The ack-ack battery spits sparks and shoots into the sky in futile competition with the clouds. I see the planes before anyone else. Five shining, three-engine efforts coming from the sea. A few cool characters discuss makes and models on a roof terrace. Most of the cars have emptied out; a bowl's been dropped in the middle of the road, a cap's lost at my feet, a metre along a corset. The planes, parallel to the sun, open fire. The sirens stop howling. Only the little ack-ack battery, chained to the spot, barks stubbornly. Not a single vehicle, dog or rooster; only the squadron approaching. Some rush off in search of a better fence. It must stun

people to think their death may be up there, approaching silently, slip-
ping through the air. They say planes go very fast, I think they always
exaggerate; they're still not overhead. Some mug starts wailing. They're
right over me. Flying by now.

'There she goes.'

A faint whistle fanning outwards. A shrill tone growing like a
pyramid being built from its pinnacle. A ray of lightning turned thunderbolt. A horrible crimson morass. A tremendous blast from the
entrails of the earth, gouging a man-made, so genuine crater, splitting
and dismantling walls, that cracks, slices and shatters beams; sunders
iron bars; fissures and flattens concrete; yellows, disgorges, disembowels,
de-legs and despatches living people over the edge who in a fraction of
a second are reduced to bits and liquid. Burns, breaks, twists, crumbles
and collapses cars, smashes their windows; squashes old wagons, pulver-
ises walls; crushes wheels, converts them into compasses; dissolves stone
into dust; dismembers a mule; guts a greyhound; de-grapes vineyards;
dislocates dead and wounded; destroys a young girl and de-brains a
customs policeman crouching opposite me; de-limbs a couple of old
men and the odd woman starting with their feet; ten metres to my
left beheads an assault guard and hangs a piece of his liver from my
branches; disembodies three children in the dyke down the lower slope;
de-leafs and de-grasses fifty metres all round and, further off, demolishes
a hovel's walls, discovers tiles from Alcora; skins the air, turns it to dust
for a hundred metres up, lops off men's ears, leaves them like the man
hanging opposite, naked, silk socks all neat and tidy, testicles driven into
his stomach, no sign of hair, bowels and intestines in the air, still pulsing;
lungs de-ribbing, face disappearing – where? – brains in place, for all to
see, gunpowder black.

My main branch is damaged and twisted, and most branches have
crashed to the ground. A black kerchief and a few coloured ribbons
hang from the one I've still got. The countryside breaks into a howl,
under clouds of dust. Cocks crow. Shrieks furrow the acrid dust. I see
people begin to stir, choking. Blood. Every bit of me hurts. The earth
is full of dust, blood, shrapnel, branches, glass. Let them prune me now,
I'm less than a third of what I was. Blood, and more blood. The dust

hovers in the air as if the air *was* dust. People start shouting their names out. Heartache, sobbing, retching, bleeding, bleeding. Scarves flash again. Acrid smells, sour smells, pungent smells. Men stir amidst yellow dust, dust on their shoulders, heads old and grey. Two are pulling a kind of bloody bag, mush hangs where a head once was, no feet either, take it off round my side. Blood-soaked earth. Ambulances drive up, turf out huge willow baskets, yellow outside, grey inside from dried blood, where they throw the chunks of flesh they find, lots of feet. Bodies stack up in another van; as there aren't enough ambulances, they pile the wounded on top of corpses.

Vans drive off ringing their bells. A company of sappers arrives and sweeps the debris and branches off the road, villagers collect firewood, people emerge from their hideouts, a mass of sobbing, loud and clear. I think I can manage without extra supports.

Two girls head towards Figueras, cut a path through the mud and the blood.

'I'm not thinking about the war; I don't want to. Someone can think for me. Everything else we must grin and bear.'

She turns to her companion: 'I don't feel in a rush.'

Re-born in a thousand places, the hazy river slowly picks itself up, the crowd gropes through the mist.

Now the peeping-toms appear, a French journalist I know, because he comes every week, in an empty car he drives back loaded with bread and parcels. The other guy is Spanish, and in a foul temper. He looks at the road, the bottle-neck to my right, and bows low before the Frenchman.

'*La paix et l'ordre dans la justice*! And what else, fat face? What else? I'm talking to you as a dead man, killed by your lot, the kind manufactured by your very own hands. A dead man. A man rotted by your peace that retreated, your non-resistance, your peace of non-intervention, your pansy peace. "If peace can be preserved at any price, then let it be!" And why shouldn't peace be preserved? Here I am, one dead, putrefying man to bear witness to that, the Czechs as well, and those who will come after us, and they will for sure, believe me. Of course I think it will be preserved, you liars, shitting yourselves blind with fear, fools permeated

by your pathetic petty-mindedness, digging holes in the ground with
your arse-licking doggy legs, nobly desiring to slip away. "And in July
1936 I gave the order to intervene." Of course, my dear Hitler,* and
we kept quiet, just in case, and *Le père* Blum, boom, boom, crying,
and us dead. Thirty months of blood and stone, thirty months thinking
that your Pyrenean rear end must be worth at least a couple of dozen
bullets and a third of a cannon. And there you all are, still in one piece,
expecting the grateful Spaniards, my dear innocent little lambs, to go
and fight with you if the sabre insists. Maybe poor idiots like me will still
think there's no choice but to fight at your side; but we'll be a very few.†
Everyone else, millions of Spaniards and Czechs, will come and smash
your faces in, make you eat your own words, and it will be a deed well
done. You bet, Don Yvole; you bet, Don Bonete; you bet, Don Blum,
boom, boom; off to the effing shit-pile, off to the effing shit-pile...'

The stroppy tyke's last words stuck in his throat he was so beside
himself; it made him retch. He banged against my trunk, head flopping
like a rag, leaning his left forearm on my bark, doing the splits, floods of
puke on the ground.

'Shame about the Pernod!' he told the Frenchman who replied, in a
friendly tone: 'You know only too well that the people don't...'

The Spaniard, wiping the gunge away with the back of his hand:
'Yes, I know. Have you got a handkerchief? Not washing with soap for
over a year is...'

The other gives him a rag, and they walk off.

'But we are right.'

'*Ça t'fait une belle jambe,*' an old Frenchie says to a lame man who's
arguing with him. A cold blast against my resentful branches, as that man
wrote: 'A cold blast cutting into your face.' Prey to a falcon, pigeons; prey
to a buzzard, partridges; prey to a hawk, sparrows; prey to an aeroplane,

*I don't understand this date; it's contradictory. The sentence quoted was uttered
by Don Adolf Hitler on 6 June 1939 on the occasion of the return to Germany of
a number of Nazi effectives sent to Spain. We shouldn't put too much trust in trees;
with their butter-wouldn't-melt-in-my-mouth airs, they only guess. And here's proof
of that.
†Another error. Many Spaniards fought side by side with the French.

women, children and rank-and-file soldiers. And it all goes awry. I've not been pruned for some time. But if the planes think their bombs will get the better of me, they're wrong: it's the sap that counts, trunk and leaves grow of their own accord. Men ought to know a severed foot will always grow back. There's more to life than budding leaves.

A blistered face says to a bandaged head: 'In the latest of their newspapers that I read, I came across an article by Pemán the bard that begins: "Consequently God, the Generalísimo of this Crusade…"'

The river of blankets spreads; ambulances ring their bells. The plump guy continues: 'Yes, like 31 December, Barcelona. At nine at night, either Burgos or Radio Nacional announces over the ether: "We've just learned the reds have received five ambulances from the reds in Buenos Aires; they won't go very far." Two hours later, to celebrate the New Year, they bombed the city centre. By this time our front-line had gone.'

The sirens again. What's the colour of fear? Is it grey or black? Fear is striped and splits men into slender tear-drops or down the middle; sunders them, silently wounds them; levels them, unites them, fuses them, undoes them; makes them forget time, want death, believe in oblivion, in miracles, resort to dreams. They chase after whatever, because fear is a great sophist. Fear is free and rushes in, vaults down from the sky, nobody knows how, infectious as the wind; it can be resisted in spring with fresh green leaves, in autumn or winter there's nothing doing.

The slow beat of marching troops slices through the silence. Where are they coming from? After the atonal, dragging noise of the crowds, what's drumming the earth, where is this hidden rumble born? People crouching down lift their heads, those hiding peer out, those who reckon they're intrepid come nearer; children run to the road-side. Troops are on the march, coming from the direction of France. What makes hope rise like steam? There they are, in full view: in rows of six, fair lads black as Castilian bread, olive-skinned lads toasted like Andalusians. Thirteen hundred men returning because they want to, a fragile respite against so much ignominy. Thirteen hundred men of the International Brigades returning, because their foreign blood is Spanish blood. One, two, one, two. As they walk, they leave their footprints, right fists scouring the air from right to left, from left to right. They smile, their strength is every-man's; the grief is Spain's.

'*No pasarán.*'

'*No pasarán.*'

A miserable, pitiful old lady sheltering by my trunk shouts to them: '*Pasarán* overhead, but *no pasarán* down below.'

'*No pasarán.*'

Nobody believes a word of it; the hoarse shouting burns their throats. They weep.

'*No pasarán.*'

They're entering Figueras now; you can hear the clamour. People stay quiet, waiting for the end of the alarm, salt in their eyes, dawn on their faces.

The tide rises again. It's night-time, the people onwards to the frontier.

'I'm going to the Centre.'

Nobody asks, when will we be back? They're all convinced it will be a few months: two, three, six at most. The world won't allow something so shameful.

'Now for sure, France will have no choice but to intervene.'

'Now they've got the Germans at their frontier...'

A girl, maybe five years old, bellows; an older child, by her side – how old is she, nine or ten?

'Shush, the aeroplanes will hear you.'

And the littl'un shushes.

⤳

Max Aub was born in Paris in 1903 to a French mother and a German father. At the outbreak of the First World War, his father was declared an enemy alien in France, so the family settled in Valencia. In 1921, Aub became a Spanish citizen and in 1929 joined the PSOE, the Spanish Socialist Workers' Party. At the outbreak of the Civil War, Aub and José Bergamín were sent to Paris as cultural attachés at the Spanish embassy. They were given the job of organizing the Republic's pavilion at the International Art and Technology Exhibition, due to open in July 1937. It was Aub who got Picasso to produce a work of art for the pavilion – the result was *Guernica*. Opening the pavilion, Aub said:

'Goya and Picasso are realist painters though they seem extravagant members of this frightening people that are the Spanish, frightening because they are the only people in Europe able to take a dagger to themselves.'

Denounced as a 'German-Jew' to the French government, Aub was twice interned in 1940 and 1941 in the Camp Vernet in the French Pyrenees and then sent to Djelfa Camp in Algeria. Released from Djelfa in 1942, Aub sailed to Mexico, where he was to live for the last 30 years of his life. Playwright, journalist, critic and novelist, Aub is best known for *The Magic Labyrinth*, a six-volume cycle about the Civil War of which only the first volume, *Field of Honour*, has been translated into English. Max Aub possessed a great sense of humour – *Jusep Torres Compalans*, his biography of a fictitious artist, included (his) paintings for the exhibition that accompanied the book. The story included here is the title story from *Enero sin Nombre* (*January Without Name*), Aub's stories about the Civil War and exile, published to critical acclaim in Spain in 1997. Much loved in Mexico, he died there in 1972.

JORDI SOLER

THE CAMP AT ARGELÈS-SUR-MER

from *The Feast of the Bear*

translated by Nick Caistor

WHEN I WOKE UP on the 14th April 2007, I was toying with the idea of getting out of a commitment I had somewhat rashly made six months earlier. Then it had seemed so far in the future that it had been easy to say yes, but now the day had arrived I was sorry I had agreed to do it. My wife and children had left home early to do their own things, while I had remained a while longer in bed. The previous night I had stayed up to watch a Russian film, and what I most felt like doing was making coffee and sitting to watch it again, notebook and pen in hand so that I could transcribe a poem that is its essence, a beautiful, striking poem spoken in Russian, a language I don't understand and whose Spanish subtitles must suffer from the shortcomings typical of that genre: subtitles are an extra indication of what the image is telling us; they have to be understood quickly at one glance, and do not permit any re-reading or much reflection, because you are immediately required to read the next one, and then the one after that. Despite all this, I had stored in my mind a verse which, even if it wasn't exactly what the Russian poet had meant, had made a profound impression on me. The commitment I had so rashly accepted was to take part in an event to be held in the south of France, in Argelès-sur-Mer, an obscure place of evil memory, a cursed spot on the map, a beach which for decades had been a taboo for me and all my family, and since I wasn't brave enough to disappoint the person who had invited me so that I could sit around in my pyjamas drinking coffee and going through the Russian film again, a few hours later, trying hard to keep my phantoms at bay, I found myself in Argelès-sur-Mer, talking yet again about the damned war, my elbows digging into the Republican flag covering the table, to a group of readers from that town. At the end of the event a woman came up to the table. She was dressed in black, her head covered in a scarf and with a brown, tattered rag round her neck that acted as a foulard. Half an hour earlier I had seen her sitting in the back row and thought she cut a really odd figure, and immediately afterwards (because the professor chairing the discussion was talking endlessly and so left me time to think about this and lots of other things) I had wondered what part of my book – which was the reason for this event – could interest this woman, who frankly looked like a tramp. She pushed her way through the dozen or so people who had come up to the table for me to sign their books. She was quite violent, but no-one dared say anything to her because she looked so strange; to be more exact, she was ugly and sinister-looking. The first thing she did when she finally reached the table was to give me a long, reproachful and sly look, made worse by the sight of her bare gums when they appeared beneath her half-smile. Still gazing at me and smiling, she began to search for something in her clothes, and at the end of several seconds of tense expectation (they could have concealed anything from a book to a fire-arm), she took out a photograph, together with a grubby piece of paper folded in four, and handed them both to me without a word. She turned on her heel and disappeared, less violently than before because the others were keeping well out of her way, leaving me with several questions on the tip of my tongue. Trying to make this weird encounter seem perfectly normal, I put what she had given me into my jacket pocket and continued signing copies and talking to my readers as if nothing had happened. However, before putting the documents away I had fleetingly glimpsed, in a blur because I was not wearing my glasses, that the photograph was an old snapshot of three soldiers in the countryside from the time of the Civil War. The instant it had taken me to see what the old woman had given me was enough to make me feel queasy, because the piece of paper was so dirty and full of stains that it seemed like a piece or scar from her battered, ruinous body. By the time twenty minutes later we went out onto the terrace to close the event with a glass of wine, I had completely forgotten the incident. After all, it's not uncommon that we writers who deal with the topic of the Civil War find people coming up to us with documents, letters and photographs, in the perfectly legitimate hope that their story, or that of their father or grandfather, that event which marked their lives and those of their descendants forever, become known and, if possible, spread more widely. I had been invited by the Association of FFREEE (Fils et Filles de Républicains Espagnols et Enfants de l'Exode), made up of the children of the Republicans who lost the war in 1939 and found themselves forced into exile on the other side of the Pyrenees, a group of enthusiasts convinced that it is essential to maintain, protect and preserve the memory of that schism which even today defines and distinguishes millions of people. The association's chairman, the man who had invited me and who for some reason or other I had not had the courage to say no to, saw my book as important because in it I describe one of the concentration camps where at the end of the Civil War the French government had interned the Spanish Republicans fleeing Franco's repression in dreadful conditions. That camp was nearby, on the beach of Argelès-sur-Mer, and as I narrate in my book, my grandfather Arcadi spent sixteen months prisoner there, enduring systematic, prolonged maltreatment that is one of the darkest episodes in the history of France: the Republicans, pursued by the fury of the Francoists, were seeking asylum in France, but the French government received them as if they were criminals, and locked them in a concentration camp. I'm explaining this in order to emphasize that the invitation to celebrate the 14th of April on that beach of ill repute seemed to me from the start to be both inappropriate and even slightly sarcastic, but the FFREEE chairman had made it impossible for me to say no, and that morning, as I was weighing up the possibility of not going and instead staying in my pyjamas to watch the Russian film, it had occurred to me that to talk about the concentration camp *in situ* in that cursed, taboo place, was an invaluable way of normalizing my relationship with that beach, and better still, was my own way of combating oblivion, an oblivion that I myself denounced in that very book, writing that the Argelès-sur-Mer beach was a kind of collective amnesia because today it is a cheap holiday resort full of bars and bodies sunbathing on the same sand, on the exact same spot where tens of thousands of Spaniards were dying of hunger, illness or cold, not that many years earlier. In reality there are very few things that can be done to ward off oblivion: raise a monument, put up a plaque, write a book, organize an event, because the natural thing is in fact to forget, and at this point, at this stage in the story I'm telling, I can only ask myself: what if all this nonsense about that damned war and its consequences isn't simply a dead weight? Besides, this is the twenty-first century, and Spain and France are no longer what they were in 1939; we don't have pesetas or francs anymore, and there isn't even a frontier between the two countries: to get to the place where the event was being held, I had climbed into my car, which was parked outside my house in Calle Muntaner in Barcelona, and driven for two hours without stopping once to Argelès-sur-Mer; in two hours I had completed the same journey it had taken my grandfather Arcadi and most of the Republican exodus several weeks to cover in 1939. The traces of that exile have been buried beneath a toll motorway you can drive along at a hundred and forty kilometres an hour, and a crowd of tourists who, smothered in cream, expose their bodies to the sun on the long beach of Argelès-sur-Mer. Very little can be done to ward off oblivion, but it is essential we do so, otherwise we will end up without foundations or perspective. That is what I thought, and that was the reason why in the end I gave up my domestic morning, took off my pyjamas and got into my car, still thinking obsessively of that verse from the Russian film I had memorized and which had robbed me of sleep; 'Live in the house, and the house will exist'.

As proof of how much things have changed, the Argelès-sur-Mer municipality is now run by the children of the men who in 1939 were imprisoned in the concentration camp. I learned this during the reception held at the end of the event on the enormous terrace looking out over the vineyards which produced the wine we were drinking and with in the background the sea, shimmering like silver in these early days of spring. It was a wonderful evening and by now I was beginning to feel I'd done the right thing in accepting the invitation, and for having done what little one can do to combat oblivion. At that moment I felt I could assert that the Civil War and its consequences are a dead weight only insofar as they are ignored, but that they are an important means for viewing the future if all the details are revealed. And so I was full of optimism when I approached the table to refill my glass; it was a long trestle set up in the middle of the terrace, covered in white tablecloths reaching to the floor. From time to time these were lifted by the breeze so that the legs were exposed and I could see what was underneath: cases of bottles, folding chairs, a pile of white tablecloths, a huge pot where some of what was being served on the table had been cooked. In the midst of all this, oblivious to the intermittent glimpses the wind offered me, two cats were fighting over a piece of chicken; they were acting out a brutal, silent battle with a fierceness and cruelty that shook me profoundly. In those few seconds, in the two glimpses allowed me by the tablecloth, I saw the cats clawing at each other, leaping in the air and rolling on the ground, before they suddenly ran off as fast as they could.

Jordi Soler was born in Mexico in 1963; there he grew up as part of a community of Catalan exiles. His writings, many of them autobiographical, chronicle the Republican diaspora in Mexico. It is estimated that over 25,000 Spaniards were given asylum in Mexico at the end of the Civil War. Soler's family were among those who founded La Portuguesa in the province of Veracruz; a coffee plantation in the midst of a hostile, tropical forest. The success of the plantation and Soler's subsequent return to Barcelona, the city from which his family had originally fled, is the subject of a moving memoir, *Los Rojos de Ultramar*, published in 2004. Soler is a writer, journalist and rock critic who now lives in Barcelona. He is founding member of the Orden del Finnegans, a group of Spanish writers who meet every Bloomsday to honour James Joyce's *Ulysses*. This extract is from *La Fiesta del Oso*, a powerful novel about exile and memory which begins at the camp at Argelès-sur-Mer where so many Republicans were interned.

JORGE SEMPRÚN

'OUR WAR'

from *Veinte años y un día (Twenty Years and a Day)*

translated by Margaret Jull Costa

'"OUR WAR",' HEMINGWAY COMMENTED. 'You all say that. As if it were the only thing or even the most important thing you have in common. Your daily bread…'

He was mumbling, talking to himself.

His voice had an unmistakably American twang.

That was two years before. Was it that long already? Yes, it was easy enough to work out: late May 1954. In El Callejón, a restaurant in Madrid.

Leidson was having lunch with Hemingway and various people from the world of bullfighting. He remembers Domingo 'Dominguín'. Not just because he was memorable, but because Domingo was the first to speak of that long-ago death.

They were sitting round the table after lunch, and the drink was still flowing. They had eaten the usual *cocido madrileño* – meat, vegetable and chickpea stew. Michael Leidson was passionate not just about recent Spanish history, but about Spanish history as a whole. He was less passionate about Spanish cuisine. Or, rather, he liked it, but it played havoc with his stomach. Stew for everyone, there was no avoiding it: the rest of the afternoon would be spent in flatulent sleep.

Hemingway had just told a story about his first return visit to Spain after the civil war. Everyone laughed. Some years later, when Leidson read *The Dangerous Summer* by Don Ernesto, he found a very different version of that same story. A less interesting one too. In the book, which chronicles the bullfighting season of 1959 and the hard-fought and inevitably bloody contest between Antonio Ordóñez and Luis Miguel 'Dominguín', the account of Hemingway's journey to Spain is given a rather solemn slant. There's even a touch of megalomania about it.

In the printed version, which is more flattering to the narrator, the policeman on the frontier at Irún recognised Hemingway at once and stood up to greet him, congratulating him on his novels, which he assured him he had read. That's a little hard to believe though. It doesn't seem plausible that in 1953 a policeman working for the dictatorship would have read, and enjoyed, Ernest Hemingway's novels.

In May 1954, however, in El Callejón, Hemingway told another version of the same story. Another version of his return to Spain. It was both more believable and more skilfully crafted. After all, one should expect from a novelist, not only a modicum of truth, but also a degree of narrative skill.

During the idle post-prandial chatter in El Callejón, Leidson heard an earlier version of that story of Hemingway's return, according to which, when the policeman checked Hemingway's passport, he commented: 'Hey, you've got the same name as that American who fought on the side of the reds during our war...' He had looked up when he said this. And Hemingway retorted: 'I have the same name as him because I am that American who fought on the side of the reds during your war...' The policeman took a step back. His eyes grew black with rage. Impotent rage. A Yankee was a Yankee, untouchable, regardless of whether he had fought on the side of the reds, the whites, or the Devil himself.

Everyone laughed, and someone else told an anecdote from the same period.

Later, Hemingway returned to the subject of the civil war.

'"Our war",' he muttered. 'You all say that, as if it were the only thing, or, rather, the most important thing, you have in common. Your daily bread. Death, that's what binds you together, the old death of the civil war.'

Leidson was on the point of saying to Hemingway that death was perhaps not the only thing the Spanish shared in their almost eucharistic memory of that war, their war, but also youth, ardour. Although perhaps death is just one of the faces of ardent youth.

Or the other way round, who knows.

But on that occasion, he said nothing. The others, however, did not hold back. The Spaniards at that lunch all had something to say. The war, our war: their youth. They had all taken part in that struggle eighteen years before. But not all of them had fought on the same side. However, none of them seemed as convinced of their reasons, or of their idealised acts of unreason, as they doubtless had been in 1936, when they were convinced enough to risk their lives.

Domingo Dominguín, so Leidson gleaned, had fought with the nationalists. With a Falangist militia. He was wounded early on in the war. Another of the guests, older than Dominguín, a former *banderillero* who had been a close friend of Dominguín's family, had fought on the side of the reds. He made affectionate fun of Dominguín and his remote Falangist past. He alluded with gentle mockery to his adventures in the field hospital. All the little nuns had fallen in love with him, said the *banderillero*, and the impudent monkey had had his way with them right there, at his leisure, lying on his bed of pain.

Everyone laughed and continued drinking.

It seemed to Michael Leidson that, for these men, the passions of the past were no longer a cause of conflict between them. At least not in the same way. Those who had fought with the nationalists – Dominguín, to look no further – seemed profoundly disenchanted. They now seemed more left-wing, more radical even, than those who had sided with the reds, and had a certain propensity to criticise the excesses and the errors of their own side.

It was then, amid the hubbub of crisscrossing conversations, that Domingo Dominguín told the story of that long-ago death.

He spoke without taking his eyes off Hemingway or Leidson. He told them the story above the noise of the other guests' anecdotes, guffaws and exclamations. He told them about that death because they were outside it, outside the experience. That is, outside the blood of the civil war, on the other side of the memory of that blood. Although still close enough to be able to understand the bloody message from the past – Sterile? Repetitive? Absurdly heroic? Unjust? Necessary?

Hemingway was warming a glass of brandy in his cupped hands, listening intently.

On 18th July 1936, said Domingo Dominguín, on a farm in the province of Toledo, the farm workers, when they heard about the military uprising, had killed one of the owners. The youngest of the brothers. The only liberal in the family, too, according to the villagers. But death does not always choose her intended. Not knowingly at least. That person is simply her intended.

Even though it was the cause of everything, the death itself was the least of it. There were so many deaths at the time. The interesting part came later. Every year, in fact, since the end of the civil war, the family – the widow and the dead man's brothers – had organised an act of commemoration each 18th July. Not just a mass or something of the sort, but a real, theatrical ceremony of atonement. The farm workers would reenact the murder, that is, they would pretend to reenact it. They would arrive mob-handed, armed with rifles, to kill again, ritually, symbolically, the owner of the farm. Or someone who took his part. A kind of allegorical religious drama, that was what it was like.

The farm workers would plunge back – or would be forced to plunge back – into the memory of that death, that murder, in order to atone for it one more time. Some, the older ones, had perhaps taken part in the original death, however indirectly. Or had witnessed it. Or had been told about it by someone or remembered it personally. The others, the majority, were too young. But each year, they found themselves submerged in that collective memory and made to feel that they were to blame. They were not the murderers of 1936, but the ceremony, in a way, made them accomplices of that death, forcing them to take responsibility for it, to bring it back into the present, to bring it alive again.

A baptism of blood, you might say.

By perpetuating that memory, the farm workers were also perpetuating their condition not only as the vanquished, but also as murderers. Or as the children, relatives, descendants of murderers. They were perpetuating the awful reason for their defeat by commemorating the injustice of that death which treacherously justified their defeat, their reduction to the ranks of the vanquished. In short, that ceremony of atonement – which used to be attended by some of the provincial authorities, civil and ecclesiastical – helped to make sacred the very social order which the farm workers, rashly no doubt – fearfully too, one imagines – had thought they were destroying in 1936 when they murdered the owner of the farm.

No one said anything when Dominguín finished his story. The silence that had been there, in the wings, so to speak, had grown perfect, transparent, dense. Michael Leidson closed his eyes and tried to imagine the landscape, the faces, the ritual of atonement. Hemingway took a long swallow of brandy and muttered something, a single sibilant syllable: 'Shit.' Yes, shit, he couldn't have put it better.

This was two years before, more or less, in El Callejón.

Jorge Semprún was born in Madrid in 1923. His father was a liberal politician who served from 1937 as the Republican government's ambassador to the Netherlands. After the war, the family went into exile in France and Semprún studied at the Sorbonne. During the Nazi occupation of France, he was active in the Resistance, arrested by the Gestapo in 1943 and sent to the Buchenwald camp. Not surprisingly, for Semprún the Civil War and the camps were the events that shaped his life and his writings – a powerful blend of the imagined and the true. 'I believe ardently that real memory, not historical and documentary memory but living memory will be perpetuated only through literature. Because literature alone is capable of reinventing and regenerating truth. It is an extraordinary weapon...' This extract is taken from the fine (as yet untranslated into English) 2004 novel *Twenty Years and a Day*, which refers to the sentence given to political prisoners in Franco's Spain. A reconstruction of the murder of a landowner by peasants at the outbreak of the war, the book shows the power past events still have over the present. From 1953 to 1962, Semprún, using the pseudonym Federico Sánchez was an important organizer of the clandestine activities of the Communist Party in Spain. He was expelled from the Party in 1964 for his critical views. Semprún died in Paris in 2011, buried in a Republican flag.

ACKNOWLEDGEMENTS

Special thanks to the translators – Peter Bush, Nick Caistor, Margaret Jull Costa and Wisiek Powaga – who gave me both invaluable advice on previously untranslated material on the Civil War and their excellent translations. To Sebastiaan Faber, Civil War historian, for generously sharing his time and knowledge. To the members of the IBMT (International Brigade Memorial Trust) who on trips to Spain were a rich source of insights. To John Davey, for his perfect blend of editorial support and criticism. To all those at Serpent's Tail and Profile who have made this book – Ruthie Petrie, Hannah Westland, Nick Sheerin, Peter Dyer, Sue Lamble, Ian Paten and Valentina Zanca. To Caroline Pretty for her heroic work in tracking down the rights holders. And to Sarah, Carla and Oscar, who, once again, helped me see the relevance of the past to the present.

PERMISSIONS

Every endeavour has been made to locate the copyright holders of the texts included here. Please could any copyright holders we were unable to locate get in touch with Serpent's Tail.

✍

Extract from *De Gernika a Guernica: Marcas* by Bernardo Atxaga is included by permission of Margarita Perelló.

Max Aub, 'Enero sin nombre', *Cuentos ciertos* © Max Aub, 1955, and Heirs of Max Aub.

'The Clash', from *The Forging of a Rebel* by Arturo Barea © Granta.

'The Civil War (1936–1939)', from *My Last Breath* by Luis Buñuel, published by Jonathan Cape, reprinted by permission of The Random House Group Limited. From *My Last Sigh: The Autobiography of Luis Buñuel* by Luis Buñuel, translated by Abigail Israel, translation copyright © 1983 by Alfred A. Knopf, a division of Penguin Random House LLC, used by permission of Alfred A. Knopf, an imprint of the Knopf Doubleday Publishing Group, a division of Penguin Random House LLC. All rights reserved.

'Las Minas de Teruel' by Pere Calders is included by permission of Edicions 62 S.A. © Heirs of Pere Calders, 1938.